HELD TO RANSOM

No one to trust, nowhere to turn...

Newly married and excited about honey-mooning near her family in the Hamptons, ghostwriter Lee Bartholomew isn't prepared for the disasters that happen when she arrives on US soil. Not only has her husband had to stay behind in London, but a botched ransom attempt on her stepbrother's adopted son brings horror into her family's midst. When a body is found close by, followed by a further kidnapping of a little boy, Lee begins to suspect a link between the crimes. It seems almost everyone in her circle could be involved – and could even pose a very real threat to her life.

HELD TO RANSOM

Held To Ransom

by

Hope McIntyre

Magna Large Print Books
Long Preston, North Yorkshire,
BD23 4ND, England.

British Library Cataloguing in Publication Data

McIntyre, Hope
    Held to ransom.

    A catalogue record of this book is
    available from the British Library

    ISBN   978-0-7505-3271-6

First published in Great Britain in 2009 by Piatkus Books

Copyright © 2009 by Caroline Upcher

Cover illustration © Mark Owen by arrangement with
Arcangel Images

The moral right of the author has been asserted

Published in Large Print 2011 by arrangement with
Piatkus Books, an imprint of Little, Brown Book Group Ltd.

Magna Large Print is an imprint of Library Magna Books Ltd.

Printed and bound in Great Britain by
T.J. (International) Ltd., Cornwall, PL28 8RW

*In memory of Marit Allen
and Randy Franken*

Acknowledgements

My thanks go to Louise Weisbord for describing her experiences as a host to Fresh Air kids in East Hampton; to Sherri Ziff Lester, founder of Los Angeles based Rock Your Life Coaching, for telling me what a life coach does and how she became one; to my friend Jimmy LaGarenne, former New York City cop and helicopter pilot – turned karaoke singer and animal trainer – for sharing his experiences working security; to my new editor Emma Beswetherick for keeping Lee on the straight and narrow; and to the very valuable Donna Condon for being my highly efficient link to London. I should also like to express my gratitude to Melissa Dolan for her careful reading of the manuscript. Without Melissa's help, Lee would have landed herself in serious trouble with the New York police.

Chapter One

It was on my watch that everything started to go wrong with Kimothy Moses. It was a sweltering July afternoon on Main Beach, East Hampton and I'd only known him for twenty-four hours. I had no experience looking after children and the fact that during that time he had barely spoken to me only served to exacerbate my nervousness.

I had flown into JFK from London two days earlier with my mother-in-law, Noreen Kennedy. The fact that I was on my honeymoon was something neither of us mentioned during the journey. I admit I'm probably the only woman in the world to find herself on her honeymoon with her mother-in-law instead of her husband. But then I'm the only person idiot enough to marry Tommy Kennedy, who, for reasons I still couldn't quite fathom, had sprung his mother on me at the last moment.

Not that I'm complaining. In fact, knowing that Noreen would be my mother-in-law had played a large part in my decision to finally agree to become Tommy's wife. And while I know I shouldn't be so morbid, I worry that we won't have her for that much longer and the more time I can spend with her, the better. Noreen is seventy-six and a cancer survivor and these days she spends a large part of her life taking naps. This was her first visit to America and her first transatlantic flight and it was touching to witness her excitement. As soon as she was settled into her seat beside me – she insisted on being by the window, fine by me, I'm terrified of flying and don't like being reminded that there's 30,000 feet between me and solid earth – and had wrapped a blanket around her knees, she announced she was hungry and buried her nose in the menu. She spent half an hour trying to decide whether to have the Salisbury steak and mashed potato with glazed carrots followed by the chocolate truffle layer cake or the seared salmon and new potatoes with cauliflower *florets au gratin* and the Georgia peach pie.

'It all sounds so delicious,' she said, the navy-blue eyes she had passed to my husband gleaming in anticipation.

'It's airline food, Noreen,' I pointed out, 'it's made of plastic. Whatever you have it'll taste the same.'

'Oh, you're such an old cynic. I'm going to enjoy it, whatever it is,' she said with the optimistic attitude to life that was so typical of her and which I was never able to emulate.

'And I want dinner and a *movie*,' she said,

finally plumping for the salmon.

We discussed the pros and cons of *Becoming Jane* versus *Factory Girl* and I tried my best to explain that she wouldn't be watching a film about a machine operator, but a biopic of a Sixties 'It' girl famous for her association with Andy Warhol.

'He's that one who wore sunglasses all the time,' she gave me a knowing look, 'and he always looked as if he'd emptied the flour bin all over his head?'

'You could put it like that, Noreen, yes.'

'I think I'll watch the one about Jane Austen. She was a writer like you. I might learn something about what you get up to.'

If only, I thought, smoothing what was left of her fluffy white hair behind her ears and gently placing the headphones over them. I'm a ghostwriter and we were on our way to Long Island where, as well as a honeymoon without a husband, my latest ghosting assignment awaited me. I'm the *as told to* or *written with* you see in miniscule type on the covers of celebrity memoirs below their name unless, as sometimes happens, they prefer to pretend they've written it themselves.

I don't mind if this happens. I'm perfectly happy to take a backseat when it comes to public profiles. It's part and parcel of my solitary loner status. I love delving into the private lives of actors and rock stars and successful business women – because more often than not I'll be hired by women – and drawing their story out of them. It's not as easy as you think. You have to win their confidence, get them to open up and spill the gossip and then fashion their story into an entertaining book while at the same time making them feel as if they've had total control from day one.

'There you go.' I summoned up the movie on her remote and tapped the screen in front of her. She watched five minutes of it and, to my relief, fell asleep. For all her feistiness, Noreen is frail and tires easily. I knew a long trip across the Atlantic without a nap would be too much for her.

Just before we landed I staggered up the aisle to the bathroom in the rear of the plane. I always do this at the end of a long flight in a vain attempt to rectify my haggard, jet-lagged appearance. It never works, I reminded myself as I stared at my reflection in the mirror. I have been told I look Italian. Or Latin, at any rate. My natural expression is rather a mournful one and my nose is long and fine. But my mouth is very wide and, although of course I never see it myself, people say I have a great smile.

My cheekbones are high and my bone structure gives my face what people call a Madonna look and they're not talking about the singer. But personally the only thing I like about my face is the grape-like colour of my eyes. I tell myself they have a soulful look, which is probably utter crap.

On my return to my seat, I reached up to the overhead locker – not a stretch, I am five feet nine – to retrieve my linen jacket. It was crumpled, but it had been worth shelling out the fortune I had paid for it. The minute I put it on, its tailored cut allowed me to assume an instant elegance – even if my face still resembled a bowl of sallow porridge.

Noreen was still asleep when we landed and I allowed the other passengers to swarm up the aisle ahead of us before I roused her gently and allowed her to disembark slowly into the wheelchair I had organized to meet us. Despite having had cancer, Noreen was amazingly fit for her age, but I had anticipated that the flight would tire her out and I had been right. She collapsed gratefully into the wheelchair. I walked along beside her and was heartened by the sight of a relatively short line in Immigration.

'What are they doing?' she asked me when the customs official looked her name up on his computer.

'They want to see if it's on a list of terrorists,' I whispered.

'Oh, it probably is,' she said cheerfully, adding much too loudly for my liking, 'very common name in Ireland, Noreen Kennedy. Bound to have been a terrorist by that name at some point.'

I hurried her along before Homeland Security had a total sense of humour failure and left her in her wheelchair by the baggage carousel while I retrieved our luggage. 'Don't fall asleep,' I warned.

We were on our way to the home of my friends Rufus and Franny Abernathy and the Lincoln Town Car Franny had organized to pick us up sped along the Long Island Expressway. I think of Rufus as my 'brother' – although he can't be my real brother because I'm an only child. He's the son of Philip Abernathy (the Phillionaire as I used to call him), an American billionaire my mother almost married – but didn't because he was killed before she could divorce my father. We passed the spot where the Phillionaire's driver had had his fatal heart attack at the wheel, and we arrived at Rufus and Franny's house just as the sun was sinking in a crimson ball over the horizon.

I had not seen Franny and Rufus since their wedding and I was looking forward to seeing the house they had chosen for the start of their married life. Other than the fact that it was reached by a driveway covering a couple of acres, his home gave no indication that Rufus was the son of a billionaire and had inherited half of his estate. It was situated deep in the heart of woods but beyond it I caught a glimpse of water. I was not expecting a McMansion – Rufus and Franny shunned ostentation of any kind – but the sprawling, almost ramshackle farmhouse that confronted me took me by surprise.

It was in good condition, no peeling paint or missing shingles, but it had a comfortable, lived-in air about it that was confirmed by the sight of a small Hispanic woman rushing out of a side door and coming towards us with arms outstretched.

'Miss Lee, I am so happy to see you.'

'You too, Lucia,' I said as I got out of the car and embraced her. Lucia had been the Phillionaire's housekeeper, and on his death, she had gone to work for Rufus.

'Miss Franny put you in the pool house,' she said, leaning into the driver's window and motioning towards a spot further down the driveway. 'More privacy for you, she say. Everything ready for you there. I left supper for you in the kitchen but first you must call Miss Franny. *Immediately*. I put number by the phone. Hello! How are *you?*' Lucia had spied Noreen in the back seat beside me.

'This is my mother-in-law, Mrs Kennedy,' I said.

'But you Mrs Kennedy too now.' Lucia looked at me and laughed. 'Gonna be hard tell you apart. Don't forget to call Miss Franny. *Urgente!*'

'I won't,' I said, wondering what was up with Franny. 'And I'm just Lee to you, Lucia. Not Mrs Kennedy.'

'And I'm Noreen. Pleased to meet you.' Noreen smiled.

'I'm gonna walk over and help Miss Noreen get settled,' said Lucia and I wanted to hug her. I had the sense that I needed to get hold of Franny before doing anything else.

Franny and Rufus and two-year-old Eliza were on vacation in France and due back the next day. The number Lucia had left was for a hotel in Paris.

'There you are. Thank *God!*' Franny's drawling voice reverberated down the transatlantic wires as if she were right there in the room with me. 'How was the flight?'

'Fine,' I said, 'We're happy to be here. But Franny, what's the problem? Lucia said it was urgent.'

'Eliza's sick.'

'Oh my God! Will she be all right? What's wrong?'

'She's got an ear infection and the doctors won't let her fly, so this means we've had to postpone our return home.'

'Oh, we'll be fine. Don't worry about a thing. We'll see you when we see you. Poor little thing, is she in a lot of pain?'

'Lee, I'm not worried about *you!* You can take care of yourself and if you can't, you've got Lucia. Did she tell you about Kimothy Moses?'

'Not a word. What kind of a name is that?'

'Timothy with a K, I suppose,' Franny sounded weary. 'Listen, I'm going to have to ask you to help me out here. He's a Fresh Air kid and–'

'He's a what?'

'They call it the Fresh Air Fund. It's an organization that arranges for kids from poor families in the city to have a vacation in the country. They live in these towering apartment buildings and there's nowhere for them to play outside except concrete playgrounds. We volunteered to take a kid for two weeks, like, you know, so we could give something back.'

I smiled. It was ironic to hear Franny talking about giving something back. Before she married Rufus, she'd lived with her teenage son and Eliza in a one-room apartment, struggling to make ends meet.

'That sounds great. When does he arrive?'

'Tomorrow.'

She waited while it sank in.

'Tomorrow! But–'

'I know. We won't be back. That's why I'm going to have to ask you to go and meet him and look after him until we do. Lucia will help you, she's–'

'Franny! This is insane. I wouldn't have a clue what to do with him. I have no experience with kids. Is somebody going to drive him out? What do I give him to eat?'

'Calm down, Lee! It's no big deal, you're

21

gonna be absolutely fine. He's just a kid, for Christ's sake.'

'That's my point,' I said. 'It's OK for you, you've raised a teenager and had two years of Eliza. How old is he?'

'Seven. I asked for a younger one but this is what they're sending me. Now here's what you do. They'll bring him out, along with loads of other kids on a bus and you'll pick him up at the white church in Southampton. The group leader will know all about you.'

'But haven't they approved *you* as the person who's taking him? Won't they have a problem with him coming to me?'

'We've called and cleared it with the local chairperson. She came to interview us and she met Lucia. He's going to be sleeping in our house and Lucia will feed him. I've told her to stock up on mac and cheese and chocolate milk and stuff like that. And she'll put him to bed so basically all you're going to have to do is keep him entertained during the day.'

'And how am I going to do that?' I said. I could feel the panic rising.

'Use your imagination, Lee. How hard can it be? We have a pool–'

'He can swim?'

'I guess. Nobody said he can't. He's going to be in and out of that pool from the moment he wakes up till he goes to bed.

22

And when he's not, you can take him to the beach. In fact, I've already made it easy for you. I've lined up a play date for him the day after tomorrow. He gets to go to the beach with Keshawn.'

'Keshawn?' Another name with a K tagged on to it.

'I told you about him. Scott and Suzette's child, the one they adopted from Malawi. He arrived with some strange name Suzette couldn't pronounce. She's supposed to be an actress but it's amazing the amount of stuff she has trouble saying. Anyway, they re-named him Keshawn.'

Scott was Rufus' brother and they were as different as they could possibly be. While Rufus went to great pains to live down his wealth, Scott flaunted it. His house on the ocean was a veritable mansion comprising a minimum of fourteen thousand square feet. I disliked Scott as much as I adored Rufus. He was brusque and condescending where Rufus was relaxed and engaging. In fact the only thing that endeared me to Scott was the fact that he was a surgeon and therefore a healer, which had to be good. But, it turned out, even there he was an elitist.

He was an orthopaedic surgeon who had once had a practice in Southampton when he lived out here. Now he had relocated to claim his father's former Manhattan apartment on Fifth Avenue, (where the Phillionaire had once lived with my mother), and to develop a much-publicized city practice where he only seemed to fix the broken bones and disintegrating joints of celebrities. He had operated on Suzette's shoulder and, after a decent interval, started dating her. I wasn't entirely sure that this was even ethical but such was Suzette's celebrity status that the hype surrounding their subsequent wedding overshadowed something as unimportant as ethics.

THE SIREN AND THE SURGEON was typical of the headlines when they were first seen out together and, if nothing else, Suzette was indeed an alluring woman. Not that I'd ever met her, but you couldn't pick up *Heat* or *Star* or any of those gossip magazines without seeing a picture of her so I knew exactly what she looked like. Her two major assets preceded her at all times and I often wondered whether Scott might not have secretly been working a little further down from her shoulder when he performed her surgery. And I also wondered if she had any idea that Rufus and Franny often referred to her as Pancake.

'Pancake?' I'd said, when I'd first heard Franny call her that.

'Wake up, Lee. *Crêpes suzette*. You know, those pancakes flamed in Cognac or whatever? The whole point being that she's not exactly flat as a—'

'OK, I get it,' I said, and of course after that I couldn't help thinking of Suzette as Pancake.

Her face was pretty enough but it had a 'made to order' look about it. The eyes were too wide open, the nose a perfect little ski lift, the lips too full and pouty. She had been catapulted to instant stardom when, as a little known MTA (*'Model turned actress, Lee, don't you know anything?'*) with one B movie to her name, she had married an actor who could greenlight a movie with just a nod of his head. Never mind that those in the know suspected that the actor was gay and that Suzette had been 'hired' to be his wife on a five-year contract, her fame was secured for long after the five years were up and she had basked in the much publicized celebrity break-up.

I'd heard enough about her from Franny to know that I had no desire to meet her and when I heard about the plans to adopt a child from Africa, my heart went out to the kid. As far as I knew, Suzette couldn't have children of her own. If there was a problem, we knew it had to lie with her for the simple reason that Scott had already fathered a child. Eliza.

It had been a one night stand after a Fourth of July picnic and, apart from the fact that it had resulted in Eliza, Franny had regretted it ever since – especially as she had subsequently fallen in love with Rufus. When Scott and Suzette had started talking about adoption, Franny and Rufus had held their breath. Would he try to claim custody of Eliza, in whom he had shown little previous interest?

But it seemed Suzette had other ideas. Franny conceded she might sound a little mean, but she said she was convinced Suzette wanted a Third World child because it was fashionable. Keshawn's adoption would feed Suzette's publicity addiction, even though the poor kid was destined to be not much more than a fashion accessory.

'Yes,' said Franny, 'Lucia will give you Scott's address. He and Pancake are out at his house for a few weeks and they'll be expecting you. Take Kimothy over there at eleven thirty on Friday and he and Keshawn can hang out at the beach for the afternoon. You'll have a ball.'

After that she hurled instructions at me, going a mile a minute until I gave up trying to write everything down and prayed that Lucia would be able to bail me out if I foundered.

Watching a stream of children emerge from the bus in Southampton the next day, I was a wreck. Noreen had elected to stay behind and have a nap, so I was on my own. As I studied the faces of the boys, wondering

26

which one was Kimothy's, I almost ran away. Surely, if there was no one to claim him, then he would be sent back where he came from, perfectly safe until Franny returned to deal with him. In fact, he'd probably be better off than he would be in my care.

The group leader had a list and one by one – and sometimes two by two – the children were selected and claimed by the members of the host families gathered at the bus stop. As the line dwindled to three, then two and Franny's name was not called out, I began to wonder if by some miracle Kimothy had been left behind. I was even starting to edge away to the car that Franny had told me to use when the group leader identified the last child.

He was tall for his age, black and possibly the skinniest kid I'd ever seen. His limbs protruded from his oversize T-shirt and baggy shorts like long twigs. I was struck by his hair, which was lighter in colour than that of the other children. It was shaven close to his head in a wiry caramel blanket and I wondered for a second if one of his parents might be white. But his facial features were distinctly African.

It took me a minute to realise that the cheeky grin on his face and the excitement with which he rushed towards me were figments of my imagination. It was how I had expected him to react to me as his saviour.

But in reality he glared at me in frank hostility and in a split second I wised up. He'd been taken to Port Authority in New York and put on a bus to travel three hours to a place he didn't know, and he was being handed over to a woman he'd never seen before. No doubt he was terrified and, what was more, he probably sensed I was too.

'Time to put your shoes on now, Kimothy,' said the group leader, and I noticed that his feet were bare.

He shook his head, still staring at me, and then he suddenly took flight, charging through the groups of families welcoming other children. One of the fathers, whose reflexes were sharper than mine, reached out to restrain him and was even quick enough to pull his hand away before Kimothy bit it.

'Where's your car?' shouted the man and when I moved towards it, he picked Kimothy up and carried him to it as the boy kicked out in all directions.

And that was how we started out, prisoner and captor sharing the car in total silence – or rather total silence on his part because I tried. I really did. *How was the ride out? Did you make any friends on the bus? Are you hungry? Shall we stop for something to eat? Do you have any brothers and sisters?* But he didn't say a word.

I thought I saw his eyes widen a little as we emerged from the woods and he saw Franny and Rufus's house and the water beyond, and when we drove past the pool he came to life as Franny had predicted, but not as I had ever seen any child behave before.

He didn't wait for me to take him into the cottage where Noreen and I were staying – Franny had called it a pool house but to me it was a most desirable little two-bedroomed guest house – but shot out of the car and rushed inside where he made straight for the kitchen as if he knew exactly where it was. He opened the door of the fridge and helped himself to a soda. He popped it open and threw his head back to toss the liquid into his mouth so that half the contents spilled onto the floor. Then he charged through the house, running in and out of every room and slamming doors behind him as he did so.

'STOP!' I went after him, trying to grab him and when I finally caught hold of him by the arm, I yanked him to a standstill. I didn't think I'd been particularly forceful, but he howled in pain and wriggled out of my grasp to run into the one room he had not yet explored, slamming the door behind him.

It was Noreen's room and she was in there and to my amazement I heard him speak for the first time. Probably more in shock than anything else.

'Who you?' he was asking Noreen as I

opened the door behind him.

'Noreen,' she said. 'You must be Kimothy. That's an interesting name.'

'I fucking hate it,' he said.

Oh, so he'd answer Noreen's questions but not mine. And I was horrified by his language.

'That's too bad. So what shall we call you?' Noreen didn't seem at all put out by the *fucking*. She reached out to pat his arm and he leapt away from her.

'They call me Mo on account of my last name.'

'It's Moses,' I said.

'Shit! I know that!' He turned on me in a fury but I was too thrilled by the fact that he'd addressed me directly to mind.

'But I don't,' said Noreen gently. 'Do you want to call your mother? Tell her you've arrived safely?'

He shook his head and his answer chilled me. 'She don't care.'

Noreen's eyes met mine for a second. 'Well, maybe I'll call her for you,' she said.

He shrugged. 'They never gave us no fucking food on that bus. I want a sandwich,' he said suddenly, not looking at either of us.

You want to learn some manners, I thought but held my tongue. Now was not the time to enforce discipline. I needed to bond with this kid before he tried to run away again.

'Peanut butter and jelly OK?' I asked him.

He shrugged again but devoured the sand-

30

wich in a flash when I handed it to him.

'Gimme another.'

'Say please,' I said.

Silence.

'Oh, go on,' said Noreen, coming into the kitchen. 'You can say please, I know you can.'

'Please,' he said. To *her*, not looking at me. And then when he'd eaten the second sandwich he opened the patio door and charged outside. I screamed, *'Wait for me!'* but within seconds the door slammed again and he was back, pulling open the freezer.

'You got ice cream?' He wasn't looking at me, but he appeared to be speaking to me. I resisted the temptation to grab him by the scruff of his neck and tell him if he didn't calm down, he was going straight back to New York.

'I don't know,' I said, and then, with infinite patience, 'take a look. And then maybe you'd like to go swimming. Do you have swimming trunks in your bag?'

He shrugged – *I don't know* – and upended the contents of his bag all over the floor.

It was a pathetic collection. Two T-shirts, two pairs of shorts, a Ziplock bag containing a toothbrush and toothpaste, a comb, a bar of yellow soap in the shape of a bear and a pair of flip-flops, which would appear to be the only shoes he had brought with him. And that was it. No pyjamas, no socks, no

31

toys of any kind. *No love*, I thought with a jolt.

And then, as I reached for the bag to replace his meagre belongings, I saw there were a couple of other things lying flat in the bottom.

A mobile phone. I held it up to him. 'Want to call your mom?'

He moved so fast I barely had time to register that the phone was no longer in my hand.

'OK, OK. Take it easy,' I said. And then I took out a large format paperback book. *My Golden Book of Bible Stories*. Before that, too, was ripped from my hands I had time to see the inscription on the title page. *For Mo. I love you. Dad.*

I tried not to flinch. 'Your dad gave you this?' I said as gently as I could. 'Was it for your birthday?'

'You got no fucking business with my stuff,' he told me and tossed the book back in the bag. 'How you know *my* dad give me this? How you know it ain't my *friend's* dad and my *friend* give me his book?' Then he stripped down to his underpants and before I could stop him, he'd raced out to the patio. 'I'm going swimming.'

The pool was fenced in to stop Eliza toddling into the water but Mo was tall enough to unlatch the gate with ease. Noreen followed him as he stood on the steps leading down into the pool and kicked a spray of water with his toe.

'Fucking cold,' he said.

'Is fucking your favourite word?' Noreen asked him, rummaging in a large cedar box filled with miscellaneous equipment and extracting a pair of orange arm bands. 'Can't be the only word you know, smart boy like you.'

Mo shook his head. Noreen advanced upon him, brandishing the arm bands. Mo hopped up the pool steps and began to back away from her. As he did so, he grinned and my heart stopped.

His eyes creased up, his mouth seemed to stretch the entire breadth of his face and the gap between his teeth gave his smile a heartbreaking vulnerability.

Noreen tried to go after him but she was no match for the speed with which his long thin legs could carry him. And as he ran, he laughed. *He's having* fun! I thought with relief. *He's finally having fun.*

I was determined to join in so I went outside and began to chase him around the pool.

'Lee, you should never run around a swimming pool,' called Noreen but I ignored her. I was bonding with Mo, we were having our own game and nothing was going to stop it. This was what he was here for.

'Can't catch me,' he taunted over his shoulder.

'Just you wait!' I did an about turn and backtracked to face him head on at the far corner of the pool. Too late he realized what I'd done and tried to back away but he couldn't outrun me.

I caught his arm and held it and he was giggling, enjoying the fun. But he began to wriggle out of my grasp.

'Oh, no, you don't,' I said, and picked him up bodily. Then, caught up in the excitement of the game, I threw him into the pool.

'That'll teach him,' I told Noreen, laughing.

But she wasn't smiling and, looking back at him, I saw why. Whatever Franny had been told, it was quite clear he couldn't swim. I could see his arms flailing and his legs thrashing around under water. He shouted something at us but I couldn't make it out before he floated down to the bottom of the pool where he seemed to crouch, face down.

It was twenty-five years since I'd taken life-saving classes at Kensington public baths in London and until that moment I'd never had an opportunity to put them to the test. But it must be like riding a bike because, when I plunged into the pool, I remembered exactly what to do and it seemed like only seconds later that I was swimming on my back to the steps, my arms clasped under Mo's, pulling him along with me.

There was a moment when I wondered

whether he had in fact been kidding because the second we reached the surface and he'd shaken his head and spluttered, he began to fight me.

'BE STILL!' I roared in his ear and felt him relax against my chest. But when we reached the shallow end he struggled out of my arms and ran up the steps and out of the pool, where he stood hopping from one foot to the other. *He's laughing at me*, I thought and I closed my eyes to concentrate on holding my temper. The shock of seeing what I had thought was a drowned child at the bottom of the pool had manifested itself in blind anger. And now he appeared to be taunting me.

Then he said something that shook me.

'You tried to kill me,' he said as I climbed out of the pool in my dripping clothes, and his eyes were two black pools of accusation.

'Of course I wasn't trying to kill. I just saved you. I thought you could swim. Why did you say you could swim when you can't?'

'I never said that,' he shouted. 'Why would I say that?'

'There's obviously been some sort of mix-up,' said Noreen.

'OK, I'm gonna use those arm bands now, get back in the pool.' He moved to take them from Noreen.

'You are NOT!' I yelled at him.

'Lee, it's what they're for,' Noreen pointed out gently. 'He should learn to use them. We can't keep him out of the pool forever.'

'I'm going to go inside and change into my swimsuit,' I said. 'Until I return you are not to go near that pool. Do you understand?'

'You talkin' to her or me?' Mo giggled.

I advanced upon him and suddenly he looked terrified. He backed away and collapsed on one of the sun loungers on the patio.

While I was changing into my swimsuit I made a quick call to the house and asked Lucia to send someone to put a padlock on the gate in the fence surrounding the pool.

I spent the rest of the afternoon standing in the shallow end while he splashed around. I let him jump in and float in the arm bands but I swam alongside him as he did so.

I'd had my wake-up call. I'd watch him like a hawk from now on. He'd be the safest kid on the east end of Long Island.

Chapter Two

When Lucia arrived at bedtime to escort him back to the main house, he refused to go with her.

'I'm staying here with you,' he told Noreen and I tried not to be upset that he so obviously preferred her. After all, we'd made a little progress, he and I. I'd made hamburgers for supper and the three of us had sat out on the patio to eat them, although I was so tense from forcing myself to stay calm that I was unable to digest more than a mouthful. I was learning fast that he knew how to press buttons, mine in particular.

'You tried to kill me.' He continued to taunt me because he'd realized he could get a reaction out of me. 'You a monster!'

I made a monster face, pulling on the corners of my mouth as far as they would go.

And he loved it. 'You a *scary* monster,' he whooped in glee.

'Who can make the scariest monster face?' I challenged, drawing poor Noreen into the game, and that was how Lucia found us when she arrived, distorting our features at each other in hideous grimaces.

Mo wouldn't go with her. He picked up his book, ran into Noreen's room and got into her bed. 'I'm sleeping here.'

I made to go after him but Noreen stopped me. 'Let me talk to him,' she said. 'Mo, this is *my* room and that's *my* bed. If you're going to stay here with us – and believe me, we'd love to have you, wouldn't we, Lee?'

I nodded frantically.

'So if you're going to be here with us you'll need your own space, won't you?' Noreen reached out her hand. 'Why don't you come out of my room and we'll take a look around and see where you should sleep.'

Whatever it was about Noreen, she had a way with her that made him respond. He took her hand and followed her out into the living area of the pool house. There was only one other bedroom – mine – so after Noreen and I had exchanged glances, we made a big show of *looking for Mo's bed*.

'What about the couch?' said Noreen, clapping her hands as if she'd only just thought of it.

'That would work,' I said, because unless he crashed on the floor, it was his only option.

But Mo wasn't interested. 'I'm gone sleep on that bed out there by the pool he said.

He was pointing to one of the sun loungers.

'You know,' I said, impressed by his ingenuity, 'that's a great idea. Come on, let's go bring it inside.'

Lucia and I made a nest for him in the hallway, which was quite spacious, allowing plenty of room for the lounger. We wheeled it into a corner and plugged in a lamp on the floor beside it that could serve as a nightlight. He wanted to be in the living room, but I had enough forethought to know how much that would inhibit any adult relaxation in the evenings.

'Now, into that bathroom with you, and clean your teeth,' said Noreen, 'and then I'll read you a story from your book.'

'No,' he said, 'I can read. I'm gone read *you* a story.'

'I'm sensing there's a problem with the mother,' Noreen whispered to me while he was brushing his teeth. 'I've tried to reach her twice on the number we have and there's no answer, not even a machine. And you'd think she would have called us.'

I told her quickly about the mobile I had found in his bag. 'I'm guessing he'll use that to call his mum,' I said.

It was clear that he was used to sleeping naked because that was how he got into bed without a shred of modesty. He picked up his book and Noreen settled herself on the edge of the lounger, motioning me to leave.

'Goodnight, Mo,' I said, trying to decide if I could risk planting a kiss on the top of his

39

head. But before I could move he made another scary monster face and I made one back and I had a feeling this would become our nighttime ritual.

'We're going to the beach tomorrow,' I told him, 'and you're going to have a play date with a boy called Keshawn.'

'He gone be scared when I make my monster face.'

I left the door open and hovered outside to listen.

He chose the story of Moses in the bulrushes.

'Pharaoh said *Every son that is born to the Israelites you shall cast into the river, and every daughter you shall save alive.*'

I was impressed at how fluently he read.

'When she saw that he was a boy child – like me!' He broke off suddenly to tell Noreen, 'She hid him for three months and when she could not hide him any longer, she laid him in a basket of bulrushes. Then she left the basket at the banks of the river and when Pharaoh's daughter came down to wash herself, she found it.'

It was a much simplified version of the story but, listening to his voice, I could tell he was taken with it. But it was what he said at the end that really shook me.

'Moses, he found at the water by Pharaoh's daughter.' It had a rhythm to it as if he was rapping. 'And Pharaoh's daughter,

40

she send for Moses' mother to take care of him. But you ain't gone send for my mother, right?'

I didn't want to hear any more. I went to pour myself a glass of wine, waving good-night to Lucia who was on her way out the door. *But you ain't gone send for my mother, right?* I'm a worrier by nature so I tried to tell myself that was the reason his words had disturbed me so. He was just a kid out to enjoy his freedom from parental discipline. But it was more than that. There was something not quite right about the way he referred to his parents – the way he had reacted when I had asked if his father gave him the book for his birthday – and now he seemed scared by the thought that we might contact his mother.

'He reads really well,' I said when Noreen joined me a few minutes later. 'Is he asleep?'

'Almost. And I'm not sure about the reading, although he may have a future career as an actor. He was holding the book upside down the whole time. Now, what are we going to do tonight?'

'I'm going to take a leaf out of your book, Noreen. Mo's worn me out. I'm going to fall into bed pretty soon.'

Noreen gave me a rueful smile. 'You go ahead, dear. Get some rest. You want to be fresh for when your honeymoon starts properly, don't you?'

41

It's fair to say that I don't do married. I've managed to reach the ripe old age of forty and remain single even though Tommy has been my boyfriend since I was thirty-one. That's nine years. You'd think we'd have tied the knot before now. As I said, you can't blame Tommy – I mean, you can if you really want to, fine by me – but as a rule people don't. He's a sweetheart – generous, understanding, handsome in an overweight puppy-dog kind of way. He's naturally gregarious, loves meeting new people, bounces up to them with a wonderfully engaging smile on his face and has the knack of drawing even the most retiring person out of their shell.

So Tommy's not the problem, I am. I'm crabby with a perilously low boredom threshold, especially when it comes to him. And I'm solitary by nature, uncomfortable sharing my space with others and yes, that includes my husband. For the first eight years of our relationship I refused even to live with him. The only reason I eventually allowed him to move in with me on a full-time basis in London was because I spent most of that year three hundred miles away in the depths of Devon, playing nursemaid to my cousin Gussie following her disastrous divorce.

But the real reason I never accepted his constant proposals of marriage was because

I'm an incurable romantic. Marriage is the kiss of death for romantics, although very few of them realize this until it's much too late. When they're at the age that most people start thinking of marriage, when they're still wide-eyed and innocent, romantics are the biggest suckers of them all. They assume that a trip down the aisle is the gateway to a life of everything they've experienced while dating. They take it for granted he's going to find you as sexy and as interesting for the next fifty years of married life as he does on day one. They think nothing's going to change and when it inevitably does – and it's often sooner rather than later – the scales that fall from their eyes jab them far harder – and much more painfully – than they do the more level headed among us.

Two things have stopped me from falling into the same trap. One is the fact that I'm such a loner I was always going to think twice before shacking up with someone. And the other reason is I've witnessed my parents' marriage at close quarters for many years and I haven't liked what I've seen.

It sort of says it all that neither of them showed up for my wedding, although as far as I'm concerned, I've never actually had a wedding. For a romantic like me, getting married in a registry office didn't count.

Tommy sprang it on me without warning. I was as close as I ever would be to marrying him for the simple reason that for the past year, whenever he had brought up the subject, I hadn't dismissed it out of hand. I'd given everybody to understand that if a wedding were organised, I'd show up for it. And here I knew I was pretty safe. My mother was a first-class organiser, but she lived in New York. My best friend Cath was too busy with two children under three and my cousin Gussie was much too involved with preparing for the first summer of her holiday farm rental. That left Tommy.

'I'm thinking Fulham,' he said cheerfully, 'or Chelsea. That church at the end of Old Church Street off the King's Road. That'd be nice, down by the Thames.'

'Why on earth would we want to go all the way down there?' I said, although I knew the answer perfectly well. It was only a hop, skip and a jump from there to Stamford Bridge football ground and if Chelsea were playing at home the day we were married, he could be there in a flash as soon as I said 'I do'.

I was mildly worried when he announced one morning, 'You know, I read you can get married at Asda. I quite fancy waiting for you by the pet food at the end of aisle seven.' But I perked up when he followed it up with, 'Or how about a country house or a castle? And we'll need an event organiser for the party afterwards. Look at this, you can get freeze-dried flower petals as confetti. Who'd have thought?' And of course I was thrilled when he started saying things like 'Fancy going out and trying on a bit of Vera Wang?' while at the same time knowing it would never happen. He jumped from one idea to the other – *Let's request donations to charities instead of a wedding list. We could get people to sponsor a llama* – while I marvelled at the irony of the fact that while he was planning our wedding, I was ghosting a book about divorce.

Mary Jane Markham's book, which I was wrapping up while Tommy pondered the attraction of a lakeside barbecue reception versus a party at Soho House (of which neither of us was a member), was the story of how she got five million pounds out of her husband when he dumped her for a younger model. She was only married for four years and there were no children but her lawyer recognised that the length of the marriage had no bearing on the loss of the abandoned spouse at the end of it. *Take Him to the Cleaners* was destined to become the potential divorcée's bible and as I neared the end of it, like all freelancers, I began to fret about what I would do next.

As it turned out, I needn't have worried. My faithful agent Genevieve had something tucked up her voluminous sleeve for me, although when she first told me about it I barely understood what she was talking about.

'A life coach? Is that a fancy name for a therapist?'

'No!' Genevieve looked quite shocked. 'Absolutely not. You go to a therapist when you're in a really dark place, when you're lonely and depressed and angry and frightened, but when you hire a life coach, you're usually in pretty good shape.'

It made no sense to me. Why would you seek help if you were in pretty good shape?

'Therapists are about delving into the painful past,' Genevieve continued, shifting her considerable weight from one side of her sofa to the other.

Genevieve is one of those rare people who make you want to be fat. Every time I went for a meeting at her office, a tiny room in Covent Garden at the top of a very narrow staircase – so narrow I wondered whether she climbed it sideways – I found myself marvelling at her porcelain skin and dainty features. She always seemed so luscious, like an exotic flower in bloom, ripe and healthy and filled with energy. I'd finally worked out that the reason she was so attractive, despite her excessive weight, was because there was nothing slothful about her, none of the lethargy that often seems to drag down overweight people. Genevieve had the zest of a lithe person – and she was a feisty and supportive agent.

'Life coaches look to the future. They help

46

you to balance your life,' she said.

Oh good. Now I knew where to go next time I felt a bit wobbly. And maybe if I stopped trying to lose weight and pigged out as much as I wanted, I'd look as good as Genevieve.

Then again, maybe not. Somehow I knew I'd also have to reinvent myself and become a naturally outgoing, self-confident, gregarious human being, and that wasn't going to happen any time this century.

'People who hire life coaches are smart enough to know that the time has come for them to make radical changes.' Genevieve was on a roll. 'Maybe they need to pursue an entirely different career or work up the courage to divorce their spouse or even–'

'What about work up the courage to marry him in the first place? Do they deal with those kind of people?'

'Oh, I'm sure they do. They help you break through your barriers, make a leap of faith, they *motivate* you.' Genevieve's tone was taking on the zeal of a revivalist preacher.

'And you think I need to go to one?'

To my intense relief she shook her head. 'No, I want you to write a book for Patience Brook O'Reilly.'

'Patience Brook O'Reilly. There's a name to conjure with. She's a life coach, I take it.'

Genevieve nodded. 'In America – but she's asked for a British ghost because she's originally from England. She needs to do a book to go with her TV series. It's called *Priorities* and it's based on her morning slot on one of the networks.'

'So she lives in America. Would I have to go there?'

'Of course you would, but here's the bit I thought would appeal to you. She's taking time out for the summer at her house in the Hamptons and that's where she wants to work on the book. Your parents are only a couple of hours away in New York, you have all those friends in the area, you'll have the summer at the beach–'

'But Genevieve, I'm getting married.'

'Yes, dear. So you said a year ago but I've yet to receive my invitation to your wedding. You need to keep working. Patience's New York agent has been in touch with me and I said I'd talk to you about it, see if you were interested. But I'm telling you, Lee, read my lips, you're interested, OK? You're perfect for the job.'

I suppose I should have suspected something when I told Tommy that evening that I'd be away for a few months on a job in the States and he took it so calmly. In fact my nose must have been totally blocked that I didn't smell the enormous rat when he said, 'The Hamptons. That's perfect. But don't sign on for another couple of weeks.'

He gave the registry office the obligatory

fifteen days' notice but he only gave me four.

'Friday morning at eleven o'clock. The Rosetti Room, first floor of Chelsea Old Town Hall. Seats fourteen people, they'll do the flowers and we can pick one piece of music and one reading. I'll take care of the music, thought I'd leave the reading to you.'

'But I'm leaving on Saturday,' I wailed.

'I know,' he said, 'it's perfect. We can have our honeymoon in the Hamptons.'

It's meant to be, I told myself over and over again as I raced round London trying to find something to wear and failing miserably. *If I don't go through with it, it'll never happen.*

Every time I tried something on, my reflection in the changing room mirror told me to take it right off again. When I called my hairdresser for a last-minute appointment, they said he was having hernia surgery and they hinted I'd be branded a traitor if I went to anyone else. When I said I was getting married, it was clear they didn't believe me. And why would they? Who books a hair appointment four days before their wedding?

In the end I opted for a five-year-old navy silk dress I'd always liked and in which, more to the point, Tommy had always thought I looked stunning. But when I pulled it out of my closet, it was alarmingly redolent of the party where I'd worn it last, which must have been a get-together of die-hard smokers.

'Don't worry, I'll drop it in the cleaners on my way to the bank,' said Tommy. 'Tell you a secret, I'm thrilled you're marrying me in this dress, much better than one of those meringues you see people in. It'll be the something old and something blue all in one and we'll get you a special bouquet to go with it.'

'What about the something borrowed and the something new?'

He hesitated for a second. 'I was actually going to wait to give you this but you can have it now, why not?' He brought a little ring box out of his pocket. 'It's Mum's. It was her engagement ring from my dad. She wants you to wear it at the wedding.'

It was a strip of gold with two sapphires and a diamond in the middle, not very big, not at all showy, but absolutely the kind of delicate jewellery I loved. I almost cried, partly because it was so typical of Noreen's thoughtfulness, but mostly because my fingers were twice the size of Noreen's and I couldn't get it on.

'Never mind,' said Tommy, ever cheerful, 'we'll get you new shoes to make up for it.'

I knew enough to put out my one and only pair of Manolos, just in case, which was just as well since when I went to pick up my dress just before they closed on the evening before the wedding, I was still waiting for the shoe-shopping expedition.

And when I presented my ticket at the cleaners, they told me my dress wasn't ready yet.

'He never said he wanted it the next day,' said the sulky girl behind the counter, 'you'll have to pick it up Monday.'

So I was married in my next best dress, a sleeveless linen shift. It was simple and boring and respectable, but at least it was white. I tried to dress it up with jazzy necklaces and floating scarves and only succeeded in making a total dog's dinner of myself. In the end I just thought, *To hell with it, I'll wear the Manolos.* Tommy had managed to put together a bouquet of extremely thorny white roses and I pricked my finger the minute I picked it up. A tiny droplet of blood landed on the skirt of my virginal white dress and I arrived at Chelsea Old Town Hall feverishly sucking my thumb to stem the bleeding.

It was a bit like getting married in an office that had been decked out like a funeral parlour with overbearing flower arrangements. Tommy and I were to sit side by side in two chairs in front of a partner's desk. Behind us, fourteen chairs were laid out in a semi-circle for our guests but twelve would remain empty. Cath's children were sick and she

51

didn't want to leave them and my mother maintained that she wasn't going to drag my father all the way across the Atlantic just to sit in a registry office, not if I was coming to New York anyway. I was hurt but not surprised. On the rare occasions when I had imagined my wedding day, my mother had somehow never featured in the picture.

Genevieve was on her summer holiday on a Kent beach and I'd been so busy fussing over what I would wear that I had never got around to calling anyone else. Noreen, bless her, arrived in a printed cotton skirt down to her ankles with a white background and coral honeysuckle all over it. With it she was wearing a white cardigan and it was all a bit dress-down Fridays, but she'd tied a bit of white chiffon around her neck in a rather jaunty fashion and she was smiling so radiantly, anyone would have thought *she* was the bride.

But the other witness was late and we couldn't start without him.

Shagger Watkins had been Tommy's best friend since they had squared off in the sandpit at primary school forty years ago. Now, along with two other former school-mates, they met up whenever Chelsea played at home, congregating at the bookie's across the road from Stamford Bridge at 2.45 on a Saturday afternoon. After the game it was always baked beans on toast at an Italian café – *Why would we order pasta? We like baked beans* – followed by a monumental piss-up in the pub.

Conversation was not Shagger's forte. *Might rain today* or *two sugars please* were typical of the more riveting exchanges I had had with him. In fact, all I really knew about him was that he was the one who bought the programmes for the match, and that all his girlfriends were inflatable.

Over the last few months, however, I had gathered from Tommy that Shagger was going through a mid-life crisis ten years ahead of his time. This had manifested itself in the unthinkable. Following Chelsea's 2-1 win over Tottenham Hotspur in the quarter-finals of the FA Cup, Shagger had announced he was defecting to Spurs. I don't know which was more bewildering to Tommy: that Shagger had gone to the match at White Hart Lane without telling him or that he'd elected to abandon Chelsea after they'd *won*.

'They'll be lost without you, mate, you know they will. Don't do this to them,' I heard Tommy pleading with him nightly down the phone as if Shagger's support could single-handedly determine Chelsea's destiny. But Shagger was adamant and what I found truly mind-blowing was that it was all on account of a woman. Shagger had fallen in love and her name was Minnie

Shaughnessy. The problem was she had six brothers and the message was clear: *You want to shag our Minnie, you've got to be a Spurs supporter.*

I could sense Tommy's mounting anxiety as we sat side by side waiting for Shagger to show up. Eventually, Tommy went outside to call him on his mobile and came back a few minutes later muttering, *'He's on his way.'* But the news didn't seem to have lightened his mood and it was only when Shagger finally did appear, wearing jeans and an open shirt, that he relaxed at the sight of the Chelsea scarf wound round Shagger's neck. *In July?* was my first thought, but I suppressed it to focus on the ceremony that could now begin. But because of the big square desk separating us from the registrar, it felt like we were having a meeting. We were going to reach agreement and sign a contract of marriage and before I had time to wonder if there was any room for negotiation, it was all over. We were man and wife.

Two things made it bearable.

In my panic I had forgotten to prepare a reading and to my utmost amazement, Tommy had anticipated this. When the time came, he slipped a piece of paper into my hands and whispered, *'Read this to me.'*

It was at moments like this that I remembered why, if I was going to marry anybody, it had to be Tommy. He knew who I was. He knew what was important to me. As he stood there in his best suit bursting at the seams – he hadn't worn it in ages and had forgotten to try it on – with his blond hair springing away from his head in an unruly mass of curls, I knew without a doubt that I loved him. And the fact that he had chosen a passage from one of my favourite books, *The Invitation* by Oriah Mountain Dreamer, confirmed it had the potential to be a lasting love.

'It doesn't interest me what you do for a living,' I read, looking into his dark-blue eyes, 'I want to know what you ache for and if you dare to dream of meeting your heart's longing–'

At the end, Noreen clapped. It wasn't entirely appropriate behaviour for a wedding ceremony but I was overjoyed to hear her. Less so the strange gulping sounds erupting from Shagger standing beside her and towering over her. It took me a second to realise he was crying.

If his choice of reading made me aware of Tommy's sensitive side, the music he had selected reminded me that he would always be a kid at heart. When Billy Idol's *White Wedding* exploded into the fake serenity of the Rosetti Room, Tommy leapt up and began to jig about. Shagger joined him and Noreen and I shook our heads in wonder at the sight of the two of them going through the full spectrum of their air-guitar moves. *This is a grown man I am marrying*, I told myself as Billy proclaimed it a 'Nice day for a white wedding, yeah, Nice day to start Agaaaaain!' And I grabbed Tommy's hand and pulled him out of the room before the registrar called security.

'Give him a call,' said Noreen, 'you know you want to.'

'Oh, no, I don't, Noreen,' I said with what I knew was ridiculous petulance, 'besides, I don't want to disturb him. He'll be busy with Shagger. I mean, if he chooses to delay his honeymoon with his new bride in favour of staying in London to boost his best mate's morale, that should tell me something about the way this marriage is going to work out, shouldn't it?'

'Now, Lee, don't be too hard on him. You've known him long enough for you to realize that's who he is, that he can't let Shagger down in his—'

'If you're going to say in his hour of need, Noreen, I'd keep your mouth shut, if I were you. Shagger was dumped by his girlfriend. It happens to everybody at some point.'

'But it's not as if Tommy's not coming at all. He'll be here in a few days, as soon as he's sorted Norman out.'

That stopped me ranting for a second. I wasn't sure I'd ever heard Shagger's real name before. 'But it's the way he did it, Noreen,' I persisted. 'Why did he have to spring it on me just as we were about to leave for the airport?'

'I know. That was a bit naughty,' Noreen conceded, 'but I expect he was scared of how you might react. You can be quite frightening, dear, when you get angry, you know? I've told you before, he fell in love with you because you were the first woman who could keep him in line.'

'If I could keep him in line, he'd be here now,' I said miserably.

'Never mind, dear. You've got me.'

I smiled at that. Poor Noreen, she'd been let down as well. By my mother, who had invited her to New York for a week so she could be there when we were in the Hamptons on our honeymoon. But at the last minute my mother had, typically, called to say she couldn't have Noreen after all. No explanation, and no apparent thought as to how disappointed Noreen would be. And I marvelled at Noreen's spontaneity in agreeing to Tommy's suggestion that she go anyway and accompany me to the Hamptons in his place.

'The thing is, Noreen,' I was determined to have the final word, 'I just don't feel *married!*'

The phone on the kitchen wall suddenly jangled. 'That'll be him,' said Noreen. 'Your *husband*,' she added pointedly.

But it was Franny, calling to find out if Mo had arrived and was safely installed and, as I reassured her that all was well, electing not to tell her about the pool incident, Mo appeared beside me.

'I'm not gonna talk to my mom,' he mouthed.

'It's not your mother,' I said. 'Sorry, Franny. He thought it was his mom calling.'

'Put him on,' she said, 'I want to welcome him, tell him I'll be there soon.'

I handed Mo the phone. 'It's not your mom. It's Franny. This is her house.'

He listened to her with surprising readiness, going *yeah* and *OK* every now and then. Then he said, 'They OK but they old. How old you?' and I decided he'd talked to her for long enough.

'He sounds cute,' she said, 'well, enjoy your day at the beach tomorrow. Scott'll be waiting for you.'

But he wasn't.

Everyone was grouchy in the morning. Noreen and I were jet lagged and Mo had had nightmares. 'I heard him in the night,' Noreen whispered to me. 'He called out for his father. What do we know about him?'

'I don't know,' I whispered back. 'I guess Franny has his case notes somewhere.'

'And he wet the bed. That sun-lounger cushion he slept on was damp. I'll bet his mother kept quiet about that when she filled out the Fresh Air forms,' she muttered and I looked at her, stunned. 'He saw me looking at it and he was very embarrassed,' she went on. 'He swore it only happened when he wasn't used to somewhere. I don't think we should make anything of it. I'll soak the patch with a sponge and leave it in the sun to dry and maybe you could have a word with Lucia?'

Still, I thought. A seven-year-old bed-wetter!

But it was a beautiful day and after settling Noreen out by the pool – *Don't go in with no arm bands*, Mo warned her – I cheered up as he and I piled into the car Franny had left for me to use and drove through East Hampton to Lily Pond Lane. Mo was silent in the backseat and, as I watched him in the rearview mirror, I was aware of him taking in the preposterous Hamptons scene, the bronzed and glossy transient pleasure-seekers parading along the sidewalks. I wondered if he'd ever seen anything like it. I didn't know exactly where he lived in the city, whether he'd ever left the projects in which he'd been raised, whether he was even familiar with places like Madison Avenue or Fifth.

His eyes widened in awe as I turned off Lily Pond and drew up at a pair of high electronic gates. *These look new*, I thought, *Scott must have installed them to protect*

Suzette. I saw a button and pressed it. An electronic squawk erupted from a microphone in a box beside it. 'Who's there?'

'Lee Bartholomew. And Mo. To see Scott.'

'You have an appointment with Mr Abernathy?'

'I do. We're here for Mo to meet Keshawn.'

'You got the code for the gate, right?' said the disembodied voice.

'No, I don't.' Franny had said nothing about a code.

'Well, I don't have you down to see Mr Abernathy and you don't have the code. Don't know how I'm going to let you in.'

'*Please* ask Mr Abernathy. His sister-in-law, Franny, she made the arrangements.'

'Miss Franny in Paris.'

'I *know* – but she said she spoke with Scott – Mr Abernathy.'

'Hold on.'

We waited for five minutes and I sensed Mo looking at me with scepticism. *Why you bring me here? Don't look like they gone let you in.* Then Scott's voice crackled at me.

'Hey, Lee, how you doing? I'm sorry, but we're not going to make it today. I just got Keshawn the new Sony PlayStation 3 and he says he wants to hang here, he doesn't want to go to the beach.'

Mo's expression showed me that he was about to go through the roof with excite-

60

ment. Six hundred dollars' worth of computer game heaven he'd probably only ever see in his dreams.

'That's OK, Scott,' I said, 'Mo'd be cool with PlayStation 3.'

There was a pause. 'Lee, you know, I'm sorry but that's not going to work. Franny never said anything about you guys coming to the house. It was just a beach deal.'

'But we've come all the way here,' I said, glancing at Mo. This was so like Scott. Mo's face had literally come alive with anticipation. I couldn't disappoint him.

'So go down the road to Main Beach,' he said. 'We'll see you another time.'

'Well, I'm going to leave the car here,' I yelled before he went, 'I don't have a beach permit yet. I assumed we'd be able to park in your driveway and access the beach from your property.' One of the more ludicrous things about the Hamptons was that you had to pay $500 just to be able to take your car to any beach worth visiting.

There was a click as he hung up and then the gates began to slowly retreat allowing us to drive in.

'Why he live on a golf course?' I heard Mo's voice behind me and glanced up at the rearview mirror to see him staring at the wide expanse of perfect lawn, peppered with sprinklers and stretching either side of the driveway as far as the eye could see. I drove

61

beyond Scott's mock Tudor McMansion, which looked more like a hotel than a home, and parked as close as I could to the ocean. When we got out I pointed to the narrow trail through the dunes.

'But we gone to the house, play the game.' Mo looked at me, the awful realisation dawning on his face.

'Not today,' I said. 'Sorry about that. Now, through there. Go on, I'll be right behind you.' I gathered up the boogie board and my collapsible seat and followed him, shooing him ahead of me as he wandered disconsolately onto the beach, scuffing sand this way and that with his bare foot. And suddenly I realised something that made me feel both uncomfortable and relieved. *He sticks out a mile. But at least that'll make it easy to keep an eye on him.*

He shed his T-shirt and self-consciously wandered down to the water in his shorts, his skinny arms wrapped protectively around his black chest, as if he were trying to hide it from view.

'Hey!' I yelled after him, 'remember the rule. No going near the water without your arm bands. And if you wait a second, I'll come and show you how to use the boogie board.' As I threw the wings to him, I held the board aloft and pointed as another boy sailed into the shallows on the crest of a wave.

Mo watched and slowly turned his head to look at me. And suddenly his face was as excited as when he had heard Scott mention PlayStation 3.

'Hey, Lee,' he said, addressing me by name for the first time, 'this place is so cool.'

When he smiled at me and waved and I waved back with the boogie board, I felt a surge of relief flood through me. *It's all going to work out. And he'll be OK with the board if I'm right there with him*, I told myself. *Better put some sunscreen on him first.* And then I silently berated myself because I was such a stupid, ignorant white person, I didn't know if he even needed it or not.

'Lee!'

I turned to see Scott striding down the beach. *Oh good*, I thought, *I can ask him what he does with Keshawn.*

But before I could say anything, Scott began to babble.

'Lee, I'm sorry. I feel bad about not inviting you to the house. Honest to God, I wish you guys could visit.'

This was typical Scott behaviour and another reason why I didn't totally hate him. He could behave like a jerk but he almost always seemed to realise what he'd done and apologise for it afterwards. Although it never stopped him being obnoxious all over again.

He stood before me now in his usual uptight fashion, as skinny as Mo, his bony shoulders hunched up almost to his ear-lobes. I was disconcerted by my own reflection in his mirrored sunglasses and I wasn't sure whether to lean forward and proffer a kiss in greeting. He was as much my 'brother' as Rufus but I felt no natural affection for him.

When he put his hand out, I realised that a formal handshake was more his style but I was surprised when he held onto my hand for a second.

'Trust me, I do feel bad,' he said, 'what you have to understand is that things have changed quite a bit since I married Suzette. She has her–' he paused as if unsure how to describe it. 'Her entourage. Her *life*.'

'But it's your house, Scott.'

'Oh sure, absolutely. But I'm protective of her, her–' again he paused. 'Her privacy. We don't want people coming to the house and staring at her – not that they'd ever get near. But we don't want strangers like–' he stopped abruptly as I shook my head slightly in warning. Mo was right behind him and he turned. 'Hey son, you doing OK?' And when Mo barely acknowledged him, he went on, 'You know what? I'm going to go back to the house and get you guys some hot dogs, how's that sound?'

'Sounds good,' I said, 'doesn't it, Mo?'

Mo shrugged and picked up the arm bands.

'Don't go too far,' I said as I helped him into them.

Scott made a few more attempts to communicate with Mo, but Mo seemed determined to punish him for denying him his dream. Finally, Scott muttered, 'Be back real soon,' and shuffled back up the beach.

I pressed my chair into the sand and flopped down, exhausted, aware that Mo had wandered down to the water. *Damn!* I had forgotten to ask Scott about sunscreen. I was careful not to doze off but it was hard to keep my eyes open. The sun was relentless and I felt the stress of my wedding, the long flight and the strain of the first twenty-four hours with Mo on top of the jet lag begin to finally dissolve. Mo was going to be fine. I could just sit here for a minute and enjoy watching him cavorting in front of me.

Except I couldn't because when I opened my eyes, he wasn't there.

I looked along the surf – to the right as far as I could see, and then back again to the left. I clambered to my feet to see if that would give me a better view. Still no sign.

I stumbled down to the water's edge and ran this way and that, shouting his name and then I stood with my back to the water and my eyes scoured every inch of the crowds on the beach right up to the dunes. I'd told myself – *he'll stand out a mile* – and I could tell at a glance that he wasn't there. How long had it been? I glanced at my watch and saw that it was 12.45. What time had we arrived at Scott's? Could I have fallen asleep without realizing it?

'Lee?'

I jumped. Scott had returned, carrying a tray with two hot dogs, two sodas and some crisps.

'What time did we get to you?' I asked him. 'Did you see Mo on your way here? Did he come back to the house?'

'I'm sorry it took so long. Chef was preparing Suzette and Keshawn's lunch. Our hot dogs had to wait–' Scott put down the tray and started pouring drinks.

'Scott! Listen to me. Mo's disappeared. How long have we been on the beach?'

'Half an hour, maybe more.'

'Half an hour! Jesus! Scott, he's gone. He's run away.'

He frowned. In my anxiety I had raised my voice and people were staring. 'He hasn't run away.' Scott patted my arm and I jumped. 'He's just wandered off, is all. He's probably hiding someplace back in the dunes, watching us. He'll be back once he sees the food.'

I took a hot dog and waved it in the air like a maniac and several people on their way down to the water gave me a wide berth. Scott took out his mobile phone.

'Sid, do me a favour. Get down here to the

66

beach, would ya? And on the way here take a look in the dunes and see if you can see a black kid anywhere. Yeah. The one who came through about half an hour ago.' He turned to me. 'Sid's coming down. He'll find him.'

'Who is he?' I was starting to panic. I had abandoned the idea that Mo had run away of his own accord. An altogether more sinister scenario was unravelling in my head.

'Sid Sharkey. He's part of Suzette's security detail. We've got him watching Keshawn.'

'Well, when will he be here?' My voice was shaking.

'Give him a break. He's going to search for your boy. Now, stop worrying. He'll turn up. Tell you what, I'll walk up the beach a bit, see if anyone's seen him. Eat your hot dog before it gets cold.'

I cringed in embarrassment as I heard him shouting out, 'Anyone seen a black kid?' On the rare occasions that Scott meant well it was usually ruined by the fact that political correctness was way over his head. Out of the corner of my eye, I saw a man stare at him and take out his mobile phone. I edged closer and heard him say, *'Suzette's husband's running up and down the beach saying a black kid's gone missing.'*

I waited about ten minutes trying to calm down. *He's hiding somewhere. He's just playing games with us. Getting back at Scott. He'll be back any moment.* I saw Scott pause further

67

up the beach and take out his phone. As he listened he began to tear through the crowd towards me. He snapped his phone shut as he reached me.

'Something weird's going on. Suzette got a call from a girl, sounded like a teenager. She told Suzette they'd got Keshawn, said she'd have to pay big to get him back.'

'He's been kidnapped?'

'That's just it. He hasn't gone anywhere. Suzette said Keshawn was right there beside her while she took the call. It's gotta be a hoax.'

'It's not a hoax,' I said slowly. 'They've got Mo. They saw him come out of your property, they saw him with you on the beach. They thought he was Keshawn. They've kidnapped the wrong boy.'

Chapter Three

'Oh, Jesus, who called the press?' Scott pointed to a man running down the beach towards us toting a hand-held camera. A sound man followed.

'Mr Abernathy? Channel 12 News. You're looking for a child gone missing on the beach? Is it Suzette's kid? Is it Keshawn? Has he run away? Has he been kidnapped?'

'No,' said Scott, 'You guys got it all wrong. It's not Keshawn. He's fine. He's up at the house with Suzette. It's just—'

I wanted to hit him. *You're wasting your time, folks. It's not a celebrity's kid that's gone missing. It's just some two-bit black kid from the projects I wouldn't even have in my house!*

'So why were you looking for him?'

'Just trying to help out.' Scott's good neighbour act might have worked better if he hadn't abruptly turned his back on the reporter and yelled, *'Sid! Over here!'* Then he turned back to him and dumped me in it. 'Lee here's my half-sister. She's from England and it's her kid that's wandered off.'

As Scott moved away to talk to a burly man in a suit, the attention switched to me. Never mind that half his information was

69

inaccurate – I wasn't any relation to him and it wasn't my kid – it was six degrees of separation, there was a connection to Suzette and that was enough for the press.

I backed away from the soundman trying to thrust a boom into my face as the reporter bombarded me with questions. *What's your kid's name? Are you staying with Suzette? How long have you been here?*

'I don't even know Suzette,' I said with a certain amount of satisfaction before the man in the suit stepped in front of me.

'Leave her alone, fellas. She has nothing to say to you. Come on, ma'am, come with me.'

He was huge, a giant beefcake of a man with the broadest chest I had ever seen straining against a white shirt underneath his jacket. His head seemed totally square, made even more so by the buzz cut of his almost white hair. I couldn't see his eyes because of his sunglasses. *Cop glasses,* I thought instantly without knowing why.

Why's he wearing a suit on a day like this? I wondered, noticing how his bulging muscles ruined the shape of the jacket. And then the jacket fell open and I saw the holster.

'Who are you?' I yelled as he hustled me up the beach towards Scott who was talking to a couple sitting on the sand just at the edge of the dunes. 'I should stay where I was. I'm here with a kid and he–'

'Yeah, I know. Mr Abernathy just told me. You're watching his brother's Fresh Air kid. Sidney Sharkey.' He held his hand across him in an awkward attempt to shake mine as we moved side by side up the beach. 'Security Sid. Part of Suzette's detail. I watch Keshawn.'

Security Sid. He said it with no irony, as if he was suggesting the form of address I should use.

'You and Sid introduced yourselves?' Scott said as we reached him. 'Listen up, these guys saw Mo go back to my house.'

I looked down at the couple sitting on the sand and then I realised they were at the very edge of the trail leading to Scott's house. 'Are you sure?' I said, 'How do you know it was him?'

'Because we were sitting right here when he came out with you.' The woman looked up at me while the man, sprawled on his towel beside her, didn't even bother to open his eyes. I resisted the urge to kick him. 'Coming back, he walked right past us with a woman about forty-five minutes ago.'

'A woman? What woman?' I was frantic.

'I thought it was you. I saw the boy but then I lay back down as the woman went by and I only saw her legs walking past and the bottom of her shorts. I'd registered her as female as she came up the beach but I didn't really look at her face.'

71

Sid had moved away to talk on his mobile. Now he shouted to us.

'I've got them searching the house. They didn't see anything on the monitors.'

We started up the trail through the dunes, Sid with his phone clamped to his ear. About halfway up, he stopped. 'They've looked in every room and they're not there. Now they're searching the basement, the garage, the pool house, everywhere. But if he'd gone to the house, they'd have known the minute he stepped on the property. Here's what I think happened.' He pointed to where the trail veered to the left to cut a path through the tall beach grass to the edge of Scott's lawn. 'When they got to here they turned right instead of left.'

I looked to the right and saw that the trail split in two. I ran along the right side without waiting for Sid to finish. Within seconds I came out a short distance down the road from the entrance to Scott's property. A car could have been waiting here, Mo could have been bundled into it and by now he could be miles away.

'We have to call the police,' I said, running back to Scott and Sid.

'Sid already did,' said Scott. 'It's kind of early to report a missing person but given Suzette had that call, I'm taking no chances.'

'I called the Juvenile desk direct,' said Sid.

72

'They're on their way.'

They must have been coming from further up the island because it took them an hour to arrive. Scott tried to make me go back to the house with him but I knew I had to stay at the beach in case by some miracle Mo appeared. I couldn't get it out of my head that something was only being done because Keshawn had been threatened. The worst part about it was not knowing whether Mo was actually in danger or not. I knew I ought to call Franny, but I didn't have the number of her hotel in Paris on me. And all the time I kept hoping that there would be no need.

By the time Sid reappeared with two other men in jackets, I was convinced that everyone on the beach must be aware that Mo was missing. I had spent the past hour trampling around each and every prone body, standing over them, blocking out their sun, forcing them to open their eyes and tell me whether they had seen Mo.

'This is Detective Pete O'Donnell and Sergeant Vincent De Serio,' said Sid, 'they're both on the Juvenile desk. Guys, this is Mrs Kennedy. Like I told you, she's taking care of the Fresh Air kid until Mr Abernathy's brother gets back from France.'

I was surprised at how violently I reacted to the *Mrs Kennedy*.

'I'm Lee Bartholomew,' I said firmly. 'I don't use my married name.' *Not least because I've barely had time to get used to it.*

The one called Pete O'Donnell crouched on the sand beside me and people turned to stare at him. Three men in jackets on the beach on a glorious summer's day could only mean one thing. I imagined I could hear the whispering begin.

'OK, what's the boy's name?'

'Kimothy Moses. But he's known as Mo.'

'How old is he?'

'Seven.'

'Can you give me a description of him?'

'African-American. Tall for his age, very skinny, long legs and arms.'

'Last seen wearing?'

'Swimming trunks, pale blue with turquoise fishes swimming all over them.'

'That's it?'

'His T-shirt and flip-flops are still here. Oh, there was something else–'

'Yes?'

'He was wearing arm bands. Orange arm bands, inflated–'

'Like this?'

I screamed. I couldn't help myself. Sid had produced something he'd been holding behind his back.

'We found this in the dunes further up the road from Scott's house, by the trail.' He showed me an orange arm band just like the one Mo had been wearing. The sight of it confirmed my worst fears.

'So you have a picture?' Pete O'Donnell had his hand out.

I shook my head.

'Back at the house?'

I shook my head again. No. I had nothing.

'No photo? What about his parents? What are their names? Has he ever run away?'

I was so ashamed at how useless I was that I couldn't look at him any more. I didn't know Mo's parents' names because I hadn't even looked at the information Franny had been given on him. Noreen had. She'd been responsible enough to try and reach his mother even if she hadn't actually managed to speak to her. I could answer only one question. *Yes, he tried to run away the second he got off the bus.*

'He seemed scared?' Detective O'Donnell tensed a little. 'What are you saying? Do you think he was trying to get away from someone on the bus?'

'I don't know,' I said, 'someone might have scared him on the way out, but he was the last one to get off the bus so they couldn't have been chasing him.'

'Where do his parents live? What's their address?'

My silence was greeted with looks of disbelief. *You're in charge of a kid and you don't even know where he lives?*

Sid came to my rescue. 'Give her a break, fellas. She's at the beach, she won't have any

75

of that stuff with her. It's going to be back at the house where the kid's staying. Scott Abernathy has a call in to his brother Rufus in Paris. He's the person the kid's supposed to be with, he'll be able to tell us where to locate this information. In the meantime, why don't you check it out with the Fresh Air Fund?'

Oh no! Now the Fresh Air people would find out how totally useless I was.

Sid must have noticed my look of dismay. 'Ms Bartholomew, they need to get his details as soon as possible. Now all you can do is go back to where you're staying and wait.'

He walked me back to Scott's house and I followed him into a room off the garage where he tried to raise Scott on the internal phone so I could say goodbye. The room had a built-in shelf-like desk running along three of the walls, with phones and security monitors on the walls. I watched, fascinated, as one by one various rooms in Scott's house came up on the monitors and then I halted on one screen and stared.

It was a luxury den with home theatre equipment laid out along one wall. I wasn't sure I'd ever seen such a big screen even in a movie theatre. Scott was on the phone and I realised he was talking to Sid right beside me. A slender boy in his pre-teens with finer features than Mo's was engrossed in a

76

computer game. Keshawn. And lounging with her feet up, her extraordinary breasts just visible, rising above the back of the couch like two upturned bowls, was Suzette. The image on the console in front of me was mute but it was clear that she was screaming silently at Scott and every now and then he turned away from the phone to answer her, causing Sid, beside me, to ask, 'Sir? Are you there?' As I watched this celebrity version of domestic bliss unfolding before me, I wondered if this was the closest I would ever come to meeting Suzette.

'Mr Abernathy's tied up right now.' Sid turned to me. 'He says for me to accompany you back to where you're staying. Your car's outside, isn't it? I'll follow you.'

As I drove away from Scott's house and up Lily Pond Lane, I was slightly mollified by the sight of several police cars passing me in the other direction and when I arrived back at the pool house, Lucia was remonstrating with a team of men who were trying to get through the door. I stopped my car, got out and gave her a hug.

'This is a forensics team,' Sid told me. 'They'll need to gather some impressions of latent fingerprints from all over the house, anything Mo might have touched. They'll have to take yours and Lucia's and those of anyone else who was here with him so they can eliminate them and isolate Mo's.

77

They're doing the same thing at the beach and at Mr Abernathy's property. Has Mo been in contact with anyone else here?'

I calmed Lucia down and led Sid and the forensic team inside.

'My mother-in-law, Mrs Noreen Kennedy, is with me,' I explained.

'On your *honeymoon?*' Sid couldn't help himself. 'Mr Abernathy mentioned you were on your honeymoon. Your husband didn't want to come to the beach?'

'My *husband*–' Did he notice the catch in my voice? '–is still in London.'

He didn't say anything and when I introduced him to Noreen, he held out his hand.

'Sidney Sharkey. Security Sid.'

'Hello.' Noreen's tiny hand was swallowed up by Sid's gigantic paw but he relinquished it with surprising gentleness. She only came up to the bottom of his massive chest and I thought how fragile she appeared beside him. She smiled and squinted up at him into the sunlight. 'Where's Mo? Stayed to play with Scott's boy?'

This was too much for me. If only Mo had been allowed to do just that. If only Scott had invited him into his precious inner sanctum so he could be watched every second on security cameras. If only he hadn't been taken to the beach by a useless person like myself who fell asleep instead of watching him like she was supposed to.

The thing I loved about Noreen was that she always took everything in her stride, even though that stride was considerably shorter than most people's. She listened to everything Sid told her about what had happened, perched on the end of one of the sun loungers like an alert little sparrow, her head cocked slightly to one side. I could see that the sun was already beginning to turn her scalp a little pink beneath what the chemo had left of her snowy white hair. I walked up behind her and placed on her head the straw bonnet she had brought with her and she reached automatically to tie the ribbons under her chin.

She didn't cry out or berate me or show any undue emotion on learning that Mo was missing. Instead she smiled and said, 'Shall we all have a cup of tea?'

The forensics team requested *ice* tea and asked where Mo had slept and could they please be given some of his things.

Noreen turned to Sid. 'Now, I'm going to make you a proper pot of tea because this is going to be hard, isn't it? We're just going to have to sit and wait for news. We're going to have to be patient, aren't we? Lee's not very good at that, are you, dear? Tell me about yourself, Security Sid, how long have you worked security?'

I saw that he puffed up – if that was possible in a person of his immense size –

when she called him Security Sid. When she made to stand up, he moved quickly to help her, his hand under her elbow. She smiled at him and allowed him to walk her into the kitchen to make the tea.

I knew that despite her fragility Noreen had no problem with her joints. Her mobility was as good as that of someone ten years younger. But she was deferring to Sid, allowing him to help her because she knew it would make him feel good.

She could read a person the minute she met them and that was one of the many reasons I liked being around her. I felt she knew exactly who I was, faults and all, and I could be myself with her. As I watched her fussing in the kitchen, allowing Sid to carry the tray, *Do you take milk and sugar? Oh, no, not cream, dear, not in tea*, I could feel my panic about Mo begin to recede a little. Noreen always had that effect on me. She met my natural tendency to fret with perpetual calm. She knew just how to handle me. She never suggested, as my own mother always did, that I might be exaggerating my problem, that I was making a fuss about nothing. Instead she always settled me down and made me talk things through with her before invariably coming up with a solution.

But this time I was prepared for her magic wand to be useless.

'I'm new to the game, ma'am,' said Sid.

'Less than a year on the job. My old captain hired me as part of the Abernathy security detail. I knew he was the boss over there and I gave him a call on my retirement.'

'So you were a policeman?' Noreen sat down and flashed me a look. *Where are you? Come and sit down. We're all worried but we just have to wait it out.* 'But, Sid, you look much too young to be retired.'

Sid grinned. 'I joined the police force right off the bat at twenty-one knowing it was a twenty-year retirement with pretty good money. But I learned pretty soon that while you're doing the job, that pension is the carrot they're hanging out on a stick to you every day. They pay you just enough to survive so even though you've got family benefits, if you want to live well you have to work a second job or a third job.'

'You've got a family, Sid? Kids?'

He made a wry face. 'I *had* a family. A wife, two kids. You're working round the clock, Christmas Day, holidays, there's a high burn-out. Wives don't always stick around.'

'I'm sorry,' said Noreen. 'Were you a cop in New York City?'

Sid nodded, his face grim. 'I worked the beat twenty years and all the time it's hell trying to make ends meet. Inflation's going up all around us, everybody's making money on the stock market but if you're a cop you gotta work two extra jobs otherwise you can't afford to make the payments on your house, a car, anything.'

'And it's so dangerous,' whispered Noreen and we both jumped as Sid exploded.

'That's exactly it! You're a target all the time! You're running in to save people, that's your job.' He mimed running, his arms going back and forth by his side. 'Two people are beating the heck out of each other and a cop's got to jump right into the middle of that. Someone's robbing a bank with a gun, you can't say *not my problem*. Cop's gotta get in there too.'

'So you're not exactly running round telling people they ought to become a cop?' Noreen said dryly.

'I'm not saying anything.' Sid looked a bit embarrassed by his outburst. 'People'll join for the same reason I joined. They want to do the right thing, they want to help people. They want to keep law and order. You're young and full of piss and vinegar and raring to go. And for some of the guys it works out fine. Look at Pete and Vince we just saw at the beach.'

'They're the detectives on Mo's case,' I explained when Noreen looked at me. *Mo's case*, I thought and my heart gave a lurch. What kind of case would it turn out to be?

Sid wasn't finished. 'But they've got problems recruiting,' he said, standing up and pacing the room. 'Oh yes! Back in eighty-one to eighty-five I was right at the end of a major hiring they had. They went from a 35,000 police force to 45,000 and so what happens? A couple of years ago everyone started hitting their twenty years and you had this mass exodus of people retiring. But they're not getting the numbers to replace them and they're lowering the standards so everybody passes the test. I wouldn't be surprised if they got functional illiterates with guns out on the beat and the worst part is who suffers? The people. The taxpayers who're paying to have a good police force.'

He was working himself back up into a state again.

'What about Pete O'Donnell and Vincent De Serio?' I asked him.

'They're good guys,' he said, standing up and giving himself a little shake as if to calm himself down. 'I've known Pete fifteen years and Vince maybe seven. They haven't been on the Juvie desk that long but I know they'll give it everything they've got.'

'Sid, you don't have to stay here with us,' said Noreen. 'We know you'll be in touch the moment there's any news.'

'It's not a problem,' he said and that's when I realised that Scott must have assigned him to protect us. 'I'm going to stick around until the boy shows up.'

He made it sound as if Mo would come running in at any minute and I knew that the sound of him slamming the door behind him would have been more welcome than anything I could think of.

'I'm going to call Franny,' I said and went to the phone. But she wasn't there and I left a message, wondering if Scott had reached Rufus. Sid took a call from Pete O'Donnell and relayed the news that they'd got Mo's mother's address from the Fresh Air Fund and sent someone round there. But she wasn't there and a neighbour said he hadn't seen her since Mo left.

Noreen made more tea, Sid paced and when I thought I was about to shoot through the roof with tension, I stripped down to my swimsuit and plunged into the pool. I stopped counting after forty laps and finally climbed out exhausted. I walked back into the house, not caring that I was dripping water everywhere. Noreen had fallen asleep on the couch and Sid was in the kitchen on the phone. As I walked by to my room, I froze when I heard Sid say.

'You're sure he's OK? We should maybe get him checked out at Southampton Hospital.'

I stood in front of him and mouthed *What's happened? Is it Mo? Have they found him?* I pulled at his sleeve and he held up his hand palm out to stop me.

'Sid!' I screamed at him. 'Tell me!'

'Hold on,' he said into the phone. 'Yes,

they've got him. He's safe. Now go wake Mrs Kennedy and I'll be there in a second to tell you what happened.'

I roused Noreen gently and sat hugging her until Sid joined us. I leapt to my feet but he motioned me to sit.

'Now you've got to stay calm but it's a bigger deal than we thought.'

'But you said he was–' I cried out.

'The boy's fine. They found him at a little ranch house over on Spring Hollow Road in Springs. A woman next door got a call from her daughter who was at the beach. The daughter said, *'Guess what? There are cops all over the beach because a black kid has gone missing and they thought it might be Suzette's.'* So a little while later the woman hears a car drive up and a lot of shouting and then she sees a kid run into the back yard. A black kid. She doesn't take much notice because the house next door is a summer rental and there have been people coming and going since Memorial Day.'

'Who was the–?'

'Lee, dear, let him finish,' said Noreen.

'But then she hears the kid crying and shouting. *No! Let me go!* Stuff like that. So she looks out her window that has a view of the back yard next door. There's a woman with her back to her and she's pulling the kid but she can't get a grip on him because of an arm band the kid's wearing. She thinks it's

85

just a mom having trouble with her kid but after a while it doesn't add up. The mom is white. And the arm band makes the woman think of the beach and her daughter's call. So she dials 911.'

'And they responded? And they found Mo. And they caught the person who took him?' I held my breath.

'The front door was open when they got there. They walked right in and at first they thought there was nobody there. Then they heard Mo. He was locked in a bedroom.'

'And the woman who took him? She got away?'

'This is the rough part.' Sid laid a hand on my shoulder. 'Mo wasn't alone in the house. They found a woman's body lying in the bathtub. Drowned.'

Chapter Four

'I have to face up to it,' said Franny. 'My life has totally changed. I've been kidding myself I'm still the same Franny Cook who grew up poor around here and that marrying my childhood sweetheart, who just happened to be the son of a billionaire, wouldn't alter a thing. But hiring a bodyguard for Eliza – that tells me something I can't ignore.'

Franny was standing in the shallow end of the pool holding her daughter by the hand as Eliza, held afloat by a rubber ring, propelled herself round and round in circles, her little legs kicking furiously. Franny blinked repeatedly as water splashed in her face. And at the far end of the pool, sitting in a chair partly obscured by a shrub, trying to look inconspicuous and failing miserably, was Security Sid.

Franny and Rufus had booked a flight back from Paris the minute Scott had reached them on the telephone. They had arrived at their house around midnight, about an hour after Pete O'Donnell and Vince De Serio had delivered Mo safely into our care.

Mo, although apparently unharmed, was exhausted by his ordeal and Noreen and I put him straight to bed. When Franny came rushing down to the pool house, I put my finger to my lips as I motioned her through the front door and pointed at him lying on the lounger in the hall.

'We'll talk in the morning,' I whispered.

I had been so relieved to see Mo when they brought him back to the pool house that I didn't even mind that he rushed straight past me into Noreen's arms. He'd been huddled in a blanket and as he ran to Noreen it fell off and I saw he was still wearing his swimming trunks and flip-flops. Sid followed with Pete and Vince.

'We'll need to question him as soon as possible,' said Pete. 'We'll be back in the morning. He kept saying he wanted to come back here so we're kinda hoping maybe he'll open up if he has you and Mrs Kennedy beside him.'

'Hasn't he been asking for his mother?' I said. 'Have you found her?'

'I don't know what it says about their relationship but he hasn't mentioned her once,' said Vince. 'Although in a way that's a good thing because there's no sign of her. She's left home and didn't leave word with her neighbours where she's gone.'

The next morning Noreen came into the kitchen and, as I handed her a cup of tea, Mo ran past us out to the patio where he slumped down at the table. I took him some juice and asked him if he wanted some eggs or a muffin but he didn't answer and by the time Pete and Vince arrived an hour later, nothing had changed.

'Mo,' Vince went outside and knelt down to the boy's level, 'we've got to have a talk, buddy, what do you say? We need to hear what happened to you.'

Mo closed his eyes and shook his head several times. Vince was about to persevere when Noreen reached out to restrain him. She whispered something to me and I nodded. Of course!

'Mo,' I said, 'look at me.' I dropped down to crouch beside Vince and I made a scary monster face. It worked. There was a moment's hesitation and then a glimmer of a smile appeared on Mo's face and he put his fingers in the corner of his mouth to distort it.

'My monster's scarier than yours.'

'Absolutely,' I said. 'Want some ice cream for breakfast? Let's all have some ice cream.'

I motioned to Pete and Vince to join Mo at the table. I put two large tubs of Ben and Jerry's before them and a scoop, some bowls and spoons.

'It wasn't my fault,' said Mo suddenly. 'I didn't do no wrong. She want me to go with her. She *invite* me.'

I froze, mid scoop.

'Who did?' said Pete gently.

'The girl on the beach,' said Mo, and then, suddenly garrulous, he rushed on, 'she ask me do I want go back to the house with her and she point to the big house where we went,' he looked at me briefly, 'and I say *We gonna get PlayStation 3?* and she say *Yeah, that's right. Come with me.* But then we get a little way up the trail and she say *We gonna go this way, we goin' drive there.* But when I get in the car, I see I left my arm band and I say *Miss, wait up, I got to get my arm band* but she drive off and she don't take me to the big house, she take me to that shitty small house. But I didn't do no wrong.'

'Of course you didn't do anything wrong,' said Noreen. 'Why ever would you think that?'

Mo looked at her in amazement. 'Because I'm black. You cops, right?' He looked at Pete and Vince. 'You come get me.'

Noreen and I looked at each other. *Did we really hear that?*

'Mo,' said Pete and nothing on his face registered surprise at what Mo had said, 'tell us about the girl. Did she tell you her name?'

Mo shook his head, *No.* 'She don't talk to me too much. She talk on her cell phone all the time. She talk 'bout me.' Mo grinned. 'She say *Yes, Keshawn's here. I got him. We're on our way home now.* Stuff like that. And I say *I ain't Keshawn.* But she take no notice and she didn't bring me home. She bring me to this dumb little house and I ask her *Where we goin'?* But she don't say nothin' to me.'

'And what happened when you got there?' Pete was trying to appear relaxed but I saw him tense as he waited for Mo's answer.

'She say *Stay in the car* while she go and unlock the front door. Then she tell me to get out and run into the house. She say *Run as fast as you can!* So I run like the scary monster's after me but instead I go round the house to the yard. She come after me. I shout *You can't catch me!* You know,' he looked at me, 'like we played round the pool?'

'But she caught you?' said Vince.

'She try!' Mo giggled. 'But she keep grabbing my arm band 'steada my arm.' He frowned suddenly, remembering. 'She got the arm band off and then she hold me so hard, she hurt my arm. I cried, I said *Let me go, you're hurting me.* But she pull me all the way to the house and she lock me in a room.'

He didn't seem unduly scared to me and I wondered if he was used to being pulled indoors and locked in a room. 'And then?' said Pete.

'I shout *Let me out!* but she don't take no notice. But I put my ear close to the door and I hear all kinds of stuff.'

I could feel the tension in the air as we waited for him to tell us what he had heard.

'There's a knock on the door, real loud, and someone say *Let me in, quick!*'

'What did this voice sound like?' Vince prompted him. 'Man or woman?'

'Woman,' said Mo, *'Old!'*

'That could mean thirty to a kid like him,' muttered Pete behind me.

'And I hear her say *Where is he?* And the girl who brought me, she say *He in there but he say he ain't Keshawn.* And the older lady get real mad and say *Who else could he be? Show me,* and they come to my room.'

'So you saw the older woman?'

Mo shook his head. 'More people come before they unlock my door, and I'm yellin' and screamin' *Let me out! Let me out!* But no one come near me again.'

'And who else arrived?'

'I hear a man.'

'That's all?' said Pete.

Mo looked anxious. 'I don't know. I couldn't *see.* I hear voices but I can't see who's there. Maybe two people, maybe five people, I don't know.'

'It's OK, Mo, you're doing great,' said Vince. 'And then what happened?'

'They all talking, making a lot of noise, then the man, he leave.'

'How do you know that, Mo, if you couldn't see anything?' said Vince.

'I hear him, he say *I'm gonna leave now, bye bye,* something like that. And then I hear talking and laughing and then suddenly it all goes very quiet. And then I get scared

92

because I know the house is empty. They done left me there and no one know where I am. How'm I gone get food?'

I put my arm around him and pushed the bowl of ice cream towards him.

'But I guess they call the police because you come and get me.' He looked at Pete and Vince. 'The ride in the cop car was pretty cool – but I ain't done nothing wrong.'

At that moment I realised that Mo had had no idea he was not alone in the house when they found him, that there had been a woman's body lying in the bathtub down the hall from him.

We heard the slam of a car door outside and a second later Security Sid walked in. Mo looked at him in alarm and I realised Sid's immense size must seem overbearing to a child.

'This is our friend, Sid,' I told Mo, holding up the palm of my hand to Pete and Vince to show them I intended to keep talking. 'Sid, this is my new friend Mo. He's out here from the city for a few days. Mo, why don't you ask Sid if he wants some ice cream?' I handed Mo the scoop.

'I guess we could take a break,' said Pete. 'Ma'am, would you mind coming outside with me for a second?'

Noreen nodded *It's okay* and moved closer to Mo. Sid helped himself to a jumbo size scoop of Butter Pecan.

Outside Pete beckoned a tall man with soulful brown eyes and a mop of curly hair who was leaning against the hood of a police car. He was dressed in a work shirt and jeans and Pete introduced him as Charlie Merriweather.

'Charlie's a detective but he's also a sketch artist,' he explained. 'He's used to working with kids and we have him dress casual so they feel comfortable with him. I'd like to have him work with Mo, see if he can get a good description of the girl who abducted him. Do you think you can persuade him to help Charlie out?'

'Noreen – Mrs Kennedy's your best bet,' I said. 'He seems to trust her more than me. Wait here a second.' I went back in the house and found a pencil and some paper. I scribbled a note to Noreen explaining about Charlie Merriweather and placed it on the table where only she could read it. She nodded at me and mouthed *Bring him in*.

'Hello, Charlie,' she said when he came in, as if she already knew him. 'Oh great, you brought your drawing things. Do you have extra paper so Mo and I can draw some pictures too?'

'She's a natural,' whispered Pete behind me, 'I may have to hire her.'

Charlie handed out paper and crayons and settled himself across the table from Mo.

'I hear you've just had an adventure,' he

94

said. 'Let's play a game. I'm going to see if I can draw the girl you met at the beach. If I get it wrong, you'll tell me, OK?'

He worked fast, sketching a girl's face, making her cheeks chubby and her eyes wide open. Mo shook his head. *You got it all wrong, she big but she have little eyes. And she got a nose that goes like this.* He brought his two forefingers together to a point in front of his own small nose with its wide nostrils.

I felt Sid's hand on my elbow. 'Let's leave them to it,' he said, 'too many people, he might get distracted. Let Charlie work on bonding with him and just leave Mrs Kennedy there in case he needs her.' He led me outside to the far end of the pool. 'By the way,' he said, 'you're going to be seeing a lot of me. Mr Rufus has asked me to run security for them now. After what's happened, he doesn't want to take any chances. I've been released from Mr Scott's detail for the time being. Now I get to watch Eliza and I'm also going to keep an eye on Mo while he's still here.'

'That's great,' I said. 'I tell you, I'll be glad to have you around even though Mo wasn't the real target. But, Sid, what happened? Whose body was found?'

'From the contents of her purse she appears to be a young local woman but they're waiting on her mother to positively ID her. And the mother, it turns out she

95

owns the house. She had construction workers living there most of the year until it came to the summer rental season.'

'And her daughter drowned in the bathtub? What was she doing there? Collecting the rent for her mother? Had she been there a while?'

'It seems she was barely dead,' said Sid, 'She must have died while Mo was in that house. It smacks of amateur night to me. The girl didn't tie him up, she could barely control him. And basically, other than lock him in a room, she didn't do him any harm.'

'Yet she managed to kill another woman,' I said.

'We don't know that yet. Sounds like there were plenty of people in that house,' said Sid. 'Until Mo gives us a description of the girl who took him from the beach, we don't know who killed whom. The woman in the bathtub might have been the girl who picked up Mo on the beach or she might have been the homeowner's daughter. We just have to wait and see.'

'What about the call she made? Can they trace it? Can't they do that with records from the phone company or something?'

'Already did,' said Sid, 'traced to a cell phone but when they contacted the owner she said her phone had been stolen the day before at the supermarket. Lifted from her purse while she waited at the checkout.

They've probably found that phone tossed away by now. She'll have switched to another once the ransom call had been made.'

'Not quite so amateur then,' I said. 'Are they saying it's definitely murder? Could it have been an accident?'

Sid made a face. *Maybe*. 'Yo!' His phone vibrated on his hip. 'Right. We'll come take a look.' He turned to me. 'Charlie's done with the pictures.'

The table was spread with discarded drawings. Mo was holding up a charcoal sketch of a woman's head. It was a foxy little face, quite pretty, I thought, but the eyes were mean. 'Look, I helped get the face right.' Mo was gleeful. Beside him Charlie surreptitiously pushed a photograph of another woman towards us, shaking his head.

'That's a picture of the woman in the tub,' he mouthed. 'Her mother gave it to us. We showed it to Mo. He said he'd never seen her before.'

I stared down at the smiling image of a fresh-faced young woman with blond hair and even teeth. It was in colour and the most striking thing about her was the almost violet blue of her eyes. It was a posed photograph, the kind that featured in displays of family members in offices, was drawn proudly out of wallets on airplane trips and affixed by magnets to refrigerator doors. Strangely impersonal, it made her look like a billion other American girls and I hoped it wasn't the only thing her relatives would have to remember her by.

So Foxy Face had lured Mo away from the beach. And presumably killed Miss All America.

'Can we come in?'

We all started as Franny poked her head around the door and without waiting for an answer, walked in carrying Eliza.

'It's your pool house, Franny,' I said, smiling at her. I looked at Pete and Vince. Surely they wouldn't insist they continue questioning Mo?

Pete nodded. 'OK. We're done for today but we'll probably be back.' He held out his hand to Mo. 'It's been nice meeting you, Mo. Thanks for helping us out.'

'You're the cops,' Mo said, slapping the palm of Pete's hand with his own. It wasn't clear whether he now thought this was a good or a bad thing. I was pretty sure Pete hadn't held out his hand to be slapped. But I was relieved to see that Mo was considerably more relaxed than he had been earlier that morning.

Charlie Merriweather was looking at the pool with longing.

'Don't even think about it, Charlie,' said Vince. 'We've got work to do.'

Charlie laughed and as he gathered up the spread-out sketches, I saw there were several of Foxy Face full length in frayed cut-off jeans and what looked like a peasant blouse, a cropped smock that flapped in the air and left her midriff bare. There were other details, earrings, flip-flops, blotches of red dabbed on the toenails, presumably to show nail polish. Charlie had clearly been busy and he had lucked into a child who was naturally observant. In one sketch she was standing alongside what had to be Mo and I noted she was tall, about my height – it was easy to see how the woman on the beach had mistaken her for me as she passed by on the periphery of her vision.

'Why have you given her pale pink hair?' I asked Charlie. 'If she's dyed it that colour, she should be pretty easy to spot.'

'It's supposed to be pale red,' Charlie laughed. 'Mo said she had hair like carrots with milk, which I thought was kind of a neat description. But when I used orange he said it wasn't right and this was as close as I could get to making him happy. I guess she might be a strawberry blonde.'

I was about to introduce Mo to Franny when he rushed past her and out to the patio.

'I wanna go in the pool,' he said, 'but I guess I can't.'

'Of course you can,' said Noreen. 'Why would you think you couldn't?'

Mo looked at her with a sly grin. 'I don't have my arm bands no more, stupid.'

'Mo, don't talk to her like that.' I was furious.

'Chill!' he said, and that sly grin was tormenting me more than ever. 'You got to learn to relax. Who you?' Now he was looking at Franny and Eliza.

'I'm Franny and it's my pool so if you want to go in it, you have to act nice. And this is Eliza. And if it's all right with Lee, why don't we all go in the pool up to our waists but no one's to go *any further!* Are we clear?'

Franny's tone was that of a drill sergeant's and Mo suddenly realised he was outdone. He was tall for his age but he was confronted by the massive Sid and what must appear to him like an Amazon woman. I was tall but, at over six feet, Franny dwarfed me with wide shoulders tapering to slim hips and excessively long legs. Standing side by side, she and Sid were like a couple of cartoon characters, the mighty warrior woman and her trusty square-jawed sidekick. Mo nodded meekly. 'I just gone splash about, OK?'

'OK, you do that, and you and I will get to know each other later. You're going to be staying with me up in the other house from now on, right? Meanwhile I need to catch up with Lee here.' Franny slung an arm around my shoulders and drew me out to the pool where she handed me Eliza and proceeded to

100

strip off her shorts and T. Underneath she had on a denim bikini and I noted with envy her washboard abs. She was a little too muscular for my liking but there was no denying she was astonishingly fit.

Noreen repaired for a much-needed nap and I noticed Sid discreetly remove himself to sit at the far end of the pool.

'Have you spoken to Scott and Suzette since you got back?' I asked her as she dunked Eliza in the water and then threw her up in the air. 'Is Keshawn aware that someone was after him?'

'Believe it or not,' said Franny, 'I actually called her to see how Keshawn was doing – not that anything happened to him but I assumed she must be worried sick about the possibility.'

'And was she?'

'Actually,' Franny made a moue of concession, 'she was. But then she amazed me by saying she was more concerned about the fact that she couldn't reach her other son. She thought kidnappers might go after him too.'

'Her other son?' This was the first I'd heard about Suzette having more children. 'Was this a kid she had by her other marriage – to the actor?'

'Earlier,' said Franny. 'This kid is in college. She had him when she was quite young and she has no idea where the father is today.'

'So who does he live with?'

Her mother, way over in somewhere like Washington State or wherever she hails from originally. He's been there since day one because, get this, she doesn't want the public to know she has a son who is college age. She puts her age somewhere in her early thirties but in fact it's closer to forty. But she was worried maybe someone had found out about him and he could be a target for kidnapping.'

'And was he safe?'

'He'd been seen at some point in the last week but he's over twenty years old. He's not exactly sitting at home every night or checking in every five minutes. She said she wasn't going to be able to sleep until she heard from him but you know why she's really worried?'

'Why?'

'Well, I'm guessing if they get him and demand a ransom, then it will all come out that he even exists.'

I didn't say anything. I adored Franny but there was no denying she was tough. Now was not the right moment to point it out to her but there was plenty in her own past that she'd kept hidden – certain sexual favours she'd granted during a spell living in Manhattan in return for the wherewithal to support herself and her own wayward teenage son. But she claimed to have kept quiet about it for her children's sake and I could see that she wasn't about to let Suzette get away with absentee motherhood for the sake of something as trivial as vanity.

She saw me looking at her and she must have noted my disapproval.

'OK,' she said, 'I guess I'm being a little unfair. And there is another reason she has to get a hold of Robby. She got the ransom call from that girl on her private cell phone and only two people have the number. Apart from Scott, that is.'

'Robby?' I said. 'And who's the other one.'

'An assistant she fired at the beginning of the summer.'

I whistled. 'Oh boy! And she never changed the number?'

Franny shook her head. 'Looks bad, doesn't it? I remember the girl. She was a real piece of work, ordered everyone around like *she* was Suzette. But even so, I can't see her pulling off a kidnapping.'

'Wouldn't Suzette have recognised her voice when she made the call?'

'You'd think,' said Franny, 'but Suzette said she couldn't be sure it was her. She said that girls of a certain age all seem to sound the same to her. Everything they say, it's a question, their voices go up at the end and they all have that nasal whine. I've got a niece, haven't seen her in months, but every

103

girl under thirty I speak to on the phone, I think it's her. It's uncanny. Speaking of missing family members,' said Franny, fixing me with a penetrating look, 'how about you explain to me how you came on your honeymoon minus your husband?'

'I want to apologise for not inviting you and Rufus to the wedding,' I said quickly, trying to deflect her. The last thing I wanted was to be subjected to an account of my disastrous four-day-old marriage. 'But, you know, it was very last minute.'

But this was Franny I was talking to. She had two middle initials: B for blunt and D for direct. And up to now they had been qualities I had appreciated in her.

'Sure I know,' she said surprising me, 'I knew you were going to get married before you did. Tommy called us in France, told us he'd booked the register office, wanted to know if we could hop on Eurostar.'

I was stunned. 'And why didn't you?'

'We absolutely intended to but then Eliza came down with her ear infection. We wanted to send flowers but Tommy never told us which registry office he'd booked and he said you guys would be leaving right after the ceremony anyway.'

'But why didn't you call *me*?'

'I didn't know if you even knew. Tommy made it sound like he was going to surprise you and I didn't want to ruin it even though

104

I sort of knew you'd probably react badly to being given no warning.'

'So did you tell him that?'

Franny backed away in denial and threw up her hands. Eliza's eyes widened in astonishment as she felt herself being let go. Franny grasped the rubber ring around Eliza's middle and gave it a reassuring tug. 'No way!' she said. 'I wanted to stay right out of it. You two have such a weird relationship. If it's taken you this long to get yourselves to the altar, it's between the two of you how you get there.'

'We didn't get to an altar,' I pointed out, 'we reached a rather ugly square partner's desk and, as I'm sure you know by now, Tommy chickened out of the honeymoon at the last minute. But I expect he's told you all about that in one of your little chats.' I was trying to keep the resentment out of my voice – she was supposed to be my friend, not Tommy's – but it was hard.

'Nope,' said Franny cheerfully. 'Not a word. I just heard it from Lucia that your mother-in-law was here – she seems like a real nice lady – but *Mr Kennedy, he no here.* So what kept him?'

I explained about Shagger's ill-advised association with a girl from a family of Spurs supporters. 'And then she went and dumped him on our wedding day and Tommy seems to have got it into his head that Shagger can't survive without him.' I exploded and waited for Franny to offer her effusive condolences.

'But isn't that just adorable of him?' said Franny and I closed my eyes in despair, 'He's taking care of his buddy. He's showing he's a warm, considerate, stand-up guy. Isn't that exactly why you married him?'

'I *didn't* marry him,' I almost yelled at her. 'At least it doesn't feel as if I did. I don't understand being married, Franny. I feel exactly the same as I did five days ago. It feels like we just went to an office in Chelsea one Saturday afternoon and had a meeting and then he put me on a 'plane and went off with his best mate to talk women and football. Business as usual.'

'Well if that's your attitude then you shouldn't have married him,' said Franny and I flinched at her candour. 'I've told you before, I just don't think you're cut out to get married, not to Tommy, not to any man. Hell, there ain't no law that says you have to get married just because most people do. You should never do things just because you feel you *oughta*. Oh, well, too late now!'

And then, as if to punctuate Franny's outspokenness, Noreen called to me from the house.

'Lee, come quick. Your husband's on the phone. He's arriving tomorrow.'

Chapter Five

'You have to have so much patience when it comes to children,' Noreen told Franny, following a particularly spectacular tantrum thrown by Eliza towards the end of the day. Eliza was exhausted, having refused, in the midst of all the excitement, to take her afternoon nap. And she was so fascinated by Mo that she was reluctant to go back to the main house and be put to bed by Franny.

'But Mo's going to be staying with us, sweetheart,' said Franny, 'he'll be coming up to the house later and he'll be sleeping in the room right next to yours.'

'No!' yelled Mo and proceeded to let rip with his own defiance. 'I want to stay here with Lee and Noreen. You a *stranger!*' He almost spat the words out at Franny, who was momentarily speechless.

I was touched that he said he wanted to stay with me as well as Noreen, especially as I had been feeling a little excluded from what had turned into a lengthy exchange between Franny and Noreen on dealing with children.

My constant requirement for solitude didn't exactly make me a natural candidate for motherhood and yet I did experience intermittent pangs of broodiness. And now that I was actually married to a man whose most passionate longing in all the time I had known him was to 'raise a lot of little Kennedys', surely I would have to face the maternity question sooner or later.

Still, with my eternal gift for procrastination, I had wilfully tuned out Franny and Noreen in a conversation they had had earlier in the day as they droned on about such diverse topics as emotional development, whether apple juice was responsible for diarrhoea, when to take away the dummy – Franny called it a *pacifier* – and how to deal with projectile vomiting. When they touched on bed-wetting, I ventured a frown in their direction because I could see Mo was all ears as he splashed about in the shallow end of the pool.

But now, when Noreen sighed and said, 'You have to have so much patience–' I snapped to attention.

'Patience! Oh, my God!'

I had been in America for five days and I had totally forgotten the main reason I was there.

It took me several minutes to locate where I had put Patience Brook O'Reilly's number but when I called, I reached her service.

'This is Patience. If you've not found me home, you probably will the next time you call. In the meantime, why don't you leave a message and your number and I'll call you back.'

I left one of those gushing, much-too-long messages, full of apology for not having called her sooner and assuring her how much I was looking forward to meeting her and probably giving her the worst possible first impression of me. To top it all, I forgot to give her my number and had to call back with more grovelling and twittering.

'When's Patience Brook O'Reilly's show on?' I asked Franny, thinking I must do some serious homework on her before she called back.

'You're asking *me?*' Franny was incredulous. 'I don't watch that New Age shit although I do know that it's not a show. She just has a five-minute morning segment on one of the TV shows and I think I read somewhere that even that had been axed recently. She had a cat fight with one of the presenters, something like that.'

'You're sure it wasn't that she was off the air for the summer so she could be out here at her home in the Hamptons?'

'Well I was reading one of those trashy gossip magazines and they wouldn't be seen dead printing anything as sensible as that. But you're right, maybe that's what's happened and they made up the other stuff to sell copies.'

And maybe Genevieve forgot to tell me or maybe I was just too busy getting married to notice, I thought with a certain amount of apprehension.

I booted up my laptop and Googled her, something I should have done weeks ago. At the back of my mind I acknowledged to myself that I wasn't really taking Patience Brook O'Reilly seriously, or rather, I couldn't quite persuade myself that being a life coach was a proper job. I probably wouldn't have even taken the job if it hadn't provided me with an excuse to hook up with Franny and Rufus on Long Island.

I felt somewhat vindicated by two video segments showing interviews with Patience on breakfast television in which the presenters echoed my sentiments by asking repeatedly, *What exactly is a life coach?*

Patience was stunningly beautiful in a rather unoriginal way. She had long dead-straight ultra blond hair falling in curtains either side of her rather mournful face. Her eyes were huge and seemed to be balancing precariously on her sculptured cheekbones. I say sculptured because her face looked as if it had been chiselled by a surgeon to the point where it could only be flattered by the intrusions of the camera.

But when she started to speak, I groaned. She babbled away with a string of vacuous clichés. *I am your personal trainer for life. I can make your life happen now. It's all about raising the bar on your creativity, breaking through your barriers, getting your life on track.*

Still, when I set off the next day for my first meeting with her, I was mildly intrigued because when she'd called me back, her voice was nothing like that of the West Coast flake I'd seen on her website, nor did it resemble the one on her answering machine. She sounded like a warm and cheerful English farmer's wife when she invited me to meet her.

'Get yourself over here, lass, and we'll get to know each other.'

Her house turned out to be even more of a surprise. If someone was on television, dealt with celebrities and had a house in the Hamptons, I automatically assumed that their home would be a minimum ten-million dollar McMansion on a par with Scott's. I began to suspect this might not be the case with Patience when I turned off the road by her mailbox (she'd told me to look out for the name *Brooks*) and found myself driving down an ever-narrowing sandy trail, full of potholes, to emerge in a clearing devoid of any landscaping. Before me stood a broken-down ranch-style cottage whose weather-beaten cedar shingles had assumed the dreary grey patina of years of neglect. Dense undergrowth and thorny briar surrounded the house but it was so lush and green that, in a tangled childlike way, it was almost romantic.

And the woman who emerged, letting the screen door bang noisily behind her, bore no resemblance to the TV Viking. She had a faded English prettiness – wispy fair hair cut at chin level framing a chubby face with sharp periwinkle eyes and a small and perfect nose. Her skin had the slight ruddy complexion of English women who live in the country, smooth and pale and creamy except for the inevitable broken veins across cheeks that had been exposed to all weathers. If her figure was a little on the dumpy side, her clothes were decidedly frumpy. I hadn't seen an Aertex shirt on anyone since my childhood and the flared calf-length denim skirt drew attention to the unfortunate width of her hips. And as my gaze travelled down to her feet, I noted that her Birkenstocks did nothing to mitigate the thickness of her ankles. I was aware that I was being overly judgemental. It wasn't that I didn't like the way she looked – far from it, her appearance suggested a warm, unthreatening persona – it was more because I couldn't reconcile it with the TV image of Patience Brook O'Reilly.

'Welcome to my world,' she said, holding out her hand, 'Patsy Brooks.'

'Nathalie Bartholomew,' I said, 'I'm looking for Patience Brook O'Reilly?'

'Sure you are, darlin'. Isn't everybody?'

She shook my hand and I flinched at her powerful grip. 'But when I'm out here I go back to the name I was born with. I dropped the "s" and added the O'Reilly because you've got to have three names in America these days if you want to get yourself a profile. Sarah Jessica Parker. Sarah Michelle Gellar. Bunch of pretentious phonys, the Americans, of course,' she winked at me, 'but they know how to reinvent themselves, I'll give them that. Mother of reinvention, me. That's what I discovered about myself when I came here. Took to it like the prover-bial duck to water skiing. I couldn't have gone from being little Patsy Brooks in the Lincolnshire wolds to Patience Brook O'Reilly, life coach to the stars, if I'd stayed in England. They'd have rumbled me in twenty seconds. But you can do that over here, can't you? Come inside, Nathalie, why don't you?'

She spoke very quickly and I was aware that I was opening and shutting my mouth like a goldfish, trying to respond. Eventually I gave up and followed her indoors mur-muring, *Please call me Lee.*

The inside of her house was yet another shock. The contrast with the outside was unbelievable. The little kitchen she led me into was spotless and stank slightly of some incongruously apple-scented disinfectant. Everything seemed somehow rather small, as if scaled down to accommodate the inhabitants of a doll's house. Her toaster wasn't one of those giant chrome affairs but a dainty little white box. Her rubbish bin was a little white pedal one. A row of white saucepans of descending sizes were arranged on a shelf above the sink with their handles all pointing rigidly in the same direction. I had the impression that when she took one down to use it, she automatically straightened any handle that might have been dislodged in the process.

Glancing through the kitchen window, I saw that the ground at the back of the house fell away sharply and I was looking out onto a slope thick with scrub oaks. *She's quite isolated out here*, I thought to myself.

'They didn't tell you, did they?' she said suddenly and I turned back to see her place a dainty white kettle on the hob.

'Didn't tell me what?' I said, 'And who are they?'

'My agent. *Your* agent. Whoever put us together. They didn't tell you what the real Patience looks like? They didn't tell you about Patsy Brooks?'

My hand clasped around my mobile in my pocket. I had half a mind to whip it out and call Genevieve. *What in the world have you got me into?*

'It was fine until the networks got involved,' said Patsy, pouring boiling water

114

into the tiny white teapot – would there be enough for two cups? – to warm it, 'it didn't matter what I looked like because no one was ever going to meet me. I work on the phone, see? No face time with anyone.'

'You *are* Patience Brook O'Reilly?' I was beginning to feel decidedly schizophrenic.

''Course I'm not. I've just told you. She's an invention. I'm Patsy Brooks – I only become Patience when I answer the phone to a client. *Hello, this is Patience. How are you today?*'

I shivered. Her mimicking of the Viking's voice was so accurate it was spooky.

'My agent said it was a natural progression to do TV. The only problem was the show's producer took one look at me and said *Yuck!* I'm not telegenic, never will be. The camera puts ten pounds on you and I look like a Teletubby. But by that time I had a following as a life coach. They'd done the research. I had the most calls, the most hits on my website and a waiting list halfway round the world. So they brought in Vicky the Viking.'

I giggled. It was such an apt description. 'She's a life coach too?'

'God, no. She was a waitress in somewhere like Flint, Michigan with aspirations to come to New York to be an actress. And now she gets to act her heart out – playing me. I write her script for her, I answer the questions from the audience for her through a feed in her ear and, to give her her due, she's pretty quick on the uptake. And by now she's learned all the stock answers to the question *So what exactly is a life coach?* She can pretty much hold her own on stuff like that.'

'And now they want you to do a book?'

'No,' she said with considerable emphasis, '*I* want to do a book. And I want to promote it and do signings myself. I want to come out of the closet,' she grinned, 'and they're not happy!'

Ah! So this was probably the real reason for the disagreement Franny had read about.

'It's amazing you haven't been outed before now,' I said.

'It is,' she agreed, 'but until now it was what we all wanted. I'm not a public person. I was quite happy to hide behind Vicky and none of us ever imagined the TV segment would last more than a season. Tell you the truth, I suspect I'd be happy to go on hiding behind her for the TV shows but I have a feeling I'll want to engage with the outside world when it comes to the book. It's going to be the real me in the book and, let me tell you, Vicky the Viking wouldn't be a good fit. When she reads what I've got to say about my life, I doubt she'll even want to be me any more.'

116

Well, this sounded intriguing from the book point of view. I opened my mouth and made some indecipherable sound if only to stake some claim on the conversation – but she rattled right along, leaving me gaping.

'I mean, what about you, Lee? How do you feel about hiding behind your ghosting subjects? Don't you ever want to step into the limelight and show them who you are?'

'*Never!*' I said firmly, and it was the truth. Professional instinct told me not to go any further, not to explain that I never actively sought people out even though I invariably found myself enjoying the company of those who managed to penetrate my wall of solitude. People shy away from the thought that someone might be a natural loner. It conjures up profiles of serial killers among other things.

'Bit scared they'll see the real you?' She laughed while I flinched at how perceptive her arrow was. I'd never thought of it like that but as soon as she said it, I knew she had a point. 'So,' she reached into a closet, 'have a ginger nut.'

She proffered a square plastic box. I shook my head. *Thank you, no.* I liked my biscuits in a scruffy, torn packet with the label displaying my favourite brand, not preserved in something as antiseptic as Tupperware. I didn't do ultra neat and tidy, in fact it made me uncomfortable. I wanted out of this clinical kitchen.

'Shall we sit outside?' I asked. 'Your yard is so beautiful.'

'Sure,' she said, cheerfully. 'Whatever you want, provided you don't mind being bugged to death. And my yard is crap. Deliberately. If anyone gets to the end of the trail by accident I want them to take one look and turn right around and go back again. I can count on one hand the number of people who know I'm here.'

Why does she trust me with her secret? I wondered.

'Tell you what,' she said, 'we'll compromise. There's a screened-in porch round the other side of the house. We'll sit in that and you can admire my crappy yard and the bugs won't get at us. I'm going to–'

But I was determined to establish some sort of two-way communication so I raised my voice a little and interrupted her as I followed: 'So are you here alone? Are you married? I'm afraid the job came up at such short notice that I just haven't researched you like I should have.' Somehow I felt I could be open with her about my inexcusable inertia. She was bound to 'rumble' me, as she put it, pretty soon in any case.

'What's the point of wasting time on research when you're going to interview someone about their life? I'd have nothing to talk about if you knew it all already.'

Somehow I doubted that given the amount of time her mouth remained shut.

'But in answer to your question,' she walked ahead of me into a gloomy wooden structure adjoining the back of the house where the mesh on the screen doors was black and seemed to blot out the sun. Maybe that was the point. 'No, I'm not married. What about you? Do you have a husband?'

The word *husband* made me hesitate and the screen door swung back behind Patsy before I could walk through. My hand went out to stop it but I only succeeded in trapping my thumb. I winced in pain and regarded the rapidly swelling flesh.

'You must have given it quite a pinch,' said Patsy, watching my thumb turn bright red. 'Come back to the kitchen, we'll put some ice on it.'

The ice might help the swelling to go down but it didn't do much to alleviate the pain. I try to be stoic about these things but I'm pretty useless and the more my thumb throbbed, the less I was able to put on a brave face.

'You need a pain killer.' Patsy started rummaging through her kitchen cabinets, drawing a blank. 'Come with me.'

She led me into a clinical white-tiled bathroom and I blinked at the gaudy array of multicolored bath towels lined up on a rail with immaculate precision. 'Don't ask,' she said when she saw me looking at them and opened her medicine cabinet to reveal tightly packed shelves of bottles and packets. 'Damn, I don't see anything immediately. I'm going to have to get all these out so I can see what's in the back. Do me a favour, while I'm searching, go into my bedroom and take a quick look in the drawer of my night-stand. I usually keep something in there for the middle of the night. Forgive the mess in there.'

There was no mess, not by my standards anyway, unless you counted an unmade king size bed that dominated the space. It was an expansive light room with a wall of glass sliders leading out to the deck and another built-in closet. I went to one of the low chests on either side of the bed that served as nightstands and pulled open the top drawer, hoping I wouldn't have to root around in her underwear for what I wanted.

What I saw gave me such a shock that for a second the pain in my thumb receded. There was nothing in the drawer except for a couple of small notepads, a pen, a TV remote – and a gun.

I know nothing about guns, but it looked like a revolver to me. Why would Patsy need a gun? It was true her house was in a pretty isolated location but still it shook me to see it lying there in the drawer. Should I say I'd seen it and ask her about it? Or would I just be making a fuss about nothing? I was in America, after all. Maybe further down the line I'd ask her for her views on gun control.

'Any luck?' she shouted from the bathroom.

I raced around to the other side of the bed, opened the drawer there, hoping I wouldn't come across a switchblade, and to my relief found a bottle of Ibuprofen. I ran back into the bathroom, rattling it.

Back in the porch, I edged gingerly through the offending screen door and swallowed a couple of pills with my tea. I bit back the words *Why do you keep a gun in the house?*

'So where were we?' She looked at me. 'Oh yes, do *you* have a husband?'

'No,' I said and almost choked. Why had I said that? 'No, I mean, *yes!* I *am* married. I'm definitely married. I was there when it happened.'

'I'm going to go with the "No" you first gave me. It sounded more real to me than the other stuff. That's part of my job, by the way, to listen to what people are *really* saying as opposed to the guff that comes out of their mouths. You're not married till you *feel* you're married and it doesn't sound like you've got there yet. Anyway, we'll get to that in due course. You've been here at least five days. How come you took so long getting in touch?'

For a split second I contemplated giving her the excuse that I was on my honeymoon but I had a feeling that somehow Patsy would *know* that my husband hadn't been with me. Indeed, when I left her, I would be continuing on up to the other end of Long Island to pick up Tommy at JFK.

And then I realized that I had a perfectly good excuse for being distracted over the last few days.

'I've been a little tied up with a kidnapping and a murder,' I said and then sat back and waited. *Let's see what you make of that little slice of life, Miss Life Coach.*

Oh, she was good! She didn't rise at all. Kept her mouth firmly shut (so, she could be silent when she wanted to), and regarded me with a quizzical look.

Of course, after a minute of silence I caved.

'OK, here's what happened. I arrived to find that the person I was staying with had left me in charge of a Fresh Air kid and he was kidnapped on the beach. Actually, it wasn't meant to be him, they were really going after Suzette's child–'

This got her attention. 'Suzette? The actress? Oh my God, Robby? They were after Robby?'

Robby? Who did she mean by Robby? Could she be talking about Suzette's older son, the one Franny had told me about? But hadn't Franny told me that Suzette was keeping quiet about him?

'Yes, Suzette, the–' I paused, unsure whether I could say the word actress with conviction '–the movie star. 'But I don't know who you mean by Robby? Her son's name is Keshawn.'

Patsy looked a little nervous for a second and I began to think maybe she did know about the other son. But then she shrugged.

'Oh, right,' she said, smiling and tapping her forehead in mock exasperation with herself, 'I must have been thinking about some other *movie star*. Can't keep them straight. So if they were after Keshawn, why did they take the Fresh Air kid?'

'It's a long story but the short version is – Keshawn's adopted, from Malawi and–'

'Do the two boys look alike?'

'Not really, Keshawn's older, he–'

'What I meant was, they're both black?'

I nodded.

Her look changed to one of concern. 'You must be beside yourself with worry, why aren't–'

'Oh, we got him back. Mo, that's his name, they found him at a house in Springs. A neighbour heard loud voices and saw a black kid in the yard and she'd heard from her daughter at the beach that a kid had gone missing so she called the police.'

'And was he OK when they found him?

You mentioned a murder? Please don't tell me–'

'He was fine, locked in a room but essentially OK. They found the daughter of the homeowner dead in the bathroom next door. The house was a summer rental and the neighbour who called the police said the place had been infested – that's the word she used, apparently – with noisy rich kids since the start of the summer season.'

I'd had a call from Sid that morning, filling me in on the latest. It seemed the neighbour was turning out to be something of a godsend for the police because she had nothing better to do with her time than spy on the folks next door.

'A new bunch arrived every two weeks,' I went on, 'driving out from the city every Friday and piling in on top of each other, sleeping four or five to a room, making constant use of the outdoor shower because there weren't enough bathrooms to accommodate them, romping naked in it at all hours of the night.'

'And of course this outdoor shower just had to be on the neighbour's side of the house and in full view of her bedroom window?' Patsy nodded knowingly. 'Probably spiced up her life no end. She must get very bored in winter time when there's no one there.'

'Oh, no,' I said, 'the place is full year

124

round. The homeowner has hordes of construction workers in there the rest of the year. But the weird thing is that the neighbour reports there was only one person at the house when the woman was found dead. A girl was there on her own, had been there about a week. And the voice on the phone call made to Suzette claiming to have abducted Keshawn sounded pretty young apparently, could even have been a teenager's. Mo briefed a police sketch artist about the person who led him away from the beach and the picture the artist produced was of a young girl.'

'And this young girl was at the house when the woman in the bathroom died?' Patsy looked at me. 'Do they think she murdered the woman as well as taking the boy?'

'Maybe. She took off in her car. But Mo said he heard other people there.'

'Could the helpful neighbour give them a description of the car?'

'No, naturally she couldn't be that helpful, she heard it leave but even though it was parked outside her house for a week, all she can remember is that she "thinks it was red".'

'Then it was probably green,' said Patsy. 'Who does the house belong to?'

'A woman in East Hampton. She's never lived in it, she bought it purely as a rental investment. But this girl who rented it from her – she was probably nineteen, twenty – she was a friend of her daughter. It was a one-off rent-to-a-friend cash situation.'

'So they've got a name,' said Patsy eagerly. 'If she was a friend of the woman's daughter's, the woman *knew* her?'

'No,' I said, 'she didn't. As I said, it was just a one-off as a favour to their daughter. *Mom, my friend wants to rent the house for a week or two, I'll take care of it, OK?* The daughter organised the whole thing and in effect her friend was just staying there. I'm not even sure rent was paid. But the daughter was on her way over there to visit her friend when–'

'Oh my God,' said Patsy, the light finally dawning, 'she's the dead woman in the bathroom and she's the only one who can identify her killer?'

I nodded. 'They'll be going through the daughter's hard drive, questioning everyone she knew to find out who the mystery renter might be.'

'I'll bet the mother must be going insane if she never got the girl's name from her daughter. Who is she, by the way, the mother?'

'Her name's Gwen Bennett.'

'The real estate broker?'

'I don't know,' I said. 'I didn't ask what she did for a living. Do you know her?'

'A woman called Gwen Bennett sold me

126

this house ten years ago,' said Patsy. 'I remember the name because she came knocking on my door not so long ago asking did I want to sell. All that land either side of the trail that leads from the road, that's mine. Probably around ten, eleven acres. I could tell she was a little shocked I hadn't upgraded the exterior but she perked up once she came inside. Said she could get me several million easy with so much land attached.'

'Are you going to sell?'

'Of course not. This is my hideaway. And God forbid she should learn I'm Patience Brook O'Reilly. She'd use it to add another million to the asking price and never give me a moment's peace.'

'Well, she'll find out when you do the book,' I pointed out. 'Which reminds me, maybe we ought to talk about what kind of book you want to do. You say you work purely on the telephone. Is that just in America or–?'

'All over the world, time differences permitting. I've had clients in Australia, London, and California all in the same week. There've been times when I've had to stay awake for nearly twenty-four hours to accommodate everybody.'

'And why do they need you? Do they just want someone to talk through their problems with when they hit a crisis in their life?'

Patsy shook her head. 'Not really. It's

127

basically about personal growth. They can be perfectly cheerful, successful people but they may have hit a place where they literally just don't know where to go next. Doesn't have to be a crisis.' She picked up the teapot and looked at me. *More tea?* I shook my head. 'Basically,' she went on, 'what I do is listen to people and ask them questions about their life and nine times out of ten they're telling me a lot of stuff but often they just don't realise the sub-text of what they're saying.'

'So what is the sub-text of what most people say?'

'They're terrified. For some reason they're often scared to change their life and they come up with all these excuses. Maybe they're scared of failure, maybe they have to hide behind a mega-salary to face the world, maybe they think people won't like them any more if they choose a different life. And that's why they need me to coach them through to the next stage of their life, to help them admit to themselves that they have these fears and then confront them.'

'And how did you know you'd be good at this?' I asked her, intrigued.

'Because I've always been intuitive. I've always found myself cutting through the bullshit when I listen to people. And I've learned how to prioritise, how to cut to the chase of what is most important in a person's life – *to that person*. That's what I want to call my book, by the way: *Priorities*.'

'Like you knew right away I didn't feel married?'

She laughed. 'Exactly! Think you might need a life coach? How long have you been married?'

'A week.' I dared not look at her.

'Well, there you are,' she said, 'you're a brand new bride. You're on the brink of the next stage of your life. You're bound to need my help to coach you on how to deal with it after the honeymoon's over.'

'It's a little more complicated than that,' I said, 'the honeymoon hasn't actually begun yet. In fact, I should probably be on my way. I have to pick my husband up at the airport in an hour.' I was proud of myself for using the word husband with no hesitation.

I heard a car door slam around the other side of the house.

'Oh, that's Eileen,' said Patsy, 'my house-keeper. Or char-lady, as we'd call her back home. She's a Scot, been with me for years. I brought her with me when I moved here.'

'How long ago was that?'

'Let's get into all of that next time.' Patsy got to her feet. 'Come on, we'll go out here and around the outside to your car. Wouldn't want to trample dirt through the house.'

'It did look awfully clean,' I admitted as she led me out through the screen door and along a disintegrating wraparound deck to the front of the house, 'almost as if Eileen had already been.'

'Careful where you step. There are broken planks everywhere. And as for the state of the house, I always clean it up a bit before she arrives,' Patsy grinned. 'You don't think I keep it like that normally, do you? When she's not here, I'm the Queen of Clutter but Eileen is a cleanliness Nazi. She's *obsessive*, she can't live with a speck of dirt *any*where. It's a bit like living in a hospital. I'm always terrified she's going to show up un-expectedly and see how I really live.'

Eileen's car was blocking my exit and as she waved – *OK, hold on a sec, I'll move it* – I studied her. She was a hefty woman in a pair of beige Bermuda shorts, a spotless white T shirt and sneakers. Her short hair was a brassy blond and cut with almost military precision and the lobster hue of her skin told me she spent too much time in the sun for someone of her fair complexion. It was hard to judge her age but I guessed her to be younger than she looked. Her face had the pinched and hard-bitten look that told of a former rough existence, one that could never be entirely wiped away by the veneer of an acquisitive new life fuelled by frequent trips to the mall. She had exchanged the fag hanging out of her mouth and the Saturday nights down the pub for the air freshener

130

and the Long Island Merlot, but just by looking at her you could still smell the smoke. Her car was a giant SUV with a large *Support Our Troops* sticker in the back window.

'Does that mean our troops or US ones?' I whispered to Patsy.

'Who knows?' she said. 'It's not a subject I get into with Eileen, if I can help it. Hi, Eileen,' she raised her voice, 'this is Lee Bartholomew. She's going to be working with me on my book.'

'Is she indeed? Must be a very clever lady. We'll have to tell the Hoover to run very quietly when she's around then, won't we?'

And then I watched as Eileen went up to Patsy and gave her an affectionate peck on the cheek which, I was intrigued to see, Patsy returned with a token pursing of her lips.

'How's the sore throat?' Eileen asked with concern. 'Did it develop into anything we need to worry about?'

'No, I'm fine this morning. I had a great night's sleep.' Patsy's smile was radiant. 'By the way those ginger nuts you bought me are truly delicious. Wherever did you find them?'

'Oh, I ordered them online from a place in the city that sells British stuff.' Eileen looked very pleased with herself.

I observed this exchange, noticing the

genuine closeness between them. These two cared about each other, although I sensed an infinitesimal awkwardness on Patsy's part and, remembering her earlier irony when speaking about Eileen, I suspected that while she valued her cleaner's devotion, she probably had less in common with her than Eileen realised.

'Now how about a cup of tea?' Eileen looked at me, including me in the offer. I shook my head.

'I made a pot about half an hour ago, Eileen, if you want to freshen it up,' said Patsy.

'I'll do better than that. I'll make myself a fresh pot,' said Eileen disappearing into the house. 'Then you'll know it's there if you decide you want a cup. Good excuse to have some more ginger nuts,' she shouted over her shoulder.

Patsy winked at me. 'All that dinky white stuff in the kitchen? It's not my taste at all,' she whispered, confirming my suspicions. 'Eileen bought it all at some discount outlet she goes to up the island somewhere. I've never had the heart to tell her it's not really me. She insists on making all the household purchases, tells me I don't have time, that it's her department, but sometimes I lie in the bath and wish I could get out and wrap myself in a plain white towel instead of something with orange fishes all over it. I can't understand it, she watches Martha Stewart religiously but never takes it in.'

I laughed, not quite sure what else to do.

'But I adore her,' Patsy said hastily, 'I'd be totally lost without her.'

I nodded and walked towards my car. 'You'll call me when you're ready to start the first session? We'll probably need to brainstorm for a couple of hours, at least.'

'Sure thing,' said Patsy, 'and I'll try and pick a time when herself's not around so we can make as much mess as we want.'

I laughed and decided I was going to enjoy working with Patience Brook O'Reilly even if she did turn out to be Patsy Brooks. But as I made the monotonous journey along the Long Island Expressway, I found myself wondering how a woman who sorted out other people's lives could allow herself to be dominated by her cleaner. The more I thought about the woman who was to be my latest ghosting subject, the more I realised I just could not pigeonhole her in any way. She was not the person she presented to the world and she had allowed someone else to impose *their* taste on her home. She had told me that she had the gift of intuition and that was what made her good at her job – but I was beginning to suspect that the one person about whom she was not intuitive was herself.

I often pondered people's backgrounds

when I was about to start working with them. I needed to get them right because I was going to have to fully inhabit that person in order to write their life story – *from their point of view*. I didn't terribly like the way I filed away the details into socio-economic compartments – were they rich or poor? Middle class or working class? But somehow it always seemed necessary if it informed their character. I told myself that people cared about these things.

The only person I knew to whom it didn't matter a jot where someone came from was Tommy. He appeared to have absolutely no discrimination as far as people were concerned and it was one of the things I loved about him. Everyone was the same to him. Of course there was another way of looking at it. Whether he slept in a palace or a one-room flat, he still managed to reduce the place to a pigsty. And the fact that he never judged a person by their bank balance meant that by the same token he had no interest in his own. How, I wondered not for the first time, was my new husband going to earn his living in the first years of our marriage.

But he'd spent money on a haircut, I noticed, as he came through the arrivals gate and waved when he saw me, before becoming swept up in the sea of people emerging from customs all around him. His blond hair was shaved on either side of his head with the exception of a single tuft sticking up on top giving him an uncanny resemblance to Tintin.

He looked so adorable, I felt my heart soften towards him. So maybe he'd taken his time getting here but he was here now and we could begin our honeymoon. I felt a sudden urge to make things right between us, to use this time together to voice my trepidation about marriage with him and ask him to help me banish my doubts about it once and for all. And it was with this new-found optimism that I pushed my way through the crowds towards him with my arms outstretched to embrace him.

But as I clasped him to me, I froze at the sight of the couple standing right behind him and all my wifely determination evaporated as quickly as it had erupted.

'You remember Shagger,' said Tommy, disengaging himself and avoiding my eye, 'and this is Minnie. They've never been to America.'

Chapter Six

Tommy offered to drive but I said no. I needed something to keep my hands occupied so that they wouldn't be able to punch his lights out. For the first half hour of the journey, Minnie Shaugnessy and I talked incessantly, except that while Minnie's squeaky little voice resounded throughout the car, everything I said remained inside my head.

*Have you no consideration for others, Tommy? Who do you imagine is going to feed Shagger and Minnie? Where do you suppose Franny is going to house them? What happened to giving people notice when you plan on availing yourself of their hospitality? Do you even understand what the word honeymoon means? First you send your mother – not that I'm complaining about her, she's a darling – then you turn up with your best friend **and** his girlfriend. How can you do this to me just when I was all geared up to be married to you – **properly** married to you, just when I–*

Tommy sat beside me in the front seat in stony silence and with a very worried look on his face. He knew me so well that he could probably hear everything I was saying even though I never opened my mouth. Every now and then he glanced over his shoulder at Shagger and asked him, 'All right, mate?'

Shagger never answered. He was sitting bolt upright in the back seat, clutching Minnie's hand and staring at her so hard he had to be thinking that if he let her out of his sight for one second, she would fly out the window. And she was such a little slip of a thing, it wasn't entirely impossible. She had ginger hair cut in a swingy bob with a fringe and a sharp featured little face, quite pretty. She was wearing a turquoise gingham sundress that left her shoulders bare, and her skin was whiter than I'd ever seen skin be and spattered with pale orange freckles. The turquoise matched the colour of her eyes, which were framed by lashes thickened with black mascara. Her lips were scarlet and constantly in motion.

I had to admit to being fascinated by her appearance and I cast surreptitious glances at her in the rear-view mirror. Until I caught sight of Shagger reaching down and giving her bare shoulder a lick, savouring it as if it were dairy ice cream, which to him I imagine it probably was.

They were a pair. He said nothing at all and I pretty soon discovered she only had one topic of conversation.

'So we're on the Long Island Expressway,

137

right?' she said. 'And where are we, Exit 82? So for the Tanger Outlets you can get off at either Exit 72 or 73. For Tanger 1 – that's got the Ralph Lauren Polo factory and Calvin Klein, and Van Heusen, Normie, for your shirts – you're better off taking Exit 73, but for Tanger II, that's Sak's Fifth Avenue and Hugo Boss and Nike for Normie – it's Exit 72, isn't it?'

Normie? I tried to remember if I'd ever actually called Shagger anything. He was one of those people that you didn't really *address* because you so seldom had a conversation with him. Maybe I should think about an alternative to Shagger. But *Normie?* No way.

'Lee?'

'What? Oh, the Tanger Outlets? I've never actually been, tell you the truth, Minnie. I should, really. I hear you can save a fortune.'

'Never been to Tanger?' Minnie made it sound as if I'd said I'd never been to the hairdresser. And actually, come to think of it, when was the last time...?

'I'm not really a mall kind of person,' I explained. 'But I know bargain hunters who go all the time and they swear by it. But how come you know about Tanger? I thought Tommy said you'd never been to America?'

'Exactly,' said Minnie in her squeaky little voice. Somehow it wasn't irritating but rather sweet because it suited her. You couldn't imagine her speaking any other way. 'This is why we had to jump at the chance to come when Tommy said he was going to Long Island. My girlfriend showed me all the stuff she bought last year. I couldn't believe it. She even gave me precise directions how to get there.'

Let me get this right, I said to myself, going very slowly in case I had a problem understanding my own words. *Minnie and Shagger have spent probably a thousand dollars each – how else could they get a last-minute ticket to New York at the height of the summer season? – on airfares for their first ever trip to one of the most spectacular continents of the world in order to save money at a discount outlet.*

'And their food court sounds terrific,' Minnie was really on a roll here. 'Listen, Normie, these sound like your favourites. Kentucky Fried Chicken, McDonald's, Taco Bell, Ragin Cajun and get this, Great Steak & Potato Co.'

'I think I'd better call Franny and warn her there'll be two extra people,' I said quickly.

'I'm really looking forward to meeting her. Tommy's told us all about her. She sounds lovely,' said Minnie and she sounded so genuine, I couldn't help smiling at her in the mirror. 'Why do you have to warn her? She does know we're coming, doesn't she?'

I lied. 'Oh, yes.' I nodded. 'I just want to

remind her.' Poor Minnie. I couldn't put her in an embarrassing position just because Tommy had pretended he'd arranged everything.

'Abernathy Residence. How may I direct your call?' Franny's voice sounded a little world weary.

'It's me,' I said, 'you sound like a hotel receptionist.'

She sighed. 'It's what I feel like since we moved in here, the place is so big compared to where I lived before I married Rufus. There are phones in every room so when you pick up, it really is a bit like answering a switchboard.'

And then I realised there was no way I could make it look as if Franny already knew about Minnie and Shagger with both of them sitting behind me, listening.

'Franny, I'm wondering if you have a guest room available at the Abernathy residence for Tommy's friends Minnie and Norman? I'm not sure we're going to be able to fit them in at the pool house.' I held my breath.

'Tommy's friends?' she repeated. I didn't say anything. *Hear what I'm saying, Franny. You're quick on the uptake. Don't let me down now.*

'Tommy's friends you didn't tell me about?' Her voice on the line dropped a little.

'Right,' I said. Very non-committal.

'Tommy's friends who, maybe, *he* didn't

140

tell *you* about?'

'Right,' I said again.

There was a pause.

'I hear you,' she said finally, 'I guess we can work something out. But, Lee, you know, it's really not a good time for this to happen.'

'I'm sorry, I'll do every–' But the line had gone dead. Franny had hung up on me. That was a first.

When we arrived back at her house, I understood why. There were a couple of trucks parked in the driveway and workmen appeared to be ripping the house apart.

'Security Sid's idea.' Franny met us in the hall. 'He says we've got to have panic buttons installed everywhere. I don't like it one bit but Rufus is insisting. So how the hell are you?' she greeted Tommy. 'Wait here,' she said before he could answer, and walked away.

She returned with a pile of bedding, which she thrust at Tommy's chest. 'Lucia's overworked enough as it is. Your friends' room, it's at the top of the stairs, turn right and go all the way to the end. I don't do breakfast.'

Minnie intercepted the sheets. 'I'm Minnie Shaugnessy. We're so grateful to you, Franny. Really, we are. Normie, upstairs, *now!*'

Shagger almost leapt in the air, picked up their bags and followed her. *Hats off to Minnie!* I thought.

'So where are we sleeping?' said Tommy.

141

'It's so good to be back with you, Franny.'

'You're not. You're down at the pool house,' said Franny, sounding about as ungracious as I'd ever heard her.

'Come and say hello to your mother,' I said quickly, dragging him away. 'Thanks, Franny. We owe you.'

'What's her problem?' Tommy got in the car.

I didn't answer. I started walking to the pool house leaving him to follow in the car. Childish, I know, but I wanted to put off for as long as possible the moment when I laid into him about Minnie and Shagger. When I didn't hear the sound of the car behind me, I turned and found he had come after me on foot.

'Wait up, I'm out of puff, what with jet lag and all.' He lumbered to a halt beside me, trying to get his breath and, when I moved on, he grabbed my arm. 'Lee, I'm sorry, all right? I know I should have called to say they were coming with me.'

'Well, why didn't you?'

'You would have said no.' He made it sound like such a reasonable excuse and it drove me into an even bigger fury.

'Of *course* I would have said no and what you have to get into your great big thick skull is that I wouldn't have been saying it for *me*. What you never seem to realise, Tommy, is how many other people are inconvenienced

142

by your thoughtlessness. Shagger and Minnie being here is going to affect Franny and Rufus, as you've just seen. Your mother will have a less relaxing time because it will be that much more crowded. We're going to have to feed them and I don't suppose you've taken into account who's going to pay for that and—'

'I'll pay for it, of course,' he said, his voice growing louder with each word, 'they're my friends. I'll take them out every day. You'll never even know we're here.'

'But I want *you* to be here, you fool.' I cried, 'We're supposed to be on our honeymoon. Just us. Together. And if you go off with them every day, we won't be. And you'll have to rent your own car because I'll need mine.'

'So I'll rent my own car. What's the big deal?'

'What with?' I whispered it, but just loud enough so he couldn't miss it. He wasn't earning. Tommy was a sound engineer by profession, but ever since he had been let go by the BBC three years ago, he had made do with a succession of part-time jobs while he chased his dream of the Next Big Thing. As they were in New York, we were lucky enough to live in my parents' London house – a veritable mansion in the middle of Notting Hill – so it wasn't as if we had a mortgage to cope with. This meant that it was feasible for us to be supported in the main by my ghostwriting, but I went to great lengths to play this down so as not to upset his dignity, Yet I could feel an occasional burst of resentment rising to the surface. He couldn't seriously think I was going to fund having my own honeymoon disrupted? 'And anyway, I thought Minnie had dumped Shagger.'

'She had,' said Tommy, 'poor sod! But when she heard that I'd invited him out to Long Island, she got all excited about that Tanger Outlet thing she was banging on about and begged to come too. Jesus, the sooner we go there, the better. Anything to stop her going on and on—'

Suddenly I began to smell an extra-ordinarily large rat.

'Just a second, exactly *when* did you invite him out here?'

'When you said you were coming out here to work. I thought it would take his mind off his troubles and—'

'And you never thought to mention it?'

'How could I tell you when you didn't even know *I* was coming with you. The wedding and that, it was all at the surprise stage then. And by the way, how can you expect me to be with you on our honeymoon when you're going to be off working as usual?'

'Oh great, put it on me, why don't you?' By now I was seething. 'Turn everything

144

around so it's all my fault. Like I'm to blame because I paid your airfare, I suppose?'

'You said it was a wedding present.'

I clenched my teeth to stop myself telling him I'd said that to make him feel OK about the fact that I'd *had* to pay for the flight he'd booked without telling me, because he'd paid for it from our joint account and at the moment the only one putting money into that was me.

'And you're going to have to rent them somewhere to sleep because there's no room where we are. There are only two bedrooms in the pool house and besides you and me there's your mother and Mo.'

'Well, Mum's going home soon so they can have that room.'

I couldn't believe it! The way he automatically assumed he could avail himself of Franny's hospitality.

'And Mo?' he added, 'Who's that?'

'He's the boy who was kidnapped. Don't you *ever* listen to anything anyone says to you?'

'I've been listening to poor old Shagger bend my ear for weeks on end.' Tommy grinned.

'Oh yes, you'll listen to *Shagger*.' I hated the petulant tone of my voice but I couldn't help it.

'Yes, I do listen to Shagger because he's my best mate and he listens to me. I've been

145

kind of hoping for the last few years that you'd step into that role and give him a break, but it's beginning to look as if it's a bit too much for you.' Now, suddenly, Tommy was the one sounding petulant and I knew we were on dangerous ground. He was as easy-going as they come – to a point. But when I pushed him beyond that point it was only a matter of time before our rows escalated into bitter stand-offs that could last for days.

'Well, he won't want you as his best mate now he's got Minnie,' I shouted at him and instantly regretted it when Tommy's face fell a mile and a half. He'd obviously never considered this eventuality.

'I'll go and get the car,' I said, 'keep going down this drive and you'll come to the pool house. You'll find your mother inside, or round the back by the pool with Mo.'

He didn't argue and shuffled off. I walked slowly back to the house to get the car and on the way I forced myself to remember something. Tommy could behave like a total jerk, but in the past I had behaved like an even bigger one. During our early years together I had treated him appallingly and he had taken it with such good grace that I knew I would always forgive him any similar obnoxious behaviour on his part. Not only had he had to put up with my neurotic lack of confidence and my over-anxious questioning of everything that happened in my life – which would have exhausted the most patient of saints and which he countered with constant gentle reassurance – but my natural loner state prompted me to banish him to his miserable bachelor pad in the East End for sometimes as many as six nights a week. He'd put up with plenty of bad behaviour on my part in the past, and I owed him. He stayed the course no matter what I threw at him and, as I began to show infinitesimal signs of finally growing up, he supported me – not financially, true, but in every other way.

An outsider witnessing the scene that had just played out between us might question why on earth he was even in my life – and they might be right – but what they wouldn't know was that I could match Tommy for childish inconsiderate behaviour. It took one to know one. We were as bad as each other and I had a feeling this was what kept us together – that and the fact that there's something very comforting knowing that someone knows exactly who you are, warts and all. What I hoped – what kept me going – was that one day we would be as *good* as each other, that we would grow and mature into two sane and stable people with never a moment's idiocy.

It might never happen, of course, but what's life without hope? To coin a phrase

Tommy himself used to say to me in my most desperate moments.

When I returned with the car, I saw Sid come out of the pool house and accost Tommy. I watched them as I parked the car. Tommy made as if to shrug Sid off and go around him and then Sid took Tommy by the shoulder and almost lifted him bodily, turning him around and sending him back down the drive the way he'd come with a hefty pat on the back.

I realised what was happening. Sid was being Security Sid. Tommy was a stranger and Sid thought he was trespassing. But why on earth hadn't Tommy said who he was?

'First you tell me who the hell *you* are,' I heard him shouting at Sid as I got out of the car. *Oh Tommy, I thought, stop being such a little boy.*

I'd always thought of Tommy as being a big hulk but standing beside Sid, he came across as a cuddly little puppy.

'Sid,' I yelled, 'It's OK. This is my husband, Tommy.'

Sid could play the little boy too. He obviously didn't relish the fact that now he'd have to climb down and allow Tommy access.

He advanced upon Tommy. 'You don't want to be leaving a beautiful little lady like Lee to spend her honeymoon all by herself?'

148

he yelled in Tommy's face. 'You don't want to be treating your wife like that. It ain't respectful.'

I felt an irresistible urge to giggle. Sid was being protective and it was rather sweet, as well as being absolutely none of his business, which of course was how Tommy saw it.

'I don't to have account to you about my wife,' he yelled back at Sid.

'Tommy, this is Sid.' I reached Tommy and took his arm. 'He's here to protect us – after the kidnapping.'

'I'm the one who'll protect you,' Tommy was beside himself. 'We don't need this jerk.'

'Except you weren't here. You left her and your mother on their own.' Sid swatted him away, taunting him.

I didn't know what to do. I didn't want to humiliate Tommy by pointing out how wonderful Sid had been but I had to make him understand Sid's importance in our midst.

'Tommy,' I began, as gently as I could, 'it's Sid's job to keep an eye on us. That's what Franny and Rufus pay him for, to watch out for Eliza – and for Mo, and us. You ought to thank him for what he's done.'

'I'll thank him to keep away from my wife!' said Tommy and then I lost it.

'You stupid thickhead! Why can't you just grow up and acknowledge that you should have been with me from the beginning? You're here as a *guest*, Tommy. When are you going to start behaving like one?'

'When you stop reminding me that I'm a useless piece of shit!'

'You *are* a useless piece of shit!' I was tearful and angry at myself for losing it – a disgusting combination. 'Enjoy your "honeymoon" with Shagger. He can be your Bridezilla from now on. I'm creating a vacancy. I'm leaving.'

Of course, then I *had* to leave. *I'm as pathetic as he is*, I thought as I stomped away from the pool house. *Now where am I going to go?* Up ahead of me I saw Minnie and Shagger come out of the main house with Franny, who pointed them in the direction of the pool house. I ducked out of sight and cut through the woods to the main gate where I collapsed against the gatepost to weigh up my options.

I'd been there only about ten minutes when Sid drew up in his car and rolled down the window.

'Get in and I'll take you for a spin. You need to cool down. I'm off duty now, we can go and have a drink.'

'*I* need to cool down? You've got to be kidding.' I got in and glared at him.

'OK, you *and* your husband need to take time out.' He laughed. 'Now call your mother-in-law and let her know you're with me so she doesn't worry. She was fixing Mo something to eat when I left and she was asking me what should she do about dinner for the rest of you?'

I called the pool house and mercifully Noreen picked up.

'Don't ask me to explain right now, Noreen,' I whispered into the line. 'As you can see, Tommy's brought Minnie and Sha – I mean Norman – without giving us any advance warning and I'm furious. Sid's taking me for a drink to calm me down. There's a lasagna in the fridge, there'll be enough for everyone. I'm sorry to dump this on you.'

'That's all the explanation you need to give me,' she said, 'and don't you worry. By the time you get back, my son will be grovelling.'

'You're a star, Noreen,' I said. Not for the first time. *Bless her!*

'I just want to swing by where I'm staying to have a quick shower and change, if that's OK with you?' said Sid. 'It's a beautiful spot. You can go sit on the beach and watch the beginning of the sunset.'

'Fine,' I said, 'and by the way, Franny told me about Suzette's assistant, the one that was fired. She was the only person besides Scott and Suzette's son Robby to have Suzette's private mobile phone number, the one the ransom call was made on.'

'Yeah,' said Sid. 'Pete and Vince, they're pretty excited. They think she could be the one who walked down that trail to the beach to lure Mo back to her car. She knew Suzette's number, and she had a reason to want to get back at her. Suzette fired her just like that, told her she didn't want her to come back the next day.'

'Did you know her?'

'Sally?' Sid frowned. 'Can't say I *knew* her. She didn't deign to speak to the likes of me. But she had a real attitude problem, which wasn't really a reason for Suzette to fire her. We wondered if maybe she'd find some way to retaliate, thought maybe she'd sue for some kind of harassment. But hey! Kidnap the boss's son – that's a good way to get some money.'

'Well, Mo should take a look at her.' Now I was as excited as Pete and Vince.

'That's why I was there just now,' said Sid. 'I wanted to have a little talk with Mo. They picked up Sally in the city yesterday and apparently she's having a pretty hard time accounting for her whereabouts over the past week. First she said she'd been in Manhattan for a month and then someone said they'd seen her shopping in East Hampton two days ago so suddenly she remembers she came out for the weekend. She's all over the place.' He threw his hand in the air in exasperation. 'Pete and Vince are driving her

152

out tonight and tomorrow we'll need Mo to ID her. I just thought I'd go over there and explain to him what he has to do ahead of time.'

'Is she a local girl?'

'Yes,' said Sid, 'and here's the kicker. She went to school with Holly Bennett and they were still in touch.'

'Who's Holly Bennett?' I said.

'The girl they found dead in the bathtub when they rescued Mo. Holly might easily have rented space to Sally – except that Holly's not around to tell us that. Scott and Suzette didn't know exactly where she was living while she worked for Suzette, but they know it was in Springs. It could have been Spring Hollow Road.'

I felt my hopes rising. 'Does she match the description Mo gave Charlie Merriweather?'

Sid shrugged. 'She doesn't have hair like "carrots and milk", but then, who does? All other respects, yes. It could be her.'

Unobtrusively I crossed my fingers as he raced along the flat expanse of Cranberry Hole Road – *Please God, let it be her* – and suddenly I knew exactly where we were going. He was taking me to the cabin.

It had been built by the Phillionaire – Rufus' and Scott's father and my mother's lover – who had used it as a retreat when he had been alive. Two years ago he had let me live there for a couple of months when I had come to the Hamptons on another job. That was when I had first met and bonded with Rufus and had become friends with the redoubtable Franny Cook. She wasn't everyone's cup of tea, I was well aware of that. Her bluntness often made people uncomfortable but I had a lot of respect for her and the way she had single-handedly raised a teenager and a baby in one room. And all in the face of harsh criticism from the judgemental locals who had not liked the way she'd dragged the run-down neighbourhood mom-and-pop store she'd inherited into the twenty-first century. When the Phillionaire had been killed in a car accident, his will had revealed that he had left the cabin to little Eliza, the result of Franny's one-night-stand with Scott and the granddaughter the Phillionaire wasn't supposed to know about. And in the meantime it was a perfect guesthouse. I'd entertained a fleeting hope that Franny would put me and Tommy there. Now I knew why she hadn't.

It stood in a clearing midway between the beach and the road, hidden from prying eyes by tall bamboo. A first impression made you think of a modern version of a pioneer log cabin. It was a simple design, about the size of a two-car garage with a flat roof, wide cedar planks and glass sliding doors leading out to the deck and, when we arrived at the end of the sandy trail, I leapt out of the car and ran onto the deck to look through the sliders.

And stopped dead. It was nothing like it had been when I'd been there. It was just one room with a shower behind a curtain and you could see everything at a glance. The expensive kitchen appliances were the same – the Viking stove, the Sub-Zero refrigerator, the stainless steel cabinetry – but the Phillionaire's books had gone and the comfortable easy chairs. And instead of the big double bed, now there was a single – so narrow it was almost a cot!

As for the rest of it – I was standing in a gym.

The place reeked of testosterone. Ugly great weight machines dominated the space. A punch ball blocked the passage to the shower. Monstrous looking barbells lurked around the skirting boards.

And underneath the kitchen bar, lined up in a row, were empty bottles of Scotch.

This was Sid's life, I realised, this was the lonely existence of a security guard who had to keep himself fit and ready for action – and who clearly had a few demons to keep at bay.

'Looks like you give yourself quite a work-out,' I said.

'Every evening when I finish my shift – and then I go for a run right around the bay.' Sid smiled. 'It's the best billet I've ever had.'

He adopted a boxer's stance and gave the punch ball a few hits, and then he hovered nervously beside the shower curtain, shifting from foot to foot. After a second it dawned on me that he was embarrassed to take a shower with me in the room. There would only be a curtain separating us and my presence would clearly inhibit him.

'I'll step outside, take a walk down to the beach,' I said. 'Give a holler when you're ready.'

I left the door open behind me and, as I beat a path through the beach grass, I heard him singing in a rich baritone. *Well, that's another area where he beats Tommy hands down,* I thought.

I gave him about fifteen minutes and then slipped back into the cabin. I could see his silhouette behind the shower curtain and I realised that having finished showering, he was now using the stall as a dressing room to change his clothes, still obscured from view. I wandered over to the bedside table, drawn to a pile of books. It intrigued me that Sid was a reader but, when I looked at the subtitles, I realised that these were not books I would be able to discuss with him. *97 Ways to Find Happiness and Success. All You Need to Know about Achieving Sustained Individual Success. How to Change your Life and Access the Power in You!* I glanced inside one or two and saw that he had written his

156

name at the top of the first page. *Sidney Sharkey*. Somehow I knew that he did this the minute he brought them home.

He'd been a bit heavy handed with the aftershave, I noticed, when we were in the car once more and heading back to Cranberry Hole Road, and he'd put a little gold ring in the lobe of his left ear, which I thought looked a bit ridiculous. Without his jacket sleeves to hide them, his pumped-up arm muscles and pecs bulged through his crisp white T-shirt. And without his shades I could see his eyes properly for the first time. They were royal blue set off by his deep tan, which in turn contrasted with his silver crewcut. A web of wrinkles spread out on either side across his cheeks and his teeth flashed square and white every time he spoke.

'By the way,' he said, 'something I ought to mention. Would you mind not telling Franny and Rufus that I invited you for this drink. I wouldn't normally associate with a principal after hours – I mean, you're not the one paying me but–'

'If I said anything – which I won't – it would be that I wanted to go for a drink and I asked you along for protection,' I said, 'and by the way, what's the latest on the girl who was killed? Did they find anything at that house?'

'Men's clothing,' said Sid.

I whistled.

'Not much.' He checked his appearance – not for the first time – in the rearview mirror. *He's quite vain,* I realised with surprise. 'Just a couple of casual shirts, a pair of shorts, swim-wear, beach shoes. A razor in the bathroom, stuff like that.'

'Could they have been left by the last lot of renters?'

'Possibly, but the renters so far this year have all been youngsters. This stuff looks like it belonged to an older guy. And Gwen Bennett, the owner, she checked the house out before her daughter's friend took it over and there was nothing left behind by the last renters. Whoever this guy is, he's been there since then.'

For some reason I expected Sid to take me to an old-style saloon bar, packed to the gills with fishermen and contractors swilling Budweiser, but he drove me to East Hampton and parked in the car park in the centre of the village behind Waldbaum's. He led me through one of the narrow alleyways to Newtown Lane, one of the two main drags, and into Cittanuova, which was definitely one of the more upscale watering holes. The bar area opened right up to spill out onto the sidewalk but Sid led me indoors to prop himself on a barstool.

'You don't mind?' he said, gesturing to the three plasma screens up on the wall above the bar, 'Mets game is just starting. Now what'll it be?'

I asked for a Sea Breeze but before it arrived, I felt Sid's hand on my elbow.

'We're moving,' he whispered in my ear, 'just follow me to the end of the bar over there.'

'But why?' I said when we were settled.

'That guy beside you was trouble.' Sid nodded his head in the direction of a what appeared to me to be an ordinary looking guy in a short-sleeved loose Hawaiian shirt, nursing a glass, eyes raised to the screen above him.

'Looks harmless to me,' I said. 'He's just watching the game like you were.'

'He's harmless now but two or three drinks down the line, he could turn nasty. And he's got a gun on him.'

'He has?' I sat up straight and stared at the man in astonishment.

'Sure,' said Sid, 'it's tucked into his pants underneath that shirt. Probably got a knife strapped to his leg too.'

'But how can you tell? You can't see them.'

'I was a cop twenty years. We're trained to have a sixth sense. The minute I walk into a place I can tell who belongs at the scene and who doesn't – and that guy definitely doesn't. It's all about his body language. I looked at him when we sat down but he wouldn't meet my eye. And his hand strayed instinctively to the gun – that's what gave him away. He's fine now, but he's edgy about something and a few drinks might exacerbate the problem. He could blow. Probably won't – but he might.'

I looked at Sid with new respect.

'So is that what's running through your mind while you're watching Eliza, watching us? You constantly on the lookout for anyone who looks suspicious. It must be a nightmare when you're in a public place?'

'It can be,' Sid acknowledged. 'For instance, I'm not looking forward to something that's on the calendar next week. Eliza's just a toddler – what is she? Two? Three? But she's been asked to an older kid's party. The birthday girl's gonna be four and the mom's taking a bunch of toddlers to see *Bambi*. Franny'll be with Eliza but I've got to go with them. I won't be sitting with them, I'll be a few rows back, probably all alone in the middle of a row, the only one wearing a jacket – to hide my gun – and conspicuous as hell. I've done this a few times before when I've been working a security detail where a kid's involved and once I got hauled out by the movie theatre manager. Someone had reported that I was a paedophile sitting there ogling the kids – and that's exactly what it must have looked like.'

'But why don't you sit with Franny and Eliza?'

Sid shook his head. 'You never crowd the

principal. That's the bitch of my job. The people being guarded, they want to know you're around if they need you, if they get into danger – but they don't want to *see* you. They want to pretend you're not there. You have to try to make yourself invisible.'

'Which do you prefer? Police work or security work?' It was sort of a dumb question. If he'd liked police work, surely he wouldn't have retired so young. But his answer surprised me.

'I hate them both but it's what I know to do. And if I'm gonna be honest with you, I'd probably say I *loved* them both equally if my wife was still with me. She took off and my life went straight into the toilet. Kinda makes it easier to do my job. It's no big deal to take a bullet for your principal if your own life has no meaning any more.'

I glanced at him. I wasn't used to going for a drink with someone and having them come out with talk like this. And then I wished I hadn't looked because he appeared deadly serious. I wagged a playful finger in front of his face.

'Enough of that. Don't go feeling sorry for yourself all evening. Where is your wife? How often do you get to see your kids?'

'You don't get it, do you? She moved to California and I never see them – and yet she's made sure I'm gonna pay for their college tuition. For a while I held out hope that

161

Gary – my oldest – would come back east to go to college so I would get to visit with him. But my ex is insisting he stays on the West Coast. He's starting at PSU in September.'

'PSU?'

'Portland State University. Oregon. Suzette suggested it to me.'

'Suzette?' I tried to keep the surprise out of my voice.

'She's a nice lady,' he said, 'you might not think it from what you read in the press, but she always took the time to say *Hello, how you doing?* She actually asked me one day if I had kids so I told her about Gary and how he was applying to colleges out west. That's when she told me about Portland. I think her mother's from around there some- where.'

'And you passed it on to Gary?'

'It was already on his list and it turned out they had accepted him. I don't think I really had anything to do with it but I thanked Suzette anyway. At least she took the trouble to discuss it with me. More than you can say about that bitch I was married to – she was a piece of ass that turned into a piece of work and I never saw it coming.' Suddenly he was on his feet. 'Come on, we're leaving. If I sit here drinking all evening, I'm going to get maudlin about my sham of a marriage and that's not the way I want to be around a brand new bride like you. Although,' he looked down at me, 'seems to me you got a few problems of your own already.'

I didn't answer. I wasn't sure it was a good idea to be gossiping with Sid about my marriage. And while he might say the man down the bar was poised to blow, I sensed a pent-up rage inside Sid that could explode if provoked.

The sun had gone down while we'd been drinking and the streets of East Hampton were filling up with vacationers out for the evening. Sid regarded them with disgust.

'This place is such a zoo in the season. If I didn't have the cabin to retreat to, I'd quit in a heartbeat.'

He drove out of the village much too fast and I saw that we were not on the road we'd come in on. 'We're going to another bar?' I said.

He shook his head. 'I'm taking you home before that tough-guy husband of yours comes looking for us. Man! That guy really scares me.'

He was grinning from ear to ear. 'But first I thought we'd drive by the house where they found Mo.'

'The crime scene?'

He smiled. 'The crime scene,' he echoed. 'If you're interested, that is?'

I wanted to see it. I was interested in spite of myself. I was scared stiff at the thought of witnessing where a woman had been killed

163

but at the same time I was in the grip of an irresistible fascination.

We drove to Springs. Springs is the most densely populated hamlet in the Hamptons and until Jackson Pollack discovered it in the Forties, it was more or less solely occupied by the 'Bubs', as the Accabonac Harbor locals were known. But in the real estate boom of the nineties, it became one of the few places where Manhattanites could still get a second home without mortgaging their entire life. Now you had weekend renters in made-over ranches living cheek by jowl with beer-bellied fishermen and contractors with fridges and skateboards all over their back yards.

Sid drew up at an innocuous-looking ranch house with vinyl siding and some fancy landscaping in the front yard that clashed violently with the litter-strewn jungle encroaching on the house on the left. The house on the right had paving stones and geraniums in tubs and I guessed this to be the nosy neighbour's.

'The lights are on,' said Sid.

'Is that bad?'

'I just didn't expect anyone to be there. Forensics are done.'

'Maybe she found new renters?'

'You think?' Sid was sceptical. 'Her daughter just died, they haven't even had the funeral yet. Would she move that fast?'

'Well, someone's in there,' I said. 'There's definitely a light on in the back.'

'Wait here,' said Sid. He got out of the car, marched up to the front door and rang the bell. Almost immediately I saw the light go off at the back of the house.

'Sid,' I hissed, 'the light went off. Whoever it is doesn't want you to know they're there.'

'Go round the left side of the house, I'll go round the right. We'll head them off at the pass.'

I stifled a giggle. I felt like we were playing a kid's game of stalking. Either that or my nerves were getting the better of me. As I crept down the side of the house, I sensed a figure inside moving to the rear. Sid and I met on the patio and waited silently as the back door opened and a woman stepped outside.

As soon as she saw us she took off round the side of the house but she was no match for Sid who reached her in just a couple of strides.

'What are *you* doing here?' I said when I saw who it was.

'Why are you running away from me, Eileen?' said Sid.

Patsy Brooks' cleaner wasn't quick enough off the mark to come up with an excuse.

'Nice to see you too, Sid,' she said. 'Come here often, do you?'

Chapter Seven

'You two know each other?' I said.

'Of course,' said Sid. 'Eileen's one of the cleaners at Scott and Suzette's.'

'You clean for Suzette?' I was astonished. For some reason I had assumed Eileen was Patsy's personal housekeeper.

'Och, yes.' Eileen's Scots accent was quite pronounced tonight. 'A lovely lady. I met her at Patsy's and she said to give her housekeeper a call if I needed a bit of extra work. Well, I called the next day, didn't I? The cost of living out here, you always need the extra work, don't you? Och, yes, a lovely lassie. She got you your job too, you know?'

I stared at her. 'No,' I said, 'my agent in London told me Patsy would be needing a ghostwriter.'

'Sure she did,' said Eileen, 'but Suzette told Patsy that Mr Scott and his brother had an English friend who was a ghostwriter. That's how Patsy first heard about you and then she contacted your agent. I was right there, cleaning Patsy's kitchen when Suzette told her. And Patsy liked the bit about you being English, said she'd feel more comfortable talking to a fellow Brit. Suzette's got

166

your name on her back burner for when she does *her* book but, in the meantime, she was generous enough to tell Patsy about you.'

Suzette's book. I made a mental note to be long gone before that little potboiler bubbled to the surface.

'I didn't know Patsy and Suzette were friends,' I said.

'I'm not sure whether you'd call them friends exactly.' Eileen pronounced it *fraynds.* 'Suzette is a client of Patsy's and one of the few who gets face time with her.'

'Patsy is Suzette's *life coach?*'

'Oh yes, Suzette's life is in a dreadful mess.'

Was it indeed?

'Are you supposed to tell me stuff like this?' I was shocked. 'Doesn't Patsy keep her client list confidential?'

'You're quite right.' Eileen gave me an engaging grin full of mock guilt. 'But she's going to tell you everything for the book anyway, isn't she?' She pulled a packet of Marlboros out of the back pocket of her shorts and sat down on the edge of the deck. 'Let's take a load off,' she said, offering the pack to me and Sid. 'Don't want one? No, you'll get a good yarn from Patsy.' She lit up, inhaled and then blew a column of smoke towards Sid. 'But you'll be careful with her?' She glanced up and looked me straight in the eye. 'Promise me that.'

'Careful?'

167

'You'll not take—' Eileen searched for the word – 'advantage of her? Make her sound bad? She's had a rough time in the past.'

'In what way?' I asked, touched by Eileen's protective instinct.

'I'll leave her to give you the details but you'll have a sob story to tell. She was never able to have bairns. It's why her husband took off, of course. Not sure whether it was because he wanted someone who would give him a family or whether he couldn't take her depression over her infertility.'

'Who is this Patsy?' said Sid.

'Someone else I clean for,' said Eileen quickly. 'The best person I clean for. I'm all over the place, I am. That's why I'm here tonight. Got to get this place shipshape after all this tairrible business.'

'You clean for Gwen Bennett?' Sid asked.

Eileen nodded. 'I do all her rentals. Nice little earner, she is. And of course I met her through Patsy too. Gwen's a realtor, as I'm sure you know, and she sold Patsy her house way back when. In fact I was the first one to see it. I told Patsy, I said this'll do you per—'

'Eileen, don't tell me you're here cleaning at eight o'clock at night,' said Sid. 'I don't buy it.'

She looked at him. 'Why else would I be here?'

'You tell me,' said Sid. 'If you were cleaning, why did you turn the light out as soon as you realised we were here? It was obvious you didn't want to be seen.'

There was an imperceptible pause. I noticed it and I was pretty sure Sid did too. Then Eileen shrugged. 'I came to get something, OK? I didn't know what would be happening with the house and I came to retrieve something.'

'Something you didn't want the police to find?' Sid leaned towards her. 'Don't you know you shouldn't tamper with a crime scene in case you contaminate the evidence? As it happens, the police won't be back. Forensics are done, but it sounds like you didn't know that. Wait a second. Was it items of men's clothing you were after, by any chance?'

Eileen reacted. She tried hard to recover quickly but she couldn't hide the fact that Sid's words had hit their mark.

'You'd better just tell me,' said Sid. 'I'm an ex-cop, remember? I'm connected to the guys investigating this death. You don't tell me, I make sure they come looking for you so you can tell them whatever it is you know.'

'I don't know anything,' Eileen blurted out. 'I just came here to get that clothing as a way of paying my respects to Holly Bennett.'

'That's Gwen Bennett's daughter, right? The one who died in the bathtub? But enlighten me,' said Sid. 'How does taking evidence away from a crime scene pay respects to the victim?'

Eileen leaned closer to him as if she thought we might be overheard. 'Holly told her parents a friend of hers wanted to rent the house but I don't think she even knew the girl. It's my guess she found her on Vacation.com or whatever it's called.'

'But why would she pretend the renter was a friend of hers?' I was mystified.

Eileen wagged a knowing finger at me. 'Because she wanted to use the house for trysts with her boyfriend – the one she didn't want her mother to know about.'

'Because?' said Sid.

'Because he was *auld!* More than twice her age and probably married. Holly confided in me, told me about the affair she was having with this man. He'd rented out here last year and she'd met him then and had been carrying on with him in the city ever since.'

Carrying on! I was amused by Eileen's slightly disapproving tone.

'So essentially the house was a shared rental?' Sid asked.

Eileen nodded. 'The room at the back is quite private and it has its own bathroom, its own entrance. The man who rented it, he was only there at weekends and he could come and go without running into the other renter. And provided Holly went round the back to his separate entrance, she wouldn't have run into the woman either.'

'But on the day she was killed, she didn't go round the back,' I said. 'She went in through the front door and she ran into the woman and Mo.'

'She did?' Eileen looked as if this was news to her. 'Who's Mo?'

I explained about him being the Fresh Air kid who had been mistaken for Suzette's son and what he had told us about hearing someone arrive at the front door.

'And who was that? Who came to the front door?' Eileen looked from me to Sid.

'He never saw her, only heard her,' I said.

'Eileen, did you ever see the woman who rented the house?' said Sid.

Eileen shook her head. 'I cleaned the house on Wednesdays from ten am until one and she was never there.'

'And Holly's assignations were only at the weekends?'

Eileen nodded. 'I never saw her either. Not there, anyway. I'd run into her in the village sometimes and she'd wink and giggle and act like the silly girl she was.'

'You didn't like her?'

'I never said that,' Eileen said quickly without looking at us. 'I was very fond of her – why else would I have helped her? I was moved that she felt she could trust me enough to confide in me. That's why I'm here tonight, isn't it? Taking the man's things away, covering up the traces of their time here together so Gwen Bennett won't find out.'

'So who was the boyfriend,' said Sid, 'the married lover from the city?'

Eileen shrugged. 'How would I know? She never told me his name. Now listen, are we done?' She stood up, flicking her cigarette into the bushes. 'I need to be on my way.'

'Don't you want to go back in and get the clothes you came for?' said Sid.

'They're not there,' said Eileen. 'I guess forensics took them away. Looks like Gwen will find out after all.'

I sensed that Sid still had more to say. He was regarding her quizzically, as if he was unsure about letting her go, but didn't quite know how to stop her. And she took advantage of his hesitation by pulling the door shut and locking it and disappearing round the side of the building with a *Nice to see you again, Sid. You're looking pretty fit* before he could stop her.

'See you at Patsy's,' she called out to me, 'I'll be keeping an eye out to make sure you treat her with respect. She tells me everything, you know. You upset her, you'll have me to answer to.'

'Bet you're quaking in your shoes,' Sid muttered as we walked back to his car.

'So what do you make of her?' I asked Sid once we were heading home.

'Eileen? Oh, she can be a real piece of

work when she wants to be.' He glanced at me. 'But I always had a sneaking admiration for her. I get the impression she's had to fight her way through life. She's a survivor but then I've always had the sense that she's a bit of a control freak. At Scott and Suzette's she was always trying to show the security detail that she had more intimate access to Suzette than we did. She'd claim Suzette confided in her about this and that, but then she'd refuse to tell us what Suzette had said. It was like she'd be happy if she could get Suzette under her thumb like she seems to have this Patsy.'

I nodded. I knew what Sid meant but I'd also sensed a genuine affection between Eileen and Patsy. But then again, Eileen had been quick to point out that Holly Bennett had confided in her too so maybe she did like pulling people close to her.

'Do you believe that stuff about wanting to shield Holly's affair from Gwen Bennett?' I said.

'Pretty much,' said Sid. 'Of course, they've discovered all about the affair and who he was from what they found on Holly's computer. She was emailing him constantly and let me tell you, he's a pretty sleazy character. He was two-timing Holly for a start. He has a string of garages and he *owns* a house out here. Whatever Eileen said, he wasn't renting that room at the house we've just left. Holly was just using it as a place for her trysts with him. But whichever way you look at him, he's probably not the kind of guy her mother would approve of. Holly was only eighteen for a start – and he was close to fifty.'

'So did they find emails from Holly to this guy, or from him to her?'

'Plenty,' said Sid, 'but there were none from anyone about renting the house on Spring Hollow Road. If Holly Bennett set that up with a friend of hers, she must have done it on the phone. There's nothing on her computer about it.'

'Weird,' I said, 'and scary, because that's the only way they can find out the girl's identity.'

I was still pondering this when we arrived back at Franny and Rufus's house.

'Want to go in, say goodnight?' said Sid.

I shook my head. 'I'd better go and find Tommy and try to make amends for calling him a useless piece of shit. Not exactly the best way to start your honeymoon.'

Sid didn't say a word. But when I looked at him, I wasn't sure whether it was because he deemed it wise to keep quiet or whether he was too distracted by the sight in front of us.

Minnie Shaugnessy was struggling down the track to the pool house with one of the giant suitcases with which she and Shagger had arrived, presumably to fill them with booty from the Tanger Outlets. Although, from the way Minnie was lumbering under its weight, her suitcase was full already.

Sid gave a gentle peep on the horn behind her and she dropped the suitcase in surprise. When she turned round, I heard Sid gasp.

He didn't follow it up with anything, didn't ask me who she was, just stopped the car and leapt out to go to her. I heard him say, 'Let me help you with that,' and within a second Minnie was in the car with us, her squeaky tones chirping at us from the back seat.

'This is ever so kind of you.' She tapped Sid on the shoulder. 'New plan, Lee. You and Tommy are sleeping in the main house now and me and Normie, we're going to share the pool house with Noreen.'

Oh, so it was Noreen already, was it? Minnie had clearly settled in well.

'What about Mo?' I asked.

'Who? Oh, the little boy? He wants to stay at the pool house with Noreen,' said Minnie. 'Poor Normie, he wasn't quite strong enough to carry my case as well as his. He said he'd come back for it but I got tired of waiting. Oh look, there he is.'

Shagger was shuffling along the track towards us from the pool house. Sid slowed down and Minnie stuck her head out the car window.

'It's all right, Normie. You've no need to get my case. We've got it here. Get in.'

She held the door open.

'I unpacked.' Shagger was unusually eloquent. 'Found I'd left my razor behind. On my way to pick it up.'

'Oh, don't bother,' Minnie tittered. 'I love a man with facial hair. I've always told you that.'

I couldn't help thinking that from the look of him, Shagger might not be able to grow a beard. Ever since I'd known him – and it had to be going on ten years – he'd always had the look of an adolescent about him. Thin and gangly with a constant eruption of unsightly pimples on the lower half of his face, he did however have wonderful eyes, soft and vulnerable looking even if they were sometimes a little pink, like a rabbit's.

But before Shagger could react, Sid pulled away, rather abruptly, I thought, towards the pool house, leaving Shagger standing there. Sid kept glancing in his rear-view mirror and I realised suddenly that his gaze was transfixed not on Shagger, but on the reflection of Minnie right behind him.

Oh Lord, I thought, *what's that expression from* The Godfather?

It was later, long after Sid had left and Shagger had returned with his razor and I had joined Franny and Rufus and Tommy for what was left of their dinner, that I remembered it.

Sid had been struck by a thunderbolt.

176

The next morning Noreen arrived on our doorstep bright and early with Mo in tow. I sensed immediately that something was wrong. Noreen has impeccable manners and she would never appear uninvited at a relative stranger's house at breakfast time without good reason.

I was in the process of laying the table for breakfast. Even though Franny and Rufus could afford to hire staff to wait on them hand and foot, Franny had laid down a house rule that Lucia was only there to take care of housekeeping. She, Franny, would do the cooking herself and, if she wasn't around, everyone had to fend for themselves.

I settled Noreen into a chair in Franny's expansive kitchen and made her a cup of tea and gave Mo a chocolate milk. 'Tommy'll be down any minute,' I said, although I wasn't holding my breath. I imagined I could hear his snores two floors above in the wonderful attic bedroom Franny had given us. It ran the entire width of the house with ceilings sloping down to the floor in places, so that you almost had to crawl on your stomach to lower yourself onto the bed. Giant skylights punctuated the roof along with heavy cedar beams for which Tommy seemed to make constant beelines, crashing his forehead into them with such force that it was a wonder he was not, as yet, concussed.

'Oh, I don't want to see Tommy,' said Noreen. 'I came to tell you that Sid came by looking for you and Mo. He said to tell you he'll be back here in twenty minutes to take Mo to the police station, and that you'll know why.' She looked at me intently. 'Something to do with Sally? Suzette's old assistant?'

'Have you told Mo?'

'Oh, yes, he's all prepared. Actually,' she added, and I thought she seemed a bit sheepish, 'I suppose we could have waited for him down there but I feel a bit strange around those two, you know, back at the pool house. They're a bit loud. The walls are rather thin. Mo was listening. I don't know, it was just–'

'They were arguing?'

And then Noreen smiled. 'Lee, wake up,' she said, patting me on the arm. 'You're my daughter-in-law, you're a married woman now. When a man and a woman get together, there are other things they do besides having a row that make a noise.'

'Shagger's always been a noisy fucker.' Tommy, appearing behind his mother in his pyjamas, had apparently stopped snoring.

'Actually, it was more her,' said Noreen. 'But I think we might take this conversation in another direction, if you don't mind.' She inclined her head slightly in the direction of Mo, who was listening with interest.

'Hey, man,' said Mo.

'Hey, Mo,' said Tommy and they slapped palms, first one, then the other and proceeded to execute an elaborate little dance of greeting, turning their backs on each other, bumping butts and offering their hands from behind. Tommy looked a little ridiculous because he was too heavy to move as fast as Mo, which resulted in him missing Mo's hand and slapping thin air more than once.

But it was clear Mo was already Tommy's biggest fan.

'Where you go last night, man?' he asked Tommy, clasping his hand and pulling on his arm. 'I thought we gone be together, be roomies, then I wake up this morning. You gone. What's up?'

'Nothing personal,' said Tommy, lifting Mo up in the air and whirling him around until he squealed for mercy. 'We boys just got to do what we're told.' A quick glance at me. 'Franny says I move in here, I move in here. I don't argue. Never argue with a woman, Mo.'

'Why not?' Mo gave Tommy's arm a jerk. 'I argue with my mom all the time. That how we talk.'

Noreen stood up. 'Tommy, get your coffee and take him outside. I need to talk to Lee.'

'What about?' said Mo.

'You,' said Noreen, pretending to give his nose a tweak, 'and what we're going to do with you.'

Tommy hoisted Mo onto his hip and carried him outside as if he were hefting a basket of laundry, Mo giggling all the while.

'He's wonderful with him,' I said, 'who would have thought?'

'You know as well as I do, Lee, that it's because he's still a big kid himself. So how did you and Tommy get on last night after you got back? It was my idea, by the way, putting you two up at the main house so you could have a bit of privacy. I called Franny and suggested it – a bit presumptuous of me, maybe – but I have to say, she agreed immediately. You and Tommy needed a bit of space. So how'd it go? Or am I being a nosy parker mother-in-law?'

'You are a bit,' I smiled, 'but I'm grateful for the interest and as a matter of fact nothing happened. I walked in as he and Franny and Rufus were finishing supper, we chatted generally for a while. It was a little awkward because there was no reference to the fact that I had rushed off. It was as if they'd made a pact not to mention it, business as usual sort of thing. And then, when we all went up to bed, your son was asleep as soon as his head hit the pillow.'

I frowned at the memory. Not only had I wanted to make things right with Tommy, I had also wanted to share my encounter with Eileen with him. Although that would have meant bringing Sid into the equation and I was pretty sure that would have set Tommy off again.

'But what we do need to sort out, Noreen,' I said, 'is what we're going to do with Minnie and Shagger. They've got to leave.'

'Actually,' said Noreen, 'it's Mo I'm more worried about.'

'Why?' I said, surprised. 'I thought he was fine now.'

'I mean when he leaves,' said Noreen.

'That's not for another week.'

'But where's he going to go?'

'Back where he came from. To his mother. Maybe she'd like to have Minnie and Shagger too, although I'm not sure I can wait that long.'

'That's what I wanted to talk to you about,' said Noreen. 'Have they located the mother yet?'

Before I could answer, Rufus came into the kitchen, marching over to the coffee machine as if his life depended on it.

I adore Rufus. Because my mother had almost married his father, I think of him as my American 'brother'. Better still, when we'd all first got to know each other, Franny and I had rejoiced in the way Tommy and Rufus had immediately bonded – two little boys rushing off to play on the beach to-gether. Of course there was a big difference between them, namely that while Tommy invariably behaved like a little boy, Rufus only looked like one. He was short and quite stocky with a surfer's muscular upper body. He was a towhead and even though he was approaching thirty, (almost ten years Franny's junior), his hair was still a pale blond and flopping over one eye and his face bore a permanently cheeky expression. But while Tommy lurched irresponsibly from one dead-end job to another, Rufus was amazingly mature for his age. He had used his father's legacy to set up a series of shelters for the homeless but he made sure that very few people knew he was behind them. To the world at large he still presented himself as a boy of the land, a fisherman, surfer and part-time construction worker. Which, essentially, he still was. He had once hired Tommy to work for him and I wondered now if he might do so again.

But this morning he was unusually brusque.

'Sid here yet?' he asked without even bidding anyone good morning.

'Haven't seen him,' I said, 'but he's–' I was about to tell Rufus that Sid would be coming by soon to take Mo to identify Sally, but he cut me off.

'Well, have him come look for me the minute he arrives. He needs to watch Eliza today. My wife took off for the city at five o'clock this morning.'

My wife! What happened to 'Franny'?

'How long will she be gone?' I said.

'She didn't tell me.'

'Rufus, I can watch Eliza,' I said. 'Sid's not a babysitter.'

Rufus gave me an uncharacteristically cold look. 'He is if I want him to be. I've hired him for the safety and protection of our child after what happened to Mo – what almost happened to Keshawn – and yet my wife spends her whole time complaining about having him around. The poor guy *has* to be around. How else is he going to make sure there isn't another kidnapping attempt. He tries to stay out of sight as much as he can but it's hard.'

Clearly there had been a major argument about Sid.

'Everything came to a head last night,' Rufus confirmed, 'because I said I wanted to hire a night detail as well as Sid during the day. Scott and Suzette have twenty-four-hour surveillance and it makes sense – but Franny totally freaked out, said it was bad enough that we even had Sid.'

'It's not Sid she minds,' I pointed out, 'she just can't get used to the idea that you have enough money to make her child a viable kidnapping proposition. Sid's presence reminds her of this, makes her nervous.'

'Don't make excuses for her,' Rufus snapped. 'You think I like it? She married

183

me, she has to adapt. Money has responsibilities. More than anything, right now I'd like to take off, go surfing for the rest of the day. But I have to spend the next few hours in meetings going over plans for the new shelter.' He saw my face and relented somewhat. 'OK, sure, you take Eliza, that would be great. Franny even suggested it as she walked out the door. Thanks, Lee,' he said and added after a beat, 'sorry.'

I hugged him because I had the feeling he needed it. The extraordinary thing about Rufus was that I knew he would probably be executing the construction of the new shelter himself once the plans had been finalised.

A wail from above signalled that Eliza was awake.

'I'll go and get her,' said Noreen and I let her. If anyone could sort out Eliza first thing in the morning, it was Noreen.

'OK, I'm off,' said Rufus. 'Oh, hi, Tommy,' he said as Tommy came in followed by Mo and, a few steps behind him, Shagger.

'Me and Shagger, we're going to take Mo out for the day,' said Tommy.

'I'm not sure that's such a good idea,' I said without thinking. 'In any case, there's something he has to do first, which may take half an hour or so. Sid's coming by soon to pick him up and take him to the police station. He's going to help out the cops by identifying the girl who took him from the beach. Maybe the beach won't work today.'

Mo's face fell and Tommy put his arm around him. 'Why not?' he said. 'Any particular reason or do you just want to make a habit out of spoiling our fun? We could follow him to the police station and take him on from there.'

He was smiling as he said this, so Mo would think he was kidding, but I sensed the hint of a barb in his tone. Just as he'd looked straight at me when telling Mo *We boys got to do what we're told.*

'Tommy,' I hissed, 'you're not exactly experienced in looking after kids.'

'And you are?'

Of course he had me there.

'I've had your mother to help me and, God knows, she's ready for anything, having raised you. But Mo is essentially Franny and Rufus's responsibility. We should maybe ask them.'

'Except they're not here,' he said. 'We'll go to the beach – just to the bay, up the road. What harm can we possibly come to there?'

'I'll take my arm bands,' said Mo, 'and I'll wear them all the time, even when I ain't in the water. Be my new look.'

'Mo, those are Eliza's arm bands,' I pointed out to him. 'They're just on loan to you because they're still too big for her.'

'I wanted it to be a boys' outing. Me, Mo

and Shagger. Just us guys together. I thought maybe Mo could use a little male bonding.' Tommy's smile – an overweight version of Jude Law's – was virtually irresistible.

'You say no, I gone get you,' said Mo and he advanced upon me with the most revolting monster face yet, his fingers pulling the corners of his mouth almost up to his earlobes and revealing an expanse of shiny pink gum.

'Norman, what do you think?' I said.

'Be awesome,' said Shagger, looking as gloomy as ever. 'You know there's a car outside?'

I froze. This was the moment of truth.

'Mo?' I looked at him. 'You know what's going to happen?'

'Sid's going to take me to look at that girl and I'm going to tell you it's her. But she won't take me away again?' I saw the fear in his eyes and hugged him to me.

'No way. Let's go and meet Sid outside.'

'Hey, Mo, how're you doin'?' Sid got out of the car as we came out of the house and gave Mo a playful punch on the shoulder. Mo tried to smile, but I could see that he was nervous.

'Can I come along with him?' I said.

'He'll be fine with me,' said Sid, 'right, Mo?'

Mo smiled and I realised Sid spoke the truth.

'Go on,' I said softly to Sid, 'get it over with. Get him back to me fast.'

'You did absolutely the right thing,' Noreen said later when we were settled at the pool. I was clutching my phone in my hand, waiting for Tommy to call me with the news that Mo had ID'd the kidnapper. Tommy and Shagger had followed Sid to the police station and the plan was that they would then take Mo from there straight to the beach.

'Lee, are you listening to me?' Noreen waved a hand in front of my face to get my attention. 'Tommy's right. That little boy probably does need to spend some time with men. But I don't mind telling you, I'm getting distinctly worried that we haven't heard from his mother. Even though I did speak to a couple of other people round here who have taken in Fresh Air kids and they told me the mothers often don't make contact. Weird, isn't it?'

'You're amazing, Noreen,' I said. 'You've only been here a few days and already you're part of the community.'

'Comes naturally to me. We're not all loners like you, dear. Not that it's a bad thing,' she said hastily. 'We're all different, aren't we? But I just know that if those other host families had called the mothers of *their* Fresh Air kids, *they* would have located them pretty quickly. Something's not right, Lee. I know it.'

My mobile rang just as Sid appeared around the side of the pool house. He shook his head at me and my spirits plummeted.

'Lee? Are you there?' Tommy's voice was loud in my ear.

'I'm here. Sid's just arrived here. He shook his head at me. I assume that means it wasn't her.'

'That's what Mo's told me,' said Tommy. 'I'm trying to buck him up. He seems to think he's done wrong in some way. Keeps asking "Did I do good?"'

'Tell him he did the best he could. I'll get the full story from Sid. Now you guys get to the beach before I change my mind. But be back here by five thirty at the latest, and Tommy, make sure Mo eats lunch somewhere. And call me on my mobile every couple of hours.'

I heard him mutter *will do* and then he hung up. I beckoned Sid and he came over.

'It was a long shot,' he said, 'but we felt he had to see her. Apparently she'd begun babbling away in a confessional manner. Turns out she was giving us the runaround because she thought we had discovered she had lifted quite a few items from Suzette's closets before she left. The bitch of it is that Suzette never even reported them missing. She's got so much stuff, she never noticed anything was gone. I'm sorry we wasted

188

your time, but we had to–'

'Of course,' I said, feeling utterly deflated by the news. 'You'll tell Scott and Suzette?'

'I'll give them a call right now,' he said, and wandered off to the end of the pool where he disappeared into the bushes, pulling out his mobile phone.

Noreen waved at him. Then she peeped over her sunglasses. 'Ooh, look, we've got company.'

The pool house had been totally silent when we had descended on it with Eliza chattering away at full pelt. *Pool. Pool. Want to go pool.* Poor Minnie didn't stand a chance of any more sleep and now she appeared on the patio.

'Mind if I join you?' she squeaked.

'Free country,' I said and felt Noreen give me a sharp kick on the shin. 'Of course,' I added hurriedly, 'move those towels off that lounger and relax. Sorry we woke you.'

I was standing waist high in the pool, holding firm to Eliza and skimming her through the water as I'd seen Franny do. As I did so, I observed Minnie, trying not to stare.

Turquoise gingham was obviously her favourite fabric although not much of it had gone into the manufacture of her miniscule bikini. She had a tiny diamond stud in her navel and I winced. Whenever I saw those things, I always immediately imagined it being inserted and felt a stab of vicarious pain. And then, without so much as a *Do you mind if I...?* Minnie whipped off the top half of her bikini and lay down on her back, her sharp little nipples pointing upwards like two rose-coloured darts.

I gasped involuntarily and looked at Noreen to gauge her reaction. OK, so everybody bared their breasts on the beach these days without a second thought, but somehow I knew I would never be able to do it comfortably in the presence of a person of Noreen's age.

Noreen got up and laid a towel over Minnie's chest. 'Skin cancer, dear. You *must* be careful. Your breasts are one of your most tender areas.'

And then there was a discreet cough as Sid emerged from the bushes at the far end of the pool. Minnie looked up, startled. 'Who's that?'

'It's Sid, he gave you a lift last night, you remember?' I explained as Minnie clasped the towel across her chest. 'He's part of the Abernathys' security detail.' And I told her about Mo's kidnapping – although I didn't mention Holly Bennett's murder, didn't want to ruin her idyllic image of the Hamptons too soon. 'Franny and Rufus don't want to take any chances with Eliza.'

'But what's he doing hiding in the bushes?' Minnie got to her feet and pattered around the pool towards Sid. 'Sid? Come out of there, you great big silly. Come and sit with us. You can't go hiding yourself away like that. You need to work on your tan, don't you? Not that it needs much work, I imagine. Get your shirt off, let's have a look at you.'

In Sid, it soon became clear that Minnie had finally found her perfect audience, not least because he knew the exact whereabouts of the Tanger Outlets. I was a little unnerved at how quickly she managed to persuade him to remove first his jacket and then his shirt. I noted how he laid the latter carefully over a chair and I caught a glimpse of the gun in its holster as he did so. Was this safe? Surely Eliza could reach it if she went over there?

He didn't have a pair of swimming trunks so he couldn't go in the pool and the sight of his hulking bare chest covered in silver fluff rising in sharp contrast above the leather belt and formal black trousers of his suit was almost comical. His naked biceps were, to me, grotesquely bulbous especially when he raised his arm to the side and flexed them, body-builder style, to squeals of encouragement from Minnie.

Minnie's constant banter and the way Sid lapped it up annoyed me for some reason. I was relieved when it was time for Eliza to take her nap after lunch. Noreen followed suit and I lay down in the cool air-conditioned living area of the pool house, cut off at last by the thick glass sliders from the sound of Minnie's inane patter. I snoozed. I was aware of her creeping past me at some point and into her room but I only opened my eyes long enough to mutter *Don't wake Eliza*, who was laid out beside me on the sofa.

I was awakened by Tommy calling to say that all was well and that they had eaten a huge lunch of lobster rolls and fish and chips at the Fish Farm on Cranberry Hole Road and were now making their way to the ocean to try a bit of surfcasting.

'But you said you'd stick to the bay,' I said, aware I was whining.

'So I lied,' said Tommy cheerfully. 'Give us a break, Lee. The bay's so calm. Mo wants some big wave action.'

'Well, just make sure he holds tight to your hand. I'm serious, Tommy. Keep an eye on him.'

'I will,' he said. 'You know I will.'

There was no sign of Minnie but the door to her room was closed so I thought maybe she was taking a nap. Noreen was now outside with Eliza again, going patiently through a pile of picture books with her. Eliza insisted on identifying each illustration, going *Ooh, cow!* and pointing at a horse and then Noreen would correct her and Eliza would look at her with immense scepticism and I could see that this could go on for some time. I went back to the main house, prepared a snack for Eliza and brought it back to the pool house on a tray. I made a cup of tea for Noreen and looked around for Sid to see if he wanted one too but there was no sign of him. I felt a slight prick of unease – wasn't he supposed to be close by at all times? – and then dismissed it. I was supposed to be relaxing, enjoying my free time before I started work on the story of Patience Brook O'Reilly.

And then, about an hour later, Tommy called again. 'Mo's gone,' he said.

'What do you mean, he's gone?' My heart began to crash about in my chest.

'We got to the ocean, drew up at the car park. I went around to the trunk to unload the fishing gear. I handed Mo a rod, told him to be very careful carrying it down to the beach, closed the trunk, rounded up Shagger and by the time we got down to the beach, Mo had gone.'

'Gone where?'

'Gone, Lee. As in not there. Disappeared. No sign of him. I've searched everywhere, asked everyone on the beach if they've seen him and all I've come up with is someone who said they saw a black kid go back to the car park and get in a car with a man but there's no saying it was Mo. There's a couple of black families here, could have been one of their kids. What do I do, Lee?'

'You stay right where you are in case he comes back,' I said, trying to sound calm. 'I'll ask Sid what to do and get back to you. Keep your mobile turned on.'

I hung up, went outside and whispered to Noreen what had happened and then yelled for Sid. No answer. I ran up to the main house but he wasn't there either.

And then I called his mobile.

'Where the hell are you, Sid?' I yelled when he answered. 'You're supposed to stay close, aren't you?'

'I'll be right there,' he said when I told him what had happened and it was only when I had disconnected that I realised he hadn't said where he was.

When he arrived back at the house, he had Minnie in the car with him. When I looked at him, he didn't offer an explanation, but he must have realised Minnie wouldn't keep her mouth shut.

'Sid took me to look at the shops in East Hampton. Bit pricey but they've got some lovely gear. Of course, we came straight back when we heard that little boy's gone missing. Is there anything I can do?'

Mo had gone missing on Tommy's watch, not Sid's, but for some reason I blamed Sid. I was furious that he had abandoned Eliza and gone off with Minnie and so I didn't answer. The tension mounted when Sid had

194

to speak to Tommy and debrief him. I could feel he was itching to yell at Tommy for losing Mo, but the way he avoided my eye told me he also felt guilty about going off with Minnie.

When Rufus came home he called Scott to check Keshawn was safe. Sid had already called Pete and Vince, the two cops investigating Keshawn's previous attempted kidnapping, and they said they'd get back to us as soon as there was any news. Tommy and Shagger came home when it began to get dark and we all sat and glared at each other, hardly daring to speak. I kept quiet about Sid and Minnie's jaunt to East Hampton because I knew Rufus would explode and the last thing we needed was more antagonism. The atmosphere between Tommy and Sid was bad enough and the knowledge that all we could do was sit and wait was almost unbearable.

'He could be dead,' I whispered to Noreen. Minnie and Shagger had gone down to the pool house but I had begged Noreen to stay with me.

'And he could just as easily be alive,' said Sid, overhearing me. 'There's only one way out of the Hamptons and that's via Route 27. Sooner or later they're going to have to go along it and then they'll be stopped. Tommy gave the police a good description and they'll be checking every car.'

195

'And what if they got away by boat?' I said miserably. 'Is there only one way out across the ocean?'

Rufus had called Franny on her mobile and she was on her way home so when we heard a car coming down the driveway, I assumed it was her and ran to the door.

But it was a truck and it went straight past the house in the direction of the pool house, followed by a police car.

We ran out of the house and down the track to the pool house.

'It's him,' I shrieked, 'it's Mo.' And I rushed to hug him, squeezing him to me in an embrace made awkward by the fact that he was still wearing his arm bands.

'See?' he said. 'I told you I wouldn't take them off.'

'That's how we found him,' Pete told Sid, getting out of the police car. 'Tommy Kennedy mentioned he might have arm bands with him and he was still wearing them, sitting in the truck.'

A tall black man was getting out of the beat-up truck in which Mo had driven up. I stared at him, not understanding.

'Is that the guy who took him?' I asked Pete. 'Why haven't you taken him into custody. Why did you let him drive Mo here without any restraint?'

'Because he's my dad,' said Mo.

Chapter Eight

Over the next few days I became so mired in domestic wrangling, I almost forgot about Holly Bennett's murder and the depressing fact that we were no closer to knowing who was responsible for it. Apparently Sally had sworn she had not divulged Suzette's private number to anyone but, as Tommy pointed out, *She would say that, wouldn't she?* All we knew was that someone else had had the number besides her and Robby.

The first thing that happened was that my mother suddenly remembered my existence.

'I thought I'd pop out to East Hampton for the weekend,' she said, purring down the phone like a Cheshire cat. It was eight o'clock in the morning and, from the rapid rise and fall of her breath, I deduced she must be calling me from Central Park as she executed her daily jog before breakfast. Even though she's not that far off seventy, my mother is as whippet thin as she was in her twenties, and determined to remain so. I don't really know why she bothers to run. The way she charges through every day, never sitting still for a second, must surely burn off enough energy to ensure that she never puts on an ounce. 'I mean, I haven't even seen you since you got married.'

And whose fault is that? I thought churlishly. *Most mothers make the effort to attend their daughter's wedding.*

'I haven't changed a bit,' I said. 'Anyway I have Noreen to keep me company.'

It was a bit below the belt but I was still pretty angry at the way my mother had let Noreen down at the last minute. Suddenly it had been 'inconvenient' for her to have Noreen to stay, yet when it suited my mother to be someone else's guest, she expected everyone to fall in with her plans.

'Oh, I'd love to see Noreen,' said my mother, as if she had completely forgotten that Noreen was actually supposed to be staying with her in Manhattan. 'And your father's away this weekend and my Saturday lunch date's just been cancelled.'

So that was the reason she'd called. She was at a loose end. But of course it didn't occur to her to invite Noreen to visit *her*.

'The thing is, Mum, I'm really sorry about this but we don't have room for you. Tommy and I are up at Franny and Rufus's as it is because Tommy's friend Norman is in our room at the pool house.' For a second I actually blessed the fact that Shagger and Minnie were there. 'And Noreen is in the other room with Mo. He's the–'

198

'The Fresh Air kid, yes, I heard all about that,' said my mother, 'but it's absolutely fine, darling. You don't need to worry about where you'll put me. I already called Rufus and he said he and Franny would be *thrilled* to have me and then I'd be right there with you newlyweds, wouldn't I?'

She was my mother. I ought to be delighted at the thought of her arrival – and ordinarily I would be. But my mother's presence generally obliterated anything else I had going on in my life and right now I had a lot on my mind.

Rufus had fired Sid. Although I never breathed a word about Sid's disappearing act, Minnie couldn't wait to tell Franny and me all about what she'd seen in the East Hampton stores. Franny and I were in the kitchen, tiptoeing around each other in a rather awkward fashion. I had come down to prepare Tommy's breakfast and found Franny staring at a cup of coffee. She said nothing to me, not even *good morning*, but because I was a guest I felt obliged to make conversation – *Lovely morning, how was your trip to the city, Eliza still asleep?* – but I got zero response apart from the occasional nod of the head.

And then Minnie came dancing in without so much as a perfunctory knock on the door, chattering away without appearing to notice the slight frost in the air. But after a minute or two, I was grateful for her intrusion. She was so genuine in her excitement, I found it infectious, and something of a relief after Franny's reluctance to engage me in conversation. I would have happily listened to her extolling the virtues of Scoop over Henry Lehr for another half an hour had she not added:

'And having Sid carry my bags for me, following me in and out of the shops, it was like I had my own personal chauffeur. I felt like a movie star, I really did.'

Franny came to life.

'Sid was with you?'

Minnie nodded.

'Where was Eliza?' Franny looked at me.

'At the pool house with Noreen and me,' I admitted.

'So this Godforsaken security guy we've hired to safeguard our child abandons her the minute our backs are turned?' Franny was on her feet.

'It was fine, Franny. I told Sid he could take Minnie shopping,' I lied.

But I could tell she didn't believe me and the next day I had a call from Sid on my mobile.

'I shouldn't be doing this,' he said, 'but I wanted to say goodbye. Or *an revoir* at least. I won't be seeing much of you from now on. I've been let go by Rufus.'

'Oh Sid, I'm so sorry,' I said, trying not to

think about how angry I had been with him when I couldn't find him following Mo's disappearance. I had been in a panic, that's all. 'I didn't tell them you weren't there, I swear.'

'I know you didn't,' he said, 'but it's not just about taking Minnie shopping. Franny was never happy about me being there, I could tell. She was looking for some kind of stick to beat me with, anything she could take to her husband, and I just handed her an opportunity on a plate. It was my own fault.'

'But what will you do?'

'What I was doing before they hired me – go back to being part of Keshawn's detail. I called my old captain, you know, the guy who now runs Scott Abernathy's security detail? And he said *absolutely, come on back*. In a way I was only on loan to watch Eliza anyway.'

'So you're still at the cabin?'

'Of course. You're welcome any time – only I'm rarely there.'

And I couldn't very well go consorting with someone Rufus and Franny had just fired.

'Sid,' I said, 'I appreciate your call and I wonder if I could ask you a favour?'

He laughed. 'Ask away.'

'Keep me posted about the Holly Bennett investigation?'

'Anything happens, you're gonna hear it

from Rufus and Franny,' he said. 'Whoever it was was after Keshawn, therefore Scott and Suzette will be kept informed. They're bound to tell Rufus.'

'Even so, I'd like to hear it from you,' I said. Somehow I knew Sid would get the real lowdown – the story *behind* the story given out for public consumption – and I wanted to know what had really happened on Spring Hollow Road the day Mo had been abducted. I was aware of an under-lying reason for my curiosity. There was a connection – albeit a tenuous one – to Patience Brook O'Reilly. The kidnappers had been after Keshawn; his 'mother', Suzette, was a client of Patsy's. The murder had occurred at Gwen Bennett's house and the victim was her daughter; Gwen Bennett had sold Patsy her house. And Sid and I had found Patsy's cleaner there. It was a purely professional need-to-know, I told myself, just in case the murder found its way into Patsy's book.

'OK,' he said. 'I'll keep you posted. I'd like the excuse to keep in touch with you, Lee, tell you the truth. You're my kind of woman – straightforward, to the point. I've been sitting here, beating myself up about how dumb I was to go off with Minnie like that. I should have been there for Eliza – for all of you. I wanted to apologise to you.'

There was nothing flirtatious in the way

he said this and I realised I felt exactly the same way about him.

'Forget it,' I said, 'it all worked out fine in the end.'

'So how's Mo holding up?' he asked, 'After his reunion with his dad?'

'Pretty good,' I said, 'considering.'

And then I changed the subject because I didn't want to talk to Sid about Mo's father and my subsequent meeting with him – even though I knew I might be getting in way above my head.

When Mo had announced that the person who had abducted him from the beach was his father, it had come as a total surprise. But once I had recovered from the shock, I had held out my hand in greeting.

'I'm Lee Bartholomew. I'm–'

'Oh, I know exactly who you are.' He loped towards me, an exceptionally tall man who was, I sensed immediately, totally at ease with his height. 'Mo's told me all about you and how you're his Fresh Air mom.'

'But I'm–' *But I'm not,* I started to say and then stopped as I realized that in reality Franny hadn't spent any time with Mo. *What's with her?* I found myself wondering suddenly. Ever since she had returned from Paris, apart from that initial day at the pool with us, she had been a little distant. OK, so Mo had refused to go and sleep in her house – but even so.

'Wynton Moses,' he said, taking my hand. 'Call me Wyn.'

His clothes were not as clean as they might be. The knees of his jeans were worn and spattered with dirt and his T-shirt had a hole on the right shoulder. But I saw the way Mo was looking from him to me and then back again. *This is my dad, ain't he great?*

'Come in and have a drink,' I said, 'I expect Mo's dying for a dip in the pool. Those arm bands have been dry for a long time.'

Out of the corner of my eye, I could see Sid gesticulating wildly at me, shaking his head, *No, don't invite him inside.* But it was too late, so what was I to do?

Pete came forward and placed an arm on Wyn's elbow. 'Time to move on now,' I heard him say. 'Say goodbye to the kid and get back in your car.'

To my surprise Wyn didn't argue, but he pulled a business card out of his pocket and handed it to me.

'I'd appreciate it if you'd get in touch,' he murmured. Then he clasped Mo to him for an instant, got back in his truck and backed away.

I turned to Sid. 'What's going on?'

'There's a restraining order against him. The mother has custody. He's not supposed to go within a hundred yards of Mo.'

'But why?'

Sid shook his head. 'Who knows? But he's

aware we're onto him now so he won't try anything again. We've told him if he does, we'll tell the mother. What'd he say to you just now?'

'Oh, he just thanked me for taking care of his son.' It was pure instinct that made me lie to Sid. I'd figure out the reason for it later on.

Mo made no fuss when he said goodbye to his father, as if he was used to him leaving. But that night when Noreen prepared for his nightly reading from *My Golden Book of Bible Stories*, he suddenly burst into tears. Noreen put her arm around him but he shrugged her off.

'Shame your father couldn't stay,' she said tentatively.

Mo didn't respond immediately. Then he sniffed loudly and looked at us with new defiance. 'He a busy man,' he said, 'and he a busy-*ness* man too. I seen his office way up in the sky. He got *money*. And it ain't no shame he leave.'

'Really,' said Noreen. 'Why's that?'

'Because he gone come back real soon. He love me.'

I felt an unexpected lump in my throat. I couldn't look at Noreen. I slipped away and left her to finish putting him to bed. And I went to look at the card Wyn Moses had given me.

Wynton P Moses. Attorney at Law.

205

Nothing else. No law firm, no address. But there was what looked like a mobile number and I dialled it. 'It's Lee Bartholomew,' I said when he answered.

'Thank you,' he said.

'I'd let you say goodnight to Mo but we're just getting him settled into bed and it might be a bit disruptive.'

'Not a problem. I spent my time with him. Can we meet?'

I suggested a cantina in Amagansett. I told Noreen I was going for a walk on the beach and said she should go ahead and fix supper for herself if she was hungry. Tommy had taken Minnie and Shagger to karaoke in Montauk and they probably wouldn't be back before two in the morning. I had been too wound up about Mo to go with them. I walked up to Franny and Rufus's to ask if I could borrow their car.

The cantina was on Main Street with a bar attached and I ordered myself a Tequila and a bowl of *pesole* while I waited for him. Heads turned when he walked in, more, I suspected, because of his height than because he was the only black person in the place. He had changed his clothes since I'd last seen him and now he looked a little more like the lawyer his card said he was. But his khaki pants were cheap and I noticed that the cuffs of his blue and white striped shirt, rolled back over his long smooth

206

forearms, were frayed. He had close-cropped hair like a soft fuzz all over his head, far darker than Mo's, as was his skin. But when he smiled at me, I saw he had the same square white teeth as his son with an identical gap in the middle.

He waylaid a server and placed an order and then slipped into the booth opposite me.

'I know about the restraining order,' I told him before he could say a word.

'So why are you here?' he said.

'I don't have much experience with kids but I sense that he cares about you. We've had absolutely no contact with his mother – it's like she's disappeared into thin air – and if she hasn't reappeared by the time he has to leave us, we don't know what will happen to him.'

And I was consumed with curiosity as to how the son of a lawyer wound up living in the projects and being shipped out to the Hamptons as a Fresh Air kid.

'How did he come to be a–' My lips were forming the question before I realized that it would be a tactless one to ask.

'To have such light skin?' Wyn misinterpreted my words. 'His grandfather was white.'

'Which explains what?'

'Pretty much everything,' he said with a grimace. 'It shouldn't, but if I tell you the

207

whole story, you just might find you agree with me. What do you do for a living?'

'I'm a writer.' I couldn't be bothered to go into the ghost thing.

'Well, then, you'll appreciate a good story.'

I held up my hands. 'I have time. But I'm guessing it's *your* story I'm going to hear, not Mo's.'

'You guessed right.' He grinned. 'You're probably wondering how a guy like me has a son like Mo. Well, forty years ago you'd have asked yourself how my father turned out a son like me. You ever go to Harlem in the old days?'

I nodded. 'But I have to confess it was in a cab on my way to the airport.'

He laughed. 'See, I'm sitting here in the Hamptons, but my father, the predominant image I have of him is as this tramp, wandering along 114th Street in the middle of the afternoon with this giant radio – this boombox – on his shoulder, and swigging from an open bottle. And that was when he was vertical. Most of the time he'd be passed out on the stoop.'

Wyn paused to gauge my reaction. I raised my eyebrows. *And?*

'And he wasn't the only one,' Wyn continued, 'most everyone was on welfare. We kids ran wild in the street, there were so many of us. It seemed the minute a girl became a teenager, she got pregnant. One, two, three, four kids by as many different fathers and those kids, some of 'em were smoking dope before they were twelve.'

'And there was crime?' I thought of the recent teenage gang shootings in England, between themselves, and the murdering of adults who tried to interfere. Killers of no more than fifteen, sixteen years of age.

Wyn nodded. 'Plenty. But don't be thinking it was all bad. Not every kid had a knife in his sock. There were parents who tried to raise their children right. There were people who had aspirations, values. But the problem was, what they didn't have was money. The only money around seemed to be drug related.' He looked at me suddenly. 'You want to hear this, right?'

I nodded. 'I do. What about your mother?'

He smiled. 'She was a good woman. She tried – she tried so hard. She was never on that stoop with my father. She was always off somewhere fighting for a better life for us. She heard they were going to close the schools, the hospital – she figured that would be the end of the community. She tried to get on the school board, she kept trying to *have her say*.'

'And what happened? Did she make a difference?'

'She died in the exact same hospital she was trying to save. Ovarian cancer. She was barely as old as I am now.'

'I'm sorry,' I said. And then, when he didn't continue, 'So how did you make it out?'

'I'll give you the long story short,' he said. 'You ever hear of A Better Chance?'

I shook my head.

'It was an organisation set up back in the early Sixties by a bunch of teachers – headmasters – from fancy prep schools to place bright young black kids from impoverished backgrounds alongside their rich white counterparts, give them the same education. They had this ad – *Which future would you rather he have?* – and the image was of two young black guys, one in jail, and the other in pinstripes behind a desk.'

'And they found you?'

'It was one of the last things my mother did before she died. She met one of the people recruiting for ABC, as it was known, and she begged him to see me. I went to Exeter and then Harvard and there I met Mo's mother.'

I remembered what he'd said about Mo's grandfather. 'She was white?'

'Half. Her mother was the stereotype big fat mama, originally from Harlem also, but her father was a civil rights lawyer. Jewish. They were New Yorkers, lived in the west Seventies. Now this you might find it hard to get your head round. *She's* the one keeping me from Mo.'

'You're right,' I said. 'I do.'

'Have you been round black people much?'

I was momentarily thrown by the question. I knew a lot of Afro-Americans – or Afro-Caribbeans, as they tended to be in London – but I didn't have any close friends who were black. Yet at school in London there'd been West Indian and Nigerian kids in my class and we'd been in and out of each other's homes all the time. But what I did acknowledge was that while black and white kids had befriended each other, the middle-class white kids had gravitated towards the middle-class black kids, leaving the children from the poorer neighbourhoods to find each other. I told him about this.

'How did it work for you at Exeter and Harvard?' I asked him. 'Did you black kids stick together?'

'I didn't stick to anyone. I kept myself to myself – *in here.*' He pointed to his chest. 'I didn't let nobody in. At first I didn't have any idea how to behave. I'd been raised in Harlem, don't forget. I'd been programmed to believe I had no power in the world and never would have, and I'd be mixing with these white kids – these *rich* white kids who took it for granted. Some of them treated me like shit – *only reason you're here is because of my daddy's money* sort of thing.'

He was a good mimic. I had no difficulty picturing the preppy young blonde with the

211

Alice band who probably said this to him.

'But I liked that better than the people who tried to make me feel like I was one of them,' he went on, 'because I wasn't, never would be. Black is different, anyone who says it ain't is dumb. But I was a kid and kids want to fit right in. They don't *want* to be different. And when I met Anna at Harvard, I felt I'd met a soul mate because of course she didn't even try to fit in.'

'She was a law student?'

'She dropped out – but not before I'd fallen in love with her. Every chance I got, I was travelling back to New York to see her. Her daddy liked me – I was going to be a lawyer just like him. And her mother, she liked me fine – to begin with. Then it all changed.'

'How come?' I was intrigued.

'Well, now, I gotta switch tracks for a minute. I graduated, right? I came out of Harvard a shining example of what they had in mind all along. I was hired right off the bat – OK, so Anna's father saw to it that I got my foot on the first rung of the ladder – but even so I did good. Anna and I were married. We got ourselves an apartment downtown in the Village.'

'And Mo was born?'

He shook his head quickly. 'Not yet. Not for quite a while. I was restless, not really ready to put down roots in the Village for

212

good. You see, if you're a black person made good – and I was well on my way to making good – you have this feeling – this *obligation* – that you should give something back. And if you don't happen to feel that way, there'll always be someone who will remind you. *Come and speak at the Boys Club, come to church on Sunday, you're a role model for the young people.* You can't keep your success to yourself, you gotta share it with the dudes who didn't *make* it. You gotta be *inspirational!*'

I was shocked at how bitter he sounded and I didn't understand it.

'Bella, my mother-in-law, she was over the moon when we told her we were moving to Harlem, that I was going to set up a practice there even though it was a safe bet most of my work would be *pro bono*. She said it was what she'd always wanted Anna's father to do but he'd resisted. Well, I should have listened to that.'

'It didn't work out?'

'What I learned pretty quick was that it's a mistake to go back because you can't communicate with them any more. You're not *black* any more. You've moved into the white guy's world, you're taking it for granted. You can't connect with people who spend their time hanging out on street corners. Harvard taught me everything but how to go back to my old neighbourhood. It wasn't immedi-

213

ate. At first I was all misty eyed with the good I could do, but then I got it. I was looking at my old neighbourhood with contempt and when I realised that, I knew I had to get out.'

'And Anna?'

He looked down at the table for a long time before answering. My *pesole* arrived and the beer he'd ordered. When he didn't look up, the server looked at me. *What should I do?* I nodded. *Put it down.*

When she'd gone, he downed it.

'With Anna it was the exact opposite. For her, even though her mother had come from there, it was the most exotic place she'd ever experienced. I'm not going to sit here and give you a blow by blow of the whole agonising period. I'll just tell you, what I shunned, she embraced. The stoops, the drinking, the street life – and ultimately, the smack.'

'*What?*' I was horrified. 'What about Mo?'

'Later. I didn't want to have a child with a junkie. We got her clean first – and I'll spare you what that was like. But it worked. In fact the first three or four years with Mo were magical – until I screwed it up.'

'*You* screwed it up.'

'I was restless again. I didn't fit into Harlem any more. I was frustrated by how little progress I was making. I wanted a better life for Mo so I said, *We're gonna get out of here.*'

214

'But Mo's still there.'

'Anna didn't want to move. Her father had died and her mother said, *Stay there, girl. That's where you belong.*'

'Even though *she'd* got out.'

'Bella never wanted to get out. She fell in love with Anna's father and that's what took her away. But she's moved back now – to a more gentrified neighbourhood in Harlem than the one she grew up in, sure. She's surrounded by white middle-class Jewish folk just like she was in the west Seventies – but she's near Anna and she can see Mo.'

He took a swig from his beer and stared into the distance. Then, just as I was about to prompt him, he started up again.

'When I left Harlem, Bella never forgave me. She stepped in and had her husband's law firm fight me tooth and nail. After the divorce Anna got custody, despite having very little income, despite having been a junkie, but Bella didn't stop there. She made Anna get a restraining order against me.'

'On what grounds?'

'That I hit Anna.'

'You didn't?'

'Of course not. Anna's got some strung-out dude she's seeing. He hits her. Mo's told me. Bella saw the bruises. Anna didn't want her to find out about the boyfriend and told Bella it was me.'

'But why haven't you fought it, told the

authorities about this other guy?'

Wyn shrugged. 'I'm biding my time. Most of my spare time is spent working out how to get Mo but Anna *is* his mother. Part of me feels a kid ought to be with his mother and providing I know he's OK, I don't want to upset his childhood too much. But as far as seeing him goes, I got lucky. Bella has a maid from the old neighbourhood and I know her. I had the maid slip Mo a cell phone and my number when he was visiting with Bella and he calls me. That's how I knew he'd be coming out here.'

'So you see him pretty regularly?'

'Yes, I do. I don't like the fact that I have to involve him in subterfuge, that he has to lie to his mother every time he sees me. And we have to involve a third party. It's mostly through Bella's maid when he visits there. She brings him to the park and we meet up there. Or there's the mother of one of his friends who's always liked me and when Mo has a play date with her kid, she lets me know so I can come over.'

'And in between he calls you on his cell phone and you catch up that way?' I said.

'That's right. One of these days we're going to be busted, his friend is going to let slip to Anna, or someone who sees us together, but until then, I'll take what I can get.'

'How long have you been out here?'

'A while. When he told me about the

216

Fresh Air plan, I went ahead and fixed my vacation so I'd be out here when he was. When you guys got together, he called me, speaking low, I guess he didn't want you to hear him. He said you were going to the beach and I said, Which one? And he said he didn't know so I took a chance it would be Main Beach and there he was, walking up the beach with a girl.'

'Me?' I laughed. 'Thanks, but I'm hardly a girl.'

'No,' he said, serious, 'this was a girl and he was going with her readily so I assumed she was one of the Fresh Air host family. Don't forget, I didn't know who they were or where they lived. I was relying on Mo feeding me information as he found it out himself.'

'Did he see you?'

'No. And I couldn't make myself known because I wasn't supposed to be anywhere near him.'

'So you saw him get into the car with this girl? Did you follow them?'

'Of course.'

He wasn't looking at me and I sensed that he was withholding something.

'Did you see them go in?'

He nodded. 'The girl got out first and went to unlock the door and then Mo got out and ran around the side of the house to the back yard and she followed him.'

'And then what did you do?'

'I left. I saw someone twitching the curtains at the house next door and I took off before they could figure out what I was doing. I knew where he was and that he'd call me when he could.'

'So when did he next call you?'

'This morning. And that's when I learned what had happened. As you can imagine, I was out of my mind with worry. I wanted to come straight over and get him but I realised I'd have better access to him in a public place. He said he'd ask to be taken to the same beach and I should go there and wait for him. When he showed up there with two men, I just waited for the opportunity to grab him. I was a fool, maybe, but–'

'I understand,' I said.

'But he told me he feels fine around you and Tommy and Noreen, is it? He's OK, he wasn't harmed. He'll be fine from now on. But what I have to ask you is, will you let me have access to him out here?'

I looked at him, wondering what to say. It would be collusion. It would probably be illegal. But he was Mo's *father*. I made a snap decision. I'd discuss it with the wise and wonderful Noreen and I'd make a plan of action based on what she said.

'I'll have to think it over,' I said. 'I'll let you know. But one thing I have to do first is find out where his mother's disappeared to. Do you have any ideas?'

'None whatsoever,' he said. 'After all I'm not supposed to be within a hundred yards of her.'

I drove away, leaving him standing on the sidewalk. I found to my surprise that I felt curiously ambivalent towards him. I had neither liked him nor disliked him. I had listened to his story but it was so outside my experience, I didn't really feel equipped to comment on it.

Without thinking, I took the long way back to Franny and Rufus's and found I was in Springs, heading towards Spring Hollow Road. On instinct I drove slowly up it and parked right outside the ranch house. It was still light and I got out of the car and stood in front of the neighbour's window. I walked towards the front door and two men stepped outside.

'Oh, hi,' I said, recognising them. It was Pete and Vince and they looked at me with guarded curiosity, as well they might. They nodded *Good evening* to me but I could see the question in their eyes. *What was I doing here at the crime scene?* Thank God they hadn't seen me half an hour earlier with Mo's father who was not supposed to have anything to do with him. I decided honesty was my best policy.

'Sid Sharkey brought me here the other night. I don't really know why I'm here again. I just thought I'd come back and take

219

another look, see if I could notice anything that might jog Mo's memory.'

I could see they didn't really buy it, but they didn't detain me. 'OK, ma'am. Say hi to Mo,' said Pete. 'Sorry about the other day.'

I wanted to ask them if they had any more news but they seemed in a hurry. As Pete followed Vince across the road to their car, I was about to turn around and go to mine when a woman appeared at the doorway and called out to me.

'Help you?' She looked me up and down.

She looked to be in her mid-sixties and I ran a probable mental profile on her. Husband dead or divorced, if she'd ever had one, and, apart from the occasional visit from her daughter, her life, as she'd once known it, was probably more or less over. She needed constant distraction and she got it from two sources: TV (I could hear it blaring inside the house), or whatever she could see through her curtains.

'You are–?'

'Rita McGill. Who are you?'

'I'm actually here about next door – someone died?' I didn't give her my name.

'You're not the police. They were just here.'

I shook my head. 'I'm a writer.'

'The press?' Now her eyes positively gleamed.

I didn't confirm or deny it. 'Can you tell me, that day, did you see a man parked outside?'

'I saw plenty of men. The place was crawling with cops.'

'No, I mean earlier. When you called your daughter on the beach. When the girl arrived with the boy?'

If she wondered how I knew so much about her movements, she didn't comment on it.

'No one came by then except my landscaper. He stopped for a minute but then he drove on. Silly fool. I guess he realised he got the day mixed up. But he's why the police were here. Seems like he's a person of interest to them.'

'Really?' If that was so then he was a person of interest to me too. 'Why was that?'

'Because I told them how friendly he was with the girl who was renting the house next door.'

'The girl who took the boy from the beach, the one you called your daughter about?' *The one who wasn't Sally*.

She nodded. 'I used to hear them chatting out back in the yard.'

'Your landscaper worked over there too?' I pointed to the house where Mo had been held.

She nodded again. 'That's what I mean. When he'd be done with my yard, he'd go over there and she'd be lying out on one of those loungers getting the sun. He helped her get the lounger out of the basement one day and I guess she'd sunbathe while he cut the grass. Anyway, those cops, they've gone to find him now, talk to him again. Seems like he was known to them in any case. And Shane Sobel, I think he came calling that day too.'

'Shane Sobel? Who's he?'

'Owns a car dealership over to Southampton. Real smooth talker. He sold me my Subaru.' She nodded to a silver car parked behind mine. 'I saw him here on a regular basis but he always went round the back. Never went in the front entrance. Started me wondering a thing or two.' She tapped her nose and winked at me. But she had no control over her eyes and she wound up squinting at me.

'And you didn't see anyone else?'

She shook her head. 'I was in my basement doing laundry. Up and down, up and down, those stairs will kill me. Someone might have come while I was down there – in fact I think they probably did. There was a whole lotta noise next door. Am I going to be in the paper?'

Once again I didn't answer her question directly. I just smiled and began to back out of the door. I waved goodbye from the gate and called *Thanks, I won't keep you any more*

222

over my shoulder. But as I got into my car, she yelled to me:

'Make sure they spell my name right. It's McGill – small c, big G.'

Chapter Nine

When he stumbled home from karaoke at whatever ungodly hour, Tommy didn't make it up the narrow staircase leading to our attic quarters. When I went downstairs the next morning, I discovered him passed out on a sofa on the landing below. Pray God Franny and Rufus were not yet up and hadn't witnessed the sight of him sprawled half on, half off the sofa, his shirt hanging open and his right hand apparently in the midst of an unconscious scratching of his balls. But his unsightly appearance was nothing to the disgusting stench of smoke and alcohol coming off him in waves as I crept past.

'Oh God, I'm sorry about Tommy, I hope you didn't–' I began as I encountered Franny in the kitchen. She had Eliza on her lap and was trying to persuade her to accept some cereal. Because of Franny's recent coldness I didn't really expect an answer so I jumped when she said, loud and clear:

'You go to karaoke in Montauk and stay till the bitter end, how else are you going to be?'

I laughed, not really sure how to react. But

then she said something that couldn't help but provoke me.

'You don't really know your husband, do you, Lee?' She cocked her head at me with a knowing expression on her face that irritated me. 'You seem to have forgotten that the last time you guys were here, he stayed on for nearly a year after you left him and ran back to England. I tell you, back then I would have been worried if Tommy had *not* passed out on the sofa every night. I've sort of come to think of it as normal behaviour for him.'

'Rufus never does anything as crass as get drunk and disorderly, I suppose?' I was aware that I sounded waspish but I was beginning to resent her rather judgemental take on my married state. Hadn't she said she didn't think I should have married Tommy in the first place? And now here she was claiming I didn't know him like she did.

'Nope, he never does. At least not any more.' But then she surprised me by adding, 'But I wish he would.'

I turned in surprise, spilling coffee grains on the counter and reaching for a cloth to wipe them away. 'You do?'

'OK, Eliza. I give up. You want to starve? Be my guest.' She dislodged her daughter from her lap, gently lowering her to the floor. Eliza tottered over to me.

'Mo?' she said.

'Sure,' I said, 'later. Franny, what do you mean, you wish Rufus would get drunk?'

She shrugged. 'Don't listen to me. I'm just mourning our lost youth. He's not the rough and tumble kid I grew up with, the one who spent all day surfing and all night drinking. He's become this goddamn pillar of the community. I just miss the way we used to be, that's all. I miss running my little country store and taking care of people's yards and knowing all their business. I hate being cooped up here in a house with security cameras spying on me the whole time. I feel like a prisoner. I hate that Rufus comes downstairs every morning dressed to go to meetings instead of to the beach. You know, I haven't seen him in shorts in over a month.'

'Why would you? You've been away in Paris. And he's had to make changes in his life since his dad died and left him all that money,' I pointed out. 'He has responsibilities now.'

'Me,' she said glumly, 'and her.' Pointing at Eliza. 'That's what we are to him, responsibilities. You can watch her for me again today, right? I have to get back to the city.'

I stared at her, furious that she would take it for granted. 'No,' I said, 'I'm sorry but I can't. I have to go to work. I told Patience Brook O'Reilly I'd be over today for our first session. In fact, I was going to bring Mo up here to you later.'

Franny shook her head automatically. *No way*.

'Franny, he's *your* Fresh Air kid, not mine,' I reminded her. I didn't need to add *and Eliza's your daughter*.

Franny flushed. 'I'm going to call Suzette. It's time we got Mo and Keshawn together. Maybe your mother-in-law could watch Eliza?'

I didn't like the way she emphasised *mother-in-law*. 'And maybe she can't,' I said. 'She's a cancer survivor in her seventies and she's here for a rest. Can't you take Eliza to the city? Why do you have to go there anyway?'

It was the wrong thing to ask. The big freeze was back. As I took my first sip of coffee, Franny picked up Eliza and pushed past me to walk out of the kitchen without another word.

I took my coffee back upstairs and woke Tommy. 'Sorry to do this to you but I need you to be on Mo duty today while I go to work.'

'After what happened last time?' He yawned in my face.

'I don't hold you responsible for that. You weren't to know the boy's father would turn up. I saw him last night, by the way.'

'The father? You let him come back to see Mo after the way he grabbed him without telling anybody?' Tommy sat up and

227

scratched his bare chest. 'Can I have some of that coffee?'

'No, you can't. You can go down and get your own. And no, I didn't let him come back, but I might.'

I outlined what Wyn had told me.

'God,' said Tommy, 'who'd be a father?'

'You, one of these days if you don't watch out.' I said it playfully but as much to gauge his reaction as anything else.

'You know I've always wanted a family.' He sounded reproachful.

'So you've always said but then you've always maintained you wanted a wedding and a honeymoon and look what we wound up with.'

He groaned. 'Well, whose fault was that? You're the one who had to come running over here to work just as I was planning your wedding.'

'But Tommy, you didn't *tell* me you were planning my wedding.'

'I wanted to surprise you.'

This could go round and round forever and I didn't have the energy.

'So will you include Mo in your plans today as well as Shagger and Minnie?'

'What about Mum? Can't she keep an eye on him?'

'No!' I said for the second time that morning, 'She can't. And it's about time you stopped taking your mother for granted. You need to give her a break. Literally. First you dump Minnie and Shagger on her and then–'

'All right! Keep your hair on. Maybe Franny can–'

I left. I didn't trust myself to respond in a civil tone. What was the matter with everybody?

It's not as if Mo's any trouble, I thought, seeing him skipping towards me as I came down the trail to the pool house. For a second I contemplated calling Wyn and having him come over and pick Mo up for the day. But I dismissed the idea almost immediately. Somehow I knew I shouldn't give Wyn the opportunity to take Mo back to New York with him. If he wanted to see his son, he'd have to come over and visit him with us.

'That's right,' said Noreen, when I told her. 'We'll have him over for a meal.'

'I've asked *your* son to come and take Mo off your hands today. He'll probably ask you to watch him but on no account are you to say yes. Is that clear, Noreen? You need a rest. And if Tommy doesn't show up, take Mo up to the house and leave him with Franny and Eliza.'

'Oh, I've already got my orders, don't you worry,' said Noreen.

'What do you mean?' I said.

'I went out for a stroll first thing,' she said.

229

'I always wake so early. And there was Franny's husband – what's his name?'

'Rufus.'

'That's it. He was sitting on the steps smoking a cigarette and–'

'Smoking a *cigarette? Rufus? Are you sure?*' Rufus had always been a health nut. He'd certainly enjoyed a drink in his time but I'd never known him to smoke.

'I told him a few home truths about what it would do to his lungs eventually and how he shouldn't be smoking with a little creature like Eliza in the house and he put it out immediately. We had a nice chat after that. He's a pleasant young man but he's not happy.'

'Noreen, how can you know that? You've only just met him and–'

'Oh, he told me. He was looking for someone to listen to him. Looks like he might have been a bit hasty marrying Franny.' Noreen nodded her head to make her point. 'She's not adapting to the switch in status the way he thought she would although what did he expect? He couldn't have imagined she'd make the leap from country store keeper to millionaire's wife overnight. He obviously didn't think it through before he married her.'

'Why do you say that, Noreen?' I was a little shocked at the stand she was taking on people she barely knew but as usual her shrewdness was beginning to make sense.

'He's grown up with money,' she went on, 'she hasn't. Having money can bring as much stress as not having it, even if they do live pretty simply. Franny probably cut herself off from the people in her old world without realising what she'd done. He told me he tries to talk to her about the strain of managing the financial responsibility that came with inheriting a fortune from his father but she just doesn't understand what he's talking about. And that's probably because *he* doesn't understand what he's talking about either. Doesn't have much experience beyond a surfboard and a chainsaw, as far as I can make out. Anyway, he said if Franny asked us to look after Eliza again because she wanted to go into the city, we were to say no. That's what I meant – I've got my orders.'

If anyone needs a life coach, it's Franny, I thought as I drove over to Patsy's, *how to adapt to life as the wife of a millionaire. Or was that billionaire?*

I had barely covered any distance on the dirt road leading to Patsy's house in the woods when I drew to an abrupt halt. A car was coming towards me, moving fast, the driver obviously not expecting to encounter another vehicle. It was a big car, a Jaguar, black, and, because there was not enough room for it to pass, I began to back

231

hurriedly up the dirt road to avoid a collision. I heard a screech of brakes but I continued looking over my shoulder in order to gauge when I would reach the road.

I don't like Jags. I know people think their lines are beautiful but I always associate them with a certain type of rich owner out to impress. I stuck my head out of my car window to get a good look at the driver as he went past and I saw a large head with swept back reddish-blond hair and an attractive face, freckled and sunburned, and just starting to turn fleshy with middle-age. He had a strong Roman nose and hefty shoulders. The collar of his navy shirt (with a little red polo player motif on his chest) was turned up in a jaunty fashion.

He glanced at me and then turned back for a longer look. I knew that look. He'd seen I was a woman and therefore worthy of appraisal. Pale-blue eyes met mine, flirted momentarily and then he was gone.

When I finally made it to Patsy's house, I opened the screen door and called, 'Hello?' but there was no reply. As the door was open I entered the house and stood in her spotless kitchen, wondering what to do.

'Jesus! You gave me a fright!' Patsy appeared a second or two later, clad in a towelling robe. 'What the hell is the time? I had no idea. I am truly sorry, I must have overslept. Help yourself to a cup of coffee

232

and I'll be back in no time.'

Overslept. So why was the Mr Coffee machine already keeping the pot warm? Didn't she want me to know about Mr Black Jag careering away from her house while she was still in bed? Who was he, I wondered?

'So how's the honeymoon going?' she asked when she returned fresh from the shower, her soaking hair scraped back in a tiny rat's tail, her rosy cheeks glowing. She was wearing a shapeless linen shift of virulent purple and flip-flops and I was reminded of her own words to describe how she'd come across on television: *I look like a Teletubby*. 'Are you married yet?'

'I was married in London over a week ago,' I said.

'Maybe,' she said, 'but do you *feel* married yet?'

'I've been with him for nine years. How can I feel any different just because we sat in a registrar's office for half an hour?'

'Because you agreed to marry him, to make a lifelong commitment to him.'

'I didn't!' I protested. 'He sprung the wedding on me. I only had four days' notice.'

'Four days to say no,' said Patsy. 'Ninety-six hours. Over five thousand minutes. Did he clamp your mouth with masking tape during that time? No? So you agreed to get married.'

'My friend Franny says I should never

have got married, that I don't ever want to get married.'

'Bullshit!' said Patsy cheerfully. 'I repeat: you didn't say no. You've been with–?'

'Tommy.'

'Tommy for nine years – that's a lot longer than many marriages last. You don't strike me as someone who does what they don't want to do. You wanted to marry Tommy. The time had finally come and your problem is you just can't believe you've actually done it. Well now it's time you wised up. Accept what you've done. Congratulate yourself. You need to give yourself some affirmations.'

'Affirmations?' I looked at her with growing suspicion. She didn't strike me as a whacko but I recalled Franny's dismissal of her TV spot. *I don't watch that New Age shit.*

'Yes. Your life affirmation is going to be *I accept that I have finally married Tommy and I want to celebrate it.* Say it ten times at least three times a day.'

Did people seriously part with thousands of dollars just to be given some kind of mantra to repeat over and over? Was it really that simple? To stave off my growing scepticism I plunged in and challenged her with something I had intended to slip in as I was leaving.

'So I understand Suzette is a client of yours?'

'Was,' she said quickly and the bright smile that had accompanied her suggestion of a life affirmation disappeared.

'But you met her? She came here? Not all your clients are at the end of a telephone? Eileen told me,' I said when I saw her shaking her head in denial.

'Eileen cleans over there,' she said as if that explained everything. And then, when she saw I still wasn't satisfied, she continued. 'OK, yes, I made an exception with Suzette. I met her at a fundraiser soon after I moved here and she was new to the area too. She'd only just married Scott Abernathy. We went to the bathroom at the same time and I found her leaning against the wall, looking wretched.'

'She was sick?'

'Troubled. Not the face she presents to the public. She didn't want to pee, she'd gone in there to take a moment to be herself.'

'And you disturbed her?'

'If you put it like that, yes. I asked her if she was OK and it was quite clear that she wasn't. Then she asked me – right out of the blue – if I had children? I said no but I must have shown some concern over the question because then she asked me if *I* was all right?'

'You?'

'Yes. You see, she'd touched a raw nerve. I can't have kids and my husband left me for that very reason. It was the last thing I wanted to talk about so I said no and immediately turned it back to her, did *she* have kids? It was before they adopted that boy from Africa and there'd been nothing in the press about her being a mother.'

'She has a son from an earlier marriage,' I said, remembering what Franny had told me.

'That's right,' said Patsy, clearly surprised that I knew. 'Robby. It all came out. She was desperate to talk to someone and who better than a stranger? She'd left him behind in somewhere like Washington State and she'd never really been a proper mother to him, she let him be raised by her own mother. And now just when she thought she could bring him into the new home she was creating with Scott, he'd told her he didn't want any baggage. That was the word he used, apparently. Baggage.'

'But how did she become a client?'

Patsy shook her head. 'I told her who I was and what I did. It's the only time I've come out of the closet, so to speak, but she was so upset and she had to go back out there and face the public at the fundraiser so I told her because I thought it was the only way I could help her. She needed coaching in her new life as Scott's wife. The guilt she felt about Robby was crippling her but she seemed to be incapable of standing up to Scott, of insisting that her son come live

236

with them.'

'So you gave her an affirmation?' I worked hard to keep the derision out of my voice. 'Because if you did, I'm not sure it worked. As far as I know he's not living with them, never has. And Scott couldn't have been against kids because they have Keshawn – and,' I hesitated, wondering whether to tell her about Eliza.

'And what? Do you mean Eliza?'

'You know about her?'

'Suzette told me he had a daughter and that she was the result of a one-night stand he'd had with his brother Rufus's wife. And she said when he told her about the little girl, she'd assumed it was because they'd be taking her on board.'

'Suzette thought she was going to be Eliza's mother?'

'Stepmother,' said Patsy. 'She thought Eliza would spend time with them as well as with Franny. But that's when she learned what Scott thought about what he called baggage. He wanted them to start anew, he wanted them to leave Eliza and Robby behind and she went along with it. But she's been guilt ridden ever since. It's weird,' Patsy went on, 'everyone assumes just because she's the famous one with money that she calls the shots. But it's not like that, according to her. I had the impression she's quite submissive as far as he's concerned.'

What was it about these Abernathy brothers? I wondered. Both of their wives were having trouble adapting to their new lives. Franny had more in common with Suzette than she knew.

'But at least Scott gets to see Eliza quite a bit,' I pointed out. 'Poor Suzette, has she seen Robby at all since she married Scott?'

'Once a year,' said Patsy. 'He comes for a summer vacation at the beach. He was here for two weeks last month. But Suzette said it actually makes it worse. Robby hangs out at the beach and barely talks to her. She says she can feel his resentment and that she hardly knows him.'

'So what was your affirmation for her?'

I love my son and I'm going to spend more time with him.

I was looking out the window at the scrub oaks, watching a blue jay flying by but when she said the affirmation I turned, because there was a catch in her voice.

'Patsy?'

'It's nothing. Ignore me.'

Hard to do when she was the only other person in the room and obviously in pain.

'You mentioned a few minutes ago that you can't have children.' It was a shot in the dark but in the initial stages of a working relationship with a ghosting subject I often take risks in order to avoid wasting time. It may sound callous but I need them to open up to me more quickly than would happen in an ordinary non-professional acquaintance.

'That's right,' she said and sniffed loudly. 'That's better. Sorry about choking up. It's just that I can't imagine what it would be like to have a son and *not* see him. I never had that choice and I wanted it more than anything.'

'And your husband left you because of it?'

'It was one of the reasons we married – to have a large family so when it didn't happen, I had to let him go – so he could.' She was in danger of breaking down again so I suggested we move on to something else.

'No,' she said, surprising me. 'I'm going to need to talk about it at some stage. It's the reason I'm doing the book. It's my story. It's what's defined me all these years. I want it out in the open. I want my husband to read the book and know that I don't bear him any ill will.'

I almost gasped. It was so different to the kind of bitterness I normally encountered in an abandoned wife.

'He has children now.' She was smiling and it was a little spooky when she said, 'I've seen them. I found out where he lived and I stalked his wife on the school run. A boy and a girl and the boy looks just like him. It gets worse,' she said, looking at me directly. 'Or rather it got worse, once, years ago. It was the real reason he left me, he was afraid of what I might do.'

I waited, sensing I had unleashed in her a bit more than I had expected.

'I stole a baby.'

I didn't say anything for a second or two, I was so shocked. Then I said gently, 'Tell me about it.'

'It was while we were trying and year after year I failed to conceive, and taking the baby, the way it happened was almost a cliché. I saw a baby in a pram outside a shop and I took it. Bob, that's my husband, was away and I took it home and looked after it for almost a week, until he came home and found us.'

'And until then—?'

'Amazing isn't it? I just carried him – it was a little boy – to my car and nobody saw us. It was as if I had been planning it subconsciously because I didn't panic, I was quite calm, I just drove home. And that's where we stayed until Bob came home. I had a son for nearly a week.'

'But what about caring for him? All the baby things you needed, a cot, baby food, diapers?'

'Eileen.'

'What?'

'Eileen. You met her the other day. She was our cleaner back then and she was there when I walked in with Michael – that's what

240

I called him. I sent her out shopping – every day till Bob came back.'

'What did Bob do?'

'He did what I asked, what I begged him to do. I knew I couldn't keep Michael and by then it was all over the papers so we knew who his parents were. I made Bob go and leave Michael somewhere where he would be found immediately.'

'You mean nobody has ever known who took him?'

'No one except Bob. Maybe he's told his new wife, I don't know. But that's something I can do in the book. I can apologise to those parents, whoever they were. It must have been the worst week of their lives.'

'And that's why you changed your name, isn't it? You came to America and became Patience Brook O'Reilly so even if Bob told people about Patsy Brooks, no one would associate the two.'

'Except Eileen,' said Patsy. 'She stuck by me when Bob left and that's why I brought her with me to America, why I let her, you know, run my life a little.' She gestured to the clinical white kitchen. 'It might not be the standard employer/employee relationship but what can I say? We need each other.'

I thought about Eileen and how she had gossiped so easily about Holly Bennett. And she had been the one who had revealed that Suzette was one of Patsy's clients. What else

241

had Eileen already let slip about Patsy's past, I wondered.

'Does Eileen know you're planning to put it all in the book?'

Patsy nodded. 'She doesn't think it's a good idea.'

I knew why. Sid had said he thought Eileen was a control freak and once the book was out, with all Patsy's secrets laid bare to the world, Eileen would no longer have any control over her. But who needed whom the most, I wondered. I couldn't overlook the way Patsy constantly referred to how much she depended on Eileen.

A door banged. 'That's her,' said Patsy, 'that's Eileen.'

But it wasn't. A tall well-built woman walked rapidly into the house, more formally dressed than most women I had seen around East Hampton. Her tailored jacket in emerald green linen and ankle-length straight skirt signalled that she was dressed for business. I have never been a fan of the ankle-length skirt look and it certainly didn't do this woman any favours. She was much too broad across the beam to carry it off successfully. Her skirt had the kind of across-the-stomach rumpling that comes from too much driving and her cleavage protruding from her too-tight jacket was crepey from sun exposure. She had peep-toe stacked mules and her nail polish was chipped. Her lipstick was painted on a millimetre of an inch outside her own lips and her curly hair was wild and unruly.

But her smile was unexpectedly warm.

'Sorry to burst in on you, Patsy. Eileen was outside and she said it would be fine to come right on in.'

'Did she now?' said Patsy mildly. 'Well, now you're here, Gwen, how about some coffee? Lee, this is Gwen Bennett. Eileen cleans for her too. Gwen, this is Lee Bartholomew.'

Patsy didn't offer any explanation as to what I was doing there and Gwen Bennett didn't ask.

I held out my hand and she shook it in a rather vague fashion and then stiffened as Patsy reached out to stroke her arm.

'I am so sorry about your daughter.'

'Oh yes,' I added, realising a little too late who this was, 'I'm sorry too. So awful for you.'

'Thank you.' Gwen Bennett backed away as if somehow wary of us. 'Holly's gone and I'm in hell but I can't bring her back so I'm working flat out. Only thing to do to take my mind off it. So you have to let me sell your house, Patsy, the location is sensational.'

It was outrageous emotional blackmail and on instinct I opened my mouth to say so but out of the corner of my eye I could sense Patsy shaking her head, just barely, just so I would see it. I tried not to stare at Gwen Bennett. She seemed alarmingly composed for someone who had just lost her daughter. I was aware that scribbling away at home, sometimes not even getting properly dressed until noon, I was probably ill-equipped to judge the behaviour of someone who had to put on a public front every day as part of their job. But I found it extraordinary that she was even working at all, even if she had just explained that doing so took her mind off what had happened to Holly.

'I guess you don't want to talk about it?' Patsy asked Gwen.

Gwen shrugged. 'I have to talk about it every day to the police, why not you?'

'Do they have any leads on what happened?' I said, wondering how far they had got since I last spoke to Sid.

'Well, we know what happened. The bastard murdered my daughter.'

'The bastard?' Patsy was agog.

'Holly had a lover that I didn't know about,' said Gwen and I tried to look as if this was the first I'd heard about it too.

'Really?' said Patsy.

'She met him at my rental house on Spring Hollow Road. She asked that we rent the house to a friend of hers but that woman has disappeared, if she was ever a friend. And Rita McGill, the woman next door, told us that Holly entertained a man in the back room on a regular basis.'

'But why do you think it was the lover who murdered her?' I asked.

'Well who else was it gonna be?' Gwen was incredulous. 'Rita McGill says Holly saw him there the day she was killed. That's why she went there. To see him. And he killed her.'

'Do the police think that's what happened?'

Gwen gave me a contemptuous look. 'They've swallowed the crap he gave them. He said he had an alibi, that he was somewhere else. With some other woman. But that's a crock.'

'Have they checked out his alibi?' I said.

Gwen shrugged again. *What do I know?*

'Have they charged him?' I asked.

'They're not even holding him. He could be halfway to Madagascar by now although I'm pretty sure I saw someone who looks just like him at a gas station on my way over here.'

'You *know* him?' said Patsy.

'Everyone knows him,' said Gwen. 'Well, probably not personally but who else are you going to buy your car from? Shane Sobel. Owns the dealership in Southampton as you turn the corner on 27. Matter of fact I knew him better than most – I rented one of my houses to him last summer. You remember him, don't you?' she called to

245

Eileen who had just come in. 'You cleaned for him over there, didn't you?'

Eileen shook her head. 'I've heard the name. But he was never there when I went over to clean. Just the way I like it,' she added, grinning. 'It's a bitch when they're lounging about under your feet when you're trying to get the place in shape. Just when you've mopped the floor they walk right back in, traipsing sand.'

As Eileen was talking, I was watching Patsy. At the mention of Shane Sobel's name, she had tensed visibly and suddenly I knew the reason why.

'You say you thought you saw Shane Sobel at the gas station on your way over,' I said to Gwen. 'What kind of car was he driving?'

Gwen flashed me a hint of a smile. 'It wasn't one of those Chevys or Lexuses you see lying around his lot at Southampton. He'd got himself some classy English wheels. It was the reason I noticed him in the first place. I wanted to know who in the world was riding around in a big black Jaguar.'

Chapter Ten

'Oh my dears, this place would be completely wonderful if you would just take the time to give it a little upgrade.'

These were the first words out of my mother's mouth when, a few days later, she arrived at Franny and Rufus's. I had dispatched Tommy to meet her off the Jitney – the luxury bus, the only other form of public transportation besides the train that enabled Manhattanites to travel to and from the city. Now Noreen, Mo, Franny and I were assembled in Franny's kitchen to form a welcoming committee, along with Rufus, who for once did not seem to have a meeting to go to. Eliza had produced a brightly coloured finger painting of what I thought was a scarecrow in drag, but which, she insisted, was in fact my mother.

And when my mother walked through the door, I flinched, because, apart from the garish colour, she bore an alarming resemblance to Eliza's portrait of her. For some reason I always blanked from my mind just how incredibly skinny she was. I suppose when she was in the city, her cadaverous frame served as the perfect clotheshorse for her expensive wardrobe. You saw the clothes, admired the cut and the fabric and were knocked out by how glamorous a woman of my mother's age could still be. But now she was wearing shorts – tailored khaki shorts reaching halfway down her thigh to be sure, but shorts all the same – and a T and flimsy sandals on her bony feet and her limbs were like twigs attached to a reed. She had a straw hat with a large out-rolled brim placed low on her forehead. Below that her eyes were hidden by giant oval sunglasses and below *them* her mouth was a vermilion gash. Beside her, Noreen, in her faded muslin blouse and ankle-length linen skirt, gathered at her tiny waist with a fraying drawstring, looked like my mother's abandoned rag doll.

'Oh, Vanessa,' said Noreen. 'There you are.'

'Oh, Noreen,' said my mother and the repetition had a faint ring of contempt to it, 'and there *you* are.'

She didn't embrace Noreen, nor did she offer any apology for reneging on her invitation to New York at the last moment. There was an awkward moment when I wondered if she was even going to embrace me, not something she did on a regular basis, but Rufus saved me from further embarrassment by enfolding her in a bear hug of his own.

'What do you mean, upgrade?' He was laughing but I could hear the hint of indignation in his voice. 'It's great to have you here, Vanessa.'

'Exactly what I say,' said my mother. 'This house is charming but you haven't fixed it up yet, have you? What are your plans for it? I can't wait to hear.'

I couldn't believe it. Nothing about Tommy and me and how exciting it was to see us newly married. No *Tell me about the wedding, I want to hear all about it*. And from the look of the little weekend bag that Tommy was carrying inside, it didn't look as if a wedding present was going to be forthcoming either.

'You'd never know her daughter had just got married,' I hissed to Tommy as he passed me.

'Oh, you're totally wrong,' he hissed back, 'I told her about the wedding in the car. She was all ears.'

So she doesn't need to hear it from me. I could feel the familiar resentment rising. *Doesn't bother coming to the wedding, barely acknowledges me the first time she sees me after it, no wonder I feel as if I've never been a bride. If my own mother's not interested in me being one, why should I be?*

'Rufus?' Franny's voice cut across my thoughts. *'Rufus!'* There was an urgency to the way she was addressing her husband that alerted me that all was not well. 'We're not planning on an upgrade. We like it just the way it is, right? *Rufus?*'

She was agitated because Rufus hadn't

answered her. He was regarding my mother thoughtfully. 'So what would *you* do with it, Vanessa?'

Later I wondered if in fact they might not have cooked the idea up between them in advance of her arrival. Nobody knew better than Rufus what my mother was capable of when it came to home makeovers. He had witnessed her complete redecoration of his father's Fifth Avenue apartment when she had been living with Philip Abernathy, and where Scott and Suzette now lived following his death. Makeovers were my mother's favourite hobby. Houses and apartments were her victims of choice but I knew she'd been itching to have a go at her daughter for the past thirty years.

This time, however, there was a slight variation on her theme because she began with the garden, probably because there wasn't one. It was one of the things I had loved about the property when I had first arrived with Noreen. It was just a big old clapboard farmhouse in a clearing in the woods, its façade of long overlapped strips of pine and cedar blending in totally with its surroundings. If you half closed your eyes, so that the driveway became a blur, you could imagine for half a second that there was nothing but a meadow before you. There was an abundance of daisies and dandelions and corn poppies, which had been left to run wild and I loved the informality of it all.

But my mother did not. The very next day she welcomed a landscaper at eight o'clock in the morning and proceeded to walk about the property with him. Snatches of their conversation filtered upwards through the attic window as I lay in bed.

'A line of birches here, maybe. And if you built up this area, dumped a ton of topsoil onto it, then you could create a hill sloping down to a retaining wall – bluestone, perhaps, with steps down to the driveway. And a border at the bottom – and of course there will have to be a deer fence all around the house.'

I got up and closed the window. I had been half hoping to engage Tommy in a little marital sex when he woke up – the first since his arrival, would it be any different to when I was single? – but there was no way I could indulge with my mother's voice in the background.

And the following morning the whole house was disturbed by the unfamiliar rumble of what sounded like a giant vehicle lumbering up the driveway.

'It's a backhoe,' yelled Franny from the landing below. 'What the hell is a backhoe doing here? *Rufus!*'

But Rufus – and my mother – were already outside and by the time I stumbled downstairs to make coffee, the driver of the back-hoe was leaving. He had just been delivering it. 'See you tomorrow,' I heard Rufus call out to him as he departed in another truck, and felt Franny stiffen beside me as we watched through the kitchen window.

I sensed an imminent showdown.

'Come down to the pool house with me, Franny,' I said, taking her by the arm and marching her out of the kitchen door, round the side of the house away from Rufus and my mother, and down a skinny path that ran through the woods, parallel to the trail we normally used.

'But Eliza–?'

'She's right behind us,' I said, and she was, tottering stark naked after her mother, straggly baby ringlets flying away from her tiny head as she bounced along, arms out-stretched. *'Mamma!'*

Franny stooped to pick her up and I went ahead to warn Noreen.

'Crisis looming back at the ranch,' I whispered ahead of Franny's arrival. 'I'll explain later but in the meantime we have to find a way to get my mother away from here. I'm thinking maybe a beach picnic. Mo would like that, wouldn't you, Mo?'

'Can we ask my dad to come along?'

Behind him Noreen nodded her head vigorously and mouthed *Great idea!*

Franny stormed in before I had a chance

to answer him.

'Can you freaking believe it, Lee? What is he *thinking?*' She pointed through the front door back towards her house. 'He wants to turn the place into just another chichi Hamptons property. As soon as the ground is totally dug up, someone's going to come in and deliver a brand new manicured garden just like everyone else's. Fully grown trees, shrubs, they'll all be in by tomorrow night, you'll see. And I just don't get it, because when we first saw the house, we both agreed we wanted it *because* it was so wild and overgrown and *natural*. He'll be suggesting we throw benefits here next. This is so *not* what I signed on for.'

I couldn't quite work out whether she was referring to her marriage or the landscaping. And I noticed she wasn't putting any of this on the person who had instigated it: my mother.

'We were just planning a beach party,' said Noreen, as if she hadn't heard a word Franny had said. 'You and Eliza and Rufus are all welcome, and we're going to invite Mo's father as well.' She put an arm around Mo as she said this and he flashed his row of square white teeth at us.

'And my mother,' I said hurriedly. 'She needs to get out and about a bit, what do you say, Franny?'

'Right,' said Franny but I could tell she

wasn't convinced. 'You mean today?'

'This afternoon,' I said. 'We're going to Lazy Point.' I was thinking on the spot. Lazy Point, a spit of land ending in a lagoon that was shielded from the bay by an island, was where Rufus had proposed to Franny, driving his truck way out into the shallows and parking before he produced the ring. And they had subsequently had their wedding there on the beach.

'Well, count me out,' said Franny and I stifled a gasp. 'The way I feel about my husband right now, Lazy Point is the last place I want to be. But you guys go right ahead and you'll take Eliza, won't you? She loves Lazy Point and I have to go to the city again.' She picked Eliza up and held her out to me.

It was blackmail. Eliza was already shouting 'Mo! 'Azy Point!' and I couldn't reject her.

Minnie and Shagger emerged from their room. Shagger, clad in an oversize T-shirt that hung down to his knees, fumbled his way toward the coffee machine, avoiding everyone's eye. Minnie, however, was disgustingly perky, prancing about in a baby doll nightie that threatened to reveal her pubic hair with every step she took.

'We're planning a beach picnic,' I said.

'Yes, I heard,' said Minnie. 'Norman'll go with you but I think I heard you say you were going to the city?' She looked at

Franny, who nodded. 'So could you drop me off in East Hampton on the way, so I can get a bit more shopping done?'

I wondered what had happened to the primary reason for her coming to America? She claimed to have been lured here by the thought of serious discount shopping at Tanger Mall, yet here she was all set to hit some of the most expensive stores in the country.

'I guess.' Franny looked a bit disconcerted. 'Come by the house in, like, a half hour or so?'

And Minnie must have done just that because she wasn't there when I returned from a quick trip to the IGA, loaded down with paper plates, cups and napkins, bags of crisps, cans of soda, hot dogs and buns and a cooked chicken whose legs and wings I planned to break off and then use the breast for sandwiches. Shagger was dispatched to find Rufus and alert him to our plans and beg a coolbox from him, and Noreen and I went to work packing up the picnic.

'We'd better find your dad and tell him where to meet us,' I told Mo.

'I'm gone do that,' he said and whipped out of his pocket the little mobile Wyn had told me about. I noted that Wyn answered Mo's call instantly and I heard Mo say Lazy Point several times.

'My dad say what time?' he said, turning

to me.

'At the rate we're going, tell him to meet us there in an hour.'

Wyn was waiting as we drove past the collection of ramshackle little fishermen's cottages that constituted Lazy Point in a convoy of assorted vehicles. Even though we were missing Franny and Minnie, we were still quite a party: Noreen, me, my mother, Eliza and Mo in my car. Tommy and Shagger in a Subaru Tommy had rented the day before and finally Rufus bringing up the rear in his truck.

Wyn was overdressed for the beach. The crisp white shirt and khaki Bermudas looked as if he'd only ripped the price tag off an hour ago. I introduced him to everyone and I noted his distinct lack of ease. Maybe he had just thought it would be me and Mo but, if so, why had he got dressed up?

He made a big show of embracing Mo and then, to get him away from the crowd, I took his arm and led him down to the water, along with Eliza and Mo.

'Help me get them into these,' I said, handing Wyn a set of water wings. 'Paddling only,' I warned the children. 'No water above your knees. Mo, you have to look after Eliza, hold her hand all the time, don't let her slip. Your dad will watch out for you.'

'I can't swim,' Wyn said. He looked terrified. 'Mo can't either.'

256

'And you think Eliza can?' I smiled re-assuringly at him. 'Don't be nervous. It's very shallow until way out into the lagoon, but just so you don't have to worry, I'll get Tommy to play lifeguard. *Tommy!*'

Tommy and Shagger were poised to rush into the water. Tommy's paunch strained against the elastic of his swimming trunks, reminding me that we had to do something about his diet. Shagger appeared to be wearing his underpants and, worse, they were the droopy cotton kind that seemed too big for his skinny frame, just like all his other clothes. Rufus, casually alighting from his truck, his muscular torso toned to perfection, put them both to shame.

I settled Noreen and my mother in beach chairs in the sand and proceeded to lay out the food on a rug. Tommy returned from his dip, emerging from the water with his shoulders hunched and arms outstretched, wading towards Mo monster fashion and eliciting the requisite squeals. Shagger followed him and after one glance, I looked away hurriedly. His flimsy underpants, now soaking wet, clung to him, leaving the outline of his enormous genitalia all but exposed to view.

'Tommy,' I hissed at him, 'wrap a towel around him or something. Why isn't he wearing swimwear?'

'I don't think he brought any.' Tommy followed my gaze and chuckled. 'It's a whopper, isn't it? Haven't you always wondered why he's called Shagger?'

As a matter of fact I had, just as I had also asked myself what a cute little button like Minnie was doing with someone as seemingly clueless as Shagger. Maybe I now had my answer and Tommy confirmed it when he added in a whisper.

'You might find this hard to believe, but Shagger has the reputation of being a sensational lover. Right back when we started chasing girls, he was always the one who scored.'

I stared at him in disbelief. 'Inflatables don't know how to say no?'

'Straight up,' said Tommy, 'he's a dark horse. Never has much to say for himself, right? And that's because he's shy – or at least he was once. Then he learned how to make his shyness work for him, how he could make himself seem vulnerable so the girls felt sympathetic towards him. That's how he operates and what he lacks in conversation, he makes up for in the kind of super tender lovemaking you women like.'

You women! 'And you know this how?'

'Word always gets back,' said Tommy knowingly, 'women talk amongst themselves. You must know that. You just haven't met the women Shagger's been involved with.'

I looked at Shagger. Had I misjudged him

all these years? Somehow I knew I was never going to make the effort to find the answer to this question.

Wyn rubbed Mo dry with a beach towel and I placed a baby sun hat on Eliza's head. Rufus had brought a little portable grill and once the hot dogs were done we all settled down to the kind of wonderful lazy picnics I had enjoyed as a child on summer holidays in Cornwall. I was so full of goodwill towards my fellow man that I forgot that I was mad at my mother and reached over to clasp her by the hand.

'Come and wander with me along the shoreline,' I said to her. 'I need to get caught up with how you are, and find out what's new with my father. We've barely had a moment since you arrived.'

She allowed herself to be hefted to her feet and I hooked my arm with hers to lead her off along the beach.

'Stop!' she yelled almost immediately, unhooking her arm and stepping away from me. But it was only to shrug off a pair of lime-green loafers and throw them one by one so they landed in the sand on the edge of the picnic area. 'Now,' she reinstated her arm, albeit with a rather tense grip on my elbow, 'let's roll. It was very good of you to allow that boy to come and spend your vacation with you, Lee. I'm proud of you.'

I have to be one of the few people in the

world for whom alarm bells start ringing when their mother says they are proud of them. My mother rarely pays me a compliment and when she does, it's invariably for something for which I cannot take credit. The problem was, I had a feeling she always knew that.

'He's Franny's Fresh Air kid, not mine,' I explained. 'She and Rufus wanted to give something back. I just help her out with Mo because she has more than enough to do running that house and taking care of Eliza and everything.'

'What do you mean, running that house?' My mother yanked her arm away again. Ah well, what had I expected? 'Why doesn't she hire staff? The place is falling apart.'

'She likes it like that. So does Rufus.'

'He does *not!*' My mother was emphatic. 'He told me this morning that I had come along in the nick of time. Said he was tired of living in a dump. Those were his words. He's thinking of running for one of those East Hampton Town boards, which will mean he'll be working to heighten his profile. It won't look good if his home is a mess.'

'He's thinking of *what?*' She had to be wrong. Rufus was surely the last person who would want to get involved with the Town. He was as anti-establishment as you could get, the eternal beach boy. Or at least he used to be. 'Does Franny know about this?'

'Well, they're married, aren't they? And married people tell each other everything.'

She said this with such bitterness that I turned to her abruptly. 'What's up, Mum?'

'You said you wanted news of your father.' She was picking her way barefoot along the water's edge, carefully avoiding the mass of dark-red seaweed that had accumulated. We were heading towards the long stretch of beach and the land that was owned by the Abernathy family.

I braced myself. I love Ed Bartholomew but I'm the first to admit he's neither a perfect husband or father, although to give him his due, being married to a category five hurricane like my mother can't exactly be a breeze. Before they retired, she was a hugely successful advertising executive and he had an antique bookstall in Portobello Market in Notting Hill that he actually seemed proud to run at a loss. He subsidised it with his small inheritance and we lived off my mother's socking great salary. Eventually she gave in to Ed's impassioned pleas that they should go and bury themselves in the French countryside for their retirement and allowed him to whisk her away to live in a glorified cowshed in the Lot, a cowshed that became the guinea pig for her first disastrous makeover.

So my mother discovered home decorating and my father discovered a French divorcée called Josiane at least twenty years his junior. She was not, I realised as I grew up and learned about the perfidious nature of men for myself, the first.

'Ed's up to his old tricks?' I said it lightly. I always called him Ed, as if I could thus ward off any notion that this wayward character was in fact my father.

'Her name is Luciane and she lives in the Village. These days they all seem to have French names even if they were born and raised in Poughkeepsie. I think he re-names them after the first fuck.'

'Mum!' Unlike what she called 'her foul-mouthed daughter', she never used language like this and it hurt me to hear her resort to it.

'Lee, she's in her thirties, for Christ's sake. She's younger than *you!* She's the daughter of friends of ours and that's not even the worst of it. She's married, herself. The last time we saw the parents, they talked about how she was trying for a baby. I nearly yelled out *With who?*'

With *whom*. I bit my lip, clamping down on the urge to correct her.

'Why do you stay with him?' I had never asked this before but then she had never opened up so quickly about his infidelities.

'He's your father,' she said simply, as if it were my fault.

'I'm a big girl,' I said, 'I could handle it if

you left him.'

'Maybe,' she said, bending to pick up a particularly invasive bit of seaweed and throw it out to sea, 'but I couldn't. I'm not like you. It would frighten me to be on my own. Unless I find someone else as wonderful as Philip Abernathy to rescue me, I'm trapped in my marriage now. Maybe I should never have gone back to your father after Phil was killed, but it's sort of instinctive behaviour for me. The single life is not for me, you know that.'

And then she dissolved into a kind of horrible yelping – sobbing, trying to stop, catching her breath and emitting a high-pitched sound that terrified me.

'We shouldn't have come here,' she said, pointing to the beach house she had shared with Philip Abernathy. 'I should have known it would upset me.'

It was the only time I had seen my mother truly happy, those few precious months she had spent with Rufus's father, the man who had rescued her when my father abandoned her for Josiane. They had even gone so far as to have a commitment ceremony on the very beach on which we were walking – they couldn't have a legal wedding because she was still married to my father – and I knew that the Phillionaire had been perhaps the only person in the world, including myself, who had truly understood my mother's

263

incapacity to show people that she loved them.

I reminded myself of this failing of hers when she said, apparently totally without guile, 'I sometimes think that the reason Phil and I were so happy was precisely because we were *not* married. Don't ever get married, Lee. Keep Tommy as your lover and you'll be much happier, believe me.'

It wasn't exactly right up there with The Best Things to Say to your Daughter on Her Honeymoon and once again I resorted to the mantra I kept having to repeat to myself whenever I was around my mother. *You know what she's like. What did you expect?*

I moved to turn her around and lead her away from the tormenting reminder of her past and back to join the others. Any minute now we would come upon an abandoned construction site, the gaping hole with the steel columns sticking out of it that was the beginning of the house my mother had never finished building. The land had been part of her inheritance from the Phillionaire, but, once she went back to my father, she lost her motivation to finish the construction. Witnessing what she had failed to achieve would only bring back more pain.

But the minute we headed back toward Lazy Point, we ran into Wyn and Mo and Rufus carrying Eliza. Noreen and Tommy were not far behind them and Shagger, to my amazement was back in the water, swimming out to a raft that was bobbing in the bay.

My mother rallied and I sent her a silent vote of confidence as she whisked Eliza from Rufus, whirled her in the air and said:

'Let's all go take a look at that funny little house Lee used to live in. Do you remember?'

She meant the cabin where Sid was now staying, and which had once been the Phillionaire's retreat. I explained about Sid staying there.

'Oh, we won't go in,' she said, 'we'll just take a walk up that sandy trail from the beach so Eliza can check on her inheritance.'

And I remembered that the Phillionaire had indeed left it in trust to Eliza. And anyway, I thought, Sid would probably be at work, camped out behind a bush somewhere, watching Keshawn.

Of course, once we were close enough, Eliza demanded to be let down so she could run up to the cabin and a few seconds later to my surprise I heard her call out 'Si, Si.'

She had difficulty with her consonants, invariably leaving them off. Sid must be there. I only hoped he wouldn't mind being invaded without warning. With luck he would have heard Eliza calling out to him and be prepared.

He hadn't heard her. That much was obvious as we arrived *en masse* at the clearing in

265

the bamboo where we had an unobstructed view through the big glass sliders into the cabin.

Sid had his back to us and he was naked except for a dish cloth thrown over his shoulder. He was standing at the stove, tossing something in a frying pan. I couldn't stop marvelling at the gigantic width of his back and the tautness of his buttocks until I heard Rufus say 'Oh shit!' behind me and I shifted my gaze a little to the right to see Minnie, equally naked, lying amidst the rumpled sheets of the bed.

I was awakened the next morning by the rhythmic tapping of a woodpecker's beak on the sill of the attic dormer window behind my bed. Tommy was not beside me and I roused myself to see him piling clothes haphazardly into his suitcase.

'What are you doing?'

'What does it look like I'm doing?' he said.

'But why? Are you moving to another room?'

'I'm moving to another country. I'm leaving for the airport with Shagger in fifteen minutes. I'm going back to London with him.'

'But you're due to stay another week – check your ticket.'

'So I changed it.' He sounded mutinous. 'And before you ask, Shagger paid the penalty fee for me.'

'You're leaving me.' The words were out before I could stop them.

'I'm not leaving *you*. I'm accompanying Shagger. He refuses to stay here another minute. The guy's in the worst state I've ever seen him.'

'Probably because you went out and got him more drunk than you've ever seen him.'

Shagger, still swimming blithely along the bay, was the only person who had not witnessed first hand Minnie and Sid in all their glory. We had stood there, frozen, until, as she often did, my mother surprised me with her quick thinking.

'Oh look,' she told Eliza, 'they're so hot they've taken their clothes off. And you know what? They're right. Let's go back to the water and cool down ourselves.'

Of course then she had to get out of stripping naked herself when Eliza called her bluff, but mercifully Rufus came to her rescue and whisked Eliza into the water. Tommy raced ahead to plunge in and head Shagger off at the pass, while the rest of us trooped back along the hot sand to the cars. Tommy called me later to tell me he was taking Shagger straight to Montauk to break the news to him and get him 'rat-assed'. I had vaguely registered him climbing into bed beside me around four o'clock in the morning so seeing him vertical and active only three hours later was the last thing I expected.

'Tommy.' I grabbed his pillows, plumped them on top of my own and propped myself up on them. 'Shagger is a grown man. He can get himself to the airport and onto a plane by himself. He doesn't need you.'

'S'more than that.' Tommy had an armful of clothes and a toothbrush in his mouth. 'Got to give him moral support after what Minnie's done. When you've known someone as long as I've known Shagger, there's a bond. You look out for each other, it's automatic.'

Like Patsy and Eileen, I wondered.

'Would he do the same for you if I left you?'

He dropped the clothes and took the toothbrush out of his mouth. 'Are you leaving me?'

'You appear to have pipped me to the post.'

'I'm not leaving our *marriage*.'

'So you've remembered we *are* married?'

'Don't start, Lee. Now is not the time—'

'Don't start what? And when can I make an appointment to start it when we've figured out what it is?'

'You know,' Tommy approached the bed and loomed over me as I lay in bed, 'if you hadn't introduced Minnie to that thug, this would never have happened.'

That thug! Sid wasn't a thug. He was a gentle and lonely man making the best of a

268

life that had clearly never been the same since his marriage had split up.

'Tommy,' I said, locking eyes with him, 'you know as well as I do that if you hadn't invited Minnie here in the first place, this would never have happened.'

He paused for a second, his lower lip protruding a little in the obstinate look he always adopted when he knew he was wrong – a look that he seemed to have perfected over the nine years I had been with him and which, I suspected, he knew always made me want to gather him up into my arms because it rendered him so vulnerable.

'There is one thing about you that I will never be able to figure out,' he said slowly, 'and that is why you always, *always*, hold *me* responsible.'

And with that he scooped up his bag, snatched his wallet from the bedside table and disappeared out the door before I could even answer him. Although what I would have said, I wasn't entirely sure because there was only one thing going through my mind.

The honeymoon was over.

Chapter Eleven

'Why didn't Tommy say goodbye to me?' Mo persisted in asking me the same question every five minutes. I was beginning to wonder if he would ever let up.

'He barely said goodbye to me either and I'm his mother,' said Noreen, turning her head slightly to address Mo in the back seat of the car.

It had been four days since Tommy had left and now we were on our way to JFK to put Noreen on her plane home to London. Then I would continue on into Manhattan where I would hand Mo over to his mother.

I had nearly dropped the phone in shock when Anna Moses had called, full of apologies for not having reached us earlier.

'I went upstate and I never checked my messages in the city till I got back yesterday,' she said brightly. Her voice was sweet and bell-like and she sounded strong. For some reason this surprised me.

'We just thought you'd like to know how Mo was doing,' I said carefully. I didn't want her to think I was judging her for not calling to check up on her son. Which, of course, I was.

'Oh, I knew he was doing fine. He called me all the time, said you guys were great.'

'He called you?' I was mystified.

'Yes. You let him use your cell phone, or someone did, anyway. Thank you for that.'

So Mo had used the phone Wyn had given him to call his mother. I admired his ingenuity but the fact that he had kept it a secret from us triggered alarm bells in my head.

'You won't forgive him?' Mo was riveted. 'Never ever? Man, Tommy, you in trouble!' He was giggling.

'Never *ever!*' I confirmed. 'In fact that's just another thing to add to my list of "non-forgives", along with inviting Minnie and Shagger to come in the first place.'

'Norman,' said Noreen automatically. 'Don't call him Shagger. Please. And I don't see what there is to forgive. You always react too strongly about him, Lee. There's nothing malicious about Norman and he's part of Tommy's life, always will be, so you might just have to get used to him.' There was just enough admonition in her tone to make me take heed. I couldn't always take what Tommy said seriously, but I knew better than to disregard what his mother said to me.

'But Noreen, it's my *honeymoon!*' I protested.

'I know, dear. But it's not as if you're just getting to know Tommy. You've been a couple for years and he was romantic enough at the wedding, wasn't he? All that stuff he found for you to read to him? And if you feel that strongly about your *honeymoon*,' the emphasis she put on the word was tinged with a hint of sarcasm, 'I suppose I should apologise to you for coming along. That must have really ruined it for you.'

'Oh, Noreen. You know I always like having you around. Isn't that right, Mo? You're going to miss Noreen, aren't you?'

'I guess,' he said, but I knew he would. The difference between the truculent kid who had tried to run away as soon as he got off the bus and the energetic little boy who, Noreen reported, now leapt out of bed each morning and charged outside in expectation, was incredible.

'It's not as if you don't know what Tommy's like,' Noreen continued. 'It's the way he's always been – he talks big, he means well and then he gets distracted and never follows through. I'll bet you gave him a piece of your mind when he cut short your *honeymoon*.'

'Oh stop!' I said. 'You know I never miss an opportunity to have a go at your son. And before you tell me I shouldn't, I read somewhere that women who swallow their anger during marital disputes are more likely to die of heart disease than women who speak their minds.'

'Ah,' said Noreen thoughtfully, 'but did you know that with men, it's having a flat-out row with a wife who answers back that's a problem for *their* coronary health.'

'My mom and my dad, they used to shout all the time. That's why they split.' Mo's little voice was a startling contribution from the back seat. Noreen glanced at me and shook her head very slightly. *Don't let's go there.*

'Lee,' she said to change the subject, 'I'm really sorry to have to tell you this but my aging bladder won't last till we get to the airport. Could you stop at the next bathroom you see, please.'

Just as well I allowed time for this, I thought, pulling into a petrol station just beyond Southampton. 'You'd better take Mo with you. He drank all that soda just before we left and it's going to have to go somewhere.'

Once they'd gone, I sat in a trance, wondering when I would next hear from my husband. I was staring through the windshield at the car dealership beside the petrol station and I wasn't registering what I was seeing until my eyes came to rest on a big black Jaguar that looked totally out of place amongst the Chevy trucks and Impalas littered all over the adjacent lot.

My gaze travelled upward to a large sign. SHANE SOBEL. And then, as if I'd pressed an invisible button that summoned him up, there he was. The man I had seen driving away from Patsy Brooks' property, Holly Bennett's lover and the man her mother assumed had killed her.

How long does it take for two people to go to the bathroom? Granted, Noreen was an elderly lady who moved slowly and took her time, and Mo had to stop and look at the petrol pumps, but they were back within ten, fifteen minutes tops. And that's how long it took for me to know that, if he asked me, I'd have a very hard time remembering I was a married woman who ought to think twice before jumping into bed with Shane Sobel.

The minute he turned his attention on me, and I looked into those eyes the colour of pale cornflower, I didn't have a prayer and I guessed this was what happened to practically every woman he spoke to. It wasn't about *his* looks, it was about the way he looked at *you*, as if you were the most delicious thing on the planet.

'See anything you like?' he asked, smiling at me in what seemed like an indulgent fashion.

I had got out of the car and wandered over for a closer look at the black Jag. 'This isn't for sale, I imagine?'

'Everything's for sale – at a price,' he said, looking right at me, flicking his eyes over me and nodding in appreciation. 'Even me. And you have excellent taste.'

'If I wanted you or the Jaguar?' Was I flirting with this man?

He laughed and his eyes creased up and his teeth flashed and for half a second I wanted to fling myself at him. 'I meant the Jag but how do you know I don't come with? By the sound of your accent, you're not a local.'

'I'm not,' I said, 'and I don't need a car. I just wanted to take a closer look at the Jaguar. I'm pretty sure it's the one I saw at a friend of mine's house the other day.'

'Is that right?' He didn't elaborate.

I nodded. 'My friend's name is Patsy Brooks.'

He winked at me. 'It's a small world.'

'And maybe we have another friend in common. Holly Bennett?'

His face was impassive. 'Are you planning on joining the club?'

'What club would that be?' Two could play at this game.

'I think you already know. Are you a friend of Patsy's from England? What's your name?'

'Lee Bartholomew'

'She hasn't mentioned you,' he said.

'Has she mentioned Holly Bennett?'

A flicker of suspicion passed across his

face, followed by one of what seemed to me genuine regret. 'Too bad about what happened to Holly.'

'Or her mother?'

'Her mother?'

'Gwen.'

'Shit!' he said, genuinely astonished. 'Gwen Bennett, the realtor? She's Holly's mother? There's a million Bennetts out here. I never made the connection.'

'Well, now you have,' I said sweetly. 'Ah, my mother-in-law's back.' Just to let him know I had a husband. 'I've got to go.'

'Good to meet you, Lee.' He held out his hand and I took it. He held on for just a fraction longer than was necessary and his touch was soft. 'Do you have a phone number? Just in case you decide you do need a car and I find I have just what you need.'

'In that case I'll call you,' I said, extricating my hand. 'In the meantime, take a tip from me. Stay clear of Gwen Bennett.'

'Smart people do.' He muttered it. He might not have even meant me to hear it. But I did. And I wondered.

'Who was that?' asked Noreen as soon as I got back in the car.

'Car salesman,' I said in as offhand a manner as I could manage. 'Whatshisname? It's on the sign up there. Why do you ask?'

'Because he stood and watched you as you walked over here. And he's still watching.

276

Looks like you made quite an impression.'

I felt absurdly pleased. Whether it was because I was smarting from Tommy having left, which made me vulnerable to someone showing me attention, I had no idea – but Shane Sobel's interest in me perked me up.

Noreen wanted me to drop her off at the kerb at JFK and leave her there. I wouldn't hear of it. I let her out and made Mo stay with her while I took the car to the car park. I told them not to move, to wait for me, but as I pulled away from the kerb, I saw them set off hand in hand for the check-in. Noreen was pulling her little suitcase on wheels behind her.

I wasn't at all convinced she should be flying on her own. Tommy might not have said goodbye to her when he left, but she had told me that he had promised to be at Heathrow to meet the flight and drive her home. But in the meantime I wanted to hang a label around her neck with her name on it, like the ones I had seen on unaccompanied children on planes. As it was, I accosted a couple waiting in line a little way behind her and surreptitiously asked them to keep an eye on her for me.

'She's not as strong as she looks,' I said, and then tried to swallow my words because of course she didn't look strong at all. She was a tiny frail little creature not much taller than Mo and with her wispy white hair she put me in mind of a puffball in a raincoat.

'Don't worry,' said the man, 'I'd be worried if my mother was flying on her own.'

'She's not my–' I began, then stopped. It would never occur to me to ask someone to watch out for my mother. Indeed, when she'd gone back to New York the day after the Minnie/Sid fiasco, it was Tommy who had taken her to the Jitney and we hadn't even kissed on parting. *What had I expected?* But as she walked out to the car I had called out *Give my love to Ed* and it wasn't until she and Tommy were halfway down the driveway that I remembered our conversation about my father at Lazy Point. How clumsy and insensitive could I be? Sometimes, it seemed, I was my mother's daughter.

Mo surprised me by clinging to Noreen as she was about to go through security, burying his face in her stomach. But when I finally managed to pull him gently away, he gave her one last scary monster face and she and I recoiled in mock fright. Then I felt her spindly arms encircling me somewhere around my midsection and heard her whisper, 'I'll be fine, and I'll talk to Tommy, don't you worry,' and then she was gone, lost amongst the hordes of other passengers anxious to board.

Mo was uncharacteristically silent on the drive into Manhattan. He sat shuffling a pack of little cards in his lap, shifting them

278

from one hand to the other. I'd seen him playing with them recently, but he always kept a tight hold on them, slipping them into his pocket or under his pillow. And when I emptied the pockets of his shorts for the laundry or removed a pillow slip, there was never any sign of them. In other words he was never parted from them.

Noreen had said they'd looked like business cards – *but he wouldn't show them to me when I asked.*

'Whatcha got there, Mo?'

'Nothin'.'

'Looks like a bunch of business cards to me.'

His reflection in the rearview mirror showed him nodding at me. 'My dad's – so I know where to reach him.'

'Why do you have so many?' I said. There were at least a dozen.

'He work a whole lotta places. He a very important man.'

'Show me,' I said, prepared for him to refuse.

But he dropped them over my shoulder into my lap. 'Here.'

I picked them up, one by one, peering at them quickly while keeping one hand on the steering wheel.

Wynton P. Moses, General Manager; Wynton P. Moses, Sales Associate; Wynton P. Moses, Director of Development; Wynton P. Moses,

Executive Editor; Wynton P. Moses, Managing Partner. And in my wallet I had *Wynton P. Moses, Attorney at Law.*

'He can't work all these places, Mo,' I said.

Mo was outraged. 'Sure he do. He take me to his offices *all* over the city. High up in the sky.' He leaned forward and looked up through the windshield at the buildings towering above us as we drove up Third Avenue. 'He take me at the end of the day so I don't disturb nobody. They all gone home. I get to sit at his desk and he have BIG desks.'

He leaned forward and yelled in my ear.

'OK, OK. Take it easy. I believe you.'

But I didn't. I had been wondering how an attorney could take what seemed like indefinite leave out in the Hamptons. And these cards – cheap designs, with just his name and title and his mobile number – it didn't add up.

I felt a little guilty about not calling my mother and letting her know I was going to be in the city. After what she had told me about my father's latest dalliance, I couldn't face staying with them. Instead I would spend the night at the Fifth Avenue apartment that the Phillionaire had left to Scott, the one that my mother had 'made over'. If Scott and Suzette had been there, I would never have gone near the place but since they were safely ensconced in East Hampton, I had no compunction about taking Rufus up on his suggestion that I stay here. He had cleared it with Scott and he didn't even need to give me a key. The doorman would take me up in the elevator that led directly into the apartment, which wasn't even locked.

But first I had to deliver Mo to his mother. I had been rather looking forward to a trip to Harlem but Anna Moses insisted on a compromise.

'You don't want to come all the way up here. I'll meet you at the 79th Street entrance to the park, near the Metropolitan Museum. I'll come down Fifth on the bus, it'll be easy for me.'

'Are you sure?' I said. 'How will I know you?'

'I think my son will recognise me. It hasn't been that long,' she said. 'Don't worry, I was about to ask you the same question before I realised that Mo would be with you.'

From her voice I expected her to be tall but she was slight and almost insignificant until you had been looking at her for a few seconds. And then it suddenly hit you how beautiful she was. She was probably in her forties but there was a girlish prettiness to her face and a fragility to her demeanour exacerbated by signs of extreme fatigue. She had fair hair, not blond and it was dead straight, parted on the side, hanging to her

281

shoulders in a bob. Only her rather sallow skin gave any indication of her bi-racial heritage. Her eyes were brown and wan above the dark circles beneath them. In fact everything about her was wan but not in a wishy-washy way because her voice was so strong and her manner so animated. And even though her clothes were faded and mismatched and had Good Will stamped all over them, she still managed to wear them with a certain *élan*.

Mo rushed to her and she patted his shoulder, a little stiffly, I thought, smiling at me over his head. He seemed delighted to see her again and it didn't jive with his attitude towards her when he had first arrived in East Hampton. When he turned around and said proudly, *'Lee, this is my Mom,'* she laughed and said, 'Who else would I be?'

It was a witty question, because as far as I could see there was not a trace of her in Mo. I hadn't realised I was staring until she said, 'You're trying to see how someone as white as me could produce Mo, aren't you?'

'I'm sorry,' I said, 'I didn't mean to stare.'

'It's OK. Everybody does. When Wyn and I were still together, it was easier to make the connection. You haven't met my husband – my ex-husband – but you only have to look at him and you see Mo.'

I saw Mo tense. Would I tell his mother

about his meeting up with his father?

'Anna,' I said, making a snap decision, 'do you have time to take a walk in the park?'

She looked surprised for a second. 'I guess,' she said after a beat. 'Mo'd like that, right, Mo? Can we walk to the Reservoir so he can show you how he can run? You know, along the track there? I like to watch my son the athlete.'

'Sure,' I said, 'good idea.'

We chatted as we walked, sharing the load of Mo's little bag. She plied me with questions as to how come I was in America, and in the *Hamptons*, and why hadn't Mo ever talked about Franny, and who exactly was Noreen – Mo had just described her as *an older lady*. I did the best I could to respond, explaining that Mo had been billeted in the pool house while Franny was up at the Big House and hoping she wouldn't ask where I slept. As she talked I began to wonder if she even knew about the kidnapping.

'Did he tell you about the time he was taken from the beach?' I said tentatively, prepared to talk her through the whole thing.

'Oh sure. He said he'd been kidnapped and I nearly died. My first thought was that Wyn had taken him but he said it was a girl and she had made a mistake and you guys showed up pretty soon after. He made it sound like quite an adventure but I guess

283

you must have been pretty worried until you found him.'

I nodded. 'We were. And we couldn't reach you.'

'Oh, I spoke to Mrs Abernathy. She re-assured me everything was fine, even said they'd hired a security person to watch over him.'

I nodded again. So Franny had been in touch with Mo's mother all along. Couldn't she have let us know down at the pool house, given we were the ones who were watching Mo for her? And what about the small technicality of Sid having been hired to watch Eliza, not Mo?

'So what happened?' Anna asked.

'Mo was mistaken for another boy,' I said.

'What boy?'

'Keshawn. Rufus – Mr Abernathy's nephew.'

'And he's OK?' She didn't need to ask if he was black, I noted.

'Yes,' I said, 'he's OK.'

'So all's well,' she said. She made it sound as if Mo had gone on a play date without telling us. I didn't mention the second time he had gone missing, when Wyn had calmly whisked him away from the beach. But now that we had reached the Reservoir, and Mo had charged ahead out of earshot, I decided it was time I turned the tables on her.

'So where did you and Mo's father meet?'

284

'At Harvard.'

'He was studying law.' I forgot to make it a question.

'He wasn't studying anything because he wasn't the student. I was.'

Wyn wasn't a student? I recovered enough to ask, 'So what was he doing there?'

'Visiting a friend. They'd grown up together as kids on the same block in Harlem and this boy had been selected for a scholarship by A Better Chance. You ever hear of that?'

I nodded. From your husband.

'Wyn came up from New York to visit with him and we met and I made the biggest mistake of my life. I fell in love with him. I was dating his friend Monroe, but once Wyn showed up, I dropped him like the proverbial hot potato. Monroe warned me about Wyn but I thought it was just sour grapes. I thought he was being snotty and patronising about Wyn, his less fortunate friend from the projects. I was so wrong.'

I was silent but inside my head my mind was racing. This story didn't run the way Wyn's had.

'What happened?'

'I'll give you the long story short,' she said. 'We dated, we married, I dropped out, we got a place in Harlem. He was already on smack. Heroin. He blew what money I brought to the marriage, he stole from my father and we were on welfare almost from the get-go.'

'Your father was a lawyer?'

She looked at me, amazed. 'How did you guess? He hated that I married a loser like Wyn. He was mad as hell when I dumped Monroe and he kept in touch with him. I think he even helped him in his career just to spite me.' Her face hardened. 'But finally, once Mo came along, I had to swallow my pride and accept that everyone had been right about Wyn. I knew I had to kick him out and manage on my own, even without my father's support. When my father died, my mother sold their apartment and moved to Harlem to be near me. She helps me out and I tell you, I don't know what I'd do without her. I sure couldn't work without her there to watch Mo.'

I wondered what kind of work she did. Somehow I had a feeling it was a far cry from what she had envisaged when she started out as a Harvard law student.

'Does Mo see his father?' I felt guilty for not coming clean with her but I felt I owed it to Mo not to betray him. I wanted to know how much she knew.

She shook her head. 'I have a restraining order against him. He's not supposed to come within a hundred yards of us.'

I frowned to show how shocked I was.

'Look,' she appealed to me, 'he's delusional

half the time. I can't let Mo see him. I'd never know if he'd be strung out and acting crazy. He can't keep a job to save his life, let alone ours, and it's like he's lost all sense of reality. All the time he's talking big about how his mega-career is right around the corner but if he gets work at all, it's as a janitor. You have to understand,' she took hold of the sleeve of my jacket and held on to it, as if she thought that was the only way she could get my attention, 'he's Mo's *father*. I *want* to think the best of him, I *want* all his fantasies to come true – but I've long since given up believing they will. And meanwhile I've got to do what's best for Mo.'

I sensed a slight defensiveness creeping into her attitude toward me. *If he gets work at all, it's as a janitor.* So what were those business cards all about?

'So did he talk much about his father?' she said suddenly, catching me off guard.

'A little,' I said, in as offhand manner as I could manage.

'It's so hard,' she said, 'I feel so guilty that he doesn't have his father there for him. But he won't talk about him with me. The night before he left to come out to Long Island, we had an argument about Wyn.'

'What happened?' I asked, remembering how Mo had reacted to any suggestion that we contact his mother.

'Mo insisted on packing for himself. He

wouldn't let me near his bag.'

Right, I thought, *he didn't want you to see the mobile and the book his father gave him.*

'But I saw he wanted to take his photo of his father and I took it from him. It was only because I wanted to take the photo out of its frame. I thought the glass might get smashed. I wanted him to take just the picture but he thought I was denying him even that. He yelled at me – *You don't want me to have a dad, you a mean bitch.* Where does he get this language? He's only seven.' She shook her head in bewilderment. 'And then he went to bed and the next morning, after he had left on the bus, I went home to change the sheets and he had wet the bed again. He's so stressed and it's my fault and yet I don't know what to do. Still,' she gave her head a decisive little shake as if to dismiss any further discussion of Wyn, 'I don't want to weigh you down with my problems. It looks like you did a terrific job with him. He sure don't look stressed now. Look at him go!' She pointed to Mo who was streaking around the Reservoir, his long legs scissoring so fast they were barely distinguishable from one another.

'It must be hard for you,' I said, aware that my words were insubstantial. *And it must be even harder for Mo*, I thought, sneaking out to see his father, probably having to listen to Wyn denigrate his mother, keeping it all secret from Anna.

She regarded me for a second. Then her gaze travelled to Mo and he started back towards her. 'No, no,' she shouted, 'you go on and play,' and she waved her hand to shoo him away. 'Don't want him to hear what I have to say. You know,' she said slowly, turning back to me, 'he really has taken a shine to you. Oh, no, don't deny it,' she added when she saw my look of surprise. 'Mo can be a tricky kid when he wants to be, as I'm sure you're aware of by now – but I could tell that he trusts you from the way he talked about the time he was having with you, what he told me on the phone.'

'He didn't at first,' I said.

'He was trouble?' Anna laughed. 'I can imagine. He knows how to press buttons like no other kid. And I felt so bad about sending him out there.'

'You did?' I was surprised. 'You didn't want him to be a Fresh Air kid?'

'Sort of,' she said, 'but it wasn't really just for his benefit. Listen, I'm going to tell you something but I hope you won't judge me too harshly.'

I waited, wondering what was coming.

'I've met someone,' she said simply. 'Mo's met him once, when he came to the apartment, and he didn't like him. He's–' She hesitated. 'He's white. I don't know if that's significant or not. But I knew from that one

289

meeting that I was going to have to tread carefully. That's where I've been these past two weeks, upstate with him. And if you're going to ask me did I fix up the Fresh Air time so I could be free of Mo, free to spend time with this new person in my life, then I guess I'm going to have to tell you, yes. I did.'

She looked at me with her chin up as if challenging me to disapprove. And I looked back at her, trying to figure out my reaction. I felt bad for Mo, caught up in his parents' tussles. But I could understand how difficult it must be for Anna to meet someone new, let alone find time to develop a relationship. Then I suddenly remembered something Wyn had said. *Anna's got some strung-out dude she's seeing. He hits her.*

'Does your husband know about this man you're seeing?'

'NO! *No* one knows.'

Bella saw the bruises. Anna didn't want her to find out about the boyfriend and told Bella it was me.

'You haven't told you mother?'

'My *mother?*' Anna was almost laughing at me. 'Why would I tell my mother? I mean, if it goes well then of course I'll want my mom to meet him but it's early days yet.'

'So why have you told me?'

'Because I'd like to spend some more time with him.' It took a few seconds for the penny to drop.

'And you'd like Mo to spend more time away?'

'He really likes you and he's not due back in school for weeks.'

I was shocked. I wondered if she'd been planning to ask me before she'd even met me and decided that she probably had. Still, her request had completely taken me by surprise. And what if this new man she was seeing did beat her? Who was I supposed to believe, her or Wyn? Did Wyn know more than Anna realised? In which case, did *Mo* know more than Anna realised and would I be performing a possible rescue act if I took Mo away again?

'Does Mo know you were going to suggest this?'

She shook her head.

'Well then, hadn't we better ask him?'

She understood my acquiescence and hugged me. 'Mo!' she shouted at him. 'Get over here.'

I literally felt warmth flood through me when she told him and Mo's face lit up in a huge smile.

'I get to go back to the beach?'

I nodded. 'If you want? By the way,' I turned to Anna, 'you told the Fresh Air Fund that Mo could swim.'

'Oh no, I never did,' she said. 'Did he tell you that? Did *he* tell you he could swim? I swear, sometimes he's as much a fantasist as his–' she stopped just in time.

But Mo hadn't heard her. He gave a whoop of glee, grabbed his bag of stuff from Anna and presented himself in front of me, grinning ecstatically in his eagerness to accompany me.

'Just one more week,' said Anna, sounding rather wistful, and I felt slightly mollified. Maybe she wasn't quite as keen as I thought to be parted from him once again.

'Two,' yelled Mo, 'three, four, five, six.'

'I'll call you every day,' I told her, but she shook her head.

'That's OK. I'm not sure where I'll be. I'll give you my cell number in case of an emergency, otherwise I'll call you to fix a time for him to come back.'

'I'll call the Fresh Air people,' I said.

'Oh, I trust you,' she said, smiling. 'Let's keep this between ourselves.'

I was so pleased by her words that I felt a momentary pang of raw guilt at the way I was deceiving her – because of course what she didn't know was that Mo would be seeing his father. But that would be for the best – for Mo – in the long run. Wouldn't it?

The arrival of a bus approaching the Fifth Avenue stop spurred Anna into action. She kissed Mo hurriedly on the top of his head, mouthed *One week and then we'll see. Call me* at me and then disappeared up the steps

292

and into the bus.

And I was left to ponder the consequences of my actions. Had I done the right thing? And would I be able to cope now Noreen was no longer around to help me out?

As Mo and I walked towards Scott and Suzette's apartment building, I prayed it would be Pedro and not Marty on doorman duty. Marty always looked at my shoes as if he could tell from their cheap leather that I was a fraud, that I didn't belong there. And how he would react to my being accompanied by Mo, I simply could not imagine.

I had parked the car in a nearby garage before meeting Anna and now I retrieved my overnight bag from it. Pedro – *thank God!* – greeted me like a long-lost friend and escorted me to the elevator, engaging in a mock fist fight with a delighted Mo along the way.

'Mrs Abernathy just arrived,' he told me, 'I just took her upstairs five minutes ago.'

Oh shit! I didn't want to stay there with Suzette. But I couldn't very well turn round and leave.

'Does she know I'm going to be there?'

'Oh sure. She's happy. Eliza, she's happy too. Ain't she grown?'

Oh, so *Franny* was here. That was different, but I wondered why she hadn't mentioned to me that she was coming in.

I stepped out of the elevator into the foyer

of the apartment and gasped. It was the first time I had been there since Scott and Suzette had taken up residence. I wondered if my mother had witnessed the total annihilation of her earlier redecoration. Before, the foyer had been a library with floor to ceiling bookshelves lining the walls. Now they were stark white and displayed huge blown-up black and white photographs of Suzette. She pouted, blew kisses, winked and smiled at me no matter where I looked.

I dropped my bag. 'Franny!' I yelled.

A maid scuttled through the swing door that led from the kitchen.

'Miss Franny in her room. You want lunch, Miss?'

'Lee,' I said, wondering if she was searching for my name. 'No thanks. Actually, wait a second. Could you maybe make a sandwich for Mo here?'

'OK,' she said. 'You want to come with me into the kitchen?'

Mo was gazing at the opulence surrounding him in total disbelief but he allowed himself to be gently ushered through the swing door into the kitchen by the maid.

I wandered down the long corridor – more pictures of Suzette, some with Scott – to the suite of guest rooms. Eliza trotted out and patted her little hands against my shins until I picked her up. Franny was stepping out of her jeans when I walked in. A chic linen shift

294

was laid out on the bed.

'Go find Mo,' I told Eliza. 'He's in the kitchen.' I escorted her back along the corridor and saw her safely through the swing door, before returning to Franny.

'Why didn't you tell me you were coming in?' I asked. 'We could have travelled in together.'

'I didn't want to have to make the detour out to JFK. Anyway, you had an agenda with Mo, right?'

'I was supposed to hand him over to his mother, yes.'

'You mean you didn't?' She looked up at me.

I nodded. 'Sure. But then I took him back again. He's here having a sandwich in the kitchen.'

She stared at me. 'Are you out of your mind?'

I didn't elaborate. Instead I asked her, 'How come you never told me you were in touch with his mother?'

Franny looked at me, genuinely astonished. 'Why should I keep you informed of who I talk to on the phone?'

There was something about her tone that irked me. 'Probably because *I* was the one taking care of her son.'

'But he was *our* Fresh Air kid,' she responded.

'So how come you never took any notice

of him?'

'Are you judging me, by any chance?' She straightened up and faced me in her underwear. *Lingerie*, I noticed. Sexy, flirty, lacy lingerie.

'Yes, I am.' I was getting angry. 'You never once took that kid to the beach, cooked him a meal, entertained him in any way. What in the world would you have done if I hadn't been there?'

'But you're so good at it,' she was almost taunting me now. 'It must thrill you that kids love you so much. I hope you don't have plans for tonight because Eliza's really looking forward to spending time with you. I was going to have the maid watch her but now you're—'

'Like she hasn't spent much time with me recently.' I was having a hard time controlling my temper. 'Like you haven't been leaving her with me at every opportunity. Why are you getting all dressed up? Where are you *going*, Franny?'

'You don't need to know. I'll be on my cell if you need me.' For a second, she disappeared from view as she slipped her dress over her head.

I lost it. I intended to grip her by the upper arms and confront her face on but I was too forceful and as her head emerged from the dress, she lost her balance and fell back on the bed.

'Tell me where you're going.' I towered over her. 'Tell me what's going on with you. Ever since you got back from Paris, you've been acting weird. You're just so–' I searched for the word– *'ungracious.* You know, Rufus told Noreen that you weren't adapting to–' I stopped, aware I'd said too much.

Franny rolled off the bed and onto her feet, advancing on me. 'Adapting to *what?* To our ridiculous marriage? To being a stupid chatelaine? You want to know where I'm going right now? Well, I'll tell you. I'm going to meet a man with whom I can have some *fun!*'

'You're going to *what?* Who is he?'

'He's someone I used to know. I ran into him in Paris. He was at that ritzy hotel Rufus booked us into, the one where we stayed while Eliza recovered from her ear infection.'

With anyone else, the words *someone I used to know* would be relatively innocent. But Franny had a past. Years ago, way before she had got together with Rufus, when she had been living in the city and struggling to raise her son by an earlier relationship, she had dated men for money. As someone had pointed out to me, you could argue it wasn't a lot different in regular relationships where the man showered the woman with gifts of expensive jewellery, clothes or foreign travel except that it was never actually stated that it was in exchange for sex. But, as far as I had been able to determine, Franny had received money *and* an extensive wardrobe, which I had discovered one day while snooping in her old apartment above the country store that she once ran. I had no idea whether or not Rufus knew about this former life of hers. I had urged her to tell him about it. Given what Noreen had told me about Rufus contemplating running for some kind of public office, details of his wife's past could be dynamite in the wrong hands.

'Oh God, take that prudish look off your face. I'm not *sleeping* with him,' she said. But the words *not yet* hung in the air.

'Are you insane?' I yelled at her. 'Did you think that being married to Rufus would mean the two of you would get to hang out at the beach all day? Get real, Franny! You ought to be relieved that Rufus is taking his role as husband and father in such a responsible fashion. Have you even talked to him about how you feel? Don't you realise how much he needs you? He knows you've had to make big changes in your life – but he has too.'

'By marrying me?' she said. 'By marrying the local tramp who's going to let him down? Well, if he didn't have this sudden ambition to raise his goddamn profile in the goddamn community, he might still be at the level he was when I married him. Back then I could handle it. Now I'm not so sure I want to. I don't do respectable, Lee. He should have known that when he married me. And anyway,' she glared at me, 'who are you to lecture me? You've been married barely a month and suddenly you're the expert?'

I didn't respond and Franny's eyes flashed in satisfaction.

'What exactly is it that you did to make Tommy walk out on you while you guys were on your honeymoon?' she said. 'And you're telling *me* I should talk to my husband. Why don't you practise what you preach on your own?'

'But what about Eliza?' I said.

'What about her?' said Franny. 'I already gave her some lunch and she likes a snack and a drink mid-afternoon and her supper is in the fridge. You can skip her bath and maybe put her down around eight?' She was deliberately misunderstanding me and it was all I needed to push me over the top.

'I am *not* watching Eliza one more second for you,' I said. 'She's your responsibility. I'm leaving.'

'Wait till you have your own,' Franny yelled after me. 'If you ever do. Bet you won't want to spend every single second with–'

But I was down the hall and through the swing door into the kitchen – *Come on, Mo, we're leaving, bring your sandwich with you –* and picking up my bag and summoning the elevator and I couldn't hear Franny any more. At least not consciously, but inside my head her remarks about Tommy walking out on me were sounding loud and clear.

I went back to the car and sat in the underground car park in a slump. Behind me, Mo was silent and I could tell he was scared by my abrupt change of mood. He sat nervously shuffling Wyn's business cards in his lap.

'Give me those,' I said suddenly. 'It's OK,' I added as he handed them over. 'I'm not mad at you.'

I picked up the top one. Wynton P Moses. Executive Editor. Below was his mobile phone number and, surprisingly, another number. I fished my own mobile phone out of my bag and dialled it out of curiosity.

'Good afternoon. Grand Central Publishing. How may I direct your call?'

'Editorial.'

'Which name in Editorial?'

'Wynton Moses.'

There was a long pause. After a while she came back. 'I have no Wynton Moses in Editorial.'

What a surprise! 'Could you put me through to Human Resources please?' I said.

When they answered, I asked if they had anyone working for the company by the name of Wynton Moses – and no, I didn't know his social. This time I was put on hold for quite some time and then I was told something that confirmed what Anna had told me.

'We had a Wynton Moses until last month. A Wynton *P.* Moses. He was one of our janitors.'

As I drove home along the Long Island Expressway with Mo slumped, fast asleep, I pictured what must have happened. Wyn would take Mo with him to the offices for which he was the janitor, going in at the end of the day when there was no one there, when he could pretend to his seven-year-old son that one of the big executive offices was his.

But whatever Mo's mother had said about her ex-husband, one thing was clear to me. Mo loved Wyn, he looked up to him, was proud of who he thought his father was. Until he was old enough to understand why his father had done what he had done, I couldn't expose Wyn's sham of a life.

When I reached Southampton and drove past Shane Sobel's car lot, I wondered once again about him and Patsy Brooks. I decided to make a pit stop at Patsy's house before going home. Mainly because I didn't really feel I could call it 'home' after my showdown with Franny. I didn't know how I was going to handle her – and Rufus – from now on and I wanted to delay my return for as long as possible.

When I saw the glimpse of yellow through the woods as I approached the turn-off to Patsy's house, I assumed it was a field of rape I had managed to overlook before, or maybe even an exotic bird.

But when I emerged from the trees and turned the corner into the sandy road, my access was blocked by a sawhorse and I saw that the yellow was a line of tape with the words *Police Line – Do Not Cross*. Beyond it, several police cars were parked along Patsy's road and I could see flashing lights up at the house itself.

Mo had woken up and I told him to stay put as I got out of my car and began to walk up the road, dodging in and out of the police cars. I was almost at the house before an officer noticed me and began to walk towards me with his hand up. But then, behind him, I saw Eileen. I waved at her.

She came over before the officer could stop her. 'They won't let you in. It's a crime scene,' she said.

'What's happened? Why have they allowed you to be here?'

'Because I called them. I found the body.'

'The *body?* Whose body?'

'That car dealer's. Shane Sobel, lying in Patsy's bed in a pool of blood. His head had been smashed in and Patsy's nowhere to be found.'

302

Chapter Twelve

'Shane Sobel is *dead?*' I advanced upon Eileen. 'But I just saw him a few hours ago. He can't be dead.'

When he heard what I said, the cop who had halted me in the driveway went back in the house and returned seconds later, followed by a man who walked with a distinct limp. He was overweight with a square open face and what I called 'twinkly' eyes. Small eyes in a chubby face could either be 'piggy' or 'twinkly' in my book, depending on whether their owner was prone to smiling or frowning. Detective Bill McCoy, as he introduced himself, was the smiling kind.

'Officer Eaton just told me you said you saw Mr Sobel a few hours ago,' he said. His face was sweating, I noticed. Probably because it was at least ninety degrees and he was wearing a sports jacket and tailored trousers in what looked to be not very light material. Then, as an afterthought, he asked, 'Why are you here?' And a beat after that, 'Who are you?'

'Is he dead?' If he wanted me to answer his questions, he'd have to answer a few of mine.

'Oh, he's dead all right,' said Eileen. She

303

was in a state of high excitement, her cheeks flushed, her eyes dancing, almost as if she was enjoying her involvement. 'I think he was dead when I arrived. I called out to Patsy and when there was no answer – usually she's right there waiting for me in the kitchen with a pot of tea – I went looking for her. When I walked into the bedroom, there he was, lying on his side in Patsy's bed with his head bashed in, blood all over the pillow. His ear was just a mass of what looked like dark-red glue, flies buzzing everywhere because the bug screen was open. We think she used a hammer, don't we, Bill?' She appealed to Detective McCoy.

I saw him react slightly to the 'Bill'.

'And from what I saw,' Eileen went on, 'maybe she used the fork end as well as the blunt. His eye was pretty much gouged out.'

I must have looked at her in sheer horror because she calmed down a little.

'Anyway,' she said, 'the hammer wasn't where it's supposed to be. When they went down to the basement to look around, I saw right away it had gone. She keeps a whole lot of handy tools hanging from hooks on the inside of the door to the basement. So that had to be what she used, right, Bill?'

He didn't comment, but I saw the 'twinklers' signal to Officer Eaton and then Officer Eaton stepped forward and led Eileen back into the house.

'She found him?' I said it automatically. Eileen was clearly made of stronger stuff than I was. If I had come upon the body of a man with his head smashed in, I would have been in no condition to hold a normal conversation.

'Sounds like it,' said Bill McCoy and I suppressed a nervous smile. 'So can we start over? Maybe with your name this time. No one's told me who you are.'

'Nathalie Bartholomew,' I said. 'I'm a writer and I'm working with Patsy Brooks on her autobiography.'

'She's writing her autobiography?' He sounded surprised. 'She's British, like you, is that right?'

I nodded.

'So is she big in England? In some way we don't know about over here? Name Patsy Brooks doesn't mean anything special to anyone, nobody I've spoken to so far knows her for anything other than a woman who lives in the city and uses this house in the summer. I mean, how come she gets to do her autobiography?'

Eileen hadn't told them who Patsy really was. Or rather who she wasn't. Well, until Patsy turned up and told them herself, or until someone in the city set them straight, I'd keep quiet on that front too. I looked at Bill McCoy and shrugged and grinned. *Who knew why people did such things?* 'It takes all sorts,' I said. 'I'm a professional ghostwriter. If someone wants to tell their story and they're not a born writer, they hire me to help them do it.'

'More people ought to hire you,' he said and, despite my unease at being so close to the scene of a murder, this time I didn't bother to hide my amusement. I liked this guy.

'Did you have an appointment with her this afternoon?' he asked me.

'No. As a matter of fact I came over here to try and fix a schedule with her. We need to get to grips with the work on her book. I guess I should have called first.'

'Probably best if someone's going to get themselves killed in her house right when you want to fix a meeting.' He glanced at me. 'So how come you saw Shane Sobel earlier today?'

'I've already been into Manhattan and back. I took my mother-in-law to JFK and on the way there we stopped at a petrol station so she could go to the bathroom. Shane Sobel's car dealership was right next door. While I was waiting for my mother-in-law, he and I got talking.'

'Why?' said Bill McCoy.

'Why what?'

'Why did you and he talk? Were you looking to buy a car?'

'No, I–' I stopped. Of course the reason I

306

had engineered a conversation with Shane Sobel was relevant to Detective McCoy's questioning. I began to explain about having seen Shane Sobel's Jaguar coming out of Patsy's driveway early in the morning that time and at that point Bill McCoy got out a pad and pen and began scribbling. As I told him about how I'd alerted Shane Sobel to the fact that I knew about not only Patsy but also his relationship with Holly Bennett, I wandered up and down and McCoy followed me, sweating all the more, his limp becoming pronounced.

Finally he stopped and leaned against a police car and waited until I wandered back to him. 'I'd be much obliged if you'd stay in one place.' His voice sounded faintly testy. 'I'm having hip surgery in a week or so. So you went to JFK – I'll need the flight number and your mother-in-law's details – and then into Manhattan. Who did you see there? Names and contact details please, and the times you were there. What time did you leave home this morning? And where are you staying?'

'Do you always get everything backwards?' I asked him.

'Pretty much.' He laughed.

This time I was unable to join him. Try as I might, the vision of Shane Sobel's blood and gore was growing in my imagination, creeping in when I least expected it.

Bill McCoy saw my face.

'Hey,' he said, 'lighten up.'

'*Lighten up?* You're telling me to *lighten up* and there's a person lying back there who had the fork of a hammer plunged into his eye and he probably saw it coming at him and–' I stopped abruptly, aware that I was making myself feel even worse. 'I suppose you see this sort of thing every day.'

'Not every day,' said Bill McCoy gently. 'So, when you're ready. What time did you see Shane Sobel in Southampton and what time did you leave him?'

'Let's start with where I'm staying,' I said. 'Rufus and Franny Abernathy's house on Cross Highway to Devon and we left there this morning at eight o'clock.'

'You're staying with Roof?' Bill McCoy smiled. 'Good for you.'

'You know him?'

'Since high school. He was in my little brother's class. Kept it on the down low that he was one of the richest kids in school but my brother once went for a sleep-over and came back with his eyes out on stalks. *They got their own movie theatre!* We were all pretty amazed when Rufus married Franny Cook, but I guess that shows you just what a down-to-earth kind of guy he really is. Coming from all that money didn't make him any different from the rest of us. You tell him I said Hi.'

I said 'Sure' but as Bill McCoy continued to question me, it was clear my association with Rufus in no way mitigated his need to eliminate me from his investigation. By the time we were done, one thing was clear: following our talk at his car lot, Shane Sobel must have gone directly to Patsy's house.

'Eileen McIntosh says she never knew Patsy Brooks and Shane Sobel were an item. She was acting pretty surprised about it when we got here.' Bill McCoy looked at me.

'Like she wasn't surprised to find him dead in Patsy's bed?' I said.

'Well, that too, but she's managed to overcome her shock to make herself an invaluable part of our investigation.'

The way he said *invaluable* told me what he thought of Eileen's involvement and I laughed. 'I guess she's only trying to help,' I said.

'So what about you? Did you know about Patsy and Shane Sobel before you saw his car leave her premises? Did you ever speak to her about him?'

'No,' I said. 'To tell you the truth I was going to ask her about him today.'

'But you knew Holly Bennett?'

'No, I didn't but I was indirectly involved with her murder.' I explained about Mo's abduction. 'Tell me, do you think Patsy killed Shane Sobel?'

Bill McCoy looked sceptical. 'The guy's

309

barely been dead half a day. I'm not ruling anything out. Maybe she's just out shopping. Maybe she went to the city. But it sounds like she doesn't go far without telling Eileen McIntosh, so the sooner she shows up and clears her name, the better it's going to look for her.'

'Am I free to go?'

'You're free to go,' he repeated, obviously amused by my use of the phrase. 'But I'd be much obliged if you didn't leave without giving someone your phone number – although I suppose I can always get a hold of you care of Rufus.'

I gave Officer Eaton my mobile number and went to tell Eileen I was leaving.

'I'll come with you,' she said. 'They won't let me do any cleaning. I might as well go home. Who's that?' she asked me as she looked down Patsy's overgrown driveway to my car where Mo was talking to a police officer.

'He's called Mo,' I said. 'He's the Fresh Air kid who was taken instead of Keshawn, the one who was held at Gwen Bennett's house.'

'Right,' said Eileen softly. 'How could anyone mistake him for Keshawn? They still didn't find the girl who took him. Wasn't he able to tell them what happened at the house?'

'He gave the police a description of the girl,' I said.

'Did he see anybody else?' Eileen asked.

I shook my head. 'Once he was locked in a bedroom he couldn't see a thing. He just heard what happened, that's all. Come say hello to him. I'm taking care of him for the next week or so and I may have to bring him with me when I come to work with Patsy.'

I said this off the top of my head as I realised I hadn't thought far enough ahead to figure out what I was going to do with Mo while I worked. It would be interesting to get Eileen's reaction.

'Och, Patsy wouldn't want that,' she said firmly, walking away from me to her car. 'I'd leave him at home if I were you.'

Who with? I thought, discouraged by her response.

I was climbing into my car when Bill McCoy came after us, hobbling out of the house, wincing in pain each time his left foot impacted on the ground.

'Wait up. Be much obliged if you'd come back for five minutes. There's something I just heard on her answering machine I want you to listen to.'

'Stay here, I won't be much longer,' I instructed Mo and followed Bill McCoy and Eileen back into the kitchen where he went to an answering machine – white, naturally – that was half hidden behind the telephone. I was horribly aware of the open door to the bedroom at the end of the long

311

corridor, and that behind it lay the bloodied and battered body of Shane Sobel. I was in awe of the fact that Eileen had been able to study it long enough to be able to describe it in detail.

Bill McCoy pressed PLAY. After the click, a high-pitched female voice began to speak, sounding very young with every sentence going up at the end as if asking a question.

'Hi, this is a message for Patience Brook O'Reilly?' There was a slight gasp and then the message continued. 'Oops! I should call you Patsy, right? My name is Rachel? And this is my first day as Joel Krickstein's assistant? He'd like you to call him back on 212–'

'What's that all about?' said Bill McCoy.

'Joel Krickstein's her producer at the network,' said Eileen.

'I'll need more than that,' said McCoy, 'what's with the Patience Brook O'Reilly and what does she have to do with a network?'

Eileen told him. He looked at me. 'You knew about this?' I nodded. 'And you were planning to tell me when?' He sounded weary, as if he were used to being given the runaround when trying to elicit information. But then maybe it was just his hip wearing him out.

When Eileen and I looked at each other, each waiting for the other to answer, he said, 'OK, we'll get into this later. You guys can leave. Much obliged.'

'Wait a second,' I said. Bill McCoy looked at me. 'There's something else,' I said. 'Did anyone take a look in the drawer of her nightstand?'

'I guess they did,' said McCoy, 'I'll check. Why? If anything of importance to the investigation had been found, I'd know about it.'

'Patsy kept a gun in one of the drawers by her bed,' I said.

'How would you know a thing like that?' Eileen gripped my arm.

'She sent me to get something from there once and I saw it,' I answered truthfully.

'Wait here,' said Bill McCoy and disappeared into Patsy's bedroom. 'It's not there – and nobody's found a gun,' he said when he returned.

'That means she's armed,' said Eileen quickly. 'And dangerous!'

'As I said before, ladies, you can go,' said McCoy, and I could see he was growing tired of Eileen's propensity for melodrama. I didn't need telling twice, but Eileen wasn't finished. I walked to my car listening to her calling to Bill McCoy – *but don't you need me to...*

There was nothing left for me to do but drive Mo back to Rufus' and Franny's in a somewhat disgruntled state. I had wanted to quiz Eileen about where she thought Patsy might have gone. I was aware of the impact Shane Sobel's death in Patsy's house might have on our book. But then, I asked myself almost immediately, would there even be a book with Patsy seemingly on the run for murder? Not unless I caught up with her before the police did.

'Why were the police there?' Mo asked me every five minutes.

'I guess they were just keeping an eye on the place,' I lied, 'it's pretty far back in the woods.' I didn't want to tell him about the murder.

Mo didn't buy it. 'I know there's trouble there,' he said, watching me closely as I drove. 'The cop who was talking to me, he said I shouldn't go inside the house, I'd be scared. Was there a real monster there?'

'Kind of,' I said. 'Just forget about it, OK, Mo?'

I had almost forgotten my altercation with Franny until I walked into the house and heard Rufus on the phone with her.

'I would have been happy to discuss it with you, Franny, but every time I tell myself today is the day I'm going to sit down with my wife and talk about where we're going with our lives, you shoot off to the city. How about discussing *that* with me?'

He saw me and waved, holding the phone to his chest for a second.

'Hi, Lee. You saw Franny when you were

in the city,' he mouthed at me.

I nodded. 'There's been a murder,' I mouthed back at him, turning away from Mo so he wouldn't see.

It was so unrelated to what he had asked me that he looked startled for a second, as if he thought maybe it was Franny who had been murdered. He said 'Franny, you there?' as if he were checking she was still alive and, when she answered, he told her 'Look, gotta go. Get back here soon, would you?'

He pointed the receiver at me a little sheepishly before replacing it.

'I guess you heard some of that and I guess you must have worked out while you've been here that Franny and I are having a few problems. But listen, who got killed?'

I signalled to him with my eyes not to say any more, standing behind Mo and pointing at him. I turned on the TV on the kitchen counter and picked Mo up and put him on a stool in front of it. I gave him the remote and told him to search for the cartoon channel. Then I took Rufus by the arm and drew him to the other end of the twenty-foot kitchen.

I told him everything that had happened at Patsy's. 'Jesus!' said Rufus. 'Shane Sobel! That guy's pretty well known around these parts. Sounds like someone really had it in for him. I guess the police were swarming all over it?' I told him about Bill McCoy and he smiled.

'Good old Bill. His brother Bobby and I were like that in high school.' He crossed his index and middle finger. 'He still say "much obliged" all the time?'

'Yes,' I said, 'as a matter of fact, he does.'

'We teased him so bad. He must've picked it up from some old guy, but I tell you, the words *thank you* were just not part of his vocabulary, even when he was a kid. All he ever came out with was *much obliged*. And he was a detective back then too. If Bobby and I only got as far as *thinking* about smoking pot or telling his mom we were going somewhere when we weren't, Bill was onto us. So who does he figure killed Shane Sobel?'

'I don't think he's got that far yet, but it's not looking good for Patsy. Or for Patience Brook O'Reilly.'

'Or for progress on your book?'

'Well, if it doesn't happen, it doesn't happen,' I said, trying to sound philosophical. 'Won't be the first time I've had to abandon something before completion. Although in this case it would be before we'd even got started. You planning on getting back on your Harley?' I asked, pointing to a motorcycle helmet and a leather biker's jacket on a chair. A few years ago, the lost days that Franny mourned, Rufus had gone everywhere on his Harley-Davidson Fat Boy, a name that had always made me smile.

'They're Sid's,' he said. 'He left them here, along with his bike. It's out there in our garage, keeping my Fat Boy company.'

'Well I don't know about the bike, but I'd be happy to take the jacket and the helmet over to him at the cabin,' I said. 'I'd like to get his take on Shane Sobel's murder. He's pretty tight with the police around here, as you probably know. Would you have any problem with my doing that – given, you know, what's happened?'

'No problem at all,' said Rufus, 'if he were still here. But he's gone, Lee. He's left town, taken Minnie with him. You didn't know?'

I was stunned for a second.

'You mean left the area? Not just the cabin? But why?'

Rufus shrugged. 'Scott fired him, I guess. I'm feeling pretty bad about the whole thing. I told Scott about what we'd seen – at the cabin, you know, with Minnie. I thought it would make him laugh, but the next thing I hear is he's told the guy who runs his security detail to let Sid go. Turns out it's not totally unwarranted. Sid was supposed to be part of the team on duty that day. Sounds like Minnie's really turned him inside out – but even so, *firing* him wasn't my idea.'

'Suzette's, I imagine,' I said without thinking.

'Now why would you say *that?*' Rufus

sounded annoyed. 'Franny's been winding you up about her, hasn't she? If my wife can't blame *me* for something, she blames Suzette.'

'Why do you keep calling Franny *my wife?*' I said. 'It's almost as though you have to keep reminding yourself that's what she is.'

'Well, if she were here a bit more, I might remember,' said Rufus, and he wasn't smiling. 'I just don't get it, Lee. She's ten years older than I am but *she's* the one who resents the fact that I'm finally starting to act like a responsible adult. What's with her? Is she regretting her own lost youth?'

'It's more than that, Rufus,' I said. 'She's uncomfortable with the fact that she's now a pretty well-off woman. It just doesn't come easily for her. Remember, you used to be that way yourself.'

Rufus looked a little shocked by my candour, then he nodded. 'You're right. I was embarrassed, running around with all the kids my age who had so little. But I can't understand why she's so freaked out around *me?* I keep trying to talk to her about how I want to come to terms with my wealth and use it to do something worthwhile. I was the one who suggested we take on a Fresh Air kid. Had to talk her into it. By the way, what's he doing here? I thought you went into the city to hand him back to his mother.'

'That's another story,' I said, 'let's get back to Franny–'

'And another thing,' he said before I could get any further, 'she's really got it in for Suzette. I guess she resents the fact that Suzette seems to have no problem dealing with *her* wealth.'

'Anyway, Suzette's got problems of her own,' I said, thinking of what Patsy had told me about her guilt over her grown-up son. 'It's probably because she's so spoiled.'

'She is NOT!' I was stunned by the vehemence of Rufus' reply. 'How can you say that, Lee? Like you've spent so much time around her, you really know what makes her tick? She can be a real sweetheart and, I tell you, I've got a lot of time for her. My brother's a much better person since he met her and while you may not share her taste in clothes or whatever, she is who she is. All that tacky publicity, it's part of her job, she can't help it. It's what she signed on for. She does the best she can.'

'But Franny's always said—'

'Who cares what Franny always said? She doesn't speak for me. And no, Suzette was not instrumental in firing Sid.' He shook his head. 'Oh no. That was definitely Scott's idea. Suzette always had a soft spot for Sid. She took an interest in his life and he appreciated it. You have to understand, Lee, that Suzette comes from a pretty humble background and what I like about her is the way she appreciates all that her high earn-

319

ings have brought her. She's never forgotten where she comes from but she's worked hard at adjusting to her wealth. Matter of fact,' he gave me one of his rueful looks, 'she could surely teach my wife a thing or two.'

I didn't say anything because all of this was a bit of a revelation. Then, after a second, I gave him a tentative smile. 'OK, so I got it wrong. I'm sorry. And if I can stay with Franny for just a second longer, you should know that she and I had a bit of a falling out when we ran into each other in the city. It'll sort itself out but, in the meantime, I think I'd better move out before she gets back.'

He grinned at me. 'She mentioned it, believe it or not. Might as well tell you, first thing she said when I called her: *Tell your friend Lee to keep her goddamned nose out of our marriage.* I'm not going to ask what that was all about and you're not going to tell me, but now that you've brought it up, I'm going to say, yes, if you could give us a bit of space, that would probably be best. But you don't have to go far. The pool house is empty now and, while I think of it, so is the cabin. How about going back to your old haunt for a while?'

A few weeks earlier this would have sounded like a dream come true, but I'd seen what Sid had done to the cabin, how he had infused it with his loneliness and bitterness.

'Is Sid's stuff still there?'

'Well, he didn't have much,' said Rufus, 'and Scott went down to take a look and said he's taken it all with him. All he left behind were some motivational books and his gym equipment because I guess even he couldn't pick that up and take it with him on a plane. That and his bike, of course.'

I thought of the weight-lifting machines and shuddered. I had a fleeting image of sleeping there and waking up in the middle of the night and seeing them looming over me like monstrous instruments of torture.

'I think I'll pass on the cabin,' I said, 'but if Mo and I could bed down at the pool house, that would be great. I'll go pack my bags.'

'*Mo* and you? What's going on, Lee?'

I began to gabble. 'It was his mother's idea. She asked if he could spend another week out here. I know I should have checked with you first but I just couldn't help it. He's had such a great time this past week and I just couldn't stand the thought of him having to go back to that concrete world. And I need to spend time around a kid if I'm ever going to think of having one of my own and–'

'And his dad's out here,' said Rufus, giving me a shrewd look. 'Look, it's OK. As long as you're out here, he can be too. Who knows, maybe we'll even get my wi– maybe we'll even get Franny to spend some time with him if she ever comes home. So give me a shout when you're ready and I'll run you guys and your bags down to the pool house in my truck,' said Rufus. 'And hey,' he said after a beat, 'give me a hug to show there's no hard feelings. We're "brother" and "sister", you and me, and it's going to stay that way, Franny or no Franny.'

I felt a twinge of superstition. He shouldn't have said the words *or no Franny*. He shouldn't have even entertained the notion. But I kept my alarm to myself when I hugged him.

Just as I made no comment about the massive plantings that were being implemented all over the property as we passed them half an hour later on the way to the pool house. My mother, I thought grimly, had certainly left her mark.

I was exhausted by the events of the last few hours and once I'd unpacked, fixed Mo some spaghetti and put him to bed, I sat mindlessly watching TV until it was time to fall asleep myself. But the next morning all I could think about was Shane Sobel and Patsy and wonder where she might have gone. I wanted to see Eileen McIntosh, but I didn't have her number so I called Rufus and asked him to get it from Suzette, pretending I wanted Eileen to come in and blitz the pool house after the invasion by Minnie and Shagger and Mo. Noreen, of course, had created so little disturbance, you would never know she had been there.

'What about Lucia?' was his first response.

'I'll square it with her,' I promised. 'Franny has always made it clear that Lucia has enough on her plate taking care of you guys up there. She'll probably be thrilled not to have to worry about clearing up our mess, but if there's even a hint of my having put her nose out of joint, I'll send Eileen packing.'

When he came back with the number a few minutes later, I called Eileen and was heartened by her enthusiasm at my call. And, as it turned out, she had something for me.

'And here I was thinking I'd have to go back to Patsy's to look up your number,' she said. 'You see Patsy left you a wee CD. I heard her talking to herself and I went into the kitchen and said, "You know what they say? First sign of madness." But she wasn't talking to herself, she was *recording* a message for you. So you get yerself here, lassie, so I can hand it over.'

There was the small problem of what to do with Mo, but as it turned out he came up with the ideal solution himself. *When am I going to see my dad?*

My first instinct was to say *No way*. Wyn would come and pick Mo up and that might be the last I would see of him. And then what would I say to Anna? But the more I thought about it – and it was clear Mo was going to keep on my case – the more I knew that one of the reasons I had agreed to bring Mo back with me was so that he could see more of his father. I had imagined that I would always be there too, but I realised there would come a time when I had to trust Wyn to do the right thing.

And that time was now. I called him on his mobile.

'Don't ask any questions,' I said when he answered, 'just know that I have Mo with me and he wants to see you. When can you come get him?'

'I'll be there in ten minutes,' he said and he was, careering down the trail to the pool house in his truck and pulling up in a cloud of dust.

'Can I keep him for the night?' he asked and I saw Mo's face light up in expectation.

I stalled before answering. Could I trust him not to disappear with Mo?

'You can,' I said slowly, 'but just don't let the police see you with him.' I looked at him meaningfully and he nodded. 'And when you bring him back tomorrow you and I are going to have a little talk.'

'We are?' he said, eyeing me warily. 'What about?'

'About your career – or careers, plural. Mo showed me all your business cards. So tomorrow, I want to hear all about it.'

I looked at him but he avoided my eyes. And then, once he'd bundled Mo into his truck and taken off again, I had another momentary pang of unease. *What if he didn't bring Mo back?*

Eileen lived in a bungalow right on the highway between Amagansett and East Hampton. It was one of half a dozen identical bungalows all joined together and I had the impression the place had once been a motel. Little waist-high walls divided the tiny yards in front of the houses and when I rang her doorbell, yapping came from inside.

Eileen opened the door with a Scots terrier under her arm who was struggling to be released. As I made to step into the house, she pointed to my feet with her free hand, a shocked expression on her face.

'Shoes off, please, while you're in the house.'

I saw the row of trainers and outdoor shoes neatly lined up by the door and slipped off my flip-flops. The dog continued barking as I stepped into the room and I saw that he had to contend with Barbara Walters. Eileen was watching *The View* with the sound turned right up and the noise was deafening.

'Wait a second while I change the channel and then he'll be quiet. He likes *Animal Planet*, don't you, Brock?' She put him down on the floor in front of the giant screen. 'Come in the back, Lee, and we'll have a cup

325

of tea.'

'Have you heard from her?' I asked as I looked around what appeared to be an exact replica of Patsy's kitchen – same white cabinets and appliances, toaster, blender, pots and pans and everything pin neat and placed just so. A small white radio blared BAB, a rock music station and I wondered why Eileen needed to surround herself with loud noise coming at her from all directions. I must have been frowning at the radio because she turned it off with a precise click.

'She's gone,' Eileen said definitively. 'She's not coming back and it's because I have *not* heard from her that I know that to be the truth.' She pronounced it *terooth*, her Scots accent surfacing for a second. 'At first I thought maybe she'd just gone out to the shops but when I saw the hammer was missing, I knew she'd done something terrible.'

'You really think she killed him?' I was seriously shocked that she appeared to suggest this.

'I don't know what to think,' she said, 'but, below the surface, she's not the bonnie lassie she appears. She's got *issues*.'

'She told me about the time she took the baby,' I said, hoping to prompt Eileen into further revelation.

'Aye,' said Eileen, 'I thought she would. It's why she wanted to do that damn book in the first place. So you can see she's capable of letting a screw go loose in her head when she wants. It's my fault,' she added and I jolted my head up to look at her.

'*Your* fault? What is your fault?'

'I told her about Holly Bennett and Shane Sobel. I was just gossiping, like you do. Patsy's more like my closest girlfriend than my employer. I'd never want to hurt her. I never meant to make her jealous.'

'But you told Detective McCoy you didn't know about Patsy and Shane Sobel.'

That surprised her. 'He told you that? What else he say about me?'

'Well, did you know?'

'Not for certain, but I had my suspicions she'd got someone coming round. Not much gets past me.'

Brock suddenly scampered into the kitchen and slurped some water from his bowl, his dripping mouth leaving a trail of puddles. Eileen swooped with a paper towel and, as I watched her, I imagined Patsy having such a person monitoring her every move. I had an awful thought. *Having Eileen McIntosh picking up after you, wherever you went, it was enough to drive a person to murder.*

'But that Irish detective, I only told him the bare minimum. And he doesn't know about this CD.' She opened a drawer and took it out.

'Have you listened to it?' I asked.

'Only for long enough to know it was the

one she meant for you. It wasn't marked, see? Normally she labelled them religiously before she gave them to me to pack up for Mr Fedex. That's how she worked. Two hours on the phone and then a follow-up CD – suckers all over the world hanging on every word she said.'

She was talking of Patsy in the past tense, I noted. *Worked. Labelled.* I took the CD and slipped it into my purse. I was feeling increasingly uncomfortable in Eileen's claustrophobic kitchen. I wasn't quite sure what I had expected from Eileen McIntosh but somehow I had imagined it would all be a little less doom laden.

I stood up to go and Brock trotted up to me and sniffed me as I passed through the living room. I wondered how Eileen dealt with the mess his muddy paws must make when it was raining. She couldn't very well say, *Shoes off, Brock.*

I turned to say goodbye, totally unprepared for the way she suddenly gripped my arm and laid her head on my shoulder. I tried not to flinch. 'Eileen, what's wrong?' I said as I saw the tears welling in her eyes.

'Whatever it sounds like, I love her. I really do. We've been together a very long time. I just can't bear to think about what she might have done.'

'Eileen,' I said, looking her straight in the eye, 'do you think she'll get in touch with

328

you? Because if she does, you have to tell Detective McCoy.'

'No,' she said, 'she'll not get in touch. I know she won't. And I'll not tell that Irishman.'

'But you'll tell me?'

'Aye,' she said after a beat. 'Aye, I'll tell ye. But,' she cried after me as I crossed her little yard to my car, 'ye'll hear nothing because I told you – she's gone.'

What would happen to Eileen when they found Patsy and proved her guilty of Shane Sobel's murder? I asked myself. *Would she go back to England?* And then I shook myself because of course I meant *if* not *when*. But did I mean if they found Patsy or if she was convicted?

My mobile was beeping in the car where I'd left it and I listened to my messages before setting off.

Tommy's voice sounded extremely apprehensive.

'Mum arrived safely. Thought you'd like to know. She was exhausted, slept all the way home from the airport. I got her home, put her to bed and–' There was a pause and I could tell he was having difficulty getting the next bit out. 'The thing is, I've moved in with her, so I can keep an eye on her, you know?'

No, you haven't, Tommy, I thought wearily, *otherwise you'd have moved in with her a long*

329

time ago. You've gone there because we had a row, you're not sure where you stand with your wife so you're running home to your mother, you great big baby.

My next message was from Sid.

'You've probably heard by now that I've left town. I'm not sure how much longer I'm going to be kept in the loop about Holly Bennett's murder now I'm thousands of miles away in Portland, Oregon, but you asked me to keep in touch – so I just wanted to make sure you had my cell number.'

I scribbled it down and slotted Patsy's CD into the machine in the dash.

'Morning, Lee.' Her cheerful voice with its slight Lincolnshire accent resounded around the inside of the car and I reached to turn down the volume. 'I'm sitting in my kitchen waiting for Eileen and I thought I'd record a little message for you. I've been thinking about your situation and wondering what we can do about it.'

You and me both, I thought.

'So have you been saying your life affirmation? *I accept that I have finally married Tommy and I want to celebrate it.* Has it helped?'

Give me a break, I muttered to myself. But what she said next surprised me.

'My guess is you think it's a load of rubbish – but that's OK. People are often a bit sceptical at first. It takes time to change

330

your life. Lee, I'd like you to do something for me and you might be surprised at how much it helps you, so give it a chance, will you?'

I nodded, as if she were right there in the car with me.

'I'd like you to make a chart for me, a life chart. It's going to look like a big wheel with lots of spokes and each spoke is going to represent an aspect of your life. Family, career, money, fitness, health, your marriage. You label each spoke and at the end of it you give it a number out of ten based on how well you feel that aspect of your life is going. Don't think too hard, just do it. And then take a look at the numbers to see which area of your life needs changing. You can give me the results next time we meet.'

I wondered how far into the tape Eileen had listened, because to me it sounded as if Patsy expected to see me again very soon.

And even if she hadn't anticipated killing her lover and running away, surely someone who could be so thoughtful and caring as to record advice for me about *my* life would not be capable of ending someone else's – of committing murder.

Chapter Thirteen

I returned Tommy's call on Noreen's number, didn't get him and put the phone down following Noreen's quavering announcement requesting that I leave my number and speak slowly and clearly. I didn't want her to hear the message I planned to leave for her son, which would have none of its expletives deleted. Then I texted Tommy on his mobile. *Pse keep an i on hse. R U paying bills?* I half expected him to text back *What with?* And was mildly perturbed when all I received was total silence. I was a bit of a stickler for paying bills on time, but that was mostly because of my constant appreciation of how lucky we – a ghostwriter and an unemployed sound engineer – were to be living rent free in my parents' ultra-expensive home in one of the most expensive areas in London. Somebody had to deal with the running of Blenheim Crescent in their – and now my – absence, although I suppose I had been overly optimistic in assuming that person would be Tommy. Still, leaving a four-storey town house empty in the middle of Notting Hill was asking for trouble. I might as well put up an ad in Tesco's. CRACK DEN AVAIL-

ABLE IN BLENHEIM CRESCENT. KEY
UNDER FLOWER POT FOURTH STEP
FROM TOP.

Getting back to Sid was much more
rewarding.

'Hey, Lee, how's it going?' He sounded
relaxed and eminently cheerful for someone
who had just lost their job.

'I'm not really sure, Sid, tell you the truth.
I've had a row with Franny and I don't
know whether you know this but Shagger –
that's Minnie's–'

'Norman, yes. I heard,' Sid interrupted.
'He took off back to London.'

'And my husband went with him.'

'No shit? I'm sorry to hear that.' Sid
sounded genuinely upset. 'Minnie spoke to
Norman in London yesterday. He never
said anything about Tommy. But then it was
a pretty brief conversation. She was trying
to apologise, but Norman hung up on her.
Even her brothers won't take her call.
Seems like they've bonded with Norman.
What's that all about?'

I contemplated talking Sid through the
vicissitudes of Tottenham Hotspur FC and
decided it wasn't worth the effort. 'It's a
soccer thing, Sid. I wouldn't worry about it.
How is Minnie otherwise?'

'She's a joy in my life,' said Sid, not exactly
responding to what I'd asked, but there was
no mistaking the happiness in his voice.

'Where the hell are you, anyway?' I asked.

'Portland, Oregon. At this precise moment Minnie's out hitting the boutiques on Northwest 23rd Avenue, said she needed some jewellery.'

And who's paying for that? I wondered. I didn't even want to begin thinking about how he was going to handle his alimony and his son's college fees, let alone a high-maintenance little miss like Minnie. I only hoped Scott had given him some kind of severance package.

'And you didn't want to go along?'

'Not my responsibility. I'm in charge of keeping us fed,' he said. 'I do the cooking and the food shopping and I'm about to go to the farmers' market. Twice a week the farmers come from all over the state and set up stands to sell their produce right here in the middle of the city. It's a beautiful sight.'

'You've rented an apartment?' Another expense.

'Actually, no. I'm a very lucky man. Suzette got a hold of me before I left, said she appreciated my situation and when I told her I was going to Portland, she said right off the bat, *You could stay in Robby's dorm. He won't be there for another week.*' He chuckled. 'So that's where we are, living right on campus at Portland State. Brand new dorm building and we're high up on the seventh floor with a sensational view of the West Hills where all the rich people live. I look up at those houses, Lee, and I imagine I'm in one of 'em, looking back down over the top of my building at Mount Hood and Mount St Helen's. Must be awesome up there.'

'So you're staying at the dorm for free?' That was something.

'Just until I get my son Gary settled in. He gets here end of the week. I'm praying his mother doesn't decide to come with him. And of course we have to give the place up to Robby any day now. Until then, Minnie and me, we're having a ball. It's just one room, twin beds pushed together, twin desks, a closet, a kitchenette and a shower, but it's all brand new. I tell you, these kids got it made. And we're studying hard,' he laughed, 'learning all about each other.'

'So what are you going to do once your son arrives? Are you staying in Portland?'

'Maybe so. There's posters up all over this building with the picture of a guy who raped someone in the hallway back at the beginning of summer. I've spoken to some of the students who have already come back to start the term and they're scared. If he cracked the security code before, he could do it again. I've told everyone I'm in the building and that I'll protect them.' He coughed and I pictured him puffing up his chest. 'So I've offered my services to PSU. We'll see what they say.'

'And where is Robby? Do you know him? Is he a good kid?' I asked.

'No, I've never met him. I was hired after he was there for his summer visit with Suzette. She said right now he's off in the mountains someplace.'

'Have you seen a picture? Does he look like Suzette?'

'Funny you should ask that,' said Sid. 'His girlfriend came by yesterday, looking for him – so I guess he's due back any minute – and we got to talking about exactly that.'

'What was she like?'

'Seemed like an OK kid, freaky looking – jet-black hair, kinda spiky, more like a boy's than a girl's – but I guess I'm just an old reactionary. She had a familiar look to her but when I mentioned it, asked her if maybe we'd run into each other, she said she was a native of Portland and she'd just met Robby three weeks ago, so I guess not. But she's sure not a fan of Suzette's.'

'Really?' I said. 'How do you know that?'

'She told me,' said Sid. 'When I suggested that from the photo I'd seen of him Robby had a look of his mom about him, she was like *How can you say that? That bitch, she never showed him the time of day, he's not like her at all.* So I said, *When did you meet Suzette?* And the kid says, *I never want to meet her. She's screwed up Robby's life so bad.* And, you know, Lee, it made me sad to hear

336

that because it means Robby's been bad-mouthing his mother and that's exactly what she used to tell me she was afraid of, that he had a negative opinion of her.

'And it's something that's always had me worried about my own kids,' he went on, 'and that's why it's important that I'm here with Gary when he starts college. I need to show him I care and that I'll be here for him when it matters. I'm kind of hoping to have a word with Robby, ask him if he'll keep an eye out for him. Do you think that would be presumptuous of me, Lee?'

'Not at all,' I reassured him, although I didn't have a clue. 'Suzette's probably told him about you. But what about Minnie? How's Gary going to feel about her?'

I couldn't help thinking that having your new much-younger lover hanging around was not exactly the best way to bond with your estranged son.

'Oh, he'll be fine with her. She already told me she's great with kids.'

He's not really a kid any more, I thought, *he's almost a man*. But I knew there wasn't any point pursuing it with Sid. Love was often deaf as well as blind.

'So I guess you heard about Shane Sobel?' I said.

Sid whistled down the phone. 'I had a call in to Pete and Vince and they told me. What a way to go, having your head smashed to

337

pulp with a hammer.'

'Did Pete and Vince have anything to tell you?'

'Nothing. They've interviewed all the employees at Scott Abernathy's, past and present, and they've had to eliminate everyone. They all had alibis for when Mo went missing and no one remembers seeing a girl on the trail to the beach. I guess she just got lucky with her timing. They're not about to give up, but they're not happy.'

'What about Holly Bennett's killer?'

'Same story. That is if you assume the girl who took Mo was the same person who killed Holly Bennett. Which I don't.'

'You *don't?*' I was intrigued. 'Are you saying you know who killed Holly?'

'I'm not saying I know for sure,' he said, 'but if I were a detective, which I'm not,' but it was clear from his tone of voice that he thought he could act like one, 'I'd bring Gwen Bennett in for questioning.'

'*Gwen Bennett?* Why her?'

'She's the only one with a motive for both murders.'

'*Both* murders?'

'Holly Bennett and Shane Sobel.'

'But she wouldn't kill her own daughter!'

'Well, she might,' said Sid with the weary rationale of someone who has seen many incomprehensible acts of violence, 'if she were sleeping with Shane Sobel too and she

338

found out he was also seeing Holly. Women have been driven by jealousy to do the unthinkable. Either that or she went to Spring Hollow Road to kill Shane Sobel and found he'd already killed her daughter. Which would give her a double motive to kill *him*. If she walked in and found him in bed with Patsy, that, and the knowledge that he had killed Holly, would be enough to tip her way over the edge.'

'Do you know a Detective Bill McCoy?'

'Spoke to him half an hour ago. Told him he'd probably find Gwen Bennett's prints all over the house.'

'Well, he probably would,' I said with a certain amount of satisfaction. 'She's trying to persuade Patsy to put the house on the market. I was there a few days ago and she started going around the rooms with a tape measure before we could stop her.'

'Is that right?' said Sid, sounding a little deflated.

'Tell me,' I said, 'how do you know Gwen Bennett was sleeping with Shane Sobel?'

'That Shane Sobel, he was a real piece of work.'

'That doesn't answer my question,' I said, reflecting that *a real piece of work* in a man's eyes often meant someone who was irresistible to women. Hadn't I felt the lure of Shane Sobel's attraction myself? 'You knew him?'

'Only in the line of work. He was the reason I got hired by Scott and Suzette in the first place.'

'*Shane Sobel?*'

'If I tell you, you gotta keep it to yourself. Don't even talk to Rufus and Franny Abernathy.' Sid sounded nervous.

I wasn't sure I liked the sound of this, but there was no way I was going to stop him telling me. 'I swear I won't tell a soul.'

'Suzette needed a new Mercedes. Shane Sobel took her for a test drive and according to my sources she tested him along with the car. But she realised the error of her ways pretty soon after and told him to get lost. Problem was he was hooked and wouldn't let go, kept coming round and wanting more.'

Shane Sobel and Suzette! I was still grappling with the mental image when Sid's voice continued.

'He was becoming a real pest. So she did the smart thing and she told Scott all about it and that's when they decided to up her security, turn it into a major deal. Which was where I came in. I turned Sobel away from the gates quite a few times.'

'Wow!' I said.

'You never heard it from me. But it's sort of the reason why Suzette and I became close. She knew I was in on her secret. And I made it part of my job to keep an eye on

Sobel. I saw him show up at Gwen Bennett's house a few times when her husband was in the city. After hours, so to speak.'

'Well, I guess he just saw sense and moved on. So what do you make of the fact that Patsy's gone missing?' I asked him.

There was a short silence. Then Sid grunted, 'You've got me there. I'll admit it doesn't look good for her.'

It didn't look good for Gwen Bennett either. I thought about what Sid had said about her after we'd chatted a while longer and then hung up. And I remembered her saying she'd seen Shane Sobel at a petrol station on her way over to Patsy's that time she'd dropped in while I was there. It could have been an accidental sighting but now that I thought about it, I had the distinct sense that Gwen Bennett might have been stalking Shane Sobel.

And then I remembered something else. Mo had said he'd heard an older woman's voice when he'd been held captive at the ranch house. Could it have been Gwen Bennett who'd found out about her daughter and Shane Sobel and gone over there just like Sid had suggested?

I wondered who I could talk to about Gwen Bennett and then I realised I knew the perfect person. Eileen McIntosh cleaned all Gwen's rental houses for her. If there was any dirt to be dished about her employer,

Eileen would surely know it.

Eileen must have left her house soon after I did because she didn't answer her phone all afternoon. I called Wyn's mobile phone to see how he was coping with Mo but there was no answer and I left a message. By the end of the day when I hadn't heard back I began to have a serious meltdown. I had handed Wyn on a plate a golden opportunity to abscond with his son, a son he was legally barred from seeing. What had induced me to take matters into my own hands and allow Mo to see his father? I had an answer to that, of course. I knew from just seeing them together that there was a special bond between Mo and his father. There was no way that Wyn would hurt Mo – but still, if I didn't hear from them by Mo's bedtime, I would have to do something about it – even if it meant calling the police on Wyn.

But in the end that wasn't necessary. Mo called me at nine o'clock to say goodnight and to make a scary monster noise down the line. 'Bet you won't sleep a wink after that!'

I left several messages for Eileen and the later ones must have sounded frantic, because when she called me back at eight o'clock the next morning, she asked me what was wrong, did I have any news, had they found Patsy?

'No,' I said. 'No news. I'd just like to chat

to you a bit more, if that's OK? About Patsy, just in case I do wind up writing this book.'

If Eileen knew I was lying, she gave no indication.

'That's not a problem, lassie, but I'm just off out to clean a house so if you're in a hurry, you'd probably best meet me there.'

'Sure,' I said, 'give me the address.'

When she told me it sounded familiar and I asked if it was someone I knew.

'Two one four Spring Hollow Road,' she said cheerfully, 'You won't have a problem coming into a house where a murder's been committed, I hope?'

Of course I had a huge problem with it but it wasn't as if I hadn't been there before. Although then I had had Sid to protect me and I had not had to go inside. It made me squeamish just to think about being in the actual room where someone had been killed, but then I reminded myself that there wouldn't actually be a body there any more. And I'd recently survived standing with just a wall between me and Shane Sobel's bloodied remains.

'Maybe I just won't go into the bathroom,' I said.

'Let me get there first and open up,' said Eileen. 'See you in about twenty minutes?'

When I arrived I paid more attention to the house than I had on my previous visits. The overlapping cedar clap-boards were grey with age and several shingles were loose on the roof. A path of flagstones veered off from the gravelled parking space across a lawn parched by the sun. I followed it around the side of the house to a small entrance porch on which stood two basket armchairs. The front door was ajar and, as I made to enter the house, Brock came at me with his teeth bared.

'Eileen!' I screamed. Somehow this scrappy little creature, who looked as if he would attack my ankles at any second, terrified me and by the time her hand came through the door and grabbed his collar, I was retreating down the path.

'What's your problem?' She was laughing at me. 'He's not an attack dog. He's just guarding me until I tell him you're my friend. Come back and let me give you a hug so he can see I'm happy to see you.'

I retraced my steps and climbed the steps up to the porch with extreme trepidation. As I gave Eileen a tentative hug, putting my arms around her but barely touching her, Brock's head under her arm was only inches from mine. Only when she drew me into the house did he relax and begin wagging his tail.

'See, he remembers you,' said Eileen. 'Now I'm going to make you a quick cup of coffee and then I'm going to ask you to follow me around while I clean. She's

344

suddenly decided to put this place on the market and I've got to give it a thorough clean one last time to make sure all traces of death are erased. Of course I've been round the place since it happened, but I just can't help feeling I may have missed something.'

I looked around as if I expected to see mangled body parts and coffins piled up against the wall.

'Figuratively speaking, of course,' said Eileen, 'does it feel to you as if someone's died in here?'

We were standing in what appeared to be the living room. Two oversized maroon-coloured couches were placed catty corner in the centre, facing a brick fireplace in the wall and with a square coffee table in front of them. They were too big for the small room with its low ceiling. The porch outside the only window blocked most of the light, making it seem as if we were in mid winter instead of late July. An opening in the far wall led to an eat-in kitchen whose appliances and cabinetry seemed to date from the 1970s. As Eileen set about making coffee, I stepped down from the kitchen into a sunroom with a glass roof, clearly a more recent add-on. It led into the back yard and I walked through the back door where Sid and I had first encountered Eileen. It had been dark then and I had not been able to see the extent to which the yard was overlooked by its neighbours. I glanced to the right and saw Rita McGill. She was inspecting a row of plantings at the end of her lawn and didn't notice me. I stood in the yard for a second or two, noting the brick patio and the glass-topped circular table and surrounding chairs. A gas grill stood over to one side.

As I moved to go back into the house, I saw another entrance to the left. I tried the door. It was locked, but through a glass panel I could see a staircase descending just inside.

'I take it you've had no word from Patsy either?' I asked Eileen when I re-entered the house.

Eileen shook her head. She was wearing a baggy pink thigh-length T-shirt over white stretch leggings and her calf muscles bulged almost indecently. She handed me a mug of coffee and returned to the living room, beckoning me to follow.

'I don't mind telling you I'm very worried,' she said as she bent over to plug in the vacuum cleaner and I tried not to look at the tiny rent in the buttock seam of her leggings. 'You see, I need her, Lee,' she said as she straightened up. 'We go way back, you know? I feel betrayed that she's not got in touch with me. I can't believe she'd do such a thing but I've this wee worm of doubt in my head and it's eating away at me.'

'What about Gwen Bennett?' I asked. 'Is she a friend too?'

'Och, no!' The vehemence in Eileen's voice was punctuated by the roar of the vacuum coming to life. She continued speaking but I stood in front of her and mimed deafness, pointing to the vacuum cleaner.

She snapped it off. 'Sorry. But I've got to get this place clean. No, I keep my distance from Gwen Bennett. She's a good source of income for me – she owns six or seven rental properties – so I keep her sweet, but I don't like her.' She glanced at me with a guilty smirk. 'You'll keep that to yourself, please?'

I nodded. 'So you discussed with Patsy that Shane Sobel was Holly Bennett's lover, the man she was seeing here in this house,' I said.

'Aye,' Eileen said, 'I did. I was just being chatty over our morning cup of tea, you know? To be honest, I was surprised by how upset it made Patsy. I knew right then that *she* was involved with him herself. She gave everything away by the look on her face.'

'Well, did you know that he was also sleeping with Holly's mother?'

I felt a certain amount of satisfaction at the look of shock on her face. *Oh yes, you didn't know I was in on the local gossip too, did you?*

'Shut *up!*' she said, recovering quickly and winking at me. 'How would *you* know a

347

thing like that?'

'I have my sources,' I said. Or rather Security Sid did. 'So why don't you like Gwen Bennett?'

'Och, I never should have said that, should I?' She gave the hem of the pink T-shirt a tug. 'I'll make you a deal. You tell me how you know she and Shane Sobel were an item and I'll tell you why she's not my favourite person.'

'Someone I know told me he saw Shane Sobel leaving Gwen Bennett's house a few mornings when her husband was away.'

'Is that so?' said Eileen. The smirk was back but without the guilt. 'And I'm guessng that someone was Sid Sharkey. Next thing you'll be telling me Suzette was sleeping with Shane Sobel.'

No I won't, I thought. I'd said quite enough already. I stared at her. *Now it's time for your side of the bargain.*

'OK,' she said. 'Believe it or not, Holly Bennett and I have something in common.'

'What's that?'

'We're both adopted.'

I was busy processing the information that Holly was not Gwen's natural child and I only half-listened to what Eileen said next.

'I'm a Scot, as you know.' She was almost muttering to herself and as I began to pay more attention I had to lean in closer to hear what she was saying. 'I was born and

348

raised in Glasgow. I'm just a wee lassie *frae* the Drum.'

'The Drum?'

'Bloody Sassenach.' She was smiling but the animosity in her tone was blunt. 'Drum-chapel. It was one of the ugliest tenement estates in Glasgow. My father took off before I was even born and my mother died when I was eight. Emphysema. Every photo I've ever seen of her, she's got a fag hanging out of her mouth.'

'I'm sorry,' I said. 'So, after she died, you were adopted?'

'By monsters,' said Eileen. 'In the disguise of my aunt and uncle who emigrated to Ontario when I was only fifteen. One slight problem, they didn't take me with them. I ran away, hitched my way south, earned my living cleaning toilets.' She shrugged. 'Nothing's changed.'

'And eventually you became Patsy's cleaner?'

'Ten years later,' she said. 'I'll spare you my sorry life in between.'

'And Gwen Bennett?' I was disturbed by the bitterness in her voice. I was sorry for her but I wasn't sure I wanted to hear any more.

'A totally different story. She adopted Holly and gave her everything she could possibly want.'

I didn't get it. Eileen sounded furious.

'What's wrong with that?' I asked her.

'Gwen Bennett spoiled Holly. All the money she made as a realtor she spent on Holly. Clothes. Vacations. Trips to Europe. With Holly, it was never a question of *Mummy, may I?* It was *Mummy, gimme*. And Gwen got out her chequebook.'

'You wish you'd had that closeness with your aunt?' I knew better than to comment on the resentment I could hear in Eileen's voice.

'Closeness?' Eileen stared at me. 'They weren't close. Holly got money from Gwen, material benefits. But that was it. Gwen wasn't a mother to Holly, she was a bank. The only way Holly could have got her mother's attention would have been if she had turned herself into a multi-million-dollar property on the ocean.'

I didn't really want to go on with this conversation. I realised I had unwittingly opened up a can of worms in prompting Eileen to reveal her grudge against the Bennett women. I wondered how much of Patsy's time had been spent sitting listening to Eileen ranting on? And had Patsy already been sleeping with Shane Sobel when Holly Bennett was killed? Maybe it wasn't such a surprise when Eileen told her Holly was his lover. Maybe the surprise for Patsy was learning that Eileen knew – and might therefore connect her to–

What was I thinking? Hadn't I persuaded

myself that someone as thoughtful as Patsy could never commit murder? Why was I now speculating that maybe as well as killing Shane, jealousy might also have made her responsible for Holly's death? Because no matter which way you looked at it, Gwen Bennett might have a motive for killing both Shane *and* Holly – and the cold and mercenary relationship between mother and adopted daughter now made this more of a possibility – but she wasn't alone. Patsy did too.

It was time I pulled myself together. At the rate I was going, I'd be accusing Suzette next.

'I need to use the bathroom,' I said, using the first excuse I could find to extricate myself from Eileen's clutches.

'Down the hall, first door on the right,' said Eileen.

It wasn't until I was sitting on the toilet in mid-flow that it dawned on me that this was probably the very bathroom in which Holly had died. The shower curtain was pulled across the tub and I stared at it, transfixed, my imagination conjuring up *Psycho*-like fantasies. And then, as I sat there, I heard a sound. It was a short, sharp human cry, like someone in pain. It seemed as if it had come from below my feet. I looked down and there was an air vent just above the skirting board. Maybe there was a shaft of some kind and sound carried up from – where? The basement? I thought of the steps I had seen when I was outside.

I reached for some toilet paper – and found there wasn't any. I searched my pockets for some Kleenex and came up empty. Finally, just as I was about to open the door a fraction and call to Eileen, there was a knock from the other side that made me jump.

'Open the door, Lee. I forgot to put any toilet tissue in there.'

The Perfect Housekeeper, I thought. *Just a bit late, that's all.*

'Where do those stairs outside lead to?' I asked her, when I came out. 'Is there a basement?'

'No, just a crawl space,' she said quickly. 'You don't want to go down there. It's full of creepy-crawlies.'

'So why the stairs?'

'The boiler's down there, and the oil tank. Hot water heater, stuff like that,' she said.

'I just heard a cry from somewhere,' I said, 'and it sounded like it came from below.'

'That was me,' she said. 'There's a cupboard in the wall halfway down that staircase where we store the loo paper,' she pointed to the roll she had just handed to me, 'and the kitchen rolls when we bulk buy from CostCo. There's a million bloody splinters in the wood and I caught one in

352

my thumb. I guess I yelped.' She was facing me now, sucking her thumb. 'OK, gotta get on.' She returned to her vacuuming.

'Was this where–?' I said, gesturing to the bathroom behind me.

'It was,' Eileen shouted over the roar of the vacuum. 'She drowned in that tub, but don't worry, I've given it a good scrub since.'

A narrow passage led off the living room with bedrooms on either side. I wandered down it, pushing open the doors and glancing inside. I tried to guess the one in which Mo had been held captive. There was a locked door at the end of the passage.

'What's this room?' I yelled back down the passage.

'It's the room at the back of the house that Holly Bennett used to entertain Shane Sobel. It's got its own bathroom and it's own entrance. Look, I'll show you.'

She switched off the vacuum and pulling a set of keys from her pocket, she leaned past me to unlock the door. 'There,' she said, showing me into a light airy room with lemon yellow walls and just a king-sized bed, 'see, I'm not hiding anything from you.'

Up to that moment I hadn't for one second assumed that she was. If she hadn't said that, I would never have doubted what she had said about the stairs to the crawl space.

But now suddenly I began to think back to

how long I had been in the bathroom. Even though I had had to wait for a new supply of toilet paper, surely I had not been there long enough for her to go outside, unlock the door, go down the stairs, open the cupboard door, receive a splinter, yelp and return. I had heard the yelp almost the second I had sat down and it had come from below me, not over on the far corner of the house where the stairs were located.

Was she lying? Or was my imagination working overtime, which wouldn't be a first? More likely the latter, but if she was hiding something, the only thing I could think was that it might be Patsy, who had contacted Eileen and asked her to shelter her. Didn't Eileen keep insisting they were friends from way back? Wasn't it highly likely that Eileen would be the first person Patsy would turn to for help?

'So what was it you wanted to talk to me about?' Eileen was coming down the passage brandishing the long suction tube of the vacuum cleaner at me. She shepherded me out of the back room and locked the door behind me.

'Oh, it doesn't matter,' I said.

'You wanted to ask me about Gwen Bennett, didn't you? You're thinking maybe she had something to do with Shane Sobel's murder, aren't you? Wouldn't that be wonderful?' She sighed.

Wonderful? I looked at her, startled.

'Well, if they arrested Gwen, then Patsy could come home.' She smiled at me.

I should have asked her flat out. *Are you shielding Patsy?* But I didn't have the nerve. Was it because I wouldn't know what to do if Patsy was indeed Shane Sobel's murderer, and by telling me Eileen would make me complicit in aiding and abetting a killer? No, better to leave and think of a way to tell Detective McCoy without making me look a total fool, and alienating Patsy and Eileen forever, if I was wrong.

'I'll leave you to get on with it,' I said and squeezed past her.

When I opened the front door, Brock escaped.

'Oh shit!' said Eileen. 'Do me a favour. Go after him and grab him for me, will you? Go on,' she said when I hesitated. 'He knows you're my friend now. He won't harm you.'

But Brock was too quick for me. He raced across the property boundary into the neighbour's back yard.

'Oh, Brock,' said Rita McGill, as she watched him relieve himself, 'don't start digging again. Those azaleas have just been planted.'

'You know him?' I was surprised.

'Oh yes,' she said. 'Eileen's a very conscientious housekeeper. She's over here every day. And you know, I was dumb. The first time Brock came over I gave him a treat so now, of course, he's going to come looking for it every day, aren't you?' She leaned down to pat him on the head.

This yard, I noticed, was beautifully maintained with a colourful assortment of shrubs adorning the herbaceous borders. I said as much to Rita McGill and she gave me a complacent smile.

'I make a point of keeping it in shape – although I have to admit, I don't do it myself. My landscaper takes care of most of it.'

'The one who does Gwen Bennett's place next door too. She'd better get them to put in a bit of work if she wants to sell the place,' I said.

'She's put it on the market?' The woman looked surprised. 'Who's going to want to buy a place where someone was just murdered?'

'Good point,' I said.

'Well, if Wyn works his magic on the yard, that'll help,' she said, 'and the siding on the house could use a power wash. Nothing like making a good first impression.'

'Wyn?'

It couldn't be!

'The name of my yard guy. Here, let me give you his card. He's a nice man, new to the area. I put him on to Gwen Bennett for all her rental properties. I wanted to find him more work so he stays out here.'

356

She reached into the pocket of her sweat-pants, withdrew a business card and handed it to me.

Wynton P Moses. Landscape Design Installation Maintenance.

Chapter Fourteen

Back at the pool house I waited with mounting tension for Wyn to bring Mo back. It was forty minutes past the time we'd fixed for Mo's return and I was worried. I padded about the place and then, to distract me, I returned to something I had begun the night before. Flattened out on the table was a brown paper bag, ripped open to form a large oblong. On it, with the help of a red felt-tipped marker, I had drawn Patsy's wheel. I had got as far as naming each of the spokes – work, health, marriage, fitness, money, family, state of mind – but then tiredness had claimed me and I had gone to bed.

Now I prepared to rate each spoke with a number from one to ten.

Work. Well, pretty disastrous really. I had come all this way for a job that had appeared to evaporate. I had barely begun to interview my subject before she had disappeared, the prime suspect in a murder investigation. Four. No, make that three.

Health. Well, I was pretty healthy and I'd give myself an eight and move on so as not to tempt fate.

Marriage. I was barely on speaking terms

with my husband of not even a month, who wasn't on the same continent as me, let alone in the same house. And, strictly speaking, as yet, our marriage had yet to be consummated. I'd say four, and that was only because neither of us had actually mentioned the word *divorce* yet.

Fitness. Hopeless. No, wait a second, what about all that swimming I'd done? I reckon that earned me a seven.

Money. I had to admit I was pretty lucky in that area but it wouldn't last long if I had to continue supporting my layabout of a husband. Better stop there and put seven.

Family. My mother didn't show up for my wedding and my father has a mistress who's younger than I am. You do the math. Five.

State of Mind. Anxious. Unfulfilled. Disappointed. How did you put a number on that?

'What are you doing?' said a voice behind me and I nearly jumped through the roof.

Franny had crept into the pool house with bare feet and I hadn't heard a sound.

'Sorry,' she said. 'What is this?' She pointed over my shoulder to Patsy's chart.

I thought fast. The last time I had seen her she had taunted me about my marriage and I had walked away from her in a state of fierce indignation. Was I prepared to let her walk back into my life as if nothing had happened?

359

Yes, I was. Because she was my friend and, despite our argument, I loved her dearly. The fact that she was here meant she was anxious to make amends – and besides, I was living in *her* pool house. I reached for the red marker and named another spoke. *Friendships*. And I gave it an eight because I reckoned, all things considered, I was truly lucky with mine.

'It's called a life chart,' I explained, grateful for the fact that she was bending over my shoulder and I didn't have to look at her. 'You consider every area of your life and award yourself points out of ten.'

'You're not doing too well on some of them,' she observed.

'Well, for God's sake, you have a go,' I said – but I smiled to show my challenge was not resentful.

'All right, I will,' she said, and sat down beside me, pulling my wheel towards her. I had no idea what was going through her head, but I was stunned to see the speed with which she awarded herself points. Moving in reverse order to me, she quickly wrote a number above mine at the end of each spoke.

Friendship. And here she suddenly leaned over and kissed my cheek before putting nine.

State of Mind six
Family eight?

Money ten
Fitness nine
Marriage four
Health seven
Work four

'So we've both got a problem with marriage and work,' I said. 'And why the question mark after the eight for family?'

'Because half of my family – Eliza – is perfect, and the other half – Rufus,' she shrugged, 'the jury's still out. And no,' she held up her hand, 'don't start berating me about Rufus again. I know we have work to do on our marriage and you know what? It began last night. Thanks to you, I ditched my hook-up with the guy in the city, stood him up cold, haven't taken any of his calls since. I spent yesterday showing Eliza New York, mostly from the Circle Line – and then I drove home to Rufus last night.'

'And?'

'And we talked. I let him tell me all about his plans to run for the Town and I listened. I really did.'

'And?' I said again.

'I was horrified and enchanted at the same time. I hate the thought of him becoming a stuffy bureaucrat but his enthusiasm was as beautiful to behold as it is when he talks about surfing. That's what's different about guys out here on the east end of Long Island. They grow up but they never really leave the beach. And you know, he could do so much good.'

'And what about you? Did he listen too? Did you tell him about the guy you've been seeing?'

She shook her head. 'It would only cause more problems than it would solve. And on the face of it, it was all totally innocent. Besides, once we were done with me listening to him, we were pretty tired and so we went to bed. And we continued making up another way, if you catch my drift. So what about your marriage? What are we going to do about that? I'm sorry for what I said in the city, by the way.'

I smiled at her. 'Forget it. And in answer to your question, I don't know what *we're* going to do. If *you* have a plan, I'd love to hear it, but *I* haven't a clue. He's called me once to say his mother got home safely, but other than that, not a word.'

'Have you called him?'

'I've tried. But he's moved out of our home, did you know that? He's gone to stay with Noreen, says he wants to keep an eye on her. But we all know why he's really there.'

'God, I'm so sorry,' said Franny, 'I had no idea. I've been so wrapped up in my own stupid problems, I guess I never even noticed things were not great between you. I mean, you guys were here on your *honeymoon*. I was even envious of you, can you imagine?'

'Listen,' I said, 'you know Tommy and you know me. We've been in this situation before and lived to tell the tale. It'll work itself out.' I wished I felt as confident as I sounded. In my mind, I had already ticked the *Separated* box in future questionnaires about my status. 'But what about you? You've got to tell Rufus what you want in this relationship. It can't be all about him. And what about the other low score you gave yourself? Your work?'

While I waited for her answer, I gave a mental nod to Patsy. However much I might think her mantras were a load of baloney, this wheel was forcing us to confront the problem areas of our lives.

'What work?' said Franny.

And then in a sudden flash of insight, I saw what Franny's solution might be.

'That's where your troubles began,' I said, 'when you left the Old Stone Market and passed the running of it to someone else. Don't you miss it?'

'Desperately,' she said, without a moment's hesitation. 'I was so proud of what I achieved with that little store. I know I didn't do myself any favours, the way I behaved with some of the customers. I know I could improve on my people skills. But in spite of that, I loved being part of the community. I loved doing the ordering and seeing which stuff sold and which didn't. And I even miss my care-taking, delivering firewood and mowing lawns.'

Franny had inherited the local family business of tending the yards of the residents of Stone Landing from her aunt and uncle. The locals had never thought she would make a go of it on top of running the store, not to mention the fact that she was a *woman*, and women didn't split logs and mow lawns. But then they'd never thought she'd marry a local millionaire either.

'So go back to it,' I said. 'What's to stop you? Surely that will be exactly what Rufus needs? A wife who's active in the community. You still own the store, don't you? It would be easy to reinstate yourself?'

'Could it be that simple?' she said, looking at me wide-eyed.

'Absolutely,' I said. 'You'll be so busy, you won't have a second to notice what Rufus is doing during the day. And you'll have a lot to talk about to each other in the evening. Eliza will be in daycare. You're bored, Franny, that's your problem. You weren't born to be an idle rich woman and you don't have to be – although I'd hang on to the rich part, if I were you.'

'So, what about your work?' she said, looking at the wheel. 'You only gave yourself a three. That's even lower than your marriage. And, by the way, it's one of the reasons I came down here. Have you seen the local paper this morning? I brought it down to show you.'

I stared at the picture that covered the top quarter of the front page. Two pictures, in fact. One of Patsy, looking decidedly homely, her thin hair scraped back behind her head. And the other was taken from the television and showed Vicky the Viking looking as stunning as she could be, long blond hair falling beyond her shoulders, her teeth flashing an inviting smile.

LIFE COACH A FRAUD, ON THE RUN FOR SUSPECTED MURDER

'Can they put that?' I said. 'Can they say she's on the run when they don't even know where she is?'

'They just did,' said Franny. 'Has she really been passing herself off as somebody else? If she'd do something as devious as that, kinda makes you think she might be capable of other stuff, doesn't it?'

'It's not like that,' I rushed to explain. 'She just wasn't comfortable being in the public eye. Not everyone is. For example, I'd hate it if I had to–'

I stopped abruptly because I had heard the sound of Wyn's truck pulling up outside. Any minute now Mo would come running in and I would have to explain to Franny what he was doing there.

But when she saw him, Franny smiled and held out her arms.

'Hey, Big Guy, I heard you were back with us. How about you come up to the house with me? Eliza really wants to see you.'

Relief surged through me. I stroked the top of Mo's head and gave his back a gentle prod towards Franny, but he stayed still. I could imagine what was going through his mind. *Why she being so nice to me? She never was that way before. And she so big!*

'There's something else,' said Franny. 'I was wondering if maybe you'd like to come with us to see Keshawn? We're going over there later today.'

Mo hesitated.

'That's the guy with the PlayStation 3,' I prompted.

'Where I was kidnapped?' said Mo and Franny and I looked at each other. He wasn't about to forget that in a hurry.

'That's right,' said Franny, 'but Rufus and I will be with you and you'll be in the house, not down on the beach where someone could grab you.'

I shook my head at her. This was a little too graphic a description. But Mo seemed convinced. 'Hey, Dad,' he shouted to Wyn who had followed him in, 'I'm going to where there's PS3. Hey,' he turned to me, 'will Sid be there to watch over me?'

'Afraid not,' I said, 'he left town. By the way,' I told Franny, 'I spoke to him. Did you know he'd gone to Portland, Oregon?'

'Oh, go on, rub it in some more.' Franny gave me a pretend hangdog look. 'He lost his job because of me.' Then she nodded. 'You know I feel bad about what's happened to Sid. If I hadn't given Minnie a ride to East Hampton, maybe she would never have hooked up with him there. She must have arranged to meet him because when I dropped her off, I saw her walk into a store. I guess she walked right out again the minute she saw me drive off, and Sid was probably waiting round the corner. Has Suzette been spreading the word that it was all my fault?'

'Nobody's been saying anything,' I said quickly. I had half a mind to point out what Sid had told me about Suzette, but I thought better of it. Franny had had ample time to make her sister-in-law her friend and it was clear that some things just weren't meant to be. In the meantime I didn't want *my* rapprochement with Franny to degenerate into an argument about Suzette.

I was suddenly aware that Mo and Wyn were listening to our exchange about Sid and Suzette. 'Franny, this is Wyn,' I said, 'Mo's father. Have you guys met? I can't remember.'

'Good to see you,' she said, 'Now I'd better get back to the house. So, Mo, are you coming or what? And Lee,' she put her arm around me, 'I wanted to tell you – stay as long as you like. I know the deal was that you guys spend your honeymoon with us, but now that's over why don't you stay on anyway? Part of me thinks you ought to go on back to London and patch things up with Tommy. But another part of me needs you here, while I patch things up with *my* husband. And who knows? Patsy may turn up tomorrow and then you'd have to go to work.'

She made it sound so easy. I knew I was a coward for putting my marital problems on hold, but I knew there was no way I was going anywhere until Patsy had been cleared of killing Shane Sobel.

So I gave her a quick hug and whispered *Thanks* as Mo said, 'How come you have to patch things up with Tommy?'

'Take him away before I have to answer that,' I said to Franny and she laughed and took his hand and led him out the door.

When I was alone with Wyn, I said nothing by way of greeting, just showed him the card with his landscaping details on it.

'I guess it's a step up from being a janitor.'

He sat down hard. 'Oh shit!'

'Oh yes,' I said. 'And you never went to Harvard and you're certainly not now or ever have been a lawyer. Or a book editor, or a general manager or a sales associate or any of those other thing on those cards you gave to Mo.'

'Why'd he show them to you?' Wyn's mouth hardened in defeat.

'Because I asked him to. He's very proud of you, said you worked in all these places. I just couldn't figure out how you could find the time?'

'It was just a game I played with him.' Wyn's eyes pleaded with me. 'Happened one time he was with me when I had to go to work, and we went up to these offices and I didn't know what to do with him. So I took him into the big corner office where the boss sat and there was a TV. I said he had to stay there, watch TV while I worked and he said *Daddy, your office is real big.* And he looked so proud of me, I couldn't tell him the truth. I had the cards made for a joke. For a *joke!*'

I was starting to feel a little uncomfortable. I had no doubt that Mo loved his father, but surely it wasn't just because he thought Wyn had a big office?

'But you didn't let Mo in on the joke, did you, Wyn? He had these cards, he genuinely thought you were everything it said on them.'

'I only wanted him to be proud of me.' Wyn's voice was barely audible.

'I told you. He *is* proud of you,' I said and the look Wyn gave me was heartbreaking.

'He is?'

'Oh, yes, I'm sure of it. I can tell by the

369

way he is with you, what he says about you. But you have to tell him the truth.'

'That I was lying, that I was just the janitor?'

'Well, maybe you don't have to go that far. Just don't lie about whatever it is you're doing now. And don't ever lie to him again.'

'Oh, I've told him the truth about the landscaping.' Wyn grinned suddenly. 'No reason to lie there. Except all I got is these cards and a leased truck and some cheap equipment. No crew or nothing. It's just me. Say,' he looked at me, 'how you find out about Harvard?'

'I met Anna. I handed Mo over to her.'

'She tell you the whole story? About our marriage?'

I nodded. 'Pretty much. We went for a walk in the park.'

'So you guys got to know each other a little.' He seemed amused by this but then he suddenly looked scared. 'You tell her I'm out here?'

'No,' I said, 'but only because that would get Mo into trouble. And I've brought Mo back so you can be with him some more.'

He grabbed my hand. 'That's a big relief. And I really appreciate being able to spend more time with him. I only came out here for the summer when I heard Mo was going to be a Fresh Air kid, so I could be near him. I wasn't on vacation, like I told you. I

370

had to work so I got me a gig mowing lawns and a bed in a house with a bunch of other guys. They made a big fuss of Mo last night.'

'But you seem to know quite a lot about landscaping,' I said, remembering how pleased Rita McGill had been with what he'd done with her yard.

'Well, yeah,' he said, smiling. 'I got lucky. I meet this old lady walking on the beach and we get talking. She say she *love* to garden so I tell her what I do and she say she help me get educated about planting and stuff. When I start a new job, I drive her round to take a sneaky look and she tells me what'll work. She gets a real kick out of it. Doesn't have much else in her life since her husband passed away.'

'So how long were you out here before Mo arrived?'

He looked a little shifty. 'I told you. A while.'

'*How* long?'

'OK, a month, maybe two. I needed to find a job so I was all set up by the time Mo arrived.'

'And how long have you been working on Gwen Bennett's yard on Spring Hollow Road?'

'Since the first week I got here. See, in the beginning I was hired as part of a crew who took care of all the yards for her rental houses. But then while I was working there

371

– where Holly was killed – I got to know Mrs McGill, the lady who lives next door. And she hired me on my own to come fix her plantings. That's when I got the card made up.'

I watched him while he spoke, saw how proud he was of what he had achieved. I looked at his open face and his wide smile and I saw how easy it was for him to charm anyone he met – the old lady on the beach, Rita McGill – into trusting him.

Suddenly he looked at me sharply. 'How you know I take care of Gwen Bennett's yard?'

'Rita McGill told me,' I said.

'You know Mrs McGill?' He was wary now.

'We've met. Wyn, when I last saw you, you told me you saw Mo being taken from the beach by a girl. You said you followed them back to Spring Hollow Road – but you gave me no indication that you *knew* the girl, that you were the landscaper at Spring Hollow Road.'

'What makes you think I did know her?'

'Mrs. McGill told me she heard the two of you talking quite a bit.'

He shook his head as if he were about to deny it, then he thought better of it.

'OK, I'm busted.' He grinned, trying to disarm me. 'Zoe. She moved in about the same time I started work there. She brought me out a cold drink when it was real hot while I was cutting the grass and we got to talking. She was real friendly.'

'Zoe who? How was she friendly, Wyn?'

'I never got her last name. How was she friendly? She listened to me. I told her why I was out here, how I was looking to meet up with my son. I told her how Anna wouldn't let me see him. And I confided in her. I told her I wanted to try and bring my son to live with me. I didn't spell it out that I was going to try and do it while he was out here, but I think she got the picture. She said why didn't I bring him to play at the house with me when I came to work. She said she'd keep an eye on him.'

'But, Wyn, why didn't you tell me this before? What have you told the police?'

He looked defeated. 'Now I pretty much told them everything. That Mrs McGill, she busted me wide open with them as well as with you. I was there at the beach that day, but I was keeping my head down, like I told you. Mo had called me and told me you all were going to the beach and I followed you, keeping way back so you wouldn't see me. I saw you fall asleep, I saw Mo wander off and suddenly I saw Zoe on the beach too. I saw her go up to Mo and start talking to him. I should have realised that she wouldn't know what he looked like. I hadn't even shown her a picture of him back then. But I didn't think.' He shook his head. 'I just didn't think.'

'What do you mean, you just didn't think? You see your son going off with a strange woman and–'

'But she wasn't strange to *me!*' Wyn looked at me. 'Don't you get it? She'd been so friendly to me, she'd suggested he come and play. I thought she was making good on her offer. It just slipped my mind that she'd never actually met him. And then when she took him to the house, I–'

'But why didn't you go in and join her, check everything was all right?'

'I was just about to, but I saw Mrs McGill peeking through her curtains, just like I said. I didn't want her to associate me with Mo, to find out he was my kid, because I knew she would tell people. So I drove up the street a ways to wait until she was done snooping. But then the cops arrived and I took off. I didn't want *them* to see me within a hundred yards of Mo.'

He leaned over and touched my hand. 'I don't want to keep having to see Mo on the sly,' he said, 'but Anna forces me to do it. I started thinking the only way I could get him for myself was if I took him. He loves me. I know he'd want to be with me.' He took a deep breath and nodded, as if re-assuring himself he was doing the right thing in talking to me.

'And did you try to get in touch with Zoe afterwards?' I asked him.

'Of course I did.' He looked pained that I should even consider otherwise. 'But I never reached her. The number she gave me, it never answered. It was like she disappeared. That's when I knew I had to take Mo for myself. Which is how I got to meet you.'

'And what did Mo tell you about what happened?'

'Well, now, I didn't talk about it too much with him.'

'Why was that?' I said.

'Because when he got in touch with me, he was excited and he talked about how he had been *kidnapped*, told me how she wasn't after him at all, that she had confused him with some other kid. By that time I'd heard there was a kidnapping attempt on Suzette's son and I'd figured out what had happened. I was pretty nervous about what I'd told Zoe about wanting to take Mo. God knows who else she talked to. Maybe even her.'

I looked to where he was pointing and my heart jumped. His finger was resting on Patsy's photo in the paper lying on the table between us.

'Why do you say that?'

'Because she turned up a couple times while I was mowing the lawn,' he said.

'Patsy came to Spring Hollow Road? You're sure?'

375

Wyn moved his chin up and down in an exaggerated nod. 'Absolutely.'

'Do you know why? To see Holly? Or Zoe?'

'Neither. She said she was looking for Eileen. The housekeeper. Said Eileen wasn't answering her phone and she thought she might find her there. But I could tell she didn't expect to see *me* there. She leapt a mile in the air when she saw me.'

'Have you told the police about Zoe and Patsy?'

He looked at me with eyes wide open. 'Sure. I just told you. When Mrs McGill busted me, I told them everything. They showed me a drawing some guy had done and I guess it looked a little like Zoe but not enough so I could be sure.'

'But you say you *saw* her take Mo from the beach. Did you tell them that?'

He shrugged. 'I guess. I don't remember.'

'But, Wyn, she might have been the person who killed Holly Bennett. Don't you realise that?'

He shook his head. 'I just can't believe that. She was so friendly to me.'

She was so friendly to me. As if that precluded her from being somewhat less friendly to someone else. But he had never got her last name so apart from seeing a slight resemblance in Charlie Merriweather's sketch, he was really no more use to the police than Mo

376

had been. They had nothing more to go on than a description that could fit thousands of women all over the country. And as for Patsy having gone to Spring Hollow Road, she had since disappeared. Grudgingly, I admitted to myself that Wyn probably had been as helpful as he could have been.

He was speaking again, interrupting my thoughts.

'It was dumb of me to try and get Mo, but one day I'm hoping Anna will let me have joint custody.' He began to move towards the door. 'I'm going to be on my way. Got work to do.'

'Wait,' I said, 'have you ever been inside that house – where Holly was killed?'

He shrugged. 'I guess. They say they found my prints in the bathroom where she was killed but that makes sense. That's the bathroom I use when I got to go.'

'So you have a key to the house?'

He nodded. 'Gwen Bennett gave it to me when she first hired me. She had an avocado plant in a pot in the living room. It had grown real big and she didn't want to move it. She wanted me to take care of it, go in and water it.'

I stared at him. If only he had gone in to take care of it when Mo had been locked inside one of the bedrooms.

'But I never used that key,' he went on. 'Only time I ever went inside the house, someone was there to let me in. Holly or Zoe, or Gwen.'

'And what about the crawl space? Did you ever go down there?'

'Crawl space?' He seemed confused.

'The outside door at the back with a staircase leading down.'

'Oh, that's not a crawl space. Those steps lead to the basement, runs the length and width of the house. I've been down there a few times – I stored some burlap down there – not recently though.'

'You had a key to that too?'

'Didn't need to. Gwen never kept it locked.'

He wouldn't stay longer than it took him to cast a quick eye around the room in the pool house where Mo had slept, which he asked to see.

'All I want,' he said as he pulled the keys to his truck from his pocket, 'is the chance to put my son to bed once again. He's too old for me to read him a story now but–'

'Actually,' I said, 'he'd read *you* a story – from *My Golden Book of Bible Stories*.'

Wyn rewarded me with a look of momentary happiness. 'He still got that? He read pretty good, huh?'

'He's a star,' I said. I couldn't bring myself to tell him Mo had memorised the stories word for word and sometimes held the book upside down.

'Thank you,' he said, suddenly serious. 'I owe you.'

When he was gone, my mind was in a turmoil, trying to make sense of all that he had told me. I had the name of the foxy-faced girl who had taken Mo, who had maybe even been responsible for Holly Bennett's death. And I said *maybe* because the fact that Patsy had gone to the house opened up another can of worms. I very much doubted she had been looking for Eileen. Either she was looking for Holly because she had found out about Holly's involvement with Shane. Or she had been looking for Shane himself for the same reason. And then, because she hadn't managed to kill Shane there, she had made a second successful attempt at her own house.

Which meant she was in hiding, and what better place to hide than at the crime scene itself where no one would think of looking? Especially now that I knew it was a basement and not a crawl space. Plenty of room to hide in a basement after the police were done with forensics there. So why had Eileen described it as a crawl space? I cursed the fact that I had been so distracted by Brock escaping from the house that I had not gone down there to take a look for myself.

And why was the door leading down to it now locked? Because Eileen was sheltering Patsy down there. *Oh God!*

And yet? What about Wyn? He had access to the house. Zoe had probably told Holly about Wyn wanting to be with Mo. What if Wyn had wanted to silence Holly? Was *that* why he wanted to elude the attention of the police? And was I making a terrible mistake in letting him have access to Mo?

When he called later in the day I assumed, when I heard his voice say, 'Lee,' that he wanted to arrange a time to see Mo again. I started to come up with an array of excuses while at the same time berating myself for even thinking of denying him access. It was only when he said more urgently, 'Lee, did you hear what I said?' that I paid attention and asked him to repeat it.

'Mo's just called me on his cell phone,' he said. 'He was whispering so I could barely make out what he said but he's over at Keshawn's, with Franny.'

'That's OK,' I said. 'Didn't you hear Franny say she was going to take him over there?'

'Yes,' said Wyn, 'but Mo says there's a woman there and he heard her speak and he recognised the voice. He says he heard it when he was shut in that room when Zoe took him.'

'But it wasn't Zoe's voice?' I said.

'No,' said Wyn, 'it was another woman. Older.'

'Well, did you ask him who it was?'

'There was a noise. Sounded like a scuffle. Then the phone was shut off, the power, everything. I can't get through to him. Can you call over there, Lee, please?'

I barely said goodbye to him in my anxiety to get him off the phone and call Franny.

'Scott,' I said when he answered the phone, 'I need to speak to Mo. Now!'

'Hey, slow down. What's the matter?' His attempt to calm me only succeeded in infuriating me.

'Scott, I'm serious. I'll explain later. Please put Mo on.'

'OK, OK. He's right here. I'll get him.'

Scott must have handed the phone to Franny because suddenly her voice was in my ear.

'What's up, Lee?'

'I have to speak to Mo.' How many more times did I have to say it?

'Scott's just gone to get him.'

'He said he was right there.'

'He is. We're in the den and he's right next door in the kitchen with Keshawn getting a snack. You should see them. They've bonded real–'

'Franny, who else is there? Who else is with you?'

'No one. It's just us.'

'Who's us?'

'Lee, what is the *matter* with you? Us. Me, Scott, Suzette, Keshawn and Mo. That's it.

381

And the security people, but they're out in the room by the garage watching us on monitors. It always kinda freaks me out to know they're–'

'And they haven't reported anything irregular? Where *is* Scott? Hasn't he found Mo yet?'

'Well, he hasn't come back in here so I guess Mo wasn't in the kitchen like we thought. Maybe Keshawn took him upstairs.'

'Franny!'

'I hear you, Lee. You hold on. I'll go and take a look myself.'

I counted while she was gone, trying in vain to quell my mounting panic. I had reached 151, well over two minutes, when first Scott's voice – and then Franny's on another extension – began to jabber in my ear.

'He's gone. He's nowhere. Everyone's looking all over the house, but it's just like before. Keshawn's here, but Mo's gone.'

Chapter Fifteen

I couldn't help myself. I screamed at them down the phone. 'Somebody must have come and taken him. Didn't Keshawn see anyone?'

Scott was firm. He made me explain what had prompted my alarm in the first instance then he said he was going to call the police. While I held on, Franny quizzed Keshawn who said he had gone to the bathroom and when he had returned to the kitchen, Mo was gone.

'But he says he didn't see any strange people.'

I asked Franny to talk to the security detail and see if anyone had come to the house, or even just to the electronic gates. In as calm a voice as I could muster, I said I assumed the grounds were being searched, and the trail down to the beach. Then I hung up and called Wyn.

'What can I do? Tell me what I can do?' He pleaded with me.

'Go to the beach and see if you can see him there. He might have wandered down the trail to the ocean.'

'But if they see me they're going to think I

had something to do with it. That I took him.'

'I'll vouch for you,' I said. 'The most important thing is to *find* Mo.'

I called Franny back.

'Scott's called Vince and Pete. They're on their way,' she said.

'What did the security people say? Did anyone come to the house since Mo's been there?'

There was a silence.

'*Franny?*'

'Yes. Someone did come here, but she didn't come by car.'

'*She?* It was a woman?'

'Yes. She walked onto the property from the trail to the beach, but she was picked up pretty quickly by the monitors and they went out to confront her immediately.'

'Was she an older woman?' I said.

'Probably,' said Franny. 'She was a real estate broker. The property next door is on the market and she was showing it. She wanted to talk to Scott and Suzette about the trail to the beach because it's shared between the two properties and she needed to know how to incorporate it into her sale. The security guys called Scott, but he didn't want to deal with it. He sent a message saying he'd get back to her later about it.'

'And she left – went back the way she came?'

'Apparently,' said Franny. 'One of the security team knew her, verified she was a real estate broker. It sounded innocent enough. In any case, what would she want with Mo?'

She'd want to silence him because he had heard her at Spring Hollow Road when she went there to confront her adopted daughter Holly Bennett for sleeping with Shane Sobel, the man she thought was her exclusive lover. And Mo must have heard her voice again while she was talking to the security guards. And recognised it. And she must have seen him and known that he knew who she was.

I cut Franny off and raced outside to my car, but once inside it, I realised I had no idea where Gwen Bennett lived. So I called Sid. He answered immediately and he sounded a little down, but when I asked him if everything was OK, he said he was tired. He'd just moved his stuff out of Robby's dorm and dragged it around the corner to a small hotel he'd found. It had taken him three trips, he said, and he was exhausted.

'So what's up?'

I told him what had happened with Mo and he whistled down the line.

'I can barely believe it.'

'And I think you were right about Gwen Bennett,' I said and told him why. 'You have to give me her address.'

'So you can go over there and wrest Mo

from her? If she's even taken him there? If it was even her? No way.'

I was stunned. 'Why not? I need to find Mo as quickly as possible.'

'I'll call Pete and Vince and the police, or I'll call Scott and have him direct them. But you are *not* to go there on your own, Lee. She might be dangerous.'

'But what about Mo?'

'Let the police go after him. They'll know what to do. I had a hunch about Gwen Bennett, but I may be wrong. Have they found Patsy Brooks? Have they discounted her?'

I had to admit to him that they hadn't and then I told him about Wyn and all he had witnessed at Gwen Bennett's house. And how he'd suggested Patsy might be the killer.

'What do you think?' I asked Sid, anxious to hear his take on this. But he surprised me. I heard his quick intake of breath and when he finally replied, he didn't mention her.

'Do you believe in coincidence?' he said.

'Yes,' I said, 'it never fails to amaze me, but I do.'

'Well, I don't,' he said. 'Wyn told you the name of the girl who took Mo that first time at the beach is Zoe?'

'Yes,' I said.

'Well,' said Sid, 'Zoe is the name of Robby's girlfriend, the one who came looking for him

386

here in his dorm the other day.'

He couldn't get me off the phone fast enough. He wanted to call Scott about Gwen Bennett and he wanted to speak to Pete and Vince and have them fax or email to him the sketch Charlie Merriweather had done of the girl Mo had described. I sensed that he was furious with himself because he could not be certain it was the Zoe he had seen until he took another look at it.

'I should have paid more attention when Charlie was doing that sketch. I just gave it a quick glance, you know?'

'Did Robby's girlfriend have a foxy face?' I asked him. 'That's the thing that sticks out in my mind about the drawing.'

'She did,' said Sid. 'Do you remember what colour hair the girl in Charlie Merriweather's drawing had?'

'Carrots with milk,' I said.

'Excuse me?' said Sid.

I laughed. 'It was how Mo described it. Charlie said he guessed it must be strawberry blond. You said Robby's girlfriend had jet-black hair? Well, she could easily have dyed it.'

'She could,' said Sid, 'but it would be dangerous to jump to conclusions. Of course I'm going to go round to the dorm immediately to see what I can get out of Robby. Maybe Zoe will even be there.'

'Call and tell me what you find out, will

you?' I said. 'And give my best to Minnie.'

I don't know why I said that. I hadn't established any noticeable bond with Minnie. But, I realised, I cared about Sid's happiness and I suppose I wanted to show him that by inquiring after Minnie.

'She's good,' he said, 'thanks for asking.' And then he was gone.

What did it mean if Robby's girlfriend *had* planned to kidnap Keshawn? Was Robby involved? He was, of course, the one other person who had Suzette's private mobile phone number. He had to be implicated somehow, because if it *was* Zoe, she had known exactly where to take Mo, using the trail through the dunes that led to Scott and Suzette's house. The same trail that Gwen Bennett – if it had been Gwen Bennett – had used to walk onto Scot and Suzette's property. You couldn't see the house from the beach and the only hint that it was there was a forbidding sign at the edge of the dunes warning trespassers to keep out.

My mind went back to what Wyn had said about there being a basement, not a crawl space, in Gwen Bennett's house and the more I thought about it, the more I knew there was one more call I had to make. I fished around in my wallet for Detective McCoy's number.

He listened to what I had to tell him about my suspicions that Eileen was harbouring

388

Patsy in the basement of the house on Spring Hollow Road. He reassured me, after I had asked him at least twice, that no, he did not think I was completely crazy. I was just about to tell him about Gwen Bennett when he stopped me and told me that I'd reached him while he was lying on a gurney in a holding bay at Southampton Hospital, waiting to be wheeled in for his hip replacement surgery. And now he was in trouble because my call had alerted them to the fact that he still had his mobile phone with him, and that was not allowed.

I was frustrated beyond belief that Sid would not give me Gwen Bennett's address. And then, on impulse, I drove into East Hampton, parked in the lot that ran parallel with Newtown Lane and walked to the real estate office where I knew Gwen Bennett worked.

I would ask the receptionist if I could see her and as soon as I was told that she was not there, I would force them to give me her home address.

But she *was* there and I was directed up a narrow staircase to the floor above. *First door on the left. You'll find her in there.*

I climbed the stairs, assuming that Gwen Bennett would have her own office where I could confront her about her visit to Scott and Suzette's property. So I wasn't prepared for the rows of desks stretching back to the end of a long room. Phones rang and brokers answered them, talking in muted voices, while staring at their screens. I moved tentatively down the wide aisle separating the two rows of desks until I found Gwen Bennett sitting over by the wall on the left.

She looked up and saw me and suddenly I realised I could not just come out and say, *Hey, Gwen, I know about you and Shane Sobel. Was he the reason you killed Patsy Brooks and your own daughter? And what have you done with Mo?* When she stood up and took my hand, on impulse I gave her the most natural reason I could think of for seeking her out.

'Gwen, forgive me dropping by without calling first. I've decided I like it round here so much that I'm thinking about staying.'

'And you'll need somewhere to live.' She smiled. 'Sit right down. How many bedrooms? What's your budget? Do you want to be on the water?'

'Oh, I don't think I could afford that. I'd prefer something quite modest. Just a simple writer's home.' I smiled back at her in what I hoped was an appealingly self-deprecating way. 'Actually, I think I know what would suit me down to the ground.'

'You do?' She beamed. 'That would make you the perfect client. What'd you have in mind?'

'Well this is going to sound weird, given the

circumstances, but that little rental house of yours – the one where your daughter – I'm sorry–'

'You want something like that?' She brushed aside any potential tactlessness on my part with bustling professionalism. 'No problem.' She turned to her screen. 'I can show you plenty of charming little ranch houses.'

'But what about *that* house?' I asked.

The smile left her face abruptly. 'One small problem,' she said. 'It's not for sale.'

'But Eileen said it was.'

Her fingers slipped from her keyboard and she turned to stare at me.

'*Eileen* said it was for sale. She must be out of her mind.' She regarded me with growing suspicion. 'And why have you been talking to Eileen?'

'She asked me to meet her there, so I went over and she was in the midst of cleaning. She said you'd asked her get the place in order because you were putting it on the market,' I said, managing to omit the reason why I'd gone to see her.

'She said *what?*' Gwen was incredulous. 'Is she insane? There can't be a single person on the east end of Long Island who doesn't know my daughter was murdered there by Shane Sobel. And I'll admit that's probably because I've told them. And before you say anything, I'm aware that some of those

391

people are probably looking at me and wondering if I had anything to do with *his* death.'

Even as she spoke, several of the other brokers turned round and looked at her, pressing the air down with their palms and raising fingers to their lips. *Keep it down!*

'What I mean is,' said Gwen, leaning closer to me and lowering her voice, 'there'd be no point putting it on the market at the moment, even if I wanted to. Nobody's going to want to buy a house where someone's been killed, unless they're a ghoul and yes, they do exist, but I'd rather not have to deal with them at this point in time. But even so, it would need the added bonus of it having been owned by a celebrity – like Patience Brook O'Reilly,' she raised her voice again, as if trying to make a point to the rest of the room, 'to make it an even remotely desirable residence.'

'So it's not on the market?' I repeated stupidly.

'Read my lips, as they say.' She pointed to her mouth. 'I don't know what's the matter with Eileen. I went over to the house yesterday to get something out of the basement and the door was locked. What's that all about? I called Wyn, that's my landscaper, and he said he knew nothing about it. She's locked me out of my own basement and now she's telling people I'm selling the place. She must be losing it. I'm going to go over and find out what's with her. I need to be able to get into that basement.'

My phone beeped to tell me I had an instant message – *Call me as soon as you get this. Sid.* I was getting nowhere fast with Gwen Bennett. She clearly wasn't hiding Mo here in this open-plan office. Would she have had time to stash him somewhere on the way over?

'Of course where I'd really like to be is right on the ocean,' I said, 'in my dreams! The property next to Scott Abernathy's is for sale. Are you handling that? What's the asking price?'

'I heard $25 million.' A note of extreme bitterness had permeated Gwen Bennett's tone. 'And no, it's not mine. One of my rivals has an exclusive on it.'

'So you weren't showing it this morning?'

'I wish,' she said. 'Why do you ask?'

'Oh, I heard there was a problem regarding the right of way for the shared trail to the beach,' I said, trying to sound as offhand as possible.

'Great!' Gwen Bennett clapped her hands. 'May it cause endless delays to any deal going through. Now why don't you come and sit beside me so I can show you a few properties within *your* budget?'

'Is it OK if I come back?' I smiled at her. 'I just came in on impulse. Let me go away and decide if I really want to do this and, if

393

I do, I'll certainly come back.'

She hid her disappointment well and assured me that by the time I came back, she'd have just what I wanted ready and waiting. On my way out I asked the receptionist if Gwen Bennett had been there all morning. No doubt she thought it was an odd question, but she answered nonetheless.

'No, she just came in, about five minutes before you got here.'

Outside on the sidewalk, walking to my car, I called Sid back.

'It's the same Zoe,' he said as soon as he answered my call.

'You saw Robby already?'

'I caught him as he was just going out and made him talk to me. I really didn't know how to go about asking him if his girlfriend was a kidnapper so I just said I wanted to say hi, and I told him I'd met Zoe.'

'Did they send you Charlie Merri-weather's sketch yet?'

'Maybe, I didn't check my laptop.'

'So how do you know–'

'Let me finish,' Sid sounded irritated. 'I asked him if he'd ever taken her back east to meet his mother? I expected him to say no because the Zoe I met said they'd only got together in the last month. But he said yes, she accompanied him when he went to see Suzette back at the beginning of the sum-

394

mer – which means Zoe was lying about how long they've known each other. But Robby didn't take her to meet his mother. He told me his grandmother in Washington had met Zoe. She told Robby he shouldn't take her along, that he needed to spend some quality time with his mother – on his own. And apparently that caused a few problems.'

'How so?'

'Zoe was angry, said it showed he thought she wasn't good enough for him – and you can sort of see her point,' said Sid. 'Eventually they arrived at a compromise. She flew east and rode out to the Hamptons with him but she rented a separate place to stay for which he gave her the money. I asked him for the address and he said he only went there once late at night and she was driving and he had no idea where he was. Some road in Springs, he thought, but since he's only ever stayed at Suzette's in the lap of luxury, he's not exactly familiar with the area.'

'It was the house where Holly was killed?'

'I don't know,' said Sid. 'But later, when he went back west, she stayed on and she had to move because he wasn't paying for her rental any more. He said she found a cheap room in a friend's house.'

'Holly Bennett's,' I said. 'So he didn't spend much time with Zoe?'

'My guess is that Zoe pretended it wouldn't work for Robby to go to her place because she was trying to engineer an invite to Suzette's. He said she mostly met him on the beach. He'd walk down that trail from the house to the ocean and she'd be waiting for him.'

'Just like she was waiting for a kid she thought was Keshawn,' I said.

'Could be,' said Sid again. 'But Robby began to realise a thing or two. He's very close to his grandmother – she raised him, after all – and he was aware that his grand-mother hadn't liked Zoe and it bothered him. And the more he saw of Zoe, the more he realised that he'd made a mistake. He said it became clear she wasn't really interested in him. She kept pressing him to introduce her to his mother. All she wanted was to hang with Suzette, she wasn't impressed by *him*, just by whose son he was. They had a row and when he went back to the west coast at the end of his vacation, he was on his own. He never expected to hear from her again and he was amazed when I said she had turned up at his dorm.'

'So you told him what we suspect?'

'He didn't want to believe it. I could tell by the way he talked about him that he really likes Keshawn. But he agreed that it didn't look good.'

'So what's going to happen?' I asked Sid.

'I've told him he has to call Zoe and invite her to his dorm, and I'm going to be there waiting for her.'

I almost chuckled. I pictured the foxy-faced girl from Charlie Merriweather's drawing knocking on Robby's door, Robby opening it and ushering her in and then Sid leaping out from behind the door in all his muscular glory.

'Have you told Pete and Vince?' I asked him.

'All in good time. I need to establish she's who we think she is first,' he said, and I sensed he was gleeful in his anticipation. Security Sid was back in action, even if he wasn't actually protecting anyone and once again he was anxious to get off the phone. I let him go, making him swear he would call me as soon as he had any further news.

And then, as I stood there thinking about what Sid had told me about Zoe, Gwen Bennett came hurtling out of the real estate offices behind me and set off at a brisk clip towards her car on the other side of Main Street. She was moving so fast that I knew she hadn't taken me in.

I didn't stop to think. I noted that she got into a black Lexus – probably acquired from Shane Sobel – and then I raced along Newtown Lane to the car park to retrieve my own car. I spun out of the car park along Main Street in time to see Gwen disappearing past the windmill out of East Hampton and along Springs Fireplace Road.

Barely aware of what I was doing, I followed Gwen, wondering if Mo could be hidden in the back of her car. When she veered sharply off Springs Fireplace onto Abraham's Path and then turned left onto the Accabonac Road, I suddenly knew where we were heading.

Sure enough, Gwen pulled up outside her rental house on Spring Hollow Road. I heard the quick *beep-beep* of her remote as she locked the car on her way up the path to the front door. She let herself in and once she was inside the house, I got out of my own car and ran across the road to look inside hers.

I couldn't see Mo anywhere. I slunk around the side and tried to open the trunk, but it was locked. I slammed my hand down on it, hoping to stir Mo to make a noise if he was in there – but I couldn't hear anything.

If Gwen chanced to look outside to the road, I was in full view so I ran over to Rita McGill's house and rang her bell. I needed a legitimate excuse to be in the area if Gwen saw me. But there was no answer.

In desperation I called Wyn and explained quickly what had happened.

'Come over here,' I said, 'please. You have a reason to be in Rita McGill's back yard.'

'No, I don't,' he said, 'nothing to do there.

No need to water, we had rain last night. And I finished putting all her plants in the ground. She never told me she bought more.'

'You don't get it,' I said, 'I *need* you to be here. Mo might be a prisoner in the house next door. I want to confront Gwen, but I'd rather have you with me when I do.'

'OK, OK, I'll be there. If Mrs McGill shows up, I'll tell her I needed to fertilise her lawn. But it's going to take me at least fifteen minutes to get there.'

'Fine,' I said, 'be as quick as you can.'

I crept around the far side of Rita McGill's house to her back yard and hid myself behind a cypress with far-spreading branches. From there I had a clear view of the back of Gwen Bennett's house and barely a minute later I was rewarded with the sight of her coming out through the back slider.

I watched as she turned immediately to the door down to the basement and rattled the handle, clearly expecting it to be locked. But it gave under her pressure and the next moment the door was swinging open.

After hesitating in momentary surprise, Gwen disappeared down the steps, leaving the door open. I left my hiding place behind the tree and tiptoed over the soft soil to cross the boundary between Gwen's property and Rita McGill's. I crept up to stand beside the open door and I listened.

I was in time to hear Gwen shout out,

'Patsy! What in the world are you doing down here? What's happened to you?' And then I heard a car draw up outside the front of the house.

I raced back behind the tree. Eileen had arrived and my sudden movement must have alerted her to the fact that someone was about because she came straight round to the back of the house. I felt her looking in my direction but she didn't appear to see me. After a minute or two, I could stand it no longer and I inched my head around the side of the trunk so I could see what was happening.

She must have seen the open door to the basement but she hadn't gone down there. She was standing beside it, waiting, listening. She must be able to hear the voices below – Gwen's, Patsy's. She must have figured out what had happened. Gwen had discovered that she was sheltering Patsy.

I needed to warn Gwen. I couldn't call Bill McCoy because he was in the middle of surgery. By the time I called Scott or Rufus or anyone else it would be too late. Wyn would be here any minute. I would have to depend on him.

Eileen leaned closer to the entrance, looking down the stairs and then suddenly jumped away again and I knew that Gwen Bennett was coming up. I watched in horror as Eileen looked around and grabbed a spade that was leaning against the wall. She raised it high above her head and when Gwen came though the door, Eileen, hiding behind it, smashed it down on Gwen's head.

I was standing in such a position that I was able to catch a glimpse of Gwen's terrified face as she emerged in the doorway and saw the spade coming towards her. And when she fell headlong back down the stairs, disappearing into the gloom below, I emitted an involuntary howl in shock.

I began to run across Rita McGill's property but Eileen saw me and came across the boundary to cut me off. I evaded her and made it out to the road to my car. She was right behind me and I expected to feel her hand on my shoulder at any moment, but instead she went to her own car.

She's getting away, I thought stupidly. *She knows she'll be arrested as an accomplice for harbouring Patsy. But I can't let her get away.*

I approached her car with caution. 'Eileen, stay here. I know Patsy's down there. I know you were only trying to be a friend to her, but it will be worse for you if you run away.'

She was reaching into her car as I drew near. I would have tackled her. I would have beaten her off and found the strength to knock her into her car and keep her there. I would have returned to help Gwen and called the authorities to come and apprehend Patsy.

But when Eileen withdrew her hand from her glove compartment, she had a gun in it. And when she pointed it at me, I turned around meekly and walked back around the side of the house to go down the steps and join Patsy and Gwen Bennett in the basement.

Chapter Sixteen

It was both a basement *and* a crawl space. The stairs were alarmingly steep and I clung to the iron railing to stop myself from stumbling, but the minute I slowed down in my descent, a sharp jab in my back propelled me onwards.

It was only as I was about four steps from the bottom that it dawned on me that Eileen wasn't jabbing me with her hand, but with the butt end of her gun.

And then I was forced to come to a dead halt to avoid falling over the prostrate body of Gwen Bennett lying at the bottom of the stairs.

Her hair was matted with fresh blood glistening like some newly applied gel. Her head was yanked sideways at an irregular angle, revealing half her face. Her eyes were closed and she was out cold. I knew this because I had stumbled into her and she hadn't stirred. I tried to discern signs of breathing and seeing none I began to panic that she was dead.

Eileen grabbed me from behind and, gripping my upper arm, stepped over Gwen's body and dragged me down into the crawl space. Because that's what we were in – an area of semi-dark with a ceiling so low that neither of us could stand up. In the gloom I could make out dusty items stacked against the wall – garden furniture, a parasol, a bed frame and – surely a relic from a former owner – a baby's highchair, wedged in with its highest point nudging the ceiling.

As I bent nearly double, thinking that at any moment I must sink to progress on my knees, Eileen urged me forward until suddenly I found myself face to face with a low door. Nudging me aside, she produced a set of keys and unlocked it.

'Get up,' she said, pushing the door open. 'Stand up.'

Even though she still had the gun in her hand, I ignored her and continued to semi-crawl through the opening until she gave me a vicious shove that landed me heavily, and painfully, on my side on the floor. While I lay there, winded, trying to adjust my eyes to the darkness, she left me and returned what seemed like only seconds later, kicking the door wide open so that the light from the stairway illuminated Gwen's body, which she was dragging towards me.

She was, I realised, immensely strong. Gwen must weigh at least 150lbs and Eileen wasn't even breaking a sweat as she hefted her under her arms and dumped her beside me. And then she straightened up, locked the door behind her and reached to flick a switch on the wall.

I gasped. The ceiling had shot up about three feet and we were now in a proper basement, a vast cement room with steel beams that were presumably holding up the entire structure of the rest of the house.

My eyes went straight to Patsy. Patsy, the killer on the run, whom Eileen was sheltering. Patsy, who had raised a hammer high above her head and smashed it down to crumple Shane Sobel's skull, who had raised it again and turned it over so that the forked end clawed repeatedly and brutally into his eye, cheekbones and nose and crushed his teeth and wrenched away his lips and–

But Patsy didn't react to my arrival, violently or otherwise, and that was because she couldn't see me. Her eyes were blindfolded with several layers of Citarella shopping bags cut into shiny plastic strips and held in place with duct tape wrapped around her head. She was on a chair in the middle of the room and she was bound to it with rope encircling her shoulders, her middle, her calves and her ankles. Her arms were behind her back and I guessed her wrists were similarly bound. As I watched, Eileen went over to her and ripped a piece of tape from her mouth.

'I like to be able to chat to her when I'm down here,' Eileen told me and I was amazed to see she was actually smiling at me, as if nothing were wrong.

I said, 'Patsy?' And she flinched and tried to move her head as she said, weakly, and barely audible, 'Lee?'

'Shut up,' said Eileen. To me. To Patsy, she began to chatter in a normal friendly manner that terrified me more than anything I had witnessed since my arrival at Spring Hollow Road.

'Sorry I've been so long, sweet. Suzette should really employ two people to clean that house. A whole team, maybe. If you ever speak to her again, maybe you could suggest it to her? It takes me forever to get round the place on my own.'

It made sickening, awful sense. Eileen had taken Mo. She'd been there cleaning and nobody had thought to mention it because her being there was such a normal, regular occurrence. But Mo had heard her voice – her Scots accent, an accent so out of place in the state of New York that an observant kid like him would not easily forget it. And she was indeed an older woman, who often went to Spring Hollow Road and could easily have done so the day Holly Bennett was killed.

But had she been there by coincidence – or design?

Now, Eileen whipped off Patsy's blindfold, her gun still in one hand. Patsy's eyes blinked and then opened wide in fear. She saw me and signalled with them furiously, unable to speak. And the way she jerked her head away as Eileen leaned in to kiss her cheek told me everything I needed to know.

Patsy was not being sheltered by Eileen. She was being held prisoner, against her will.

'How about a nice cup of tea?' said Eileen, and I saw there was a makeshift kitchen along the far wall, a counter with a kettle and a microwave, and below it a fridge. Eileen laid the gun down on the counter and plugged in the kettle and I noticed that even down here she had retained the meticulous order of her other domains. White mugs were lined up just so on the counter, their handles all pointing in exactly the same direction. Cutlery was laid out in rows and, even without the use of a ruler, I knew there would be an identical measurement between each fork and knife and spoon.

'But first things first,' she said, coming at me suddenly and kicking me so hard and viciously in the shin that I yelped. 'Sit down,' she said, pulling up a hard kitchen chair. 'Now!' when I didn't move. She rammed the chair into the backs of my knees until I collapsed onto it and then she forced my ankles together. I felt rope being tied around them and I reached down and clawed at her hair, her face, anything I could find.

It was a futile gesture. I had been right about her exceptional strength. She only had to reach up and grab my shoulder, gripping me with brute force, for me to know that I had no hope of overpowering her. But it didn't stop me yelling abuse at her and demanding to know what she'd done with Mo and how could she leave Gwen Bennett lying there when she could be–

Eileen slapped my face so hard I could feel my skin turning vermilion from the stinging. She bound my shoulders and arms and calves and ankles, just like Patsy's, but she left my eyes unobstructed.

And my mouth – so that when she had brewed up a pot of tea, she was able to hold a steaming mug to my lips and force me to swallow. As she did with Patsy.

'So aren't you a lucky girl to have some company?' she asked her. 'I'm going to leave Lee here with you for a while.'

'What about Gwen?' I said.

'What about her?' said Eileen.

'She's hurt. She needs medical attention.'

'I'm sure you're right,' said Eileen, 'but she's not going to get it. The next person to attend to her will likely be a mortician.'

'Eileen, *please!*' I begged her.

'Have another sip of tea.' She upended the mug and forced the liquid between my lips until I choked and spluttered. 'Patsy?' I appealed.

'Patsy can't help you. Patsy can barely keep her eyes open. I've made her nice cups of tea these past few days but I've not given her much to eat. Have I, duck?' Eileen rubbed Patsy's cheek with the back of her hand in a weird combination of affection and menace. 'But you needn't worry. I wouldn't let anything terrible happen to you, would I, sweet? We'll be together forever, right Patsy? We're—'

Eileen stopped and froze mid-sentence. We heard the sound of a car pulling up outside.

'HERE! WE'RE DOWN HERE! HELP!' I yelled as loud as I could, but then I heard the car pull away.

Even so, Eileen went into action. She ripped off a strip of duct tape and stuck it over my mouth, and then continued unwinding the roll until it was wrapped several times around my head. She retrieved her gun from the kitchen counter and slipped out through the door, locking it behind her. I heard her open the door to the crawl space and then there was silence.

But in her haste to get away she had forgotten to muzzle Patsy.

I looked over at Patsy and could see her eyes raised upwards. Together, we listened for the sound of Eileen returning, but after a minute or two we heard her footsteps going around the side of the house and moving down the path to the road. Then silence.

And then Patsy began to speak.

But her voice was so weak, I couldn't hear what she was saying, so I moaned and signalled with my eyes for her to *Wait*.

Bound and gagged as I was, I was able to struggle to my feet and, taking care not to topple over, I hobbled with my chair strapped to me, inch by inch over to where she sat.

I leaned back as slowly as I could and my chair slumped with a crash to the ground, taking me with it into a sitting position.

Patsy began again.

'I need to tell you what happened in case…'

She stopped. I leaned closer. She began again.

'I was in bed with Shane. We overslept. He was out cold – we had awakened earlier and had sex and he had fallen back to sleep afterwards. But I was dozing so I heard Eileen come in.' She was speaking in short economic sentences to save her breath. 'She was calling my name as she always does. I shouted, "Don't come in" but it was too late. She saw us. She left, she came back with the hammer. She attacked him, turning the hammer over, smashing the forked end down again and again. She wouldn't stop, Lee, she wouldn't…'

Again she faltered, then she took a deep breath and regained control of herself. Her chin was up in a stoic and determined manner. *I'm not going to react to what I'm saying. I'm not going to break down. I have to tell you what happened.* The duct tape strapped around my head prevented me from reacting. All I could do was listen.

'I was in shock for thirty seconds,' Patsy went on, her voice barely above a whisper, 'then I went for my gun in the drawer of my nightstand. She saw me. She wrenched it out of my hand and turned it on me. Shane was just a mass of blood, unrecognisable. He had not uttered a sound. This was a man who had made love to me only half an hour earlier. I could still feel him. The skin I had touched, that I had *stroked*, was now shredded by the forked end of that hammer. It was slimy with his blood. I thought, *She's going to kill me too*. But I was wrong.

'She had the gun on me all the time. We left the bedroom, went out of the house to her car. She brought me here, to this basement. It was all ready – someone had been living here before me. See–'

She jerked her head and for the first time I noticed a commode in a far corner. And a cot with pillows and blankets.

'But I don't think that person was a prisoner, because Eileen wasn't prepared for me. She didn't have rope ready. She had

411

to go fetch it and while she was gone I screamed and screamed down here but nobody came. No one would hear me unless they were in the house upstairs. She was gone a long time.'

Of course she was, I thought. *She went back to your house, Patsy, and she called the police and told them she'd found Shane's body and that you had killed him and were on the run. She was an unbelievably cool customer.*

I recalled the almost manic state of excitement Eileen had been in after her 'discovery' of the body. I remembered how I had almost admired the way she had had no qualms about looking at the body. *Of course she didn't, she was revelling in her own handiwork.*

'And then when she did come back and tie me up, she told me why she'd done it.'

My mind jerked back to what Patsy was saying. *She did it because she was crazy, surely.*

'It started last summer. Gwen had rented one of her houses to Shane Sobel.' Patsy made a rueful face. 'At the very least Eileen's opened my eyes as to what a shit Shane was. I guess he always had to have somewhere to take women if they couldn't entertain him at their homes. Anyway, Eileen was cleaning for him last year and he seduced her. I swear to you, Lee, while she was telling me this, it was as if she'd completely forgotten I'd been seeing Shane too. Whatever happened between them last year, she's still completely besotted with him. She genuinely believed he was in love with her, that her cleaning days would soon be over. She looked upon him as her *saviour!*'

Patsy shook her head at Eileen's gullibility.

'We'd get quite girly sometimes, you know? After a few drinks. I didn't make a habit of it but, because she'd been with me for so long, every now and then I'd invite her over for a meal. And once or twice I'd ask her about men – in a roundabout kind of way, of course. Nothing too direct or intrusive. She was no innocent. I sensed there was stuff in her past that was pretty horrific. She was on her own for a long time before she found me – when she was a young girl. *Very* young. Probably unable to defend herself. She did let slip that later on she'd gone on some kind of assault training, and she's strong as an ox now. But emotionally, I had the feeling she was terrifyingly naive. You know, if someone took the trouble to be tender with her, to *seduce* her instead of slamming her up against a brick wall in some dark alley, to flatter her as Shane probably did – then in her mind she was married to them.'

Patsy shut her eyes for a second.

'She wouldn't admit to me that he grew tired of her, but she first began to suspect what a shit he was when she started cleaning for Suzette this summer and got wind that

Shane was seeing *her*. There was a lot of gossip below stairs, so to speak, and Shane started showing up at the gates and suddenly there was a new bodyguard on the scene who sent him packing.

'That started Eileen on the path of revenge,' Patsy's voice was gaining strength, 'but she didn't target Shane. She looked for some way to get her own back on Suzette – and she found it when Suzette's son, Robby, came for his annual visit. Eileen told me the tension between mother and son was out there for everyone to see. And then she followed Robby down to the beach one day and watched him with some cheap little girlfriend he used to meet on the quiet. Well, that was when Eileen knew she'd found her accomplice. "It takes one to know one," she said to me.'

I sat up. *Zoe!*

'Eileen said this girl was as bent on vengeance as she was, albeit for different reasons, but together they cooked up a plan to kidnap Keshawn and extract a fortune out of Suzette.'

Patsy cleared her throat. I sensed she was adjusting to be able to speak again, to her mouth being free again. I could feel my own jaw muscles beginning to ache from being strapped so tight with the duct tape.

'Then Robby and Zoe break up,' said Patsy, switching to the present tense, which

414

gave her story even more immediacy. 'Robby goes back west, Zoe stays on. And Eileen finds her a new place to rent. Holly Bennett has confided in her about how she needs a place to take a lover Gwen wouldn't approve of, and she has hit on the idea of using Spring Hollow Road. But she needs to find a "friend" to rent it as a cover. Eileen says she has the perfect person – and Zoe moves in.

'Eileen overhears Scott talking to Franny, fixing up a play date on the beach between Keshawn and Mo. She tells Zoe to wait at the end of the trail to the beach, but of course Eileen isn't there the day that you and Mo turn up so she doesn't know that Keshawn never makes it to the beach.

'So Zoe takes Mo by mistake. She has found Suzette's private number in Robby's phone and she uses it to make the ransom call. Well, you know what happened. Zoe took the wrong kid.

'But Eileen doesn't know this. She gets a call from Zoe – *I've got the kid, meet me at Spring Hollow Road*. Eileen comes here and starts to realise Zoe's hopeless. She hasn't even put the kid in the basement as agreed. Eileen got so worked up when she was telling me this. *How could Zoe have been so dumb?* And she's just about to go to the bedroom – when she would have discovered it was Mo and not Keshawn – when there's a

415

knock on the door and it's Holly. She's locked herself out of her separate entrance at the back, can she walk through the house to her room? Eileen lets her in and then she sees Shane right behind her. And she runs to him, Lee, she's totally over the moon, she thinks he's come to see *her!*'

I had listened to the story unfold with sickening predictability. The fact that Patsy continued to recount what happened in an even, almost flat monologue, virtually devoid of emotion, made it all the more harrowing.

'I felt sorry for her, Lee.' Patsy nodded her head to confirm what she was saying. 'I did. When she told me how she ran towards him with her arms outstretched, waiting for the moment when he would hold her – I just couldn't bear it. And the way she had no compunction about telling me how she was humiliated after that. "He just turned and ran away, Patsy. He didn't want to see me. And those girls, they saw it all. They knew what I felt for him, and they were laughing."'

I knew what was coming.

'I don't know if she meant to kill Holly, or just stop her laughing,' said Patsy. 'She lost control and rushed at her. Holly backed away into the bathroom and fell and hit her head on the tub. She was out cold, but Eileen was taking no chances. She told me she sent Zoe away from here and told her to go and lie low at her house. Then she tipped Holly into the tub and turned on the taps until the bath was full. She said she knew she had to get out of there fast and she left what she thought was Keshawn in the house. Whether she planned to go back later and get him, I don't know, but once she learned it was Mo, she abandoned the idea. She hid Zoe at her house until the forensics were done with this place and then she moved her into this basement and hid her here, cool as a cucumber, until things calmed down and she could put her on a plane back to Oregon.'

Eileen had nerves of steel, I reckoned. When Sid and I had found her here that night, she must have been visiting Zoe in the basement. It was a perfect hiding place – the scene of the crime *after* it had been searched by the police. I wondered if Sid had found all this out for himself by now.

'I told Eileen she had to–' said Patsy, and then she recoiled. As did I.

Because somewhere above us, outside, towards the road, we had heard the distinct *crack* of a gun shot.

And then a few seconds later there was another, followed by a car door slamming and an engine revving up.

'Jesus!' whispered Patsy.

I jerked my wrists this way and that to no

avail. I stood up again and hobbled over to the wall where I tried to bash the chair into it, trying to free myself from it.

'No,' shrieked Patsy, 'you'll wind up with nothing to sit on. You'll exhaust yourself.' Then she suddenly turned her head away from me and looked up to the ceiling. 'There's someone coming.'

It was true. I could hear footsteps running up the path. Then the front door was opened and someone ran through the house, moving very fast. We heard the doors to all the rooms being opened and I even thought I heard my name being called, but it was probably wishful thinking.

Then the footsteps came out of the back of the house and we heard the door to the crawl space being opened. But the feet coming down the stairs were not Eileen's. They were lighter, faster.

We waited, terrified, for whoever it was to unlock the door from the crawl space. It was clearly somebody who hadn't been here before, because two keys were tried before the door swung open.

MO! I screamed as he ran into the basement – although it came out as an unintelligible moan.

I heard Patsy gasp. The front of his T-shirt was drenched in blood. I could see he was shaking and his face was wet with tears. I strained to see what had caused the blood.

Had he been hit?

'My dad's been shot,' he cried. 'My dad's hurt.'

And then his foot stumbled into Gwen lying on the floor before him and he squealed in fright.

I thought fast. I rolled my eyes at Patsy, signalling to her.

'Mo,' she said, 'rip the tape off Lee's mouth. Do it NOW!'

He started at the urgency in her voice but he obeyed her. We were lucky he was tall for his age. I bent my head and he searched for the end of the roll of tape. When he found it and tugged, he had to walk around me three times before my head was free. I braced myself for the strip covering my mouth to be removed and sure enough it was ten times worse than having a band aid pulled off. I had the feeling I was losing several layers of skin, let alone facial hair I never knew I had.

'Mo,' I said, now my mouth was free, 'do you have your mobile?'

'My what?'

'Your mo – your cell phone.'

'I got it, but the battery go flat. I forgot to charge it. I'm sorry.'

'Never mind,' I reassured him. It was a long shot. If he had had it, he would have surely called for help before now. 'Go back outside, find my car. It's unlocked. Open the door and look in the dash for my cell phone. Bring it back down here as soon as you find it. Are you OK about going back outside?'

'But my dad–'

'Mo, if he's been shot we need to call an ambulance right away. Go get the phone and then you can tell me what happened. Go *on!*'

'What if the shooter's still out there,' I said to Patsy as soon as he had left and we could hear him running up the stairs.

Patsy didn't answer and we sat in tense silence until we heard footsteps on the stairs once again.

Mo ran in with my phone.

'My hands are tied, Mo. Dial 911 and hold the phone to my face so I can talk into it,' I told him. I asked that they send an ambulance immediately to 214 Spring Hollow Road. 'A man has been shot out in the road,' I looked at Mo for confirmation and he nodded, 'and we have an injured woman down in the basement.'

I hung up wondering how soon they would get to us.

'Mo, you're the best person in the world we could have hoped to see,' I told him and a glimmer of a smile played across his face. 'We have to help your dad and Gwen over there. Can you go over to the kitchen and take a look in the drawers and see if there's a knife?'

'Sure thing,' he said.

He came back with three and I nodded at a bread knife with a serrated edge. He began attacking the rope behind my back with a little too much vigour and I imagined my wrists being slit at any second. 'Careful,' I admonished, 'take it slow, a little bit at a time. So what happened out there?'

He confirmed what I had suspected. He had recognised Eileen's accent and she had overheard him calling Wyn. Then she had led him out to her car on the pretext of showing him something and the next thing he knew she had thrown him into the back seat and was driving him away.

'She took me to her house first, said she had to feed her dog.'

Even though the tape had been removed from my face, I was speechless. Eileen seemed to be able to continue life as normal in the midst of extreme criminal activity.

'She left me locked in her car and I yelled and banged on the windows, but there was nobody there. She even brought her little dog out to show me. She held him up outside the window, lifted his paw, made him wave at me. *Hi Mo!*'

'Then what happened?' said Patsy. 'Did she bring you here?'

'Yes,' said Mo. 'I been here a long time. She leave me in the car again, but she make me lie down on the floor in back and she say

421

if I move an inch, she's gonna shoot me. She show me her gun. I get down in the back of her car and I think, *I'm gonna die.*'

I was shocked beyond belief. It must have been truly petrifying for Mo. And I realised he must have been hiding in the car when Eileen reached into it and retrieved her gun to scare me into going down to the basement. He must have been too frightened to even make a sound.

'But how did you find us down here?' I asked him. 'Did you hear my voice?'

Mo shook his head. 'My dad told me. He gave me the keys. After he got shot.'

'How'd that happen, Mo?' Patsy said gently.

'While I'm lying in the back of the car I start thinking I gotta do something. I figure when she come back, when she open the door, I'll roll out before she can grab me and shoot me.'

'Oh, Mo!' I closed eyes at the thought of how close he must have come to being killed.

'When I hear the door open, I'm ready. But I get confused, I forget to duck down. I sit up instead a slidin' out and she's right there. But then I hear my dad's voice. He's shoutin' at her and she turns and shoots *him*. I see him fall down in the road. I think she's gonna drive off with me again and kill me, but she say, "Get outta the car." I get outta the car, and then she drive off. I run over to my dad. I know I gotta help him. But he say no, go to my truck, look for my cell phone and then you go find Lee – and he give me all kinds a keys. I look upstairs for you and then I try this door at the back, like my dad told me.'

He had finally freed my hands and I pointed to my ankles.

'Mo, how bad was your dad shot?' I felt bad asking him this, forcing his mind back to the horror of seeing his father wounded, but I had to know.

'Bad,' said Mo. 'She shoot him twice because the first time it was just in his leg. But then she send a bullet into his chest.' He shut his eyes tight, as if trying to squeeze the image out of them. 'I saw blood,' he shivered, 'all over the road.'

'But you found his cell phone?'

'No,' said Mo. And he began to cry again. 'I couldn't find it. And when I go back to him, it's like he dead. He's lying in the road and he's not movin'. I get down on the road and I give him a hug but he won't speak to me. That's when I come looking for you, Lee. And that's where he's at now. Maybe he already dead?'

Chapter Seventeen

I had Mo with me when I went to meet Anna off the train from New York. I was glad of his presence, because I knew she was less likely to lay into me in front of her son.

She stepped down from the train, pale and formal in her thrift-shop cotton dress with its three-quarter length sleeves and a hem-line around her calves. It was Friday afternoon and she stood out amongst the tanned weekenders escaping the Manhattan heat, as they erupted onto the platform in their sleeveless tops and bare midriffs, buff legs extending from shorts, the sound of their flip-flops slapping towards the gate.

Anna didn't hug Mo when he ran to her with his arms outstretched. Her glare was so intense, for one awful second I thought she was going to cuff him about the head. She merely stood there while he wrapped his arms around her waist and pushed his face into her chest. Then she gently disengaged herself and walked towards me in silence, leaving Mo to follow. I recognised this behaviour. It mirrored the distance my own mother often chose to put between herself and her husband – or herself and her child. *I can't deal with you. I may be angry with you. I may even be choked up with love for you, but I am not capable of showing emotional feeling. I am going to immerse you in silence and let you make of it what you will.* I caught the look on Mo's face and saw that he was devastated, but from the dead look in his eyes a moment later, and the way he fell into step beside her, I knew that, like me, he had learned to adjust.

As I drove her to Southampton Hospital, Anna didn't give me much more than perfunctory answers to my questions – *How was the ride out? Have you been out here before?* – questions that blatantly avoided the chasm of resentment that existed between us. And when we arrived at the hospital, she was out of the car before I had had time to fully bring it to a standstill. Before closing the passenger door, she held out the flat palm of her hand towards me as if to halt any further movement on my part.

'I want to see Wyn alone. Just me and Mo.'

And then she was gone. Mo scrambled out of the car and ran after her, turning to wave shyly at me.

I opened my window and yelled after them. 'Room three one three. Third floor.'

Wyn had undergone surgery to remove the bullets from his chest and leg after which he had remained in intensive care for forty-eight hours. It was only when he was pronounced to be in a stable condition that I had driven Mo to Southampton to visit him.

Wyn was asleep when we knocked softly on the door and entered his room. With my arm around Mo, I drew up a chair to the bed, trying not to look at the monstrous collection of tubes that seemed to me to be attached to every part of Wyn. I was a coward as far as hospitals were concerned, barely able even to stomach more than fifteen minutes of an episode of ER. Now as I stared at Wyn lying in the bed, he appeared shrunken and lifeless, but then suddenly he opened his eyes and saw us. The look on his face when he saw him made me realise that bringing Mo to see him would probably expedite his recovery more than anything else. And Mo, too, needed to see for himself that his father was alive. In spite of my constant reassurance, Mo had been coming into my bed every night where he whimpered in his sleep beside me.

I slipped out of the room and left them alone together for twenty minutes and then I enlisted the help of a passing nurse, asking her if she would have Mo go assist her at the nurses' station while I had a quick word with Wyn in private.

'Thank you,' he said, when I settled myself once again in the chair beside him.

'Mo will be fine now he's seen you.' I smiled. 'Do you feel up to telling me what happened?'

'Wait a second,' he said, 'no one's told me. Did they get her?'

'Eileen?' I nodded. 'They got her, thanks in part to Mo.'

Wyn's eyes widened in alarm. 'He chase after her?'

'No, no, nothing like that. But he told them to look out for a woman with a little black dog. They went straight to her house to see if Brock was still there and when he wasn't, they put out an APB for a woman travelling with a Scots terrier. They picked her up at Wainscott, on the Jitney, can you believe it? They let you take small dogs if you keep them in one of those portable pet carriers. Brock was just small enough and his presence gave her away. She was sitting at the rear of the bus and she had taken him out of his case and had him on her lap. She gave herself away when she saw them coming and tried to barricade herself in the bathroom at the back of the bus, but they stopped her. Just as well they got to her before the bus took off on the Long Island Expressway otherwise she would have disappeared into New York at the other end.'

I had been stunned at Eileen's audacity when I heard this, the way she brazenly defied being caught by doing everything in plain sight. She had returned to the scene of the crime to hold her prisoners in the basement of Spring Hollow Road, and now she

427

calmly tried to evade the police on public transportation. They would have had a good description of her to give out, but adding Brock to it made it twice as effective.

'He's a wondrous little boy,' said Wyn softly. 'I've been beating myself up knowing I was sitting in my truck waiting for you when all the time you were tied up down in the basement and he was cowering in the back seat of Eileen's car right across the road. I could have saved him. I just didn't know.'

'You were *waiting* for me when I was already there?' I didn't understand what he was saying.

'You called me, you told me to meet you in Mrs McGill's back yard. But when I got there, I didn't find you, I figured you weren't there yet so I went back to my truck to wait for you.'

'But didn't you see my car parked outside?'

'How I know what car you drive?' he said. 'You never driven me anywhere. I'm thinking maybe I oughta let myself into Gwen Bennett's house, check Mo ain't there but then I figure maybe I better call you first, see where you are, so I go back to my truck and then Eileen comes out of Gwen Bennett's house and I think, *Well, that's good. That means Gwen Bennett don't have Mo in there like Lee thought.* So I'm walking towards

428

Eileen's car and she opens the door and then suddenly Mo sits up in the back and – Boom! – I put it all together and I'm running to get him and she shoots me. I go down, that's the last I remember.'

'Well. She'll go down too, Wyn. It's the only consolation I can give you. She's been arrested for Holly Bennett's murder, and for Shane Sobel's.'

And maybe for Gwen Bennett's.

When I left Wyn, promising to bring Mo to see him the next day, explaining as gently as I could that Anna would be arriving and had said she wanted to see him, I walked out of the hospital, wondering on which floor Gwen was fighting for her life.

I felt guilty about Gwen. All my attention had been focused on getting Wyn to hospital as quickly as possible. And yet Gwen Bennett had been lying at my feet all the time we had been imprisoned in the basement, her life in even more danger than Wyn's.

The blow to her head as she fell down the stairs had cracked her skull and she had been in a coma ever since. But I knew that Gwen had plenty of people to worry about her. After all, in East Hampton, an assault on a prominent real estate broker was much bigger news than a black man found lying in the road.

Now, I contemplated going into the hospital to try and find Gwen while I waited for Anna and Mo. But I had no idea how long they would be. I searched in the car and found an old copy of the *New York Times* Sunday magazine lying under the seat, but as I tried to read it I couldn't concentrate. It had taken three calls to track Anna down and when I had finally reached her, she was full of apology for not calling me back sooner. But when I told her why I was calling and she began to understand the enormity of what had happened, she began to scream insults at me. *I trusted you! You're a lying bitch! I confided in you! You let me tell you about my marriage and my problems with Mo's father and all the time you were meeting him, talking to him. You agreed to take Mo back with you so he could see Wyn, didn't you? And now you tell me you let Mo go with someone who let him be kidnapped right out of their house.*

The truth was she was right. I *had* considered that Mo would be able to continue seeing his father if I took him back to Long Island. I had kept quiet about the fact that she had been the one to suggest he go with me in order that she might spend more time with her new boyfriend. I knew the guilt she must be feeling about that. Finally, she had hung up on me, calling back an hour later and leaving a message telling me which train she would be on and requesting that I bring Mo with me to meet her.

I tried to think of the approach I would

take with her when we finally sat down to talk about what I had done. I needed to make her understand that I had never intended to come between her and Wyn, that I had not wilfully decided that Mo should seek out his father. I would explain to her how Wyn had taken Mo and been apprehended and I would concede that yes, I *had* gone to meet Wyn at his request, but that had been because I had seen how happy Mo had been to see his father, and I had wanted to find about more about him. I would try to make her understand that I had facilitated Mo seeing his father for Mo's sake, *not* because I was on Wyn's side.

But I was not able to tell her any of these things.

Having waited in the car with mounting frustration for nearly an hour, I went in to the hospital and up to Wyn's floor. I asked at the nurses' station if somebody would go into Wyn's room and find out how much longer Anna and Mo would be – and they looked at me with some surprise and told me that they had left about half an hour ago. The nurses had not known anyone was waiting for them, because Anna had asked them for the number of a taxi service. She needed to get to the train station, she explained. She and her son were returning to New York.

Anna must have left by another entrance so as to avoid being seen by me. I asked where the station was and drove there in frantic haste, but I was too late. A train had left some ten minutes earlier and they must have been on it, because they were nowhere to be seen.

I went back to the hospital and sat in silence with Wyn for a while.

'I didn't know,' I told him, 'I just had no idea she would do this.'

'It wasn't all bad,' he said. 'She probably thought it didn't show, but I know her well enough to see that she was shocked by what had happened to me, and what it meant to Mo. I think she'll lift the restraining order from now on.'

'Well she already has,' I said. 'She's broken the rules herself by coming to see you.'

I wondered at what point Anna would tell him about the new man in her life and whether her desire to develop this relationship might not have something to do with her change of heart about Mo visiting him in the future.

'I'll be back tomorrow,' I said and left him.

I began to cry almost as soon as I left the hospital. I drove home with only one hand on the steering wheel, wiping my eyes with a tissue with the other. I paused in the driveway outside Franny and Rufus's house, but then I drove on down to the pool house. Franny was my friend, but she was a tougher nut than I was and I wasn't sure I could count on her for the kind of comfort I craved. I knew who I had to talk to. It would be five o'clock in the afternoon in London. I searched for the number.

Noreen answered my call at the first ring, as if she had been waiting by the phone. She listened patiently as I told her what had happened in weepy fits and starts. It took quite a while to cover everything from Shane Sobel's murder to Wyn being shot and Anna coming out from the city and taking Mo.

'She can't do that,' I concluded. 'Noreen, she has no right to take him away from me. I never even had a chance to say goodbye.'

'She has every right, dear,' said Noreen quietly. 'She's his mother, Lee.'

'But she can't just cut me off from seeing him like that. He's been crawling into bed with me these past few nights, Noreen. He's been cuddling up to me for comfort. He really needs me.'

'He *needed* you, Lee. I am sure he did and you were there for him, but he has his mother now.'

'But she didn't care about him. I just told you. She sent him off back here with me so she could be with her boyfriend. And Mo doesn't even like this boyfriend. He needs to be with his father.'

Noreen wouldn't budge. 'That's not for you to decide. He's not your child, Lee.'

'I know but it feels – it's begun to feel as if–'

'As if nothing. You have to let go.'

'But, Noreen, I may never see him again.'

There was a short silence before Noreen said, 'No, you may not. But that's OK. You know you gave him a wonderful time and he knows that you cared for him. Sometimes people come into your life, Lee, and then they leave, for whatever reason – and you have to let them.'

'But–'

'No buts, dear.' She was talking to me as if I were five years old and yet I listened to her. 'He'll be all right, Lee. Anna and Wyn, I'm sure they both love him in their own way and somehow he'll be taken care of. Think about it. If you were in Anna's situation with Tommy, and you had a child, would you want to hand him over to someone like you. Someone who wasn't even family? Be reasonable, Lee.'

I felt anything but reasonable.

'Is Tommy there?' I asked her. I realised I hadn't even thought about him until she had invoked his name.

'No, he's out.' She didn't say anything more.

'Why has he come to stay with you?' I said. 'Why isn't he at Blenheim Crescent?'

Again there was a silence. Finally she said, 'I'll tell you if you really want to know.'

'Of course I want to know.'

'Blenheim Crescent isn't his home.'

'It *is*,' I said. 'Well, it almost is. It belongs to my parents, but they're in New York as you know and my mother has told me they have every intention of making it over to us as a wedding present. They just haven't got around to it yet.'

'Don't let them,' said Noreen, so quietly I wasn't sure I had heard her correctly.

'*Whaaat?*'

'Lee, Tommy is a north London boy. He's grown up in Islington, all his family are dotted about the place round here. I know he lived in the East End for a minute before he moved in with you, but he's never really going to be comfortable anywhere else but north London.'

'But he's never said—'

'He never would. Just as he'll never say how awkward he feels about the fact that you come from a – that you don't really have to worry about money. He doesn't want you to have to give up what you have and make do with what he could provide for you.'

'He doesn't have to provide for me. I can—'

'I know you can, dear,' Noreen cut in. 'That's just it. He'd like to pay his way but he knows he's a long way from making the kind of money that will buy another house like Blenheim Crescent.'

'But my parents would include him in the—'

'He wouldn't let them do that. He wants

to be his own man for you.'

'So you're saying–?'

'I'm saying just think about giving him a chance to do that. Try letting *him* decide where you're going to live and what's going to happen in your lives.' She didn't actually say the words *for a change*, but I heard them just the same. 'I'm not saying you'll like what he suggests, Lee, not at first at any rate. But you might find you like making him happy. You might find out how rewarding it is.'

'I thought he was–'

'He's happy because he loves you and he's married you. What I'm saying is that he needs you to show him that you've married him, too.'

Her voice was barely audible now and I suddenly realised how frail it sounded. She was exhausted. I had kept her on the phone for a long time, babbling away about myself and my problems.

'I'm so selfish, Noreen,' I said. 'I haven't even asked you how you are?'

'Tired,' she confirmed. 'I think I'm ready for a little nap now, if you don't mind, dear? I'm so pleased you phoned. I was wondering what had become of you. Shall I ask Tommy to give you a bell when he gets in?'

'That would be kind,' I said. 'Yes, tell him to ring me.' Suddenly I realised I really wanted to talk to him. 'And you get some rest now.'

'I love you, dear,' she said, 'and Tommy does too. And it makes me happy to know he'll be with you.'

I didn't exactly sit by the phone, but I hung about the pool house, tidying up, moving Mo's sun lounger bed back out to the patio, keeping myself busy while I waited for Tommy to call.

He didn't, not that night and not the next morning. I could call him, I told myself, of course I could, but why the hell should I? Maybe Noreen hadn't given him the message. But the more I thought about that, the more I knew she would have told him she'd spoken to me the minute he walked in the door.

I walked up to see Franny and Rufus, believing that as soon as I returned, there'd be a message waiting for me.

'I need to ask you what to do about Mo's things,' I said, ready with an excuse for bursting into their kitchen unannounced. 'Anna took him back to New York straight from the hospital. There's not much, just his little bag of stuff, but what should I do with it once I've gone?'

After Noreen's wise words I was making a big effort to keep my feelings in check – but I didn't fool Franny.

'Mo's *gone?* That's not possible. Oh, sweetie, that must be such a wrench. You and he had grown so close.'

Of course then I felt the tears welling up again.

'I'm never going to see him again,' I wailed.

'Don't be too sure about that,' said Rufus. I saw him look at Franny. 'Shall we tell her?'

'Tell me what?'

'You may have noticed the way our property has changed quite a bit since your mother's visit,' said Franny.

I didn't say anything. I hoped Franny wasn't preparing to work herself up into a state again about the plantings my mother had instigated.

'The thing is,' said Rufus, 'someone's going to have to maintain the grounds. Nothing's going to water or prune or transplant itself.'

I stared at him. What did this have to do with Mo? And then slowly I made the connection. *Could he really be thinking what I thought he was thinking? If so, it was just too good to be true.*

'You think Wyn's a good man, don't you?' Franny asked me. 'In spite of the problems he's had in the past.'

'I genuinely, honestly do,' I said. 'I'd vouch for him any day.'

'And you know others who could give him references?'

I nodded. *There was Rita McGill, and Gwen*

Bennett when she recovered. If she recovered. Oh God! 'He'd be your landscaper?'

'Yes,' said Rufus, 'and we'd give him the pool house to live in – once you had no further need of it, of course.'

'And Mo would visit?'

'And Mo would visit,' said Franny.

'Well, it solves the problem of what to do with his stuff,' I said. 'I'll just leave it down there until he comes out here next.'

No one, I noticed, raised the question of when I might be moving on. It all depended on Patsy and I could do nothing until I had seen her. When I went back to the pool house and found there was still no word from Tommy, I called her.

She invited me over on the pretext of wanting to return to work on the book, but when I got there it was clear what she needed was more complicated than that. She was recovering well from her ordeal in the basement of Spring Hollow Road – physically. But mentally was another story.

'It's my fault,' she said suddenly as she was pouring me a cup of tea in her kitchen – a very different kitchen now that it was no longer tended by Eileen. Dirty dishes were stacked waiting to be loaded into the dish-washer. The handles of mugs pointed every which way. And, as was the case throughout the rest of the house, dust was accumulating everywhere.

Pretty soon I realised that while Patsy might be a self-proclaimed Queen of Clutter, the real reason for the mess was infinitely more disturbing. She was seriously depressed.

I remained silent when she said it was her fault, dreading what was coming, but knowing I had to listen.

'I knew all along that there was something wrong with her,' said Patsy. 'But I refused to acknowledge it. Sometimes at three o'clock in the morning, I'd be there worrying about how crazed she would become if I tampered with the way she'd arranged everything in the house. But then I'd force myself to bury it and go back to sleep and wake up in the morning and pretend it was nothing.

'Or I'd tell myself she needed me,' she turned to me and I nodded, unsure what to say. 'That as long as she had me, as long as I gave her love and shelter, she'd be all right. And the truth is, I needed her too. She'd been with me at the worst time of my life and she'd helped me come through it. I owed her. But I didn't love her, Lee.'

I reached across the table and put my hand on her shoulder as I heard the catch in her voice.

'In a way, I think I maybe even hated her, resented her for the hold she had over me. Do you think that's possible?'

I shrugged. I didn't feel capable of committing myself either way. And then the enormity of what she was saying struck me.

'Do you mean that you suspected she might kill someone?' I said.

Patsy shook her head. 'I don't think so. I never wanted to admit to myself what I thought she was capable of, but if anything I feared she might harm *herself*. I just knew she needed help beyond that which I could give her – professional help.'

'Did you ever suggest that to her?'

Patsy stared at me. 'You don't understand what I'm saying. She wouldn't have listened. She thought *I* was the one who needed help.'

But you didn't suggest it, did you? I thought. *And that's why* you *can't forgive yourself.* Still, it was too late now. She couldn't spend the rest of her life blaming herself. I needed to redirect her to a more positive attitude.

'But you're a life coach. You sort out other people's lives.'

'Go on, laugh. I know you don't believe in what I do.' Patsy was smiling, but I sensed the edge in her voice.

'Actually, I do,' I said, and told her about my attempt, and Franny's, to assess our lives via her wheel, but Patsy cut me off short. She still wasn't finished with Eileen.

'I miss her. I can't bear to think what's going to happen to her now. I lie awake at three a.m., imagining her in jail, wondering how they're treating her, because, you know,

441

I wouldn't – I wouldn't–' And then she dissolved into uncontrollable sobbing, and I knew why.

When it came to it, Patsy had delivered as blatant a statement as she possibly could that she wanted to sever all relations with Eileen. She had refused to post Eileen's bail, knowing full well that there was unlikely to be anyone else who would come forward for her.

I decided it was time I ventured a little life coaching of my own.

'Get away from here, Patsy,' I suggested. 'Go back to New York. Get yourself re-connected with the network.'

'Oh, they don't want me any more,' she said, sounding surprisingly cheerful. 'Now I've been outed. I think they're trying to train Vicky the Viking to speak for herself. Good luck to them! No, I've been looking in another direction, as a matter of fact. I think the time has come for me to go home, to go back to England and see if I can re-start my life coaching over there. What do you think?'

'Brilliant idea,' I said.

'And of course we need to get your married life sorted out. Are you ready for a bit of coaching?'

She needed to be needed, I thought. She was one of those people who was uncom-fortable leaning on someone else for long. That was why she had remained in such a blinkered state about Eileen. And now she was turning to me.

I drove home thinking that if anybody could have been a life coach, it was Noreen. I was going over in my mind what she had said about making Tommy happy so I was thrilled when Franny ran out of her house to waylay me and tell me that he had called three times since I had left, trying to reach me.

'But why didn't you tell him to call me at Patsy's?' I said.

'I did,' said Franny, 'but he said he wanted to be sure you were alone when you talked.'

I drove my car much too fast down to the pool house, scattering a few startled squirrels. I took the phone out to the patio and collapsed on one of the loungers to dial Tommy's number. I looked out over the pool as the number began to ring, recalling visions of Mo splashing about in his water wings.

'Tommy, I am so happy you called,' I said when he finally picked up the phone. 'I've been meaning to call, every day I've thought of it, I swear. I said some stupid things, I know I did. I need to be with you, Tommy, I–'

'Lee,' he said, his voice so faint I felt my ear beginning to throb as I pressed it hard against the receiver in an effort to hear him, 'I am not calling about us.'

Noreen had died with the minimum amount of fuss. She'd suffered a stroke quietly and unassumingly upstairs in her bedroom while Tommy was downstairs watching television. He didn't discover what had happened until he took her up the mug of cocoa she liked every night to get her off to sleep.

It must have happened within a few hours of my phone call, I realised, as I flew over the Atlantic, huddling miserably under a blanket, missing her already, missing Mo, buoyed only by the fact that I would soon be reunited with Tommy.

But here again I was in for a shock. Tommy was not there to meet me at Heathrow. I searched for his chubby face, his Tintin topknot sticking up above the heads of the waiting crowds behind the barriers as I pushed my baggage trolley along the wide aisle in Arrivals. But I searched in vain because he wasn't there.

'I've got a funeral to organise,' was his only excuse when I called him from the taxi, stalled in traffic on the Hammersmith flyover. 'You never said you needed to be met.'

I didn't know I had to, I muttered to myself, *why do you think I texted you my flight arrival time?* Into the phone, I said, 'What can I do to help?'

'Nothing,' he said, 'I've got it pretty much under control. Just show up tomorrow morning. It's that church near the Caledonian Road. Eleven o'clock.'

'But what about tonight?' I began and stopped when I realised I was speaking to a dial tone.

So I went to Blenheim Crescent and stayed there alone. I had called my mother in New York to tell her that Noreen was gone and it had depressed me how quickly she had got me off the phone. Now, sitting in the kitchen at Blenheim Crescent and fighting jet lag, I kept myself awake by calling a florist on her behalf, even though she hadn't asked me to. I felt she ought to be seen to be mourning Noreen, so I ordered a wreath from her and Ed.

Then I went upstairs and gazed in horror at the unholy mess Tommy had left behind in our bedroom. It looked as if he had come home from America, upended his bags and emptied his dirty clothes all over the bed – and then left everything to go and be with his mother in Islington.

I was too tired to be angry. In fact, I found myself thinking just before I fell asleep, *If I can put up with this, it means I really love him.*

I dressed carefully for the funeral, wanting to do Noreen proud. I put on a simple black linen dress with cap sleeves and a boat neck. It had little tucks just below the waist that pushed the line of the skirt out into the shape of a tulip. I wore a silver bracelet she

445

had given me and, as I secured the clasp, I kissed it in her memory.

Tommy was nowhere to be seen when I arrived at the church and I walked over to inspect the wreaths. My own little posy of daisies was just what I had wanted, but the stunning arrangement of cornflowers and baby's breath lying next to it somehow did a much better job of evoking Noreen. As I leaned over to see who it was from, I felt a hand on my shoulder.

'It's from your mother,' said Tommy behind me. 'She called me last night to offer her condolences and she asked me to order them. She was very specific, said it had to be cornflowers because of Mum's eyes. I was quite touched by that, I have to say.'

I squeezed his hand, marvelling at how my mother never ceased to surprise me.

'Who on earth sent that monstrosity?' he said, pointing to a giant wreath of garish blooms that had just been delivered. 'Take a look for me, would you?' he said to Shagger, who was right beside it.

'In loving memory from Ed and Vanessa,' he read out slowly, as I had known he would the minute I saw it.

'I suppose she didn't think I was reliable.' Tommy shot the wreath a dirty look and walked away, leaving me alone with Shagger.

I prepared myself for the usual two-line conversation with him – *Doubt we'll see the*

446

sun today or *Keeping well, are you?* – and then I had a minor epiphany. Noreen had always encouraged me to get the point of Shagger. Even if she wasn't there to see it, I knew I would be pleasing her if I made an effort with him now.

'So, Norman, what a sad day. You know, Noreen was terribly fond of you. She was saying as much only the other day when you were out on Long Island.' It was a bit of a stretch but I meant well. I was searching for something else to say, assuming that Shagger would be his normal monosyllabic self, when he more or less knocked me off my perch by coming out with the longest sentence I had ever heard him utter.

'I'm chuffed you told me that. I really am, Lee. And you know what? She rated you pretty high too. Told me so when you and Tommy were first seeing each other, said you were the best thing that ever happened to him. And,' he glanced at me shyly, 'I agree.'

'Do you really?' What a revelation!

'Straight up. Tommy and me, we were always pretty crap at relationships. Never thought we had what it took to keep a woman interested in us for more than one night. Nothing's changed – not for me at any rate.' He looked miserable for a second or two.

'But Tommy knew right from the start that he was going to try really hard to make it

447

work with you. I remember him telling me one night down the King's Arms, he said all he wanted to do was make you smile, that you didn't smile enough. He said it was because you didn't have a mother like Noreen and it had really screwed you up.'

'He said *what?*'

'He did, honest.' Shagger looked mildly offended at my questioning him. 'He said your mum didn't realise how smart you were, didn't appreciate you and it had made you all prickly and insecure. But he knew how to fix that.'

'He knew how to de-prickle me and build up my confidence? I never knew he was an amateur psychologist.'

'Well, what's wrong with that?' said Shagger. 'We could all use someone who cares enough about us to see through the defences we put up in order to get through the day, someone who accepts us for who we really are. You've got that with Tommy and you ought to be bloody grateful. He's the best mate anyone could ever ask for.'

'I appreciate you telling me this, Norman,' I said carefully, knowing perfectly well that I was getting pricklier by the minute, 'and I am especially glad that we've been able to talk like this. I know we don't have much in common, but–'

'What do you mean?' Shagger was shifting his neck inside his collar, his body clearly chafing at the formality of his funeral attire. 'We've got Tommy in common. What else do we need?'

And suddenly I realised he was absolutely right. What else *did* we need? And at that moment I felt an unexpected rush of fondness for him. I wanted to reach out and try and say something meaningful to him.

'I'm so sorry about Minnie,' was what came out. 'You know, it was probably for the best that she did what she did. She wasn't right for you, Norman. She didn't care enough about you to see through to the real you – like you were just saying about Tommy – she–'

'Yeah, yeah, yeah.' Shagger brushed aside my attempts to bond with a shrug and a frown. 'Speaking of that, do *you* care enough about Tommy to know the real *him?*'

I had always thought the wonderful thing about Tommy was that what you saw was what you got. There *was* no other side to him. Was Shagger trying to tell me I'd been wrong all these years? That underneath Tommy's cheerful uncomplicated exterior there lurked a moody and tortured soul striving to be understood?

'Come on,' he said, taking my arm – another first – 'the service is starting.'

Shagger and I stood either side of Tommy in the front pew and I couldn't help it, I kept bending forward and looking beyond

Tommy to this new and loquacious Shagger, until Tommy turned to glare at me. *Will you stop?* But I just couldn't believe what I'd heard come out of Shagger's mouth.

I had forgotten how extended Tommy's family was. The minute the service was over and Noreen's casket was hoisted onto the shoulders of several strapping relatives, he was surrounded by an impenetrable wall of Kennedys and I couldn't get near him. It occurred to me that so small an affair had our wedding been, and so recent, that many of them probably had no idea I was his wife.

It was the same at the wake, as Tommy insisted on calling it, at the pub down the road and as I looked around, it suddenly shook me that I didn't know any of them. These people were my family – by marriage, true, but even so – and yet they were total strangers. As I fought my way through the crush, introducing myself here and there, I could tell by the looks of polite surprise, that they were just as bemused as I was. I couldn't make head nor tail how they were related to Tommy and in the end I did what I always did at a party – I crept to one side of the room and stood alone, silently watching.

I slipped away eventually, trying hard not to feel neglected by Tommy. This wasn't about him and me, this was about Noreen, and I went back to Blenheim Crescent to spend a second night alone, mourning her, crying for her, wondering if I would grieve half as fiercely when my own mother died.

Chapter Eighteen

The telephone beside my bed woke me in the morning, dragging me from the depths of a different time zone. To my surprise I heard Shagger's voice.

'Tommy's not here,' I said automatically, barely awake.

'I know that,' said Shagger, 'he's here with me. He got so totally rat-arsed last night I brought him home to kip at my place, didn't trust him to make it back to Bewdly Street safely on his own. He wants to speak to you, but I just thought I'd chip in first and say I was ever so pleased we had that chat yesterday. Anyway, here he is–'

'Shagger,' I said, 'don't go, I–'

'Don't call him Shagger,' said Tommy, loud in my ear.

'*You* do,' I protested.

'Yeah, but I'm his mate.'

'So am I,' I said with sudden conviction. All these years I'd been a snotty idiot. Instead of dismissing Shagger as Tommy's moronic football-crazy drinking companion, if I'd only bothered to make an effort to have a proper conversation with him, I'd have discovered what I discovered yesterday at

Noreen's funeral – that we were more than capable of forging a bond for Tommy's sake. It was a mistake having preconceived ideas about people and it was time I stopped being so judgemental.

'Sorry I mislaid you yesterday,' said Tommy. 'Are you mad at me?'

'Your mother died, Tommy. How could I be mad at you?'

'Easily, if you wanted to be,' he said, but he laughed. 'Listen, I was wondering, could you meet me round at Mum's later on this morning? I need to pack up her things and you might know better than me what to do with some of her stuff, what's worth hanging on to, what needs to be chucked out.'

It was a sweet gesture on his part to include me, but as it turned out it was totally superfluous. I arrived at Noreen's tiny artisan's cottage – two up, two down with a kitchen and a bathroom tagged on at the back – and Tommy and I hugged wordlessly before turning our attention to the contents of the house.

Twenty minutes later we faced each other in the kitchen, each of us holding a couple of black garbage bags. Because that was it, that was the pathetic sum total of Noreen's life.

'Now don't start blubbing,' said Tommy when he saw my face. He put down his bags and took me into his arms, patting my back as if I were a baby he was trying to wind.

'But it's so sad.' I gestured to the bags. 'That her life should be reduced to this. She was so,' I searched for the right word and came up with something woefully ironic, *'alive!* And now there's nothing left of her.'

'It's often like that when somebody dies,' said Tommy, 'especially with someone like Mum who wasn't a hoarder. She never had many possessions. You probably never noticed because whenever you came here you were focusing on *her.* And she was such a vibrant little person even though she was so frail to look at, and so tiny. I mean, I'm – I *was* – six inches taller than her, yet she could literally tower over me if she wanted to tear me off a strip. But I was with her when a couple of my aunties died, clearing out their houses, and it was exactly the same. Once a person's gone, their possessions are somehow meaningless without them. As you say, there's nothing left.'

He pointed to Noreen's house keys lying beside her scuffed little wallet. He opened it and took out two one pound coins and her bus pass and it was just so pathetic that even he had a hard time holding back the tears.

'You think she knew?' I whispered. 'I spoke to her only hours before she died. Do you think she had any idea?'

Tommy shook his head. 'I don't think she knew precisely when it would happen, but I think she was ready. She had all her affairs in order, as they say. You know Mum, she liked everything neat and tidy. Not something I've inherited from her, I'll get that out there before you do. But she was tired when she came back from America. She was different somehow. I noticed it and that's why I came up here to be with her.'

'Oh God, you think she shouldn't have gone there? Did we wear her out? Did I–?'

'Lee, will you give it a rest?' he shook his head at me. 'She wouldn't have missed going to America for all the tea in China. She told me she loved it, she loved being with you.'

'Really?'

'Really. We're both only children, you and I. I don't know about Vanessa, but Mum often went on about what it would have been like to have more kids, particularly what it would have been like to have a daughter. It really used to piss me off. But I'll tell you something, once you came along, she stopped all that. She didn't have to speculate any more.'

'Were you lonely as a kid?' I said, realising with a start that it was something I had never asked him.

'What, with all that lot you saw yesterday all around me?' He rolled his eyes. 'I had cousins coming out of my ears. How could I be lonely?'

'You grew up with all those people? They lived round here?'

'Highbury, Islington, Camden, all over north London.'

'And you must miss them?' I said, thinking back to what Noreen had told me.

'Now and then,' he tossed it off but I heard the wistful note in his voice, 'but I confess I've always seen a big family in my future.'

'Which was why you married a loner like me?'

'It's all right,' he said, 'I'm not talking about the *immediate* future. I'm not going to start banging on again about when we're going to start a family.'

I didn't say anything.

'Hey,' he said, after a beat, 'that was a joke. I'm serious. There's no way I'd even think about having a kid until I knew I was in a position to be able to fully support it. You're safe for a while yet.' But I wasn't. What I knew Tommy hadn't taken into account was the fact that I was forty and he was even older than that. We didn't have a second to waste and I didn't even want to dwell on how disappointed he would be if I didn't manage to get pregnant at all.

'I'll have to wait a few years at least before I know whether my new business is going to be a going concern,' he said, 'always assuming the bank sticks with me.'

'Your new business,' I repeated slowly, grateful for an excuse not to have to continue the conversation about having children. Not to mention the fact that the words *Tommy* and *business* didn't belong in the same sentence.

'Mum's left me two properties,' he said, sitting down on Noreen's little sofa and patting the space beside him. His considerable bulk didn't leave me much room and in my attempt to squeeze myself into it, I landed on his lap. And stayed there.

'*Two* properties?' I leaned my head on his shoulder and settled myself against his ample chest.

'This house and Uncle Bernie's lock-up down near the Angel. I'm going to turn it into a recording studio. For the local talent.'

'You're *what?*' I nearly fell off his lap.

'Don't sound so stunned. Think about it, Lee. It's what I know how to do. I'm a sound engineer.'

'The local talent?'

'I'm a local boy,' he said as if that explained everything. 'I went to see the bank the day before Mum's funeral. That's why I didn't come to meet your flight. I knew I needed to get this sorted so I could present it to you. *And they said yes to a loan!* There's a million conditions, of course, but it's a start. I'm going to call it Kennedy Sound. I can't wait to show you the place, Lee. It's going to need a total do-over, but it's a great space.'

'So you're going to go there, to work – like – every day?'

'Well – *yes, duh!* It's what most people do when they go to work. Just because you get to fall out of bed and pad over to your desk in your smelly jim-jams and sit there all day, it doesn't mean that's what the rest of us do.'

I biffed him on the arm.

'But yeah,' he said, 'I know, it'll be a bit of a hike to get up here from Notting Hill every day, but it's not *that* much further than when I was travelling to Broadcasting House when I worked at the Beeb.'

'I've got a better idea,' I said, trying to stop myself shaking as I said the words that were about to change my life, 'you could live here in this little house that Noreen's left you, then you'd be just around the corner.'

'Oh, right, that's a great idea,' his voice had taken on a distinctly sardonic tone, 'and you'd be sitting in solitary splendour once again in Blenheim Crescent. It'd be like we were in the beginning, when I was still living in the East End and you graciously allowed me to spend one night a week with you in Notting Hill.'

'No, I'd move here too.' I lifted my head and said it loudly, right in his face, because I knew if he asked me to repeat it, I'd

458

chicken out.

But before he could react, his mobile began to ring. He'd left it lying on the kitchen table beside Noreen's wallet and he offloaded me gently from his lap to go and answer it.

Within a few seconds I could hear his voice raised in consternation.

'Shagger, don't do this to me, mate. You'll regret it. You will. You'll ruin your life. *Shagger!*'

He came back looking morose.

'What's up?' I said, feeling a mild sense of relief that I didn't have to confirm what I had just said about moving to Islington.

'I haven't had a chance to mention this,' he said, not looking at me, 'but Shagger sat beside this girl on the plane coming home from New York.'

'Don't tell me–' I began.

Tommy nodded. 'Totally besotted. I have no idea what's the matter with him these days. First Minnie, now – I forget her name, not that I'm ever going to bother to remember it.'

'You don't like her?'

'I *HATE* her!'

I jumped. This was a bit strong for Tommy. Then I got it. 'She's not a Chelsea supporter?'

'It's worse than that,' he said, turning to look at me now. 'She doesn't like football *at*

459

all. Do you know what Shagger's just told me. He says maybe he'll give it a rest for a bit, too. Maybe he won't be coming to the games with me next season. Maybe it's time to move on. Is he *insane?*'

I got to my feet and went into the kitchen muttering something about a cup of tea – but mainly so he wouldn't see my smile.

'That's the only good thing about Blenheim Crescent,' he shouted after me. 'It's closer to Chelsea Football Ground.'

The only good thing. Interesting that he'd never put it like that before. As I boiled the water, I thought about the incongruity of a north London boy like Tommy being a Chelsea supporter. But then I remembered that it had been Shagger who had drawn him south to Stamford Bridge in the first place. Shagger's family had moved from Islington when the two of them had been in their teens and Shagger had become a Chelsea supporter. And now Shagger had deserted him.

I suppose I wasn't really thinking when I came out of Noreen's tiny galley kitchen – you could fit it into the one at Blenheim Crescent three times over – and said to Tommy as I handed him a brimming mug of tea:

'Tell me, when you have a son, what will he be? If he grows up round here, how can he not support Arsenal – or even Tottenham? Or will you be dragging him all the way across London to the game at Stamford Bridge every week?'

It was the *when* – as opposed to the *if* – that surprised me, more even than the fact that I was already assuming our child would grow up in Islington.

Tommy didn't say anything for a very long time and when he did speak, he'd got a little ahead of me.

'How do you imagine we're going to fit a football into this house, let alone a budding Chelsea supporter? There's barely enough room for you and me. Speaking of which, I–'

'We can work it out when the time comes,' I said, amazed at how simply everything was beginning to slot into place in my head. 'By that time your business will be doing so well, we'll be able to afford to buy a bigger house. Isn't that what you said just now? That you didn't want to think about having a kid until you knew you could support it?'

Neither of us, I noticed, had mentioned the multi-million pound elephant in the room, my parents' Notting Hill mansion that was waiting to be made over to us. As far as I was concerned, that was something else we could deal with when the time came.

'What's made you change your mind? If Mum hadn't died, would we be even having this conversation?' Tommy had begun to

461

pace Noreen's living room – which took him all of four steps and back.

'You mean about moving to Islington?' I said. 'Probably not. But don't ask me to explain, because I might start thinking twice about it.'

'Actually,' he said, coming back and drawing me into his arms, 'it's the fact you've brought up having kids that's surprised me more than anything. If you really mean it, knowing that we might have her grandchild one day is the one thing that will help ease the pain of Mum's death. So thank you for that. If you mean it?' he repeated nervously.

Don't thank me, I thought, as I made the scariest monster face yet, with my head pressed into his chest so he wouldn't see it, *thank Mo wherever he is, because he was the one who made me see what I've been missing all this time. Pray God I haven't left it too late.*

The publishers hope that this book has given you enjoyable reading. Large Print Books are especially designed to be as easy to see and hold as possible. If you wish a complete list of our books please ask at your local library or write directly to:

Magna Large Print Books
Magna House, Long Preston,
Skipton, North Yorkshire.
BD23 4ND

This Large Print Book, for people
who cannot read normal print,
is published under the auspices of

THE ULVERSCROFT FOUNDATION

... we hope you have enjoyed this book.
Please think for a moment about those
who have worse eyesight than you ...
and are unable to even read or enjoy
Large Print without great difficulty.

You can help them by sending a
donation, large or small, to:

**The Ulverscroft Foundation,
1, The Green, Bradgate Road,
Anstey, Leicestershire, LE7 7FU,
England.**
or request a copy of our brochure for
more details.

The Foundation will use all donations
to assist those people who are visually
impaired and need special attention
with medical research, diagnosis
and treatment.

Thank you very much for your help.